NARCISSUS

an ascetic monk; a rigorous intellectual remains in the monastery to become an abbot; the epitome of the masculine, analytical mind.

GOLDMUND

romantic, dreamy, flaxen-haired boy; celebrates the lush, lyrical, rapturous, sensuous quality of women; leaves the monastery to find his true nature; he epitomizes the feminine mind.

NARCISSUS AND GOLDMUND

two antithetical natures, the best of friends, who understand and assist each other.

"Hesse lifts the contrapuntal play of conflicting forces into a plane as close to music as words will come. What lingers in the reader's mind is a melancholy melody, a romantic "lied" full of wanderlust for a trip into the id."
—Saturday Review

NARCISSUS AND GOLDMUND
HERMANN HESSE
Translated by Ursule Molinaro

BANTAM BOOKS
TORONTO • NEW YORK • LONDON • SYDNEY • AUCKLAND

This low-priced Bantam Book
has been completely reset in a type face
designed for easy reading, and was printed
from new plates. It contains the complete
text of the original hard-cover edition.
NOT ONE WORD HAS BEEN OMITTED.

NARCISSUS AND GOLDMUND

*A Bantam Book / published by arrangement with
Farrar, Straus and Giroux, Inc.*

PRINTING HISTORY

*Translated from the German, Narziss und Goldmund.
Copyright 1930, 1957 by Hermann Hesse, Montagnola.*

*Farrar edition published 1968
Nine printings through 1969*

*Bantam edition / January 1971
17 printings through February 1987*

All rights reserved.
*Copyright © 1968 by Farrar, Straus and Giroux, Inc.
This book may not be reproduced in whole or in part, by
mimeograph or any other means, without permission.
For information address: Farrar, Straus and Giroux, Inc.,
19 Union Square West, New York, N.Y. 10003.*

ISBN 0-553-26686-1

PRINTED IN THE UNITED STATES OF AMERICA

KR   26 25 24 23 22 21 20 19 18 17

NARCISSUS AND GOLDMUND

Outside the entrance of the Mariabronn cloister,
whose rounded arch rested on slim double columns, a chestnut tree stood close to the road. It
was a sweet chestnut, with a sturdy trunk and a
full round crown that swayed gently in the wind,
brought from Italy many years earlier by a monk
who had made a pilgrimage to Rome. In the
spring it waited until all the surrounding trees
were green, and even the hazel and walnut trees
were wearing ruddy foliage, before sprouting its
own first leaves; then, during the shortest nights of
the year, it drove the delicate white-green rays of
its exotic blossoms out through tufts of leaves,
filling the air with an admonishing and pungent
fragrance. In October, after the grape and apple
harvests, the autumn wind shook the prickly chest-
nuts out of the tree's burnished gold crown; the
cloister students would scramble and fight for the
nuts, and Prior Gregory, who came from the south,
roasted them in the fireplace in his room. The
beautiful treetop—secret kin to the portal's slender
sandstone columns and the stone ornaments of the
window vaults and pillars, loved by the Savoyards
and Latins—swayed above the cloister entrance, a
conspicuous outsider in the eyes of the natives.

Generations of cloister boys passed beneath the
foreign tree, carrying their writing tablets, chatting, laughing, clowning, and squabbling, barefoot
or shod according to the season, a flower or a nut

between their teeth or a snowball in their fists.
There were always newcomers; and the faces
changed every few years, yet most of them resembled one another, if only for their blond and curly
hair. Some stayed for life, becoming novices and
monks; they had their hair shorn, donned habit
and cincture, read books, taught boys, grew old,
died. Others after finishing their studies were tak-
en home by their parents to castles, or to mer-
chants' and artisans' houses, and then went out into
the world and lived by their wits or their crafts.
They returned to the cloister occasionally as grown
men, bringing their little sons to be taught by the
priests, stood for a while smiling pensively at the
chestnut tree, then vanished once more. The cells
and halls of the cloister, between the thick round
window vaults and the trim double columns of red
stone, were filled with life, with teaching, learning,
administration, ruling; many kinds of arts and
sciences—the pious and worldly, the frivolous and
somber—were pursued here, and were passed on
from one generation to another. Books were written and annotated, systems invented, ancient
scrolls collected, new scrolls illuminated, the faith
of the people fostered, their credulity smiled upon.
Erudition and piety, simplicity and cunning, the
wisdom of the testaments and the wisdom of the
Greeks, white and black magic—a little of each
flourished here; there was room enough for everything, room for meditation and repentance, for gre-
gariousness and the good life. One interest would
usually outweigh another, predominating in accord with the personality of the incumbent abbot
or the tendency of the day. At times the cloister's
reputation for exorcism and demon-detecting
would attract visitors; at other times the cloister
would be known for its fine music, or for a holy
monk who had the power to heal and perform
miracles, or for the pike soup and stag-liver pies

served in the refectory. And among the throng of monks and pupils, whether pious or lukewarm, fasting or fat, who came and lived there and died, there would always be one or another who was special, whom all loved or all feared, who seemed to be chosen, of whom people spoke long after his contemporaries had been forgotten.

Even now the cloister of Mariabronn had in its midst two persons who were out of the ordinary, one old and one young. Among the many brethren who flocked to the dormitories, chapels, and classrooms were two of whom all were aware, whom all respected: Abbot Daniel and Brother Narcissus. Though the latter had only recently entered on his novitiate, he had, because of his gifts, been appointed a teacher, mainly of Greek, against all tradition. These two, the aging Abbot and the novice, had special standing in the house; they aroused curiosity and were watched, admired, envied, and sometimes slandered.

Most brothers loved the Abbot for his kindness, simplicity, and humility. Only the learned were a trifle condescending in their affection for him, because, for all his saintliness, Abbot Daniel would never be a scholar. He had the simplicity of wisdom, but his Latin was modest and he knew no Greek whatsoever.

The few who permitted themselves an occasional smile at their Abbot's simplicity were all the more enamored of Narcissus, the handsome prodigy who possessed elegant Greek, impeccable manners, quietly penetrating thinker's eyes, and beautiful, sharply outlined lips. The scholars admired him for his extraordinary Greek; almost all the others, for his nobility and refinement. Many quite simply loved him, but there were inevitably those who resented his extreme reserve, self-control, and exquisite manners.

Abbot and novice, each bore his fate and ruled

and suffered in his own way. They felt closer and more drawn to each other than to anyone else in the cloister, yet neither found the way to the other or felt at ease in the other's presence. The Abbot treated the young man with the greatest solicitude, worried about him as though he were a rare, sensitive, perhaps dangerously precocious younger brother. The young man accepted the Abbot's every order, counsel, and good word with perfect equanimity, never argued or sulked, and if the Abbot was right in finding that Brother Narcissus's only sin was pride, Narcissus was a master at concealing it. There was nothing to be said against him; he was perfect and no one was a match for him. Yet, apart from the learned, he had few friends; his distinction surrounded him like a chilling draft.

Once, after confession, the Abbot said to him: "Narcissus, I admit that I am guilty of having judged you harshly. Often I have considered you arrogant, and perhaps I have done you an injustice. You are very much alone, my young brother, you have admirers, but no friends. I wish I had reason to scold you from time to time, but I have none. I wish you would misbehave occasionally, as young people of your age often do. But you never misbehave. I worry about you a little, Narcissus."

The young novice fixed his dark eyes on the old Abbot.

"I wish above all not to worry you, gentle father. It may well be that I am arrogant. If so, I beg you to punish me. Sometimes I feel an urge to punish myself. Send me to a hermitage, father, or assign me lowly chores."

"You are too young for either, dear brother," said the Abbot. "Besides, you are eminently gifted in speech and thought. To assign you lowly chores would be wasting these God-given talents. In all probability you will become a teacher and a scholar. Is that not your own wish?"

"Forgive me, father, I am not certain what my own wishes are. I shall always take pleasure in study, how could it be otherwise? But I do not believe that my life will be limited to study. A man's wishes may not always determine his destiny, his mission; perhaps there are other, predetermining, factors."

The Abbot listened gravely. Still, a smile played about his old face as he said: "Insofar as I have come to know people, we all have a slight tendency, especially while we are young, to confuse our wishes with predestination. But tell me, since you believe that you have foreknowledge of your destiny, tell me what you believe yourself destined for?"

Narcissus let his dark eyes close until they disappeared in the shadows of his long black lashes. He did not answer.

"Speak, my son," the Abbot ordered after much waiting.

In a low voice, his eyes on the ground, Narcissus began: "I believe, gentle father, that I am destined above all else for cloister life. I believe that I shall become a monk, a priest, a prior, perhaps an abbot. I do not believe that this is because I wish it. I do not wish for offices. They will be laid upon me."

Both were silent for a long time.

"What gives you this belief?" the old man asked hesitantly. "What talent is there in you, other than learning, that expresses itself in this belief?"

"It is a capacity to sense the characters and destiny of people," Narcissus said slowly, "not only my own destiny, but that of others as well. It obliges me to serve others by ruling over them. Were I not born for cloister life, I should have to become a judge or a statesman."

"Perhaps," nodded the Abbot. "Have you tested

your capacity to recognize people's characters and destinies? Have you examples?"

"I have."

"Are you willing to give me an example?"

"I am."

"Very well. Since I do not wish to pry into the secrets of our brothers without their knowledge, you might perhaps tell me what you think you know about me, your Abbot Daniel."

Narcissus raised his lids and looked the Abbot in the eye.

"Is that an order, gentle father?"

"An order."

"I find it difficult to speak, father."

"And I, my young brother, I find it difficult to force you to speak. And yet I do. Speak."

Narcissus bowed his head and said in a whisper: "I know little of you, gentle father. I know that you are a servant of God who would rather watch over goats and ring the bell in a hermitage and listen to peasants' confessions than head a large cloister. I know that you have a special love for the Holy Mother of God and that most of your prayers are addressed to her. Occasionally you pray that Greek and similar subjects that are studied in this cloister do not lead the souls in your care into confusion and danger. Occasionally you pray for continued patience with Prior Gregory. Sometimes you pray for a gentle end. And I think that your prayer will be heard and that your end will be gentle."

It was very still in the Abbot's small office. At last the old man spoke.

"You are a romantic and you have visions," said the old gentleman in a friendly voice. "But even pious, friendly visions may trick us; do not rely on them any more than I rely on them.—Can you see, my romantic brother, what I think about this matter in my heart?"

"Father, I can see that you have very friendly

thoughts about it. You are thinking the following: 'This youthful scholar is slightly in danger. He has visions. Perhaps he meditates too much. Perhaps I could impose penance on him; it would do him no harm. But the penance that I shall impose on him, I will also impose on myself.' That is what you are thinking."

The Abbot rose and smiled. He waved to the novice to take his leave.

"All right," he said. "Do not take your visions altogether too seriously, my young brother. God demands much else of us besides visions. Let us assume that you have flattered an old man by promising him an easy death. Let us assume that, for an instant, the old man was glad to hear this promise. That is sufficient for now. You will say a rosary tomorrow morning, after early mass. You will say it humbly and with devotion, not superficially. And I shall do the same. Go now, Narcissus, there have been words enough."

On another occasion Abbot Daniel had to settle a disagreement between the youngest of the teaching fathers and Narcissus on the point of the teaching method. Narcissus passionately urged the introduction of certain changes and justified them with convincing arguments; but out of a kind of jealousy Father Lorenz refused to hear of any changes, and each new discussion would be followed by days of ill-humored silence and sulking, until Narcissus, who was sure he was right, would broach the subject once more. Finally Father Lorenz, mildly offended, said: "Well, Narcissus, let us put an end to this quarrel. As you know, the decision is mine and not yours. You are not my colleague, you are my assistant, you must do as I say. But since this matter seems so important to you and since I am your superior only by rank and not by knowledge or talent, I will not take the decision upon myself. We shall submit the matter to our father the Abbot and let him decide."

This they did. Abbot Daniel listened with gentle patience as the two learned men argued about their conceptions of the teaching of grammar.

After each had stated his point of view and defended it, the old man looked at them with an amused air, shook his gray head softly, and said: "My dear brothers, neither of you thinks that I know as much of these matters as you do. I commend Narcissus for having a keen enough interest in the school to want to improve the teaching method. However, if his superior holds a different opinion, Narcissus must be silent and obey, because no improvement of the school would make up for the slightest disturbance of order and obedience in this house. I reprove Narcissus for not knowing how to give in. And I hope that you two young scholars may never lack superiors who are less intelligent than you; it is the best cure for pride." With this amiable jest he dismissed them. But during the next few days he did not forget to keep an eye on the two teachers to see if harmony had been restored.

And then it happened that a new face appeared in this cloister which had seen so many faces come and go, a new face that did not pass unremarked and unremembered. An adolescent, previously enrolled by his father, arrived one day in spring to study at the cloister school. Father and son tethered their horses under the chestnut tree; the porter came out to meet them.

The boy looked up at the tree still bare with winter. "I've never seen a tree like that," he said. "What a strange, beautiful tree. I wonder what it is called."

The father, an elderly gentleman with a worried, slightly pinched face, paid no attention to his son's question. But the porter, who liked the boy immediately, told him the tree's name. The young man thanked him in a friendly voice, held out his hand, and said: "I am Goldmund, I'll be going to school here." The porter smiled and led the new-comers through the portal and up the wide stone steps, and Goldmund entered the cloister with confidence, feeling that he had already met two beings in his new environment with whom he could be friends, the tree and the porter.

Father and son were received first by the priest who headed the school, then, toward evening, by the Abbot himself. Both times the father, who was in the service of the Emperor, introduced his son Goldmund and was invited to stay for a while as a guest of the cloister. But he accepted only for a night, saying that he had to ride back the next day. He offered one of his two horses to the cloister as a gift, and it was accepted. His conversation was courteous and cool; but both abbot and priest looked with pleasure upon the respectfully silent Goldmund. They had taken an immediate liking to the delicate, good-looking boy. Without regret, they let the father depart the following day; they were glad to keep the son. Goldmund was taken to see the teachers and given a bed in the students' dormitory. Sad-faced and respectful, he said good-bye to his father and stood gazing after him until he had disappeared through the narrow arched gate of the cloister's outer wall, between the gra-nary and the mill. A tear hung on his long blond lashes when he finally turned away; but the porter was there to give him a friendly pat on the shoul-der.

"Young master," he said consolingly, "don't be sad. Most everyone is a little homesick at first, for his father, his mother, his brothers and sisters. But you'll see: life isn't bad here either, not bad at all."

"Thank you, brother porter," said the boy. "I

have no brothers or sisters, and no mother; my father is all I have."

"You'll find schoolmates here to make up for him, and books and music and new games you never played before, all kinds of things, you'll see. And if you feel the need for a friend, come to me."

Goldmund smiled at him. "Thank you very much. Would you do me a favor then, please, and show me where I can find the horse my father left behind. I'd like to say hello to him and see if he is happy here."

The porter led him to the stable beside the granary. The lukewarm twilight smelled strongly of horses, manure, and oats, and in one of the stalls Goldmund found the little brown horse that had carried him to the cloister. He wrapped both arms around the neck of the animal, which was stretching a long head toward him in greeting; he put his cheek to the wide dappled forehead, caressed it tenderly, and whispered into an ear: "Hello there, Bless, my dear, my good horse, are you happy? Do you love me still? Have you been fed? Do you still remember our home? Bless, my little horse, my friend, I'm so glad that you've stayed, I'll come to see you often." From the cuff of his sleeve he pulled a slice of bread that he had hidden there, broke it into small pieces, and fed it to the horse. Then he said goodbye and followed the porter across a courtyard as wide as the marketplace of a large city, shaded in places by linden trees. At the inner gate he thanked the porter and shook his hand. Then he realized that he no longer knew the way to the classroom he had been shown yesterday, laughed a little, blushed, and asked the porter to take him there, which the porter was glad to do. He entered the classroom, where a dozen boys and young men were sitting on benches, and the assistant teacher, Brother Narcissus, turned his head.

"I am Goldmund," he said, "the new scholar."

Narcissus nodded to him, and briefly, without a smile, indicated a seat on the rear bench and went on with the lesson.

Goldmund sat down. He was surprised to find the teacher so young, only a few years older than himself, surprised and deeply delighted to find this young teacher so handsome and refined, so stern, yet so charming and likable. The porter had been nice to him; the Abbot had given him a friendly reception. Not far away in the stable was his Bless, a little bit of home, and now there was this surprisingly young teacher, grave as a scholar, polished as a prince, with his cool, controlled, matter-of-fact yet compelling voice. He listened gratefully, although without at first understanding the subject of the lesson. He began to feel happy. He was among good, likable men and was ready to seek their friendship. In his bed that morning he had awakened with a feeling of anguish, still tired from the long journey. And saying goodbye to his father had made him cry a little. But now all was well, he was happy. Again and again, for long moments, he looked at the teacher, took pleasure in the straight, slender figure; the cool, sparkling eyes; the firm lips that were forming clear, precise syllables; the inspired, untiring voice.

But when the lesson was over and the pupils stood up noisily, Goldmund started and realized a little shamefacedly that he had been asleep for quite some time. And he was not the only one to realize it; the boys on the bench beside him had noticed too and passed it on in whispers. As soon as the young teacher had walked out of the room, they nudged Goldmund and pulled at him from all sides.

"Had a nice nap?" asked one of them with a grin.

"A fine scholar!" jeered another. "He's going to be a true pillar of the church, falling asleep during his first lesson!"

"Let's put the baby to bed," proposed another. And they seized his arms and legs to carry him off with mocking laughter.

Goldmund was startled; it made him angry. He struck out at them, tried to free himself, got punched several times, and was finally dropped to the ground, one of the boys still holding him by a foot. He kicked himself free, threw himself upon the boy who happened to be standing nearest, and was soon involved in a violent fistfight. His adversary was strong; everyone watched the fight eagerly. When Goldmund stood his ground and landed a few well-aimed blows, he made a few friends among his classmates before he knew a single one by name. But suddenly they all scattered and were hardly gone when Father Martin, the head of the school, entered and faced the boy, who was still standing on the same spot, alone. Astonished, he looked at the boy, whose embarrassed blue eyes were looking out of a flushed, somewhat scarred face.

"What has happened to you?" Father Martin asked. "Aren't you Goldmund? Have they been rough with you, the scoundrels?"

"Oh no," said the boy. "I got even with him."

"With whom?"

"I don't know. I don't know anyone by name yet. One of them had a fight with me."

"He did? Did he start it?"

"I'm not sure. No, I guess I started it myself. They were teasing me and I got angry."

"An auspicious beginning, my boy. Now you listen to me. If I catch you once more fighting in the classroom, you'll be punished. Now off with you to supper!"

With a smile he watched the embarrassed Goldmund run off, trying to smooth his tousled blond hair with his fingers as he ran.

Goldmund thought that his first act in the cloister had been ill-mannered and foolish; rather dejectedly, he looked for his classmates at the supper table. But they welcomed him with friendship and respect. He made an honorable peace with the enemy and from that moment on he felt that he belonged to the school.

2

Although he was on good terms with everyone, he had not made a real friend. There was no one among his classmates for whom he felt any particular affinity, let alone fondness. And to their amazement, the others discovered in the fistfighter they had first taken for a rowdy a peace-loving companion, a model student who seemed to be striving for scholarly laurels.

There were two men in the cloister to whom Goldmund's heart reached out, who filled his thoughts, whom he admired and revered: Abbot Daniel and the assistant teacher, Brother Narcissus. He felt that the Abbot was a saint. He was immensely attracted by his kind simplicity, his clear, concerned eyes, by the way he gave orders and made decisions, humbly, as though it were a task, by his good, quiet gestures. He would have liked to become the personal servant of this pious man, to be in his presence constantly, obedient and serving, to bring him the sacrifice of all his youthful need for devotion and dedication, to learn a pure, noble, saintly life from him. Goldmund wished not only to finish the cloister school but to remain in the cloister, indefinitely perhaps, dedicating his life to God. This was his intention, as it was his father's wish and command and, most likely, God's own decision and command. Nobody seemed aware of the burden that lay upon the handsome radiant boy, an original burden, a secret destiny of atonement and sacrifice. Even the Abbot was not aware of it, although Goldmund's father had dropped several hints and clearly expressed the wish that his son remain in the cloister forever. Some secret flaw seemed attached to Goldmund's birth, something unspoken that sought expiation. But the Abbot felt little sympathy for the father, whose words and air of self-importance he had countered with polite reserve, dismissing the hints as not particularly important.

The other man who had aroused Goldmund's admiration had sharper eyes and a keener intuition, but he did not come forward. Narcissus knew only too well what a charming golden bird had flown to him. This hermit soon sensed a kindred soul in Goldmund, in spite of their apparent contrasts. Narcissus was dark and spare; Goldmund, a radiant youth. Narcissus was analytical, a thinker; Goldmund, a dreamer with the soul of a child. But something they had in common bridged these contrasts: both were refined; both were different from the others because of obvious gifts and signs; both bore the special mark of fate.

Narcissus took an ardent interest in this young soul, whose character and destiny he had been quick to recognize. Fervently Goldmund admired his beautiful, outstandingly intelligent teacher. But Goldmund was timid; the only way he knew to court Narcissus was to exhaust himself in being an attentive, eager student. But more than timidity held him back. He sensed a danger to himself in Narcissus. It was impossible to emulate simultaneously the kindly humble Abbot and the extremely intelligent, learned, brilliant Brother Narcissus. Yet every fiber of his youthful soul strove to attain these two incompatible ideals. It caused him much suffering. There were days during his first months at the cloister school when Goldmund's heart was so torn, so confused, he felt strongly tempted to run away or to take his anguish and anger out on his classmates. Sometimes a bit of innocent teasing or a prank would stir such a wild rage inside this warm-hearted boy that the utmost control was required to hold it in; he would close his eyes and turn away, silent and deathly pale. Then he would go to the stable to find Bless, lean his head against the horse's neck, kiss him and cry his heart out. Gradually his suffering increased and became noticeable. His face grew thinner; his eyes became dull; he rarely laughed the laugh all liked so much.

He didn't know what was happening to him. He honestly wished, was honestly determined, to be a good scholar, to begin his novitiate as soon as possible, and after that to become a quiet, prayerful monk of the cloister. He firmly believed that all his strength and talent drove toward this mild, pious goal; he knew nothing of other drives. How strangely sad then to find this simple, beautiful goal so difficult to attain. Occasionally he would be discouraged, bewildered to detect hateful moods and tendencies in himself: he'd feel distracted, unwilling to learn. He'd daydream or drowse through a lesson, rebel with sudden distaste against the Latin teacher, be cranky and impatient with his classmates. And what was most confusing was that his love for Narcissus seemed to fight his love for Abbot Daniel. Yet at moments he felt almost certain that Narcissus loved him also, that he was concerned about him, was waiting for him.

Narcissus's thoughts were far more occupied with Goldmund than Goldmund imagined. He wanted the bright boy as a friend. He sensed in him his opposite, his complement; he would have liked to adopt, lead, enlighten, strengthen, and bring him to bloom. But he held himself back, for many reasons, almost all of them conscious. Most of all, he felt tied and hemmed in by his distaste for teachers or monks who, all too frequently, fell in love with a pupil or a novice. Often enough, he had felt with repulsion the desiring eyes of older men upon him, had met their enticements and cajoleries with wordless rebuttal. He understood them better now that he knew the temptation to love the charming boy, to make him laugh, to run a caressing hand through his blond hair. But he would never do that, never. Moreover, as a mere tutor, with the rank but not the position or the authority of a teacher, he had become especially cautious and watchful. He was used to conducting himself with pupils only a few years younger than himself as though he were twenty years their senior, to forbidding himself sternly all partiality toward a pupil, to forcing himself to particular fairness and concern for those pupils who were naturally repugnant to him. His was the service of the mind, and to that he dedicated his strict life. Only secretly, during his most unguarded moments, did he permit himself the pleasure of arrogance. No, no matter how tempting a friendship with Goldmund seemed, it could only be a danger; he must never let it touch the core of his existence. The core and meaning of his life was to serve the mind, to serve the word: the quiet, superior, self-negating guidance of his pupils—and not only of his pupils—toward high spiritual goals.

For a year or more, Goldmund had been a student at the cloister school of Mariabronn. He had played some hundred times with his classmates under the linden trees in the courtyard and under the beautiful chestnut tree—ball games, races, snowball fights. Now spring had come, but Goldmund felt tired and sick and often had headaches; he found it hard to stay awake in class, hard to concentrate.

Then one evening Adolf came up to him, the classmate he had first met during a fistfight and with whom he had begun to study Euclid that winter. It was in the hour after supper, an hour of recreation when the boys were permitted to play in the dormitories, to walk and talk in the outer cloister yard.

"Goldmund," he said, pulling him down the stairs after him, "I want to tell you something, something funny. But you're such a model student— you'll probably end up a bishop one of these days. First you must give me your word of honor that you won't tell the teachers on me."

Goldmund immediately gave his word. There was cloister honor and student honor, and occasionally one contradicted the other, Goldmund was well aware of that. But, as anywhere else in the world, the unwritten law defeated the written one; he would never try to evade student laws and codes while he was himself a student.

Adolf dragged him outside the arch under the trees. There was, he whispered, a group of good, strong-hearted classmates—he himself was one of them—who were carrying on an old student tradition, of reminding themselves that they were not monks. They would occasionally steal away from the cloister for an evening in the village. It was the kind of prank or adventure no decent fellow could avoid taking part in; later during the night they would sneak back again.

"But the gates are locked at that hour," Goldmund objected.

Of course they were locked. Precisely. That was the fun of the whole thing. But there were secret ways to get back inside unnoticed; it wouldn't be the first time.

Goldmund recalled hearing the expression: "going to the village." It stood for boys' nocturnal escapades, for all kinds of secret adventures and pleasures which were forbidden on pain of heavy punishment. He froze inside. "Going to the village"

was a sin, something forbidden. At the same time
he understood only too well that that was precisely
why the "regulars" considered it a point of honor to
take the risk and that it was a certain distinction to
be asked to join in this adventure.

He would have liked to say no, to run back and go
to bed. He felt tired and weak; his head had ached
all afternoon. But he felt slightly embarrassed in
front of Adolf. And who could tell: perhaps there
would be something new, something beautiful outside the cloister, something that might make one
forget headaches and listlessness and all kinds of
pain. It was an excursion into the world—although
secret and forbidden, nothing to feel proud of. Still,
perhaps it would bring release, be an experience.
He stood undecided while Adolf continued to talk;
suddenly he laughed and said yes.

Unobserved, they slipped out under the linden
trees in the vast darkening courtyard; the outer
gate had already been locked. Adolf led him to the
cloister mill through which one could easily sneak
out, unseen in the twilight, and unheard because of
the constant whirring of wheels. In complete
darkness they climbed through a window onto a
pile of slippery-wet planks, one of which they
pulled out and used as a bridge to cross the little
stream. And now they were outside, on the pale
glistening road that disappeared into the dark forest. All this was exciting and secret; he enjoyed it
very much.

At the edge of the forest they found a third
classmate, Konrad; they waited for a long time and
were joined by a fourth, big Eberhard. All four
tramped through the forest. Nightbirds rose
above them in a rustle of wings; a few stars peeked
wet and bright through quiet clouds. Konrad chat-
tered and joked. Occasionally he'd make the others
laugh, but there hung above them the solemn anx-
iety of night that made their hearts beat faster.

After barely an hour they came to the village on the other side of the forest. It seemed asleep. The low gables shimmered faintly, criss-crossed by dark ribs of timber; there wasn't a light anywhere. Adolf led the way. Silent, on tiptoe, they circled several houses, climbed a fence, stood in a garden, sank into the soft earth of a flower bed, stumbled over steps, stopped by the wall of a house. Adolf knocked at a shutter, waited, knocked again. There was a sound inside. Soon a light shone, the shutter opened, and one after the other they climbed into a kitchen with a black hearth and an earthen floor. A tiny oil lamp was standing on the stove, its feeble flame flickering on a thin wick. And there was a girl, a haggard servant girl, who stood holding out her hand to greet the intruders. Another girl stepped out of the shadows behind the first one, a young thing with long black braids. Adolf had brought gifts for them, half a loaf of white cloister bread, and something in a paper sack, a handful of stolen incense perhaps, thought Goldmund, or candle wax or the like. The young girl with the braids went out of the kitchen, groped her way through the darkness to the door, stayed away for a long while, returned with a jug of gray clay with a blue flower painted on it and offered the jug to Konrad. He drank from it, passed it on. They all drank; it was strong apple cider.

In the light of the tiny lamp they sat down, the girls on rigid little stools and the students around them on the floor. They spoke in whispers, with interruptions for sips of cider, Adolf and Konrad making most of the conversation. From time to time one of them would get up and caress the hair and neck of the older girl, and whisper into her ear; no one touched the younger girl. The big one was probably the maid, Goldmund thought, and the smaller, pretty one the daughter of the house. But what difference did it make. It was none of his business and he would never come back here. The secrecy of the escapade, the walk through the night forest had been beautiful, out of the ordinary, exciting but not dangerous. Forbidden yes, but even so the transgression did not burden one's conscience. Whereas this, visiting girls at night, was more than just forbidden; he felt it was a sin. Perhaps for the others even this was only a small adventure, but not for him; he knew that he was destined for the ascetic life of a monk, and playing with girls was not permitted him. No, he would never come back here. But his heart pounded with anguish in the flickering half light of the poor kitchen.

The others were showing off in front of the girls and spiking their talk with tidbits of Latin. The servant girl seemed to like all three; they would sidle up to her with their awkward little caresses, a timid kiss at most. They seemed to know exactly how much was permitted. And since the whole conversation had to be held in whispers, there was something rather silly about the scene, but Goldmund did not see it that way. He crouched on the floor and stared into the flickering flame of the lamp, not saying a word. Occasionally a slightly eager side glance would catch one of the caresses the others were exchanging. Stiffly he stared straight ahead again. More than anything else he would have liked to look at the younger girl with the braids, at no one but her, but that especially he forbade himself. And every time his will slackened and his eyes strayed to the sweet quiet face of the girl, he found her dark eyes riveted on his face, staring at him as though she were spellbound.

An hour may have passed—never had Goldmund lived through a longer hour. The students had exhausted their conversation and caresses; they sat in embarrassed silence; Eberhard began to yawn. The servant girl said it was time to leave. They stood up, shook her hand—Goldmund

last. Then they shook hands with the younger girl—
Goldmund last. Konrad was first to climb out
through the window, followed by Eberhard and
Adolf. As Goldmund was climbing out, he felt a
hand hold him back by a shoulder. He could not
stop; once outside on the ground he slowly turned
his head. The younger girl with the braids was
leaning out of the window.

"Goldmund!" she whispered. He stood and
waited.

"Are you coming back?" she asked. Her timid
voice was no more than a breath.

Goldmund shook his head. She reached out with
both hands, seized his head; her small hands felt
warm on his temples. She bent far down, until her
dark eyes were close before his.

"Do come back!" she whispered, and her mouth
touched his in a child's kiss.

Quickly he ran through the small garden, top-
pled across the flower beds, smelled wet earth and
dung. A rosebush tore his hand. He climbed over
the fence and trotted after the others out of the
village toward the forest. "Never again!" commanded his will. "Again! Tomorrow!" begged his heart.

Nobody surprised the night owls. Nothing hin-
dered their return to Mariabronn, across the little
stream, through the mill, across the square of linden trees, along secret passageways, over gables,
around window columns, into the cloister and the
dormitory.

Big Eberhard had to be punched awake in the
morning, he was sleeping so heavily. They were all
on time for early mass, morning soup and assembly
in the auditorium; but Goldmund looked pale, so
pale Father Martin asked him if he were ill. Adolf
shot him a warning glance and Goldmund said he
felt all right. But during Greek, around noon, Narcissus did not take his eyes off him. He, too, saw
that Goldmund was ill, but said nothing and

watched closely. At the end of the lesson he called him, sent him on an errand to the library to avoid rousing the students' curiosity, and followed him there.

"Goldmund," he said, "can I help you? I see you are in trouble. Perhaps you're not feeling well. In which case we shall put you to bed and send you some soup and a glass of wine. You have no head for Greek today."

For a long while he waited for an answer. The pale boy looked at him out of troubled eyes, hung his head, raised it again. His lips quivered; he wanted to speak but could not. Suddenly he sank to one side, leaned his head on a lectern, between the two small oak angels' heads that framed the lectern, and burst into such violent weeping that Narcissus felt embarrassed and averted his eyes for some time before touching the sobbing boy to raise him up.

"All right," he said in a voice that was friendlier than Goldmund had ever heard from him. "All right, *amicus meus*, you just weep; it will soon make you feel better. There, sit down; there is no need to speak. I can see that it has been too much for you. It was probably difficult for you to stay on your feet all morning without letting anyone notice; you've been very courageous. Weep now, it is the best you can do. No? All finished? Back on your feet so soon? All right, we'll go to the infirmary then and you'll lie down, and by evening you'll feel much better. Let's go."

He led Goldmund to the sick room, careful not to pass any study halls on the way. He pointed to one of two empty beds and left the room when Goldmund obediently began to undress, and went to the superior to have the boy put on the sick list. He also ordered the promised soup and a glass of wine at the refectory, two special treats the cloister habitually allowed the ailing, who enjoyed it greatly when they did not feel too sick.

Goldmund lay on the bed in the sick room, trying to think himself out of his confusion. Something like an hour ago he could perhaps have explained to himself why he felt so indescribably tired today, what deathly strain on the soul drained his mind and made his eyes burn. It was the desperate, constantly renewed, constantly failing effort to forget last night—but not the night itself, not the foolish, enjoyable escapade from the locked cloister, or the walk through the forest, or the slippery makeshift bridge across the little black stream behind the mill, or the climbing over fences in and out of gardens, through windows, sneaking along passageways, but the single second outside the dark kitchen window, the girl's words, her breath, the pressure of her hands, the touch of her lips.

But now something new had occurred, another shock, another experience. Narcissus cared for him, Narcissus loved him, Narcissus had taken trouble over him—the refined, distinguished, intelligent young teacher with the narrow, slightly sarcastic mouth—and he, Goldmund, had let himself break down in front of him, had stood before him in stammering embarrassment, and had finally started to bawl! Instead of winning this superior being with the noblest weapons, with Greek and philosophy, with spiritual heroism and dignified stoicism, he had collapsed in disgraceful weakness. He'd never forgive himself for it. Never would he be able to look Narcissus in the eye again without shame.

But his weeping had released the great tension. The quiet loneliness of the room and the bed were doing him good; the despair had lost more than half of its impact. After an hour or so, one of the lay brothers came in, brought a gruel soup, a piece of white bread, and a small mug of red wine which the students normally drank only on holidays. Goldmund ate and drank, emptied half the plate, pushed it aside, started to think again, but couldn't, reached for the bowl once more, ate a few more spoonfuls. And when, somewhat later, the door quietly opened and Narcissus came in to look after his patient, Goldmund was asleep and a rosy glow had already returned to his cheeks. Narcissus looked at him for a long time, with love, curiosity, and also a slight envy. He saw that Goldmund was not ill; there would be no need to send him wine tomorrow. But he knew that the ice was broken, that they would be friends. Today it was Goldmund who needed him, whom he was able to serve. Another time he himself might be weak and in need of assistance and love. And from this boy he would be able to accept it, were it to come to that some day.

3

It was a curious friendship that had begun between Narcissus and Goldmund, one that pleased only a few; at times it seemed to displease even the two friends.

At first it was Narcissus, the thinker, who had the harder time of it. All was mind to him, even love; he was unable to give in to an attraction without thinking about it first. He was the guiding spirit of this friendship. For a long time he alone consciously recognized its destiny, its depth, its significance. For a long time he remained lonely, surrounded by love, knowing that his friend would fully belong to him only after he had been able to lead him toward recognition. With glowing fervor, playful and irresponsible, Goldmund abandoned himself to this new life; while Narcissus, aware and responsible, accepted the demands of fate.

For Goldmund it was a release at first, a convalescence. His youthful need for love had been powerfully aroused, and at the same time hopelessly intimidated, by the looks and the kiss of a pretty girl. Deep inside himself he felt the life he had dreamed of up to now, all his beliefs, all the things for which he felt himself destined, his entire vocation, threatened at the root by the kiss through the window, by the expression of those dark eyes. His father had decided that he was to lead the life of a monk, and with all his will he had accepted this decision. The fire of his first youthful fervor burned

toward a pious, ascetic hero-image, and at the first
furtive encounter, at life's first appeal to his
senses, at the first beckoning of femininity he had
felt that there was an enemy, a demon, a danger:
woman. And now fate was offering him salvation,
now in his most desperate need this friendship
came toward him and offered his longing a new
alter for reverence. Here he was permitted to love,
to abandon himself without sinning, to give his
heart to an admired older friend, more intelligent
than he, to spiritualize the dangerous flames of the
senses, to transform them into nobler fires of sacrifice.

But during the first spring of this friendship he
ran up against unfamiliar obstacles, unexpected,
incomprehensible coolness, frightening demands. It
never occurred to him to see himself as the contradiction, the exact opposite of his friend. He thought
that only love, only sincere devotion was needed to
fuse two into one, to wipe out differences and
bridge contrasts. But how harsh and positive this
Narcissus was, how merciless and precise! Innocent
abandonment, grateful wandering together in the
land of friendship seemed unknown and undesir-
able to him. He did not seem to understand, to
tolerate dreamy strolls on paths that led in no particular direction. When Goldmund had seemed ill,
he had shown concern, and loyally he helped and
advised him in all matters of school and learning;
he explained difficult passages in books, opened
new horizons in the realm of grammar, logic, and
theology. Yet he never seemed genuinely satisfied
with his friend, or to approve of him; quite often
he seemed to be smiling, seemed not to take him
seriously. Goldmund felt that this was not mere
pedantry, not just the condescension of someone
older and more intelligent, but that there was
something else behind it, something deeper and
important. But he was unable to recognize this

deeper something, and this friendship often made him feel sad and lost.

Actually Narcissus recognized his friend's qualities only too well; he was not blind to the budding beauty, the vital force of nature in him, his flowering opulence. He was no pedant bent on feeding Greek to a fervent young soul, on repaying an innocent love with logic. On the contrary, he loved the blond adolescent altogether too much, and this was dangerous for him, because loving, to him, was not a natural condition but a miracle. To fall in love was not permitted him; he could not be content with the joyful contemplation of those eyes, with the nearness of this golden light. Not even for a second could he let this love dwell upon the senses. Because where Goldmund *felt* himself destined for monkish asceticism and a lifelong striving for saintliness, Narcissus *was* truly destined for that life. To him, loving was permitted only in its highest form. Narcissus did not believe in Goldmund's calling to be an ascetic. He knew how to read people more clearly than most, and here love increased his clarity. He recognized Goldmund's nature and understood it deeply, in spite of the contrasts, because it was the other, the lost half of his own. He saw that this nature was armored by a hard shell, by fantasies, faults of upbringing and paternal words; he had long sensed the whole, uncomplicated secret of this young life. He was fully aware of what he must do: reveal this secret to its bearer, free him from the shell, give him back his true nature. It would be hard, and the hardest was that perhaps it would make him lose his friend.

With infinite caution he drew closer to his goal. Months went by before a serious approach became possible between the two, a deep-reaching conversation. In spite of their friendship, they were so far apart, the bowstring was so taut between them: a seeing man and a blind man, they walked side by side; the blind man's unawareness of his own blindness was a consolation only to himself.

Narcissus made the first breakthrough when he tried to discover what the experience had been that had driven the boy toward him at a weak moment. It turned out to be less difficult than he had expected. Goldmund had long felt the need to confess the experience of that night, but there was no one, outside the Abbot, whom he trusted enough, and the Abbot was not his confessor. And when Narcissus reminded his friend, at a moment he judged favorable, of the very beginnings of their bond and gently hinted at the secret, Goldmund immediately said, "If only you were an ordained priest and able to confess me; I would have liked to free myself of that matter in confession and I would gladly have done penance for it. But I couldn't tell my confessor."

Carefully, shrewdly, Narcissus dug deeper; the vein had been found. "You remember the morning when you seemed to be ill," he ventured. "You can't have forgotten, since that was when we became friends. I think of it often. Perhaps you didn't notice, but I was rather helpless that morning."

"You helpless!" cried his friend, incredulous. "But *I* was the helpless one! It was I who stood there, swallowing, unable to utter a word, who finally began to weep like a child! Ugh, to this day I feel ashamed of that moment; I thought I could never face you again. You had seen me so disgracefully weak."

Narcissus groped ahead.

"I understand," he said. "It must have been unpleasant for you. Such a firm, courageous boy breaking into tears in front of a stranger, and a teacher at that, it was quite out of character. Well, that morning I merely thought you were ill. In the throes of a fever, even a man like Aristotle may behave strangely. But you were not ill. You had no fever! And that is why you feel ashamed. No one feels ashamed of succumbing to a fever, does he? You felt ashamed because you had succumbed to something else, to something that overpowered you? Did something special happen?"

Goldmund hesitated a second, then he said slowly: "Yes, something special did happen. Let's pretend you're my confessor; sooner or later this thing must be told."

With bowed head, he told his friend the story of that night.

Smilingly, Narcissus replied: "Well yes, 'going to the village' is of course forbidden. But one can do all kinds of forbidden things and laugh them away, or one can confess them and that is that; they need no longer concern one. Why shouldn't you commit these little foolishnesses like other students? What is so terrible about that?"

Angrily, without holding back, Goldmund burst out: "You do talk like a schoolmaster! You know very well what it is all about! Of course I don't see a great sin in breaking the house rules for once, to play a student prank, although it's not exactly part of the preparatory training for cloister life."

"Just a moment, my friend," Narcissus called sharply. "Don't you know that many pious fathers went through precisely that kind of preparatory training? Don't you know that a wastrel's life may be one of the shortest roads to sainthood?"

"Oh, don't lecture!" protested Goldmund. "It wasn't a trifling disobedience that weighed on my conscience. It was something else. It was that girl. I can't describe the sensation to you. It was a feeling that if I gave in to the enticement, if I merely reached out to touch the girl, I'd never be able to turn back, that sin would swallow me like the maw of hell and not give me up ever. That it would be the end of every beautiful dream, of all virtue, of all love of God and good."

Narcissus nodded, deep in thought.

"Love of God," he said slowly, searching for words, "is not always the same as love of good. I wish it were that simple. We know what is good, it is written in the Commandments. But God is not contained only in the Commandments, you know; they are only an infinitesimal part of Him. A man may abide by the Commandments and be far from God."

"But don't you understand?" Goldmund complained.

"Certainly I understand. You feel that woman, sex, is the essence of everything you call 'world' or 'sin'. You think yourself incapable of all other sins; or, if you did commit them, you think they would not crush you, that you could confess them and be whole again."

"Yes, that is exactly how I feel."

"You see, I do understand. You're not so terribly wrong after all; the story of Eve and the serpent is certainly no idle tale. And yet you are not right about this, my dear friend. You *would* be right if you were the Abbot Daniel, or your baptismal saint, the holy Chrysostom, or a bishop, or a priest, even a simple monk. But you aren't. You are a student, and although you wish to remain in the cloister for life, or your father wishes it for you, still you have not taken any vows; you have not been consecrated. If some pretty girl were to tempt you one of these days and you were to give in to the temptation, you would not have broken any vows."

"No written vows!" Goldmund cried heatedly. "But an unwritten one, the most sacred, something I carry inside me. Can't you see that this may apply to many others but not to me? You have not been consecrated either, nor have you taken any vows yet, but you would never permit yourself to touch a woman! Or am I mistaken? Isn't that how you are? Or aren't you the man I thought you were? Didn't you long ago, in your heart, make the vow that has not yet been made with words before superiors, and don't you feel bound by it forever? Aren't you exactly like me?"

"No, Goldmund, I am not like you, not in the way you think, although I, too, am keeping an unspoken vow—in that respect you are right—but I am in no way like you. Some day you will think of what I am going to say to you now: our friendship has no other purpose, no other reason, than to show you how utterly unlike me you are."

Goldmund was stunned; Narcissus's expression and tone permitted no contradiction. He was silent. Why had Narcissus said these words? Why should Narcissus's unspoken vow be more sacred than his own? Didn't he take him at all seriously? Did he see nothing but a child in him? The confusions and griefs of this strange friendship were beginning all over again.

Narcissus no longer had any doubt about the nature of Goldmund's secret. It was Eve who stood behind it, the original mother. But how was it possible that the awakening of sex met with such bitter antagonism in such a beautiful, healthy, flowering adolescent? There must be a secret enemy who had managed to split this magnificent human being within himself and turn him against his natural urges. This demon had to be discovered, had to be conjured up and made visible; only then could it be defeated.

Meanwhile Goldmund had been more and more neglected by his classmates, or rather they felt neglected by him, betrayed. His friendship with Narcissus pleased no one. The slanderers, those who had themselves been in love with one or the other, said the whole thing was against nature. Even those who were certain that no vice could be suspected here shook their heads. No one wanted to see these two friends together. It seemed that they were setting themselves apart from the others by this friendship, arrogantly, as though they were aristocrats for whom the others were not good enough; that was unbrotherly, not in keeping with the cloister spirit, not Christian.

Many things about the two—rumors, accusations, slander—reached Abbot Daniel. He had seen many friendships between young men in over forty years of cloister life; they belonged to cloister life and were a pleasant tradition, sometimes amusing, sometimes a danger. He waited, watched, did not intervene. Such a violent, exclusive friendship was rare, probably not undangerous, but since he did not for an instant doubt its purity, he decided to let it take its course. If it had not been for Narcissus's exceptional position among students and teachers, the Abbot would not have hesitated to place a few separating rules between the two. It was not good for Goldmund to have withdrawn from his classmates and to be in close association only with someone older, with a teacher. But was it permissible to disturb the extraordinary, highly gifted Narcissus, whom all teachers considered their equal if not their superior, in his privileged career and relieve him of his teaching position? Had Narcissus not proved himself as a teacher, had this friendship led to partiality and neglectfulness, the Abbot would have demoted him immediately. But there was nothing to be held against him, only rumors and others' jealous suspicions. Moreover, the Abbot knew of Narcissus's special gifts, of his curiously penetrating, perhaps slightly presumptuous, insight into people. He did not overestimate these gifts, he would have preferred Narcissus to have other gifts; but he did not doubt that Narcissus had noticed something unusual in the student Goldmund, that he knew him far better than he, or anyone else in the cloister. He himself, the Abbot, had not noticed anything unusual about Gold-

mund, apart from his winning nature, and perhaps
a certain eagerness, a somewhat precocious zeal
that made him conduct himself, still a student
and a boarder, as though he belonged to the
cloister and was one of the brothers. He saw no
reason to fear that Narcissus would encourage
this immature though touching zeal or that he
would spur it on. He feared rather, for Goldmund, that his friend might infect him with a
certain spiritual pride and erudite arrogance; but
this danger seemed unlikely for this particular pupil; it was all right to wait and see. When he
thought how much simpler it was for a superior,
how much more peaceful and comfortable, to rule
over average rather than strong or exceptional
characters, he had to sigh and smile. No, he was
not going to let himself be infected by suspicions;
he did not wish to be ungrateful for the two exceptional human beings entrusted to his care.

Narcissus pondered a great deal about his
friend. His special gift of spotting and emotionally
recognizing the nature and destiny of others had
long since told him about Goldmund. All that was
alive and radiant in this young man spoke only too
clearly: he bore all the marks of a strong human
being, richly endowed sensually and spiritually,
perhaps an artist, but at any rate a person with a
great potential for love, whose fulfillment and happiness consisted of being easily inflamed and able
to give himself. Then why was this being with such
rich and perceptive senses so set on leading the
ascetic life of the mind? Narcissus thought at great
length about it. He knew that Goldmund's father
favored his son's determination. Could the father
have inspired it? What spell had he cast over his
son to make him believe that this was his destiny,
his duty? What sort of a person was this father?
Narcissus had often intentionally touched on the
subject of this father—and Goldmund had frequent-

ly spoken of him—and yet he could not imagine him, could not see him. Was it not strange and suspicious? Whenever Goldmund told a story about a trout he had caught as a boy, when he described a butterfly, imitated the call of a bird, spoke of a friend, a dog, a beggar, he created a vivid picture. Whenever he spoke of his father, one saw nothing. No, if his father had really been such an important, powerful, dominant figure in Goldmund's life, he would have been able to describe him differently, to conjure up vivid images of him. Narcissus did not think highly of this father, he did not like him; sometimes he wondered if he were really Goldmund's father. But what gave him such power? How had he succeeded in filling Goldmund's soul with dreams so alien to his soul?

Goldmund also brooded a great deal. He did feel warmly loved by his friend, and yet he often had the unpleasant sensation of not being taken seriously, of being treated a little like a child. And what did it mean when his friend insinuated, again and again, that he was not like him?

Yet thinking did not fill all of Goldmund's days. He was not able to think for too long at a time. There were other things to be done in the course of a day. He often went to see the friar porter, with whom he was on excellent terms. He'd beg and coax for an opportunity to ride the horse Bless for an hour or two, and he was very popular with the few nearby cloister tenants, especially with the miller. He'd often stalk otters with the miller's man, or they'd bake pancakes with the finely ground prelate's flour, which Goldmund could tell from all other kinds of flour, eyes closed, just by the smell of it. Although he spent time with Narcissus, there still remained a number of hours in which he pursued his old habits and pleasures. And usually the service was also a joy to him. He loved to sing in the student choir; he loved to say a rosary in front

of a favorite altar, to listen to the solemnly beautiful Latin of the mass, to see the gold of the receptacles and ornaments glitter through clouds of incense, and the quiet venerable saints' figures standing on columns, the evangelists with the beasts, St.
Jacob with his hat and pilgrim's satchel.

He felt drawn toward these wood and stone
figures; he liked to think that they stood in secret
relationship to him, perhaps like immortal, omniscient godfathers who protected and guided his life.
He felt the same secret bond and love for the
columns and capitals of the windows and doors, for
the altar ornaments, for the beautifully profiled
staves and wreaths, for the flowers and thickets of
sprouting leaves that burst from the stone of the
columns and unfolded so eloquently and intensely.
It seemed a valuable, intimate secret to him that,
outside of nature with its plants and creatures,
there existed a second, silent, man-made nature:
these men, beasts, and plants of stone and wood.
He spent many of his free hours copying these
figures, animal heads and leaf clusters; sometimes
he also tried to draw real flowers, horses, human
faces.

And he was very fond of the hymns, especially
of those in honor of Mary. He loved the firm severe
pace of these songs, their constantly recurring
rhythms and praises. He could follow their reverent
meaning adoringly, or he could forget their meaning and become engrossed in the solemn cadence
of the verses and let himself be filled by them, by
the deep, drawn-out notes, the full sound of the
vowels, the pious refrains. Deep down in his heart
he had no love for learning, grammar, and logic,
although they, too, had their beauty. His real love
was for the image-and-sound world of liturgy.

And every so often, for brief moments, he'd
break the estrangement that had set in between
him and his classmates. It annoyed and bored him

in the long run to find himself surrounded by rejection and coolness. Every so often he'd make a grumpy bench companion laugh or start a taciturn bed neighbor chatting; he'd work at it for an hour, ingratiating himself and winning back a couple of friends for a while. Twice these approaches brought him, much against his intention, an invitation to "go to the village." Then he'd become frightened and quickly draw back. No, he was not going to the village again, and he managed to forget the girl with the braids, never—or almost never —to think of her any more.

4

Narcissus's long siege had not succeeded in bringing Goldmund's secret out into the open. For a long time he had apparently labored in vain to awaken him, to teach him the language in which the secret could be told.

Goldmund's description of his home and childhood gave no clear picture. There was a shadow-life, faceless father whom he venerated, and then there was the legend of a mother who had vanished, or perished, long ago, who was nothing but a pallid name. Narcissus, the experienced reader of souls, had gradually come to recognize that Goldmund was one of those people part of whose lives have been lost; pressure of circumstances or some kind of magic power has obliterated a portion of their past. He realized that nothing would be gained by mere questioning and teaching, that he had overestimated the power of logic and spoken many useless words.

But the love that bound him to his friend and their habit of spending much time together had not been fruitless. In spite of the vast differences of their characters, each had learned much from the other. Beside the language of reason, a language of the soul had gradually come into being between them; it was as if, branching off the main street, there are many small, almost secret lanes. Gradually the imaginative power of Goldmund's soul had tracked such paths into Narcissus's thoughts and expressions, making him understand—and sympathize with—many of Goldmund's perceptions and feelings, without need for words. New links from soul to soul developed in the warm glow of love; words came later. That is how, one holiday, in the library, there occurred a conversation between the friends that neither had expected—a conversation that touched at the core and purpose of their friendship and cast new, far-reaching lights.

They had been talking about astrology, a forbidden science that was not pursued in the cloister. Narcissus had said that astrology was an attempt to arrange and order the many different types of human beings according to their natures and destinies. At this point Goldmund had objected: "You're forever talking of differences—I've finally recognized a pet theory of yours. When you speak of the great difference that is supposed to exist between you and me, for instance, it seems to me that this difference is nothing but your strange determination to establish differences."

Narcissus: "Yes. You've hit the nail on the head. That's it: to you, differences are quite unimportant; to me, they are what matters most. I am a scholar by nature; science is my vocation. And science is, to quote your words, nothing but the 'determination to establish differences.' Its essence couldn't be defined more accurately. For us, the men of science, nothing is as important as the establishment of differences; science is the art of differentiation. Discovering in every man that which distinguishes him from others is to know him."

Goldmund: "If you like. One man wears wooden shoes and is a peasant; another wears a crown and is a king. Those are differences, I grant you. But children can see them, too, without any science."

Narcissus: "But when peasant and king are dressed alike, the child can no longer tell one from the other."

Goldmund: "Neither can science."

Narcissus: "Perhaps it can. Not that science is more intelligent than the child, but it has more patience; it remembers more than just the most obvious characteristics."

Goldmund: "So does any intelligent child. He will recognize the king by the look in his eyes, or by his bearing. To put it plainly: you learned men are arrogant, you always think everybody else stupid. One can be extremely intelligent without learning."

Narcissus: "I am glad that you're beginning to realize that. You'll soon realize, too, that I don't mean intelligence when I speak of the difference between us. I do not say, you are more intelligent, or less intelligent; better or worse. I merely say, you are different."

Goldmund: "That's easy enough to understand. But you don't speak only of our difference in character; you often speak also of the differences in fate, in destiny. Why, for instance, should your destiny be different from mine? We are both Christians, we are both resolved to lead the life of the cloister, we are both children of our good Father in heaven. Our goal is the same: eternal bliss. Our destiny is the same: the return to God."

Narcissus: "Very good. True, in the view of dogma, one man is exactly like another, but not in life. Take Our Saviour's favorite disciple, John, on whose breast he rested his head, and that other disciple who betrayed him—you hardly can say that they had the same destiny."

Goldmund: "Narcissus, you are a sophist. We'll never come together on that kind of road."

Narcissus: "No road will bring us together."

Goldmund: "Don't speak like that."

Narcissus: "I'm serious. We are not meant to come together, not any more than sun and moon were meant to come together, or sea and land.

We are sun and moon, dear friend; we are sea and land. It is not our purpose to become each other; it is to recognize each other, to learn to see the other and honor him for what he is: each the other's opposite and complement."

Goldmund was perplexed. He bowed his head, and his face was sad.

Finally he said: "Is that why you so often don't take my thoughts seriously?"

Narcissus hesitated before he answered. His voice was clear and hard when he said: "Yes, that is why. I take only you seriously, dear Goldmund; you'll have to get used to that. Believe me, there isn't an intonation in your voice, not a gesture, not a smile that I don't take seriously. But your thoughts I take less seriously. I take seriously all that I find essential and necessary in you. Why do you want particular attention paid to your thoughts, when you have so many other gifts?"

Goldmund smiled bitterly: "You've always considered me a child; I've said it before."

Narcissus remained firm: "Part of your thought I consider a child's thought. Remember what we said earlier: an intelligent child need not be less intelligent than a learned scholar. But when the child wants to assert its opinion in matters of learning, then the scholar doesn't take it seriously."

Goldmund said with violence: "You smile at me even when we don't discuss matters of learning! For instance, you always act as though all my piety, my efforts to advance my studies, my desire to become a monk were so many childish fantasies."

Narcissus looked at him gravely: "I take you seriously when you are Goldmund. But you're not always Goldmund. I wish nothing more than to see you become Goldmund through and through. You are not a scholar, you are not a monk—scholars and monks can have a coarser grain. You think you're not learned or logical or pious enough for me. On the contrary, you are not enough yourself."

Perplexed and even hurt, Goldmund had withdrawn after this conversation. And yet a few days later he himself wished to hear more. And this time Narcissus was able to give Goldmund a picture of their different natures that he found more acceptable.

Narcissus had talked himself into a fever; he felt that Goldmund was accepting his words more openly and willingly, that he had power over him. His success made him give in to the temptation to say more than he had intended; he let himself be carried away by his own words.

"Look," he said, "I am superior to you only in one point: I'm awake, whereas you are only half awake, or completely asleep sometimes. I call a man awake who knows in his conscious reason his innermost unreasonable force, drives, and weaknesses and knows how to deal with them. For you to learn that about yourself is the potential reason for your having met me. In your case, mind and nature, consciousness and dream world lie very far apart. You've forgotten your childhood; it cries for you from the depths of your soul. It will make you suffer until you heed it.

"But enough of that! Being awake, as I've already said, makes me stronger than you. This is the one point in which I am superior to you, and that is why I can be useful to you. In every other respect you are superior to me, my dear Goldmund—or rather, you will be, as soon as you've found yourself."

Goldmund had listened with astonishment, but at the words "you've forgotten your childhood" he flinched as though pierced by an arrow. Narcissus didn't notice; he often kept his eyes closed for long moments while he spoke, or he'd stare straight ahead, as though this helped him to find his words. He did not see Goldmund's face twitch suddenly.

"I . . . superior to you!" stammered Goldmund, feeling as though his whole body had been lamed.

"Why, yes," Narcissus continued. "Natures of your kind, with strong, delicate senses, the soul-oriented, the dreamers, poets, lovers are almost always superior to us creatures of the mind. You take your being from your mothers. You live fully; you were endowed with the strength of love, the ability to feel. Whereas we creatures of reason, we don't live fully; we live in an arid land, even though we often seem to guide and rule you. Yours is the plenitude of life, the sap of the fruit, the garden of passion, the beautiful landscape of art. Your home is the earth; ours is the world of ideas. You are in danger of drowning in the world of the senses; ours is the danger of suffocating in an airless void. You are an artist; I am a thinker. You sleep at the mother's breast; I wake in the desert. For me the sun shines; for you the moon and the stars. Your dreams are of girls; mine of boys . . ."

Goldmund listened, wide-eyed. Narcissus spoke with a kind of rhetorical self-intoxication. Several words struck Goldmund like swords. Toward the end he grew pale and closed his eyes, and when Narcissus became aware of it and asked with sudden fear what was wrong, the deathly pale boy said: "Once I broke down in front of you and burst into tears—you remember. That must not happen again. I'd never forgive myself—or you! Please go away at once and let me be alone. You've said terrible words to me."

Narcissus was overcome. His words had carried him away; he had felt that he was speaking better than usual. Now he saw with consternation that some of his words had deeply affected his friend and somehow pierced him to the quick. He found it hard to leave him at that moment and hesitated a second or two, but Goldmund's frown left him no choice. Confused, he ran off to allow his friend the solitude he needed.

This time the extreme tension in Goldmund's soul did not dissolve itself in tears. He was still, feeling deeply, desperately wounded, as though his friend had plunged a knife into his breast. He breathed heavily, with mortally contracted heart, a wax-pale face, limp hands. This was the old pain, only considerably sharper, the same inner choking, the feeling that something frightful had to be looked in the eye, something unbearable. But this time there was no relief of tears to overcome the pain. Holy Mother of God, what then could this be? Had something happened? Had he been murdered? Had he killed someone? What had been said that was so frightful?

He panted, pushing his breath away from him. Like a person who has been poisoned, he was bursting with the feeling that he had to free himself of something deadly, deep inside him. With the movements of a swimmer he rushed from his room, fled unconsciously to the quietest, loneliest parts of the cloister, through passages, down stairways and out into the open. He had wandered into the innermost refuge of the cloister, into the court of the cross. The sky stretched clear and sunny over the few bright flower beds; the scent of roses drifted through the cool stony air in sweet hesitant threads.

Without knowing it, Narcissus had accomplished his long-desired aim: he had named the demon by which his friend was possessed; he had called it out into the open. One of his many words had touched the secret in Goldmund's heart, which had reared up in furious pain. For a long time Narcissus wandered through the cloister, looking for his friend, but he could not find him.

Goldmund was standing under one of the massive stone arches that led from the passageway out into the little cloister garden; on each column three animal heads, the stone-carved heads of dogs and wolves, glared down at him. Pain was raging inside him, pushing, finding no way toward the light, toward reason. Deathly fear clutched at his throat, knotted his stomach. Mechanically he looked up, saw the animal heads on the capital of one of the columns, and began to feel that those three monstrous heads were squatting, glaring, barking inside him.

"I'm going to die any moment," he felt with terror. "I'll lose my mind and those animal snouts will devour me."

His body twitched; he sank down at the foot of the column. The pain was too great; he had reached the limit. He fainted; he drowned in longed-for oblivion.

It had been a rather unsatisfactory day for Abbot Daniel. Two of the older monks had come to him, foaming with excitement, full of accusations, bringing up petty old jealousies, squabbling furiously. He had listened to them altogether too long, had unsuccessfully admonished them, and dismissed them severely with rather heavy penances. With a feeling of futility in his heart, he had withdrawn for prayer in the lower chapel, prayed, and stood up again, unrefreshed. Now he stepped out into the court a moment for some air, attracted by the smell of roses. There he found the pupil Goldmund lying in a faint on the stones. He looked at him with sadness, frightened by the pallor and remoteness of the usually winsome face. It had not been a good day, and now this to top it all! He tried to lift the young man, but was not up to the effort. With a deep sigh the old man walked away to call two younger brothers to carry Goldmund upstairs and to send Father Anselm to him, the cloister physician. He also sent for Brother Narcissus, who soon appeared before him.

"Have you heard?" he asked.

"About Goldmund? Yes, gentle father, I just heard that he has been taken ill or has had an accident and has been carried in."

"Yes, I found him lying in the inner court, where actually he had no business to be. It was not an accident that he fainted. I don't like this. It would seem to me that you are somehow connected with it, or at least know of it, since you are so intimate. That is why I have called you. Speak."

With his usual control of bearing and speech, Narcissus gave a brief account of his conversation with Goldmund and of its surprisingly violent effect on him. The Abbot shook his head, not without ill humor.

"Those are strange conversations," he said, forcing himself to remain calm. "What you have just described to me is a conversation that might be called interference with another soul, what I might call a confessor's conversation. But you're not Goldmund's confessor. You are no one's confessor; you have not been ordained. How is it that you discussed matters with a pupil, in the tone of an adviser, that concern no one but his confessor? As you can see, the consequences have been harmful."

"The consequences," Narcissus said in a mild but firm voice, "are not yet known to us, gentle father. I was somewhat frightened by the violence of his reaction, but I have no doubt that the consequences of our conversation will be good for Goldmund."

"We shall see. I am not speaking of the consequences now, I am speaking of your action. What prompted you to have such conversations with Goldmund?"

"As you know, he is my friend. I have a special fondness for him and I believe that I understand him particularly well. You say that I acted toward him like a confessor. In no way have I assumed any religious authority; I merely thought that I knew him a little better than he knows himself."

The Abbot shrugged.

"I know, that is your métier. Let us hope that you did not cause any harm with it. But is Goldmund ill? I mean, is anything wrong with him? Does he feel weak? Has he been sleeping poorly? Does he eat badly? Has he some kind of pain?"

"No, until today he's been healthy. In his body, that is."

"And otherwise?"

"His soul is ailing. As you know, he is at an age when struggles with sex begin."

"I know. He is seventeen?"

"He is eighteen."

"Eighteen. Well, yes, that is late enough. But these struggles are natural; everybody goes through them. That is no reason to say that he is ailing in his soul."

"No, gentle father. That is not the only reason. But Goldmund's soul has been ailing for a long time; that is why these struggles hold more danger for him than for others. I believe that he suffers because he has forgotten a part of his past."

"Ah? And what part is that?"

"His mother, and everything connected with her. I don't know anything about her, either. I merely know that there must lie the source of his illness. Because Goldmund knows nothing of his mother apparently, except that he lost her at an early age. I have the impression that he seems ashamed of her. And yet it must be from her that he inherited most of his gifts, because his description of his father does not make him seem a man who would have such a winsome, talented, original son. Nothing of this has been told me; I deduced it from signs."

At first the Abbot had smiled slightly at this precocious, arrogant-sounding speech; the whole matter was a troublesome chore to him. Now he began to think. He remembered Goldmund's father as a somewhat brittle, distrustful man; now, as he searched his memory, he suddenly remembered a few words the father had, at that time, uttered about Goldmund's mother. He had said that she had brought shame upon him and run away, and that he had tried to suppress the mother's memory in his young son, as well as any vices he might have inherited from her. And that he had most probably succeeded, because the boy was willing to offer his life up to God, in atonement for his mother's sins.

Never had Narcissus pleased the Abbot less than today. And yet—how well this thinker had guessed; how well he really did seem to know Goldmund.

He asked a final question about the day's occurrences, and Narcissus said: "I had not intended to upset Goldmund so violently. I reminded him that he does not know himself, that he had forgotten his childhood and his mother. Something I said must have struck him and penetrated the darkness I have been fighting so long. He seemed beside himself; he looked at me as though he no longer knew himself or me. I have often told him that he was asleep, that he was not really awake. Now he has been awakened. I have no doubt about that."

He was dismissed, without a scolding but with an admonition not to visit the sick boy for the time being.

Meanwhile Father Anselm had ordered the boy put to bed and was sitting beside him. He had not deemed it advisable to shock him back into consciousness by violent means. The boy looked altogether too sick. Out of his kind, wrinkled face, the old man looked fondly upon the adolescent. Meanwhile he checked his pulse and heartbeat. The boy must have eaten something impossible, a bunch of sorrel, or something equally silly; that kind of thing happened sometimes. The boy's mouth was closed, so he couldn't check his tongue. He was fond of Goldmund but had little use for his friend, that precocious, overly young teacher. Now it had come to this. Brother Narcissus surely had something to do with this stupid mishap. Why had this charming, clear-eyed youngster, this dear child of nature, picked the arrogant scholar, the vain grammarian, who valued his Greek more highly than all living creatures of this world!

When the door opened much later, and the Abbot came in, Father Anselm was still sitting beside the bed, staring into the boy's face. What a dear, trusting young face this was, and all one could do was to sit beside it, wishing, but probably unable, to help. It might all be due to a colic, of course; he would prescribe hot wine, perhaps some rhubarb. But the longer he looked into the greenish-pale, distorted face, the more his suspicions leaned toward another cause, a much more serious one. Father Anselm was experienced. More than once, in the course of his long life, he had seen men who were possessed. He hesitated to formulate this suspicion even to himself. He would wait and observe. But if this poor boy had really been hexed, he thought grimly, we probably won't have to look far for the culprit, and he shall not have an easy time of it.

The Abbot stepped up to the bed, bent over the sick boy, and gently drew back one of the eyelids. "Can he be roused?" he asked.

"I'd rather wait a bit longer. His heart is sound. We must not let anyone in to see him."

"Is he in danger?"

"I don't think so. There aren't any wounds, no trace of a blow or fall. He is unconscious because of

a colic, perhaps. Extreme pain can cause loss of
consciousness. If he had been poisoned, he'd be
running a fever. No, he'll come to and go on living."

"Do you think it could be his soul?"

"I wouldn't rule that out. Do we know anything?
Has he had a shock perhaps? News of someone's
death? A violent dispute, an insult? That would
certainly explain it."

"We know of nothing. Make sure that no one is
allowed to see him. Please stay with him until he
comes to. If anything should go wrong, call me,
even if it's in the middle of the night."

Before leaving, the old man bent once more over
the sick boy. He thought of the boy's father, of the
day this charming blond head had been brought to
him, how everyone had taken to him from the
start. He, too, had been glad to see him in the
cloister. But Narcissus was certainly right in one
respect: nothing in the boy recalled his father. Ah,
how much worry there was everywhere, how in-
sufficient all our striving! Had he perhaps been
neglectful of this poor boy? Was it right that no
one in the house knew this pupil as thoroughly as
Narcissus? How could he be helped by someone
who was still a novice, who had not yet been
consecrated, who was not yet a monk, and whose
thoughts and ideas all had something unpleasantly
superior about them, something almost hostile?
God alone knew whether Narcissus too had not
been handled wrongly all this time? Was he concealing something evil behind his mask of obedience, hedonism perhaps? Whatever these two
young men would some day become would be
partly his responsibility.

It was dark when Goldmund came to. His head
felt empty, dizzy. He knew that he was lying in
bed, but not where. He didn't think about that;
it didn't matter. But where had he been? From

what strange land of experience had he returned?
He had been to some far-away place. He had seen
something there, something extraordinary, something sublime, but also frightful, and unforgettable
—and yet he had forgotten it. Where had it been?
What was it that had appeared to him, huge, painful, blissful? That had vanished again?

He listened deeply inside him, to that place from
which something had erupted today, where something had happened—what had it been? Wild tan-
gles of images rose before him, he saw dogs' heads,
the heads of three dogs, and he sniffed the scent of
roses. The pain he had felt! He closed his eyes. The
dreadful pain he had felt! Again he fell asleep.

As he awoke from the rapidly vanishing dream
world that was sliding away from him, he saw it.
He rediscovered the image, and trembled with pain
and joy. His eyes had been opened: he saw Her. He
saw the tall, radiant woman with the full mouth
and glowing hair—his mother. And at the same
time he thought he heard a voice: "You have forgotten your childhood." But whose voice was that?
He listened, thought, found it. Narcissus's voice.
Narcissus? In a flash everything came back: he
remembered. O mother, mother! Mountains of rubbish collapsed, oceans of forgetfulness vanished.
The lost woman, the indescribably beloved, was
again looking at him with her regal light-blue eyes.

Father Anselm had dozed off in the armchair
beside the bed; he awoke. He heard the sick boy
stir, he heard him breathe. Gently he stood up.

"Is someone in the room?" Goldmund asked.

"It is I, have no fear. I'll put the light on."

He lighted the lamp, its glow fell over his well-
meaning, wrinkled face.

"But am I ill?" asked the boy.

"You fainted, son. Hold out your hand, let's take a
look at your pulse. How do you feel?"

"Fine. Thank you, Father Anselm, you're very

kind. Nothing's wrong with me now. I'm just tired."

"I bet you are. And you'll go right back to sleep. But first you'll have a sip of hot wine; it's all made and ready. Let's drain a mug together, my boy, to good fellowship."

He had kept a small pitcher of hot wine in readiness.

"So we both had a nice nap," laughed the physician. "A fine night nurse, huh, who can't keep awake. Well, we're all human. Now we'll take a sip of this magic potion, my boy. Nothing's more pleasant than a little secret drinking in the middle of the night. *Prosit.*"

Goldmund laughed, clinked cups, and tasted the warm wine. It was spiced with cinnamon and cloves and sweetened; he had never tasted such a drink before. He remembered his previous illness, when Narcissus had taken care of him. Now it was Father Anselm who was caring for him. It was all so pleasant and strange to be lying there in the lamplight, drinking a mug of sweet warm wine with the old father in the middle of the night.

"Have you a pain in your stomach?" the old man asked.

"No."

"I thought you probably had the colic, Goldmund. You don't then. Let's see your tongue. Well, fine, your old Anselm's proved his ignorance once again. Tomorrow you'll stay in bed and I'll come and take a look at you. Already through with your wine? Fine, may it do you good. Let's see if there is more. Half a mug each, if we share and share alike.—You really gave us a scare, Goldmund! Lying in the court like a child's corpse. And you really have no stomach ache?"

They laughed together and shared what was left of the convalescent wine. The father joked; gratefully, delightedly Goldmund looked at him. His eyes were clear again. Then the old man went off to bed.

Goldmund lay awake awhile longer. Again the images rose up inside him; his friend's words flamed up again. The blond radiant woman, his mother, appeared again in his soul. Like a warm south-wind, her image swept through him: like a cloud of life, of warmth and tenderness and innermost enticement. "O my mother! How was it possible, how was I able to forget you!"

5

Up to now, the few things Goldmund knew of his
mother had come from what others had told him.
Her image had almost faded from his memory. Of
the little he thought he knew of her, he had told
Narcissus next to nothing. Mother was a subject
he was forbidden to mention—something to be
ashamed of. She had been a dancer, a wild beautiful woman of noble, though poor, birth; Goldmund's father said that he had lifted her from
poverty and shame; and since he couldn't be sure
she was not a heathen, he had arranged to have
her baptized and instructed in religion; he had
married her and made her respectable. But after a
few years of domesticated and ordered existence,
she had remembered her old tricks and crafts, had
started to make trouble and seduce men, had
strayed from home for days and weeks at a time,
had acquired the reputation of a witch, and, after
her husband had gone to find her and taken her
back to his house several times, she had finally disappeared forever. Her reputation had stayed alive,
a wicked reputation that flickered like the tail of a
comet, until it had been extinguished. Slowly her
husband recovered from the years of disorder, fear,
and shame, of the never ending surprises she
sprang on him. In place of the unredeemed wife,
he educated his little son, who greatly resembled
his mother in features and build; he grew nagging
and bigoted, instilling in Goldmund the belief that

he must offer up his life to God to expiate his mother's sins.

This was the tale Goldmund's father told of his lost wife, although he preferred not to speak of her. He had hinted at it to the Abbot the day he brought Goldmund to the cloister. It was all known to the son as a terrible legend, but he had learned to push it aside and had almost forgotten it. The real image of his mother had been completely forgotten and lost, an altogether different image that was not made of his father's and the servants' tales and dark wild rumors. He had forgotten his own true living mother-memory. And now this image, the star of his earliest years, had risen again.

"I can't understand how I could have forgotten," he said to his friend. "Never in my life have I loved anyone as much as I loved my mother, unconditionally, fervently. Never did I venerate or admire anyone as I did her; she was sun and moon to me. God only knows how it was possible to darken this radiant image in my soul, to change her gradually to the evil, pallid, shapeless witch she was to my father and to me for many years."

Narcissus had recently completed his novitiate and had donned the habit. His attitude toward Goldmund was strangely changed. Because Goldmund, who had often before rejected his friend's hints and counsel as cumbersome superiority and pedantry, was now, since his deep experience, filled with astonished admiration of his friend's wisdom. How many of his words had come true like prophecies, how deeply had this uncanny man seen inside him, how precisely had he guessed the secret of his life, his hidden wound, how deftly had he healed him!

At least Goldmund seemed to be healed. Not only had the fainting spell been without evil consequences, but all that was unformed and unauthentic in Goldmund's character had somehow melted away, his mistaken vocation to monkhood, his belief that he was obliged to render particular service to God. The young man seemed to have grown younger and older all at once. He owed it all to Narcissus.

But Narcissus was now conducting himself with a strange caution toward his friend. He looked upon him with great modesty, no longer in the least condescending or instructing, while Goldmund admired him more than ever. He saw Goldmund fed from secret sources to which he, himself, had no access; he had been able to further their growth, but had no part in them. Though he was glad to see his friend freeing himself of his guidance, he also felt sad. He saw that this friendship, which had meant so much to him, was nearing its end. He still knew more about Goldmund than Goldmund knew about himself. Goldmund had rediscovered his soul and was ready to follow its call, but he did not know where it would lead him. Narcissus knew this and felt powerless; his favorite's path led to regions in which he himself would never travel.

Goldmund's eagerness to learn had decreased considerably, as had his desire to argue with his friend. Shamefacedly he remembered some of their former discussions. Meanwhile Narcissus began to feel the need for seclusion; either because he had completed the novitiate or because of his experience with Goldmund, he felt drawn to fasting and long prayers, frequent confessions, voluntary penitence, and Goldmund understood this, could almost share in it. Since his cure, his instincts had been sharpened. Although he had no inkling of where his future would lead him, he did feel strongly, often with anguishing clarity, that his destiny was shaping itself, that this respite of innocence and calm was coming to an end, that all within him was taut and ready. These premonitions were often blissful, kept him awake half the night like a sweet infatuation; at other times they were full of darkness and suffocation. His long-lost mother had come back to him: that was deep happiness. But where was her enticing call leading him? Into uncertainty and entanglement, into need, perhaps into death. It did not lead to quiet, mildness, security, to the monk's cell, to collective cloister life. Her call had nothing in common with his father's orders, which he had for so long confused with his own wishes. Goldmund's piety fed on this emotion; it was often as strong and burning as a violent physical sensation. He would repeat long prayers to the holy Mother of God, letting flow the excessive feelings that drew him toward his own mother. But often his prayers would end in those strange, magnificent dreams of which he had so many now: day-dreams, with half-awake senses, dreams of her with all his senses participating. The mother-world would spray its fragrance about him, look darkly from enigmatic eyes of love, rumble deep as an ocean, like paradise, stammer caressing, senseless endearments, or rather endearments that filled his senses with a taste of sweetness and salt and brushed his hungry lips and eyes with silken hair. His mother meant not only all that was graceful; not only were her gentle look of love and sweet, happiness-promising smile caressing consolations; but somewhere beneath this enticing exterior lay much that was frightful and dark, greedy and fearful, sinful and sorrowful, all that gave birth and all death.

The adolescent would sink deeply into these dreams, into these many-threaded webs of soul-inhabited senses. Enchantingly they resurrected not only the beloved past: childhood and mother love, the radiantly golden morning of life; but in them also the future swung, menacing, promising, beckoning, dangerous. At times these dreams, in which mother, Virgin, and mistress all fused into

one, seemed horrendous crimes to him afterwards,
blasphemies, deadly, unpardonable sins; at other
times he found in them nothing but harmony and
release. Life stared at him, filled with secrets, a
somber, unfathomable world, a rigid forest bristling
with fairy-tale dangers—but these were mother
secrets, they came from her, led to her, they were
the small dark circle, the tiny threatening abyss in
her clear eye.

So much of his forgotten childhood surged up
during these mother dreams, so many small flowers
of memory bloomed from the endless depth of forgetfulness, golden-faced premonition-scented memories of childhood emotions, of incidents perhaps,
or perhaps of dreams. Occasionally he'd dream of
fish, black and silver, swimming toward him, cool
and smooth, swimming into him, through him,
coming like messengers bearing joyous news of
a more gracious, more beautiful reality and vanishing, tails flipping, shadowlike, gone, having
brought new enigmas rather than messages. Or
he'd dream of swimming fish and flying birds, and
each fish or bird was his creature, depended on
him, could be guided like a breath, radiated from
him like an eye, like a thought, returned to him. Or
he'd dream of a garden, a magic garden with fabu-
lous trees, huge flowers, and deep blue-dark caves;
the eyes of unknown animals sparkled in the grass,
smooth-muscled serpents slid along the branches;
giant moist-glistening berries hung from vine or
bush, he'd pick them and they'd swell in his hand
and leak warm juices like blood, or they had eyes
which they'd move with cunning seduction; groping, he'd lean against a tree, reach for a branch,
and see and feel between trunk and branch a
curling nest of thick tousled hair like the hair in
the pit of an arm. Once he dreamed of himself, or
of his name-saint, he dreamed of Goldmund of
Chrysostom, who had a mouth of gold, who spoke

words with his golden mouth, and the words were small swarms of birds that flew off in fluttering groups.

Once he dreamed that he was tall and adult but sat on the floor like a child, that he had clay in front of him and was modeling clay figures, like a child: a small horse, a bull, a tiny man, a tiny woman. The modeling amused him and he gave the animals and men ridiculously large genitals; it seemed wonderfully witty to him in his dream. Then he grew tired of the game and walked off and felt something alive at his back, something soundless and large that was coming nearer and when he looked around he saw with great astonishment and shock, but not without joy, that his small clay figures had grown and come to life. Huge mute giants, they marched past him, continuing to grow, monstrous, silent; tower-high, they traveled on into the world.

He lived in this dream world more than in the real one. The real world: classroom, courtyard, library, dormitory, and chapel were only the surface, a quivering film over the dream-filled superreal world of images. The smallest incident could pierce a hole in this thin skin: a sudden hint in the sound of a Greek word during a tedious lesson, a whiff of scent from Father Anselm's herb satchel, the sight of a garland of stone leaves protruding from the top of a column in a window vault—these small stimulants were enough to puncture the skin of reality, to unleash the raging abysses, streams, and milky ways of an image world of the soul that lay beneath peacefully barren reality. A Latin initial changed to his mother's perfumed face, a long note in the *Ave* became the gate to Paradise, a Greek letter a galloping horse, a rearing serpent that quickly slithered off through the flowers, leaving the rigid page of grammar in its place.

He rarely spoke of it, only occasionally did he give Narcissus a hint of his dream world.

"I believe," he once said, "that the petal of a flower or a tiny worm on the path says far more, contains far more than all the books in the library. One cannot say very much with mere letters and words. Sometimes I'll be writing a Greek letter, a theta or an omega, and tilt my pen just the slightest bit; suddenly the letter has a tail and becomes a fish; in a second it evokes all the streams and rivers of the world, all that is cool and humid, Homer's sea and the waters on which Saint Peter wandered; or it becomes a bird, flaps its tail, shakes out its feathers, puffs itself up, laughs, flies away. You probably don't appreciate letters like that very much, do you, Narcissus? But I say: with them God wrote the world."

"I do appreciate them greatly," Narcissus said sadly. "Those are magic letters, demons can be exorcised with them. But for the pursuit of science they are, of course, unsuitable. The mind favors the definite, the solid shape, it wants its symbols to be reliable, it loves what is, not what will be, what is real and not what is possible. It does not permit an omega to change to a serpent or a bird. The mind cannot live in nature, only against nature, only as its counterpart. Do you believe now that you'll never be a scholar, Goldmund?"

Yes, Goldmund had long since begun to believe it, resigned himself to it.

"I'm no longer intent on striving for a mind like yours," he said, half jokingly. "I feel about mind and learning the way I did about my father: I thought I loved him very much and wanted to become like him and swore by everything he did. But as soon as my mother reappeared, I knew the meaning of love again and my father's image had suddenly shrunk next to hers and become joyless, almost repugnant. And now I'm inclined to regard all things of the mind as father-things, as unmotherly, and mother-hostile, and to feel a slight contempt for them."

He spoke in a joking tone, and yet he was not able to bring a happy expression to his friend's face. Narcissus looked at him in silence; his look was like a caress. Then he said: "I understand you very well. There's no need for us to quarrel ever again; you are awakened, and now you recognize the difference between us, between mother-heritage and father-heritage, the difference between soul and mind. Soon you'll probably also realize that cloister life and striving for monkhood were a mistake for you, an invention of your father's. He wanted you to atone for your mother's memory, or perhaps avenge himself on her in this way. Or do you still believe that it's your destiny to remain in the cloister all your life?"

Goldmund looked pensively at his friend's hands. How distinguished they were, severe as well as delicate, bony and white. No one could doubt that they were the hands of an ascetic and a scholar.

"I don't know," he said in the lilting, slightly hesitant voice he had recently acquired and that seemed to dwell lengthily on every sound. "I really don't know. You judge my father somewhat harshly. He has not had an easy life. But perhaps you're right in this too. I've been in the cloister school for over three years, and he's never come to see me. He wants me to stay here forever. Perhaps that would be best, I thought I wanted it myself. But today I'm no longer sure what I really want and desire. Before, everything was simple, as simple as the letters in my textbook. Now nothing is simple any more, not even the letters. Everything has taken on many meanings and faces. I don't know what will become of me, I can't think about that now."

"Nor need you," said Narcissus. "You'll find out

where your road will lead you. It began by leading you back to your mother, and it will bring you closer to her still. As for your father, I'm not judging him too harshly. Would you want to go back to him?"

"No, Narcissus, certainly not. If I did, it would have to be as soon as I finished school; right now perhaps. Since I'm not going to be a scholar anyhow, I've learned enough Latin and Greek and mathematics. No, I don't want to go back to my father . . ."

Deep in thought, he stared ahead of him. Suddenly he cried out to Narcissus: "How on earth do you do it? Again and again you say words to me, or pose questions that shine a light into me and make me clear to myself. You merely asked if I wanted to go back to my father, and suddenly I knew that I didn't want to. How do you do it? You seem to know everything. You've said so many words that I didn't quite grasp when I heard them but that became so important to me afterwards! It was you who said that I take my being from my mother, you who discovered that I was living under a spell and had forgotten my childhood! What makes you know people so well? Couldn't I learn that too?"

Narcissus smiled and shook his head.

"No, my dear Goldmund, you cannot. Some people are capable of learning a great deal, but you are not one of them. You'll never be a student. And why should you be? You don't need to. You have other gifts. You are more gifted than I, you are richer and you are weaker, your road will be more beautiful and more difficult than mine. There were times when you refused to understand me, you often kicked like a foal, it wasn't always easy, I was often forced to hurt you. I had to waken you, since you were asleep. Recalling your mother to your memory hurt at first, hurt you very much; you were found lying in the cloister garden as though dead. It had to be. No, don't stroke my hair! No, don't! I don't like it."

"Can't I learn anything then? Will I always remain stupid, a child?"

"There will be others to teach you. What you could learn from me, you child, you have learned."

"Oh no," cried Goldmund, "we didn't become friends to end it now! What sort of friendship would that be, that reached its goal after a short distance and then simply stopped? Are you tired of me? Have you no more affection for me?"

Narcissus was pacing vehemently, his eyes on the floor. Then he stopped in front of his friend.

"Let that be," he said softly. "You know only too well that my affection for you has not come to an end."

With doubt in his eyes he studied his friend. Then he began pacing once more, back and forth; again he stopped and looked at Goldmund, his eyes firm in the taut, haggard face. His voice was low, but hard and firm, when he said: "Listen, Goldmund! Our friendship has been good; it had a goal and the goal has been reached; you've been awakened. I would like it not to be over; I would like it to renew itself once more, renew itself again and again, and lead to new goals. For the moment there is no goal. Yours is uncertain, I can neither lead you nor accompany you. Ask your mother, ask her image, listen to her! But my goal is not uncertain, it lies here, in the cloister, it claims me at every hour. I can be your friend, but I cannot be in love. I am a monk, I have taken the vows. Before my consecration I shall ask to be released from my teaching duties and withdraw for many weeks to fast and do exercises. During that period I'll not speak of worldly matters, nor with you either."

Goldmund understood. Sadly he said: "So you're going to do what I would have done too, if I had joined the order. And after your exercises are over and you have fasted and prayed and waked enough—then what will be your goal?"

"You know what it is," said Narcissus.

"Well, yes. In a few years you'll be the novice-master, head of the school perhaps. You'll improve the teaching methods; you'll enlarge the library. Perhaps you'll write books yourself. No? All right, you won't. But what is your goal?"

Narcissus smiled faintly. "The goal? Perhaps I'll die head of the school, or abbot, or bishop. It's all the same. My goal is this: always to put myself in the place in which I am best able to serve, wherever my gifts and qualities find the best soil, the widest field of action. There is no other goal."

Goldmund: "No other goal for a monk?"

Narcissus: "Oh, there are goals enough. One monk may find his life's goal in learning Hebrew, another in annotating Aristotle, or embellishing the cloister church, or secluding himself in meditation, or a hundred other things. For me those are no goals. I neither want to increase the riches of the cloister, nor reform the order, nor the church. I want to serve the mind within the framework of my possibilities, the way I understand the mind; no more. Is that not a goal?"

Goldmund thought for a long while before he answered.

"You're right," he said. "Did I hinder you much on the road toward your goal?"

"Hinder me! Oh Goldmund, no one furthered me as much as you did. You created difficulties for me, but I am no enemy of difficulties. I've learned from them, I've partly overcome them."

Goldmund interrupted him. Half laughingly, he said: "You've overcome them wonderfully well! But, tell me: when you aided me, guided and delivered me, and healed my soul—were you really serving the mind? In so doing you've probably deprived the cloister of an eager, well-intentioned novice, maybe you've raised an enemy of the mind, someone who'll strive for, think and do the exact opposite of what you deem good!"

"Why not?" said Narcissus in deep earnest. "Dear friend, how little you know me still! Perhaps I did ruin a future monk in you, but in exchange I cleared the path inside you for a destiny that will not be ordinary. Even if you burned down our rather handsome cloister tomorrow, or preached a mad doctrine of error to the world, I would not for an instant regret that I helped you on the road toward it."

With a friendly gesture he laid both hands on his friend's shoulders.

"See here, little Goldmund, this too is part of my goal: whether I be teacher, abbot, father confessor, or whatever, never do I wish to find myself in the position of meeting a strong, valuable human being and not know what he is about, not further him. And let me say this to you: whatever becomes of either of us, whether we go this way or that, you'll never find me heedless at any moment that you call me seriously and think that you have need of me. Never."

It sounded like a farewell; it was indeed a foretaste of farewell. Goldmund stood looking at his friend, the determined face, the goal-directed eyes; he had the unmistakable feeling that they were no longer brothers, colleagues, equals; their ways had already parted. The man before him was not a dreamer; he was not waiting for fate to call to him. He was a monk who had pledged his life, who belonged to an established order, to duty; he was a servant, a soldier of religion, of the church, of the mind. Goldmund now knew he did not belong here; this had become clear to him today. He had no home; an unknown world awaited him. His mother had known the same fate once. She had left house and home, husband and child, community and order, duty and honor, to go out into uncertainty; she had probably long since perished in it. She had had no goal, and neither had he. Having goals was a privilege he did not share with others. Oh, how well Narcissus had recognized all this long ago; how right he had been!

Shortly after the day of their conversation, Narcissus seemed to have disappeared, to have become suddenly inaccessible. Another instructor was teaching his courses; his lectern in the library stood vacant. He was still present, he was not altogether invisible, one saw him walk through the arcade occasionally, heard him murmur in one of the chapels, kneeling on the stone floor; one knew that he had begun the great exercise, that he was fasting, that he rose three times each night to exercise. He was still present, but he had crossed over into another world; he could be seen, although not often, but he could not be reached. Nothing could be shared with him; one could not speak with him. Goldmund knew: Narcissus would reappear, he would be standing at his lectern again, sit in his chair in the refectory, he would speak again—but nothing of what had been would be again; Narcissus would belong to him no longer. As he thought about this, it became clear to him that Narcissus alone had made the cloister, the monkish life, grammar and logic, learning and the mind seem important and desirable to him. His example had tempted him; to become like Narcissus had been his ideal. True, there was also the Abbot, whom he had venerated; he had loved him, too, and thought him a high example. But the others, the teachers and classmates, the dormitory, the dining hall, the school, exercises, mass, the entire cloister no longer concerned him without Narcissus. What was he still doing here? He was waiting, standing under the cloister roof like a hesitant wanderer caught in the rain who stops under any roof, a tree, just to wait, for fear of the inhospitality of the unknown.

Goldmund's life, during this span, was nothing but hesitation and bidding farewell. He visited the different places that had become dear and meaningful to him. He was surprised that there were so few persons and faces it would be hard for him to leave. Brother Narcissus and old Abbot Daniel and good dear Father Anselm, the friendly porter maybe, and their jovial neighbor, the miller—but even they had already become unreal. Harder than that would be saying farewell to the tall stone madonna in the chapel, to the apostles of the portal. For a long time he stood in front of them, in front of the beautiful carvings of the choir pews, of the fountain in the cloister garden, the column with the three animal heads; he leaned against the linden trees in the courtyard, against the chestnut tree. One day, all of this would be memory to him, a small picturebook in his heart. Even now, while he was still in its midst, it started to fade away from him, lose its reality, change phantomlike into something that no longer was. He went in search of herbs with Father Anselm, who liked to have him around; he watched the men at work in the cloister mill; every so often he let himself be invited to a meal of wine and baked fish; but already it felt strange to him, half like a memory. In the twilight of the chapel and the penitence of his cell, his friend Narcissus was pacing, alive, but to him he had become a shadow. The cloister now seemed to be drained of reality, and appeared autumnal and transient.

Only the life within him was real, the anguished beating of his heart, the nostalgic sting of longing, the joys and fears of his dreams. To them he belonged; to them he abandoned himself. Suddenly, in the middle of a page or a lesson, surrounded by his classmates, he'd sink into himself and forget everything, listening only to the rivers and voices inside himself which drew him away, into deep wells filled with dark melodies, into colorful abysses full of fairy-tale deeds, and all the sounds were like his mother's voice, and the thousands of eyes all were his mother's eyes.

6

One day Father Anselm called Goldmund into his pharmacy, his pretty herb pantry full of wondrous smells. Goldmund knew his way around there. The monk showed him a dried plant, neatly preserved between two sheets of paper, and asked him if he knew its name and could describe it accurately, the way it looked outside in the fields. Yes, Goldmund could; the plant was John's-wort. He was asked for a precise description of its characteristics. The old man was satisfied and gave his young friend the mission of gathering a good bundle of these plants during the afternoon, in the plant's favorite spots, which he indicated to Goldmund.

"In exchange you'll have the afternoon off from your classes, my boy. You'll have no objection to that, and you won't lose anything by it. Because knowledge of nature is a science, too—not only your silly grammar."

Goldmund thanked him for the most welcome assignment to pick flowers for a couple of hours rather than sit in the classroom. To make his joy complete, he asked the stablemaster to let him take the horse Bless, and soon after lunch he led the animal from the stable. It greeted him enthusiastically; he jumped on and galloped, deeply content, into the warm, glowing day. He rode about for an hour or more, enjoying the air and the smell of the fields, and most of all the riding itself, then he

remembered his errand and searched for one of the
spots the father had described to him. He found it,
tethered the horse in the shade of a maple, talked
to it, fed it some bread, and started looking for the
plants. There were a few strips of fallow land,
overgrown with all kinds of weeds. Small, wizened
poppies with a last few fading petals and many
ripe seed pods stood among withering vetch and
sky-blue chicory and discolored knotweed. The
heaps of stones between the two fields were inhabited by lizards, and there, too, stood the first, yel-
low-flowered stalks of John's-wort; Goldmund began to pick them. After he had gathered a sizable
bunch, he sat down on a stone to rest. It was hot
and he looked longingly toward the shadowy edge
of the distant forest, but he didn't want to go that
far from the plants and from his horse, which he
could still see from where he sat. So he stayed
where he was, on the warm heap of stones, keeping
very still to see the lizards who had fled come out
again; he sniffed at the John's-wort, held one of its
small leaves to the light to study the hundred tiny
pin pricks in it.

Strange, he thought, each of these thousand little
leaves has its own miniature firmament pricked
into it, like a delicate embroidery. How strange and
incomprehensible everything was, the lizards, the
plants, even the stones, everything. Father Anselm,
who was so fond of him, was no longer able to pick
his John's-wort himself; his legs bothered him. On
certain days he could not move at all, and his
knowledge of medicine could not cure him. Perhaps he would soon die, and the herbs in his
pantry would continue to give out their fragrance,
but the old father would no longer be there. But
perhaps he would go on living for a long time still,
for another ten or twenty years perhaps, and still
have the same thin white hair and the same funny wrinkle-sheaves around the eyes; but what

would have become of him, Goldmund, in twenty
years?

Oh, how imcomprehensible everything was, and
actually sad, although it was also beautiful. One
knew nothing. One lived and ran about the earth
and rode through forests, and certain things looked
so challenging and promising and nostalgic: a star
in the evening, a blue harebell, a reed-green pond,
the eye of a person or of a cow. And sometimes it
seemed that something never seen yet long desired
was about to happen, that a veil would drop from
it all; but then it passed, nothing happened, the
riddle remained unsolved, the secret spell unbro-
ken, and in the end one grew old and looked cunning like Father Anselm or wise like Abbot Daniel,
and still one knew nothing perhaps, was still waiting and listening.

Ho picked up an empty snail house, it made a
faint tinkling sound among the stones and was
warm with sun. Absorbed, he examined the wind-
ings of the shell, the notched spiral, the capricious
dwindling of its little crown, the empty gullet with
its shimmer of mother-of-pearl. He closed his eyes
and felt the shape with probing fingers, which was
a habit and a game with him. He turned the shell
between loose fingers, slidingly retracing its con-
tours, caressingly, without pressure, delighted with
the miracle of form, the enchantment of the tangible. One of the disadvantages of school and learning, he thought dreamily, was that the mind
seemed to have the tendency to see and represent
all things as though they were flat and had only
two dimensions. This, somehow, seemed to render
all matters of the intellect shallow and worthless,
but he was unable to hold on to this thought; the
shell slid from his hand; he felt tired and drowsy.
His head sank over the herbs, which smelled
stronger and stronger as they wilted, he fell asleep
in the sun. Lizards ran over his shoes; the plants

wilted on his knees; under the maple, Bless waited and grew impatient.

From the distant forest someone came walking, a young woman in a faded blue skirt, with a red kerchief tied around black hair, and a tanned summer face. The woman came closer; she was carrying a bundle; a fire-red gillyflower shone between her lips. She noticed the sitting man, watched him from afar for a long while, curious and distrustful, saw that he was asleep, tiptoed closer on naked brown feet, stood in front of Goldmund and looked at him. Her suspicions vanished; this fine young sleeper did not look dangerous; he pleased her greatly—what had brought him out here to these fallow fields? With a smile she saw that he had been picking flowers; they were already wilted.

Goldmund opened his eyes, returning from a forest of dreams. His head was bedded softly; it was lying in a woman's lap. Strangely close, two warm brown eyes were looking into his, which were sleepy and astonished. He felt no fear; no danger shone in those warm brown stars; they looked friendly. The woman smiled at his astonishment, a very friendly smile, and slowly he, too, began to smile. Her mouth came down on his smiling lips; they greeted each other with a gentle kiss, and Goldmund remembered the evening in the village and the little girl with the braids. But the kiss was not over yet. The woman's mouth lingered, began to play, teased and tempted, and finally seized his lips with greed and violence, set fire to his blood, made it throb in his veins; in slow, patient play the brown woman gave herself to the boy, teaching him gently, letting him seek and find, setting him afire and stilling the flames. The exalted, brief joy of love vaulted above him, burned with a golden glow, sank down and died. He lay with eyes closed, his face against the woman's breast. Not a word had been said. The woman didn't move, softly she stroked his hair, gave him time to come to himself. Finally he opened his eyes.

"You!" he said. "You! But who are you?"

"I'm Lise," she said.

"Lise," he repeated after her, tasting her name. "Lise, you are sweet."

She brought her mouth close to his ear and whispered into it: "Tell me, was this the first time? Did you never love anyone before me?"

He shook his head. Abruptly he sat up and looked across the fields and up into the sky.

"Oh!" he cried, "the sun is almost down. I must get back."

"Where to?"

"To the cloister, to Father Anselm."

"To Mariabronn? Is that where you belong? Don't you want to stay with me a little longer?"

"I'd like to."

"Well, stay then!"

"No, that would not be right. And I must pick more of these herbs."

"Do you live in the cloister?"

"Yes, I'm a student. But I'll not stay there. May I come to you, Lise? Where do you live, where is your home?"

"I live nowhere, dear heart. But won't you tell me your name? —Ah, Goldmund is what they call you. Give me another kiss, little Goldmouth, then you may go."

"You live nowhere? But where do you sleep?"

"If you like, in the forest with you, or in the hay. Will you come tonight?"

"Oh, yes. But where? Where will I find you?"

"Can you screech like a barn owl?"

"I've never tried."

"Try."

He tried. She laughed, satisfied.

"All right, come out of the cloister tonight and

screech like a barn owl. I'll be close by. Do you like me, little Goldmouth, my darling?"

"Oh, Lise, I do like you. I'll come. Now go with God, I must hurry."

It was twilight when Goldmund returned to the cloister on his steaming horse, and he was glad to find Father Anselm occupied. A brother had been wading barefoot in the brook and cut himself on a shard of crockery.

Now it was important to find Narcissus. He asked one of the lay brothers who waited at table in the refectory. No, he was told, Narcissus would not be down for supper; this was his fasting day; he'd probably be asleep now since he held vigils during the night. Goldmund hurried off. During the long exercises, his friend slept in one of the penitents' cells in the inner cloister. Goldmund ran there without thinking. He listened at the door; there wasn't a sound. He entered softly. That it was strictly forbidden made no difference now.

Narcissus was lying on the narrow cot. In the half light he looked like a corpse, rigid on his back, with pale, pointed face, his hands crossed on his chest. His eyes were open; he was not asleep. He looked at Goldmund without speaking, without reproach, but without stirring, so obviously elsewhere, absorbed in a different time and world, that he had difficulty recognizing his friend and understanding his words.

"Narcissus! Forgive me, dear friend, forgive me for disturbing you. I'm not doing it lightly. I realize that you ought not to speak to me, but do speak to me, I beg you with all my heart."

Narcissus reflected, his eyes blinked violently for a moment as though he were struggling to come awake.

"Is it necessary?" he asked in a spent voice.

"Yes, it is necessary. I've come to say farewell."

"Then it is necessary. You shall not have come in

vain. Here, sit with me. I have fifteen minutes before the first vigil."

Haggard, he sat on the bare sleeping plank. Goldmund sat down beside him.

"Please forgive me!" he said guiltily. The cell, the bare cot, Narcissus's strained face, drawn with lack of sleep, his half-absent eyes—all this showed plainly how much he disturbed his friend.

"There is nothing to forgive. Don't worry about me; there's nothing amiss with me. You've come to take leave, you say? You're going away then?"

"I'm going this very day. Oh, I don't know how to tell you! Suddenly everything has been decided."

"Has your father come, or a message from him?"

"No, nothing. Life itself has come to me. I'm leaving without father, without permission. I'm bringing shame upon you, you know; I'm running away."

Narcissus looked down at his long white fingers. Thin and ghostlike, they protruded from the wide sleeves of the habit. There was no smile in his severe, exhausted face, but it could be felt in his voice as he said: "We have very little time, dear friend. Tell me only the essentials, tell me clearly and briefly. Or must I tell you what has happened to you?"

"You tell me," Goldmund begged.

"You've fallen in love, little boy, you've met a woman."

"How do you always know these things?"

"You're making it easy for me. Your condition, *amicus meus*, shows all the signs of that drunkenness called being in love. But speak now, please."

Timidly Goldmund touched his friend's shoulder.

"You have just said it. Although this time you didn't say it well, Narcissus, not accurately. It is altogether different. I was out in the fields, and I fell asleep in the heat, and when I woke up, my head was resting on the knees of a beautiful woman and I immediately felt that my mother had come to take me home. I did not think that this woman was my mother. Her eyes were brown and her hair was black; my mother had blond hair like mine. This woman didn't look in the least like her. And yet it was my mother, my mother's call, a message from her. It was as though an unknown beautiful woman had suddenly come out of the dreams of my own heart and was holding my head in her lap, smiling at me like a flower and being sweet to me. At her first kiss I felt something melt inside me that hurt in an exquisite way. All my longings, all my dreams and sweet anguish, all the secrets that slept within me, came awake, everything was transformed and enchanted, everything made sense. She taught me what a woman is and what secrets she has. In half an hour she aged me by many years. I know many things now. I also suddenly knew that I could no longer remain in this house, not for another day. I'm going as soon as night falls."

Narcissus listened and nodded.

"It happened suddenly," he said, "but it is more or less what I expected. I shall think of you often. I'll miss you, *amicus*. Is there anything I can do for you?"

"Yes, if you can, please say a word to our Abbot, so that he does not condemn me completely. He is the only person in this house, besides you, whose thoughts about me are not indifferent to me. His and yours."

"I know. Is there anything else?"

"Yes, one thing, please. Later, when you think of me, will you pray for me from time to time? And— thank you."

"For what, Goldmund?"

"For your friendship, your patience, for everything. Also for listening to me today, when it was hard for you. And also for not trying to hold me back."

"How could I want to hold you back? You know how I feel about it. —But where will you go, Goldmund? Have you a goal? Are you going to that woman?"

"Yes, I'm going with her. I have no goal. She is a stranger—homeless, it seems; perhaps a gypsy."

"Well, all right. But do you know, my dear Goldmund, that your road with her will be extremely short? I don't think you should count on her too much. Perhaps she has relatives, a husband perhaps; who knows what kind of reception awaits you there."

Goldmund leaned against his friend.

"I know," he said, "although I had not thought of it yet. As I told you, I have no goal. This woman who was so very sweet to me is not my goal. I'm going to her, but I'm not going because of her. I'm going because I must, because I have heard the call."

He sighed and was silent. They sat shoulder to shoulder, sad and yet happy in the feeling of their indestructible friendship. Then Goldmund continued: "Do not think that I'm completely blind and naïve. No. I'm happy to go, because I feel that it has to be, and because something so marvelous happened to me today. But I'm not imagining that I'll meet with nothing but joy and mirth. I think the road will be hard. But it will also be beautiful, I hope. It is extremely beautiful to belong to a woman, to give yourself. Don't laugh if I sound foolish. But to love a woman, you see, to abandon yourself to her, to absorb her completely and feel absorbed by her, that is not what you call 'being in love,' which you mock a little. For me it is the road to life, the way toward the meaning of life. Oh, Narcissus, I must leave you! I love you, Narcissus, and thank you for sacrificing a moment of sleep to me today. I find it hard to leave you. You won't forget me?"

"Don't make us both sad! I'll never forget you. You will come back, I ask it of you, I expect it. If you are in need some day, come to me, or call to me. Farewell, Goldmund, go with God!"

He had risen. Goldmund embraced him. Knowing his friend's aversion of caresses, he did not kiss him; he only stroked his hands.

Night was falling. Narcissus closed the cell behind him and walked over to the church, his sandals slapping the flagstones. Goldmund followed the bony figure with loving eyes, until it vanished like a shadow at the end of the corridor, swallowed by the darkness of the church door, claimed by exercises, duties, and virtues. How extraordinary, how infinitely puzzling and confusing everything was! This, too—how strange and frightening: to have come to his friend with his heart overflowing, drunk with blossoming love, at the very moment his friend was in meditation, devoured by fasting and vigils, crucifying his youth, his heart, his senses —all offered up in sacrifice; at the very moment his friend was subjecting himself to the most rigorous obedience, pledging to serve only the mind, to become nothing but a minister *verbi divini!* There he had lain, tired unto death, extenuated, with his pale face and bony hands, corpselike, and yet he had listened to his friend, lucid and sympathetic, had lent his ear to this love-drunken man with the smell of a woman still on him, had sacrificed his few moments of rest between penances. It was strange and divinely beautiful that there was also this kind of love, this selfless, completely spiritualized kind. How different it was from today's love in the sunny field, the reckless, intoxicated play of the senses. And yet both were love. Oh, and now Narcissus had gone from him, after showing him once again, clearly, at the last moment, how utterly different and dissimilar they were from one another.

Now Narcissus was bent down in front of the altar on tired knees, prepared and purified for a night of prayer and contemplation that permitted him no more than two hours' sleep, while he, Goldmund, was running off to find his Lise somewhere under the trees and play those sweet animal games with her once more. Narcissus would have said remarkable things about that. But he was Goldmund, not Narcissus. It was not for him to go to the bottom of these beautiful, terrifying enigmas and mazes and to say important things about them. For him there was only giving himself and loving, loving his praying friend in the night-dark church as much as the beautiful warm young woman who was waiting for him.

As he tiptoed away under the lime trees in the courtyard and out through the mill, his heart beating with a hundred conflicting emotions, he had to smile at the memory of that evening with Konrad when he had left the cloister once before by the same secret path, when they were "going to the village." How excited and secretly afraid he had been, setting out on that little forbidden escapade, and today he was leaving for good, taking far more forbidden, dangerous roads and he was not afraid, not thinking about the porter, the Abbot, the teachers.

This time there were no planks beside the brook; he had to cross without a bridge. He pulled off his clothes and tossed them to the opposite bank, then he waded naked through the deep, swirling stream, up to his chest in the cold water.

While he dressed again on the other side, his thoughts returned to Narcissus. With great lucidity that made him feel ashamed, he realized that he was merely executing now what the other had known all along, toward which he had guided him. Very distinctly he saw Narcissus's intelligent, slightly mocking face, listening to him speak so much foolishness, the man who had once, at a crucial moment, painfully opened his eyes. Again he clearly heard the few words Narcissus had said to him at that time: "You sleep at your mother's breast; I wake in the desert. Your dreams are of girls; mine of boys."

For an instant his heart froze. He stood there, utterly alone in the night. Behind him lay the cloister, a home only in appearance, yet a home he had loved and to which he had grown accustomed.

But at the same time he had another feeling: that Narcissus had ceased to be his cautioning, superior guide and awakener. Today he felt he had entered a country in which he must find his own roads, in which no Narcissus could guide him. He was glad that he realized this. As he looked back, the days of his dependence seemed shameful and oppressive to him. Now he had become aware; he was no longer a child, a student. It was good to know this. And yet—how hard it was to say farewell! To know that his friend was kneeling in the church back there and not be able to give him anything, to be of no help, to be nothing to him. And now he would be separated from him for a long time, perhaps forever, and know nothing of him, hear his voice no longer, look into his noble eyes no longer.

He tore himself away and followed the stony little road. A few hundred steps from the cloister walls he stood still, took a deep breath, and uttered the owl call as best he could. A similar call answered in the distance downstream.

"Like animals we call to each other," was the thought that came to him as he remembered the hour of love in the afternoon. Only now it occurred to him that no words had been exchanged between him and Lise, except at the very end, after the caresses were over, and then only a few and they had been insignificant. What long conversations he had had with Narcissus! But now, it seemed, he had entered a wordless world, in which one called to one another like owls, in which words had no meaning. He was ready for it. He had no more need for words today, or for thoughts; only for Lise, only for this wordless, blind, mute groping and searching, this sighing and melting.

Lise was there; she came out of the forest to meet him. He reached out to feel her, framed her head with tender, groping hands, her hair, her neck and throat, her slender waist, her firm hips. One arm about her, he walked on with her, without speaking, without asking where to. She walked with sure step in the dark forest. He had trouble kooping up with hor. Liko a fox or a marton, oho seemed to see with night eyes, walked without stumbling, without tripping. He let himself be led into the night, into the forest, into the blind secret wordless, thoughtless country. He was no longer thinking: not of the cloister he had left behind, not of Narcissus.

Like two mutes they moved through the dark forest, sometimes on soft moss upholstery, sometimes on hard root ribs. Sometimes the sky shone light through sparse high treetops; at other times the darkness was complete. Branches slapped his face; brambles held him back. Everywhere she knew her way and found a passage; she seldom stopped, seldom hesitated. After a long time they arrived in a clearing of solitary pines that stood far apart. The pale night sky opened wide before them. The forest had come to an end; a meadow valley welcomed them with a sweet smell of hay. They waded through a small, soundless creek. Out here in the open the silence was still greater than in the forest: no rustling bushes, no startled night beast, no crackling twigs.

Lise stopped in front of a big haystack.

"We'll stay here," she said.

They sat down in the hay, taking deep breaths at first and enjoying the rest; they were both a little tired. They lay back, listening to the silence, feeling their foreheads dry and their faces gradually cool off. Goldmund crouched, pleasantly tired. Playfully he bent his knees and stretched them straight again, took deep breaths of the night air and the smell of hay, and thought neither backward nor forward. Slowly he let himself be drawn and enticed by the scent and warmth of the woman beside him, replied here and there to her caressing hands and felt joy when she began to burn and pushed herself closer and closer to him. No, here neither words nor thoughts were needed. Clearly he felt all that was important and beautiful, the youthful strength, the simple, healthy beauty of the female body, felt it grow warm, felt its desire; he also felt clearly that, this time, she wished to be loved differently from the first time, that she did not want to guide and teach him this time, but wanted to wait for his attack, for his greed. Quietly he let the streams flow through him; happily he felt the boundless fire grow, felt it alive in both of them, turning their little lair into the vital, breathing center of all the quiet night.

He bent over Lise's face and began to kiss her lips in the darkness. Suddenly he saw her eyes and forehead shine with a gentle light. He looked in surprise, watched the glow grow brighter, more intense. Then he knew and turned his head: the moon was rising over the edge of the long black stretch of forest. He watched the white gentle light miraculously inundate her forehead, her cheeks, slide over her round, limpid throat. Softly, delighted, he said: "How beautiful you are!"

She smiled as though a present had been made her. He sat up; gently he pulled the gown off her shoulders, helped her out of it, peeled her until her shoulders and breasts shone in the cool light of the moon. Completely enraptured, he followed the delicate shadows with eyes and lips, looking and kissing; she held still as though under a spell, with eyes cast down and a solemn expression as though, even to her, her beauty was being discovered and revealed for the first time.

7

It grew cool over the fields. The moon climbed higher by the hour. The lovers lay on their softly lighted bed, absorbed in their games, dozing off together, turning toward each other anew upon awakening, kindling each other, entangled once more, falling asleep once more. They lay exhausted after their last embrace. Lise had nestled deep into the hay, breathing heavily. Goldmund was stretched out on his back, motionless; for a long time he stared into the moon-pale sky; a deep sadness rose in both, which they escaped in sleep. They slept profoundly, desperately, greedily, as though for the last time, as though they had been condemned to stay awake forever and had to drink in all the sleep in the world during these last hours.

When Goldmund awoke, he saw Lise busy with her black hair. He watched her for a while, absent-minded, still half asleep.

"You're awake?" he said finally.

Her head turned with a start.

"I've got to go now," she said, embarrassed and somewhat sad. "I didn't want to wake you."

"Well, I'm awake now. Must we move on so soon? After all, we're homeless."

"I am," said Lise. "But you belong to the cloister."

"I no longer belong to the cloister. I'm like you, completely alone, with nowhere to go. But I'll go with you, of course."

Lise looked away.

"You can't come with me, Goldmund. I must go to my husband; he'll beat me, because I stayed out all night. I'll say I lost my way. But he won't believe me."

Goldmund remembered Narcissus's prediction. So that's how it was.

"I've made a mistake then," he said. "I had thought that you and I would stay together. —Did you really want to let me sleep and run off without saying farewell?"

"Oh, I was afraid you might get angry and beat me, perhaps. That my husband beats me, well, that's how things are, that's normal. But I didn't want you to beat me, too."

He held on to her hand.

"Lise," he said, "I won't beat you, not now, not ever. Wouldn't you rather stay with me than with your husband, since he beats you?"

She tugged to get her hand free.

"No, no, no," she said with tears in her voice. And since he could feel that her heart was pulling away from him, that she preferred the other man's blows to his good words, he let go of her hand, and now she really began to cry. At the same time she started to run. Clasping both hands over her streaming eyes, she ran off. He stood silently and watched her go. He felt sorry for her, running off across the mowed meadows, summoned and drawn by who knew what power, an unknown power that set him thinking. He felt sorry for her, and a little sorry for himself as well; he had not been lucky apparently; alone and a little stunned, he sat in the hay, abandoned, deserted. But he was still tired and eager for sleep; never had he felt so exhausted. There was time to be unhappy later. Immediately he went back to sleep and woke only when the sun stood high and made the air hot around him.

He felt rested now; quickly he got up, ran to the brook, washed, and drank. Memories came gushing forth; love images from the night exhaled their perfume like unknown flowers, evoked many gentle, tender feelings. His thoughts ran after them as he began to walk briskly. Once more he felt, tasted, smelled, touched everything over and over. How many dreams the unknown woman had fulfilled for him, all the buds she had brought to flowering, stilled so many wonderings and longings, roused so many new ones in their place!

Field and heath lay before him, dry, fallow stretches and dark forest. Beyond it might be farms and mills, a village, a town. For the first time the world lay open before him, wide and waiting, ready to receive him, to do him good or harm. He was no longer a student who saw the world through a window; his walking was no longer a stroll ending with the inevitable return. Now the wide world had become a reality, he was part of it, it contained his fate, its sky was his sky, its weather his weather. He was small in this large world, no bigger than a horse, an insect; he ran through its blue-green infinity. No bell called him out of bed, to mass, to class, to meals.

Oh, how hungry he was! Half a loaf of corn bread, a bowl of milk, some gruel soup—what delicious memories! His stomach had come awake. He passed a cornfield, with half-ripe ears. He stripped them with fingers and teeth; avidly he chewed the tiny, slimy kernels, plucked more and still more, stuffed his pockets with ears of corn. Later he found hazelnuts. They were still quite green, but he bit into them joyfully, cracked their shells, and put a handful in his pocket.

As he entered the forest, he saw pines and an occasional oak or ash, and soon he found blueberries in unending abundance. He rested and ate and cooled off. Blue harebells grew in the sparse, hard forest grass; brown, sunny butterflies rose and vanished capriciously in ragged flight. Saint Genevieve had lived in a forest like this; he had always loved her story. How much he would have liked to meet her. Or he might find a hermitage in the forest, with an old, bearded father in a cave or a bark hut. Or perhaps peat diggers lived in the forest; he would have liked to speak to them. Or even robbers; they would probably not harm him. It would be pleasant to meet somebody, anybody. But he was well aware that he could walk in the forest for a long time, today, tomorrow, several days more, without meeting anyone. That, too, had to be accepted, if it was his destiny. It was better not to think too much, to take things as they came.

He heard a woodpecker tapping and tried to find it. For a long time he tried in vain to catch sight of the bird. At last he succeeded and watched it for a while: the bird glued to the trunk of the tree, all alone, tap-tap-tapping, turning its busy head this way and that. What a pity that one couldn't speak to animals. It would have been pleasant to call a greeting up to the woodpecker, to say a friendly word and learn something about its life in the trees perhaps, about its work and its joys. Oh, if one could only transform oneself!

He remembered how he used to draw sometimes, during his hours of leisure, how he used to draw figures with the stylus on his writing tablet, and flowers, leaves, trees, animals, people's heads. He'd amuse himself that way for hours. Sometimes he had created creatures of his own imagination, like a small God, had drawn eyes and a mouth into the chalice of a flower, shaped figures into a cluster of leaves sprouting on a branch, placed a head on top of a tree. For whole hours those games had made him happy, spellbound, able to perform magic, drawing lines that often surprised him—a figure he had started suddenly turned into a leaf or a tree,

the snout of a fish, a foxtail, someone's eyebrow.
That's how one ought to be able to transform
oneself, he thought, the way he had been able to
transform the playful lines on his tablet. Goldmund
longed to become a woodpecker for a day perhaps,
or a month; he would have lived in the treetops,
would have run up the smooth trunks and pecked
at the bark with his strong beak, keeping balance
with his tail feathers. He would have spoken woodpecker language and dug good things out of the
bark. The woodpecker's hammering sounded sweet
and strong among the echoing trees.

Goldmund met many animals on his way through
the forest. There were quite a number of hares;
at his approach they'd bound out of the underbrush, stare at him, turn and run off, ears folded
back, white under the tail. He found a long snake
lying in a clearing. It didn't move; it was not a
live snake, only an empty skin. He picked it up
and examined it carefully: a beautiful gray and
brown pattern ran down the back; the sun shone
through it; it was cobweb thin. He saw blackbirds
with yellow beaks; frightened, they'd look at him
from stiff, narrow eyeballs, fly off close to the
ground. There were many red robins and finches.
He came to a hole, a puddle filled with thick green
water, on which long-legged spiders ran in eager,
frenzied confusion, absorbed in an incomprehensible game. Above flew several dragonflies with deep-
blue wings. And once, toward nightfall, he saw
something—or rather, he saw nothing except frantic
leaves, branches breaking, clumps of mud slapping
the ground. A large, barely visible animal came
bursting through the underbrush with enormous
impact—a stag perhaps, or a boar; he couldn't tell.
For a long time he stood panting with fright. Terrified, he listened in the direction the animal had
taken, was still listening with pounding heart long
after everything had grown silent again.

He couldn't find his way out of the forest; he was
forced to spend the night there. He picked a sleeping place and built a bed of moss, trying to imagine what it would be like if he never found his way
out of the forest, if he had to stay in it forever.
That would surely be a great misfortune. Living on
berries was after all not impossible, nor was sleeping on moss. Besides, he would doubtless manage
to build a hut for himself eventually, perhaps even
to make a fire. But living alone forever and ever,
among the quietly sleeping tree trunks, with animals that ran away, with whom one could not
speak—that would be unbearably sad. Not to see
people, not to say good morning and good night to
anyone; no more faces and eyes to look into; no
more girls and women to look at, no more kisses;
never again to play the lovely secret game of lips
and legs, that would be unthinkable! If this were
his fate, he thought, he would try to become an
animal, a bear or a stag, even if it meant forsaking
the salvation of his soul. To be a bear and love a
she-bear would not be bad, would at least be much
better than to keep one's reason and language and
all that, and vegetate alone, sad and unloved.

Before falling asleep in his bed of moss, he listened to the many incomprehensible, enigmatic
night sounds of the forest, with curiosity and fear.
They were his companions now. He had to live
with them, grow accustomed to them, compete
with them, get along with them; he belonged to
the foxes and the deer, to pine and fir. He had to
live with them, share air and sunshine with them,
wait for daybreak with them, starve with them, be
their guest.

Then he fell asleep and dreamed of animals and
people, was a bear and devoured Lise amid
caresses. In the middle of the night he awoke with
a deep fear he couldn't explain, suffered infinite
anguish in his heart and lay thinking for a long

time, deeply disturbed. He realized that yesterday
and today he had gone to sleep without saying his
prayers. He got up, knelt beside his moss bed, and
said his evening prayer twice, for yesterday and
today. Soon he was asleep again.

In the morning he looked about the forest with
surprise; he had forgotten where he was. Now his
fear of the forest began to dwindle. With new joy
he entrusted himself to the life around him; and all
the while he continued to walk, taking his direction from the sun. At one point he came to a
completely smooth stretch in the forest—hardly any
underbrush, nothing but very thick old straight
pines. After he had walked around these columns
for a while, they began to remind him of the
columns in the main cloister church, the very same
church into which he had watched his friend Narcissus disappear through the dark portal the other
day—how long ago? Was it really only two days
ago?

It took him two days and two nights to reach the
end of the forest. Joyfully he recognized signs of
human habitation: cultivated land, strips of field
with barley and oats, meadows through which a
narrow footpath had been trodden; he could see
sections of it here and there. Goldmund pulled out
a few stalks of barley and chewed on them. With
friendly eyes he looked at the tilled land; everything felt warm and human to him after the long
wilderness of the woods: the little footpath, the
oats, the wilted, bleached cornflowers. Soon he
would meet people. After a short hour he came to
a crucifix at the edge of a field; he knelt and
prayed to the feet. Coming around the protruding
nose of a hill, he suddenly found himself in front of
a shady lime tree. Delighted, he heard the music
of a well from which water ran through a wooden
pipe into a long wooden trough. He drank cold
delicious water and noticed with joy a couple of

thatched roofs seemingly coming out of the elderberry trees; the berries were already dark. The lowing of a cow touched him still more than all these signs of friendliness; it sounded so pleasantly warm and hospitable, like a greeting that had come to meet him, a welcome.

He investigated a bit and then approached the hut from which the lowing had come. Outside the door, in the mud, sat a small boy with reddish hair and light-blue eyes. An earthen pot was beside him, filled with water, and with its mud and water he was making a dough. His bare legs were already smeared with it. Happy and earnest, he kneaded the wet mud between his hands, watched it squish through his fingers, made it into balls, used one knee for pressing and shaping.

"God bless you, little boy," Goldmund said in a very friendly voice. The little boy looked up, saw the stranger, opened his mouth, puckered his plump face, and ran bawling, on all fours, through the door. Goldmund followed him and came into a kitchen; it was so dark after the bright noon glare, he could not see anything at first. He said a Christian greeting, just in case, but there was no reply; but the screaming of the frightened child was finally answered by a thin old voice that comforted the boy. Finally, a tiny old woman stood up in the darkness and came closer; she held a hand to her eyes and looked at the stranger.

"God bless you, mother," Goldmund cried. "May all the dear saints bless your kind face; I haven't seen a human being in three days."

The little old woman gaped at him, a bit simple, from farsighted eyes, not understanding.

"What is it you want?" she asked suspiciously.

Goldmund took her hand and stroked it lightly.

"I want to say God bless you, little grandmother, and rest awhile, and help you make the fire. And I won't refuse a piece of bread if you offer me one, but there's time for that."

He saw a bench built into the wall and sat down on it, while the old woman cut off a piece of bread for the boy, who was now staring at the stranger with interest and curiosity, but still ready to cry and run off at any moment. The old woman cut a second piece from the loaf and brought it over to Goldmund.

"Thank you," he said. "May God reward you."

"Is your belly empty?" asked the woman.

"Not really. It's full of blueberries."

"Well, eat then. Where do you come from?"

"From Mariabronn, from the cloister."

"Are you a preacher?"

"No. I'm a student. I'm traveling."

She looked at him, half chiding, half simple, and shook her head a little on her long, wrinkled neck. She let Goldmund take a few bites and led the boy back outside into the sunshine. Then she came back and asked curiously: "Have you any news?"

"Not much. Do you know Father Anselm?"

"No. Why, what's with him?"

"He's ill."

"Ill? Is he going to die?"

"Who knows? He has it in the legs. He can't walk too well."

"Is he going to die?"

"I don't know. Maybe."

"Well, let him die. I must cook my soup. Help me chop the kindling."

She handed him a pine log, nicely dried beside the hearth, and a knife. He cut kindling, as much as she wanted, and watched her lay it on the ashes, and bend over it, and wheeze and blow until the fire caught. According to a precise, secret system, she piled now pine, now beechwood. The fire shone brightly in the open hearth. A big black kettle hung in the chimney on a sooty chain; she pushed it into the flames.

At her behest Goldmund drew water from the well, skimmed the milk pail. He sat in the smoky twilight and watched the play of the flames and the bony, wrinkled face of the old woman appearing and disappearing above them in the red glow; he could hear the cow rummage and thump on the other side of the wall. He liked everything. The lime tree, the well, the flickering fire under the kettle, the snuffing and munching of the feeding cow, the dull thuds she made against the wall, the half-dark room with table and bench, the small, ancient woman's gestures—all this was beautiful and good, smelled of food and peace, of people and warmth, of home. There were also two goats, and the old woman told him that they had a pigsty in the back; the old woman was the farmer's grandmother, the great-grandmother of the little boy. His name was Kuno. Every so often he came inside; he didn't say anything and still looked a little frightened, but he was no longer crying.

The farmer arrived, and his wife; they were greatly surprised to find a stranger in the house. The farmer was all set to start cursing. Distrustfully, he gripped the young man by the arm and pulled him toward the door to see his face in the daylight. Then he laughed, gave him a well-meaning slap on the shoulder, and invited him to eat with them. They sat down; each dipped his bread into the common milk bowl until the milk was almost gone and the farmer drank up what was left.

Goldmund asked if he might stay until tomorrow and sleep under their roof. No, said the man, there wasn't enough room, but there was enough hay lying around all over the place, outside, for him to find a bed.

The farmer's wife sat with the boy by her side.

She did not take part in the conversation; but during the meal her inquisitive eyes took possession of the stranger. His curls and eyes had made an impression on her and she noticed with pleasure his lovely white neck and smooth, elegant hands with their free, beautiful gestures. How distinguished and imposing he was, and so young! But most of all she felt drawn by the stranger's voice. She fell in love with the singing undertone, the radiating warmth and gentle wooing in the young man's voice; it sounded like a caress. She would have liked to go on listening to his voice much longer.

After the meal, the farmer busied himself in the stable. Goldmund had gone outside to wash his hands under the well; he was sitting on its low edge, cooling himself and listening to the water. His mind was undecided; there was nothing for him to do here any more, yet he regretted having to move on so soon. Just then the farmer's wife came out with a bucket in her hand; she placed it under the gullet and let it run full. Half loud she said: "If you're still around here tonight, I'll bring you some food. There's hay back there, behind the long barley field; it won't be taken in before tomorrow. Will you still be there?"

He looked into her freckled face, watched her strong arms lift the bucket; her clear large eyes looked warm. He smiled at her and nodded; she was already walking away with the full bucket, disappearing in the darkness of the door. He sat, grateful and deeply content, listening to the running water. Some time later he went in, looked for the farmer, shook hands with him and with the grandmother, and thanked them. The hut smelled of fire, soot, and milk. A moment ago it had still been shelter and home; now it was already foreign territory. With a farewell, he went out.

Beyond the hut he found a chapel, and nearby a

beautiful wooded area, a clump of sturdy old oaks in short grass. He remained there, in their shade, strolling among the thick trunks. How strange it was with women and loving! There really was no need for words. The farmer's wife had said only a few words, to name the place of their meeting; everything else had been said without words. Then how had she said it? With her eyes, yes, and with a certain intonation in her slightly thick voice, and with something more, a scent perhaps, a subtle, discreet emanation of the skin, by which women and men were able to know at once when they desired one another. It was strange, like a subtle, secret language; how fast he had learned that language. He was very much looking forward to the evening, filled with curiosity about this tall blond woman, the looks and sounds she'd have, what kind of body, gestures, kisses—probably altogether different from Lise. Where was Lise at this moment, with her taut black hair, her brown skin and little gasps? Had her husband beaten her? Was she still thinking of him? Or had she found a new lover, as he had found a new woman today? How fast things happened, everywhere happiness lay in one's path, how beautiful and hot it was, and how strangely transitory! This was a sin, adultery. Not so long ago he would have died rather than commit this sin. And now a second woman was waiting to come to him and his conscience was calm and serene; not so calm perhaps, but neither adultery nor lust were troubling and burdening it. Rather a feeling of guilt for some crime one had not committed but had brought along with one into the world. Perhaps this was what theology called original sin? It might well be. Yes, life itself bore something of guilt within it—why else had a man as pure and aware as Narcissus subjected himself to penance like a condemned felon? And why did he, himself, feel this guilt somewhere deep inside him? Was he not a happy, healthy young man, free as a bird in the sky? Was he not loved by women? Was it not beautiful to feel allowed to give the woman the same profound joy she gave him? Then why was he not fully, not completely happy? Why did this strange pain penetrate his young joy, as it penetrated Narcissus's virtue and wisdom, this subtle fear, this grief over the transitory? Why was he made to muse like this, every so often, to think, when he knew he was no thinker?

Still, it was beautiful to be alive. He plucked a small purple flower in the grass, held it to his eyes and peered into the tiny, narrow chalice; veins ran through it, hair-thin tiny organs lived there; life pulsated there and desire trembled, just as in a woman's womb, in a thinker's brain. Why did one know so little? Why could one not speak with this flower? But then, even human beings were hardly able to speak to each other. Even there one had to be lucky, find a special friendship, a readiness. No, it was fortunate that love did not need words; or else it would be full of misunderstanding and foolishness. Ah, how Lise's half-closed eyes had looked almost blind at the height of ecstasy; only the white had shown through the slits of twitching lids—ten thousand learned or lyrical words could not express it! Nothing, ah, nothing at all could be expressed—and yet, again and again one felt the urge to speak, the urge to think.

He studied the leaves of the tiny plant; how daintily, with what strange intelligence they were arranged around the stem. Virgil's verses were beautiful, and he loved them; still, there was more than one verse in Virgil that was not half as clear and intelligent, beautiful and meaningful as the spiraled order of those tiny leaves climbing the stem. What pleasure, what ecstasy, what a delightful, noble, meaningful task it would be for a man to be able to create just one such flower! But no man was able to do that—no hero, no emperor, no pope or saint!

When the sun had sunk low, he got up and found the place the farmer's wife had indicated. There he waited. It was beautiful to be waiting like this, knowing that the woman was on her way, bringing him so much love.

She arrived, carrying a linen cloth in which she had tied a chunk of bread and a piece of lard. She unknotted it and laid it out before him.

"For you," she said. "Eat!"

"Later," he said. "I'm not hungry for bread, I'm hungry for you. Oh, let me see the beautiful things you've brought me."

She had brought him a great many beautiful things: strong thirsty lips, strong gleaming teeth, strong arms that were red from the sun, but on the inside, below the nook and further down she was white and delicate. She didn't know many words but made a sweet, luring sound in her throat, and when she felt his hands on her, his delicate, gentle hands so full of feeling, the like of which she had never felt before, her skin shivered and her throat made sounds like the purring of a cat. She knew few games, fewer games than Lise, but she was wonderfully strong; she squeezed as though she wanted to break her lover's neck. Her love was childlike and greedy, simple and still chaste in all its strength; Goldmund was very happy with her.

Then she left, sighing. With difficulty, she tore herself away, because she could not stay.

Goldmund remained alone, happy as well as sad. Only much later did he remember the bread and the lard and ate it in solitude. Now it was completely dark.

8

Goldmund had been walking for quite some time; he rarely spent two nights in the same place. Everywhere women desired him and made him happy. He was dark from the sun and thin with walking and frugal meals. Many women said farewell in the early hours of the morning, and left him, some in tears. Occasionally he thought: "Why doesn't one of them stay with me? Why, if they love me and commit adultery for the sake of a single night of love—why do they all run back to their husbands immediately afterwards, even though most of them are afraid of being beaten?" Not one had seriously begged him to stay, not one had asked him to take her along, had loved him enough to share the joys and hardships of his wandering life. Of course he had never asked that of them, had never even hinted at it to any of them, and, when he questioned his heart, he knew that he cherished his freedom. He could not remember a single woman for whom he had not stopped longing in the arms of the next. Still, it seemed a little odd and sad that love had to be so extremely short-lived wherever he went, his own love as well as that of the women, and that it was satiated as rapidly as it was kindled. Was that how it should be? Was that how it was always and everywhere? Or was it because of him: was he perhaps fashioned in such a way that women thought him desirable and beautiful but did not wish to be with him longer than the brief, wordless span in the hay or on the moss? Was it because he lived a wanderer's life, because the settled have a terror of the homeless? Or was it solely because of something in himself, because of him as a person? Did women desire him as they desired a pretty doll, to hug to their hearts, only to run back to their husbands afterwards, in spite of the beatings that awaited them? He couldn't tell.

He did not grow tired of learning from women. Actually he felt more drawn to girls, to the very young, as yet without husbands, who knew nothing. With them he could fall in love longingly. But most young girls were out of reach; they were the cherished ones, timid and well protected. But he also enjoyed learning from the women. Every one left him something, a gesture, a way of kissing, a particular play, her own special way of giving herself, of holding back. Goldmund gave in to everything; he was as insatiable and pliable as a child, open to every seduction: and only for that reason was he so seductive. His beauty alone would not have been enough to draw women to him so easily; it was his childlike openness, the inquisitive innocence of his desire, his absolute readiness for anything a woman might wish of him. Without knowing it, he was to each woman the lover she had wished for and dreamed of: delicate and patient with one, fast and greedy with another, a boy who experiences love for the first time, or again artful and knowing. He was ready to play, to wrestle, to sigh and laugh, to be chaste, to be shameless; he did nothing but what the woman desired, nothing that she did not prompt him to do. This was what any woman with intelligent senses soon perceived in him, and it made him their darling.

All the time he was learning. In a short time he learned many kinds of love, many arts of love, absorbed the experiences of many women. He also

learned to see women in their multiplicity, how to
feel, to touch, to smell them. His ear grew sensitive to every tone of voice; with certain women a
certain tone infallibly told him the type and scope
of their amorous capacities. With unending delight
he observed their infinite variety: how the head
was fastened to the neck, how the forehead
emerged from the roots of the hair, the movement of a knee. He learned to tell one type of
hair from another in the dark, eyes closed, with
discreetly probing fingers, one kind of skin, of
down, from another. Quite soon he began to
notice that the purpose of his wandering lay,
perhaps, in this distinguishing, that he was perhaps driven from woman to woman in order to
learn and exercise this gift of recognizing and
differentiating still more subtly, more profoundly, with greater variation. Perhaps his destiny
was to learn to know women and to learn love in a
thousand ways, until he reached perfection, the
way some musicians were able to play not only
one, but three, four, or a great number of instru-
ments. But to what purpose he knew not, nor
where it would lead him; he merely felt that this
was his road. He had been able to learn Latin and
logic without being particularly gifted for either—
but he was gifted for love, for this game with
women. Here he had no difficulty learning; he
never forgot a thing. Here experience accumulated
and classified itself.

Goldmund had been walking the roads for a
year or two when he came to the homestead of a
prosperous knight who had two beautiful young
daughters. It was early autumn; soon the nights
would be getting cool. He had had a taste of cold
weather during the last autumn and winter and he
was worried about the months ahead; wandering
was difficult in winter. He asked for food and a bed
for the night, was received with courtesy, and

when the knight heard that he had studied Greek, he called him away from the servants' table and over to his own and treated him almost as an equal. The daughters kept their eyes cast down. The older was eighteen; the younger just sixteen: Lydia and Julie.

The next day Goldmund wanted to continue on his road. He could not hope to win one of these beautiful blond young ladies, and there were no other women who might have enticed him to stay. But after breakfast the knight drew him aside and led him to a room furnished for a special purpose. Modestly the old man told the young one of his weakness for learning and books, and showed him a small chest filled with scrolls he had collected, a writing desk he had had built for himself, and a stock of the most exquisite paper and parchment. By and by Goldmund learned that this pious knight had been a scholar in his youth but had completely abandoned his studies for the sake of warfare and worldly affairs until, during a grave illness, God had prompted him to go on a pilgrimage and repent the sins of his youth. He had traveled as far as Rome and Constantinople, had found his father dead upon his return, the house empty, had settled down then and married, lost his wife, raised his daughters, and now, at the beginning of old age, he had begun to write a detailed account of his long-past pilgrimage. He had written several chapters, but— as he confessed to the young man—his Latin was somewhat faulty; it held him up constantly. He offered Goldmund new clothes and free shelter if he agreed to correct and copy out all that had been written so far, and also to help him complete the book.

Goldmund knew the realities of wandering in the cold, nor were new clothes to be scorned either. But most of all the young man enjoyed the prospect of staying in the same house with the two beautiful sisters for many months to come. Without another thought, he said yes. A few days later the housekeeper was asked to unlock the wardrobe, and in it they found a bolt of fine brown cloth, from which a suit and cap were ordered for Goldmund. The knight had fancied black, a kind of scholar's gown, but his guest would not hear of it and knew how to coax until a handsome-looking outfit, half that of a page, half that of a huntsman, was made for him. It suited him well.

His Latin was not too rusty either. Together they went over all that had been written. Goldmund not only corrected the many imprecise, faulty expressions; he also rounded out the knight's clumsy, short sentences here and there and made them into pleasing Latin constructions, with solid grammar and neat, consecutive tenses. It gave the knight great pleasure and he was not stingy with praise. Every day they worked at least two hours.

Goldmund had no trouble passing his time in the castle—which was in reality a spacious, fortified farmhouse. He went hunting, and huntsman Heinrich taught him how to use a crossbow; he made friends with the dogs and was allowed to ride as much as he pleased. He was rarely alone; he'd either be talking to a dog, or a nag, or to Heinrich, or Lea, the housekeeper, a fat old woman with a man's voice who liked a laugh and a jest, or the kennel boy, or a shepherd. It would have been easy for him to start a love intrigue with the miller's wife who lived close by, but he held himself aloof and played innocent.

He took great joy in the knight's two daughters. The younger was the more beautiful, but so prim she hardly spoke to Goldmund. He treated both of them with great respect and courtesy, but both felt his presence to be a continuous courtship. The younger one shut herself off completely, stubborn

with shyness. Lydia, the older, found a special tone
for him, treated him with a mixture of respect and
mockery, as though he were a monster of learning.
She asked him many curious questions, and also
about his life in the cloister, but there was always a
slight irony in her tone, and the superiority of the
lady. He gave in to everything, treated Lydia like a
lady and Julie like a little nun, and whenever his
conversation detained the girls a little longer than
usual at the table after meals, or if Lydia spoke to
him outside the house, in the yard or in the garden, and permitted herself to tease him, he was
content and felt that he was making progress.

That autumn the leaves stayed late on the tall
ash in the courtyard and there were still asters in
the garden, and roses. One day visitors arrived. A
neighbor with his wife and horseman came riding
in; the mildness of the day had tempted them to
travel farther than usual. Now they were there and
asked shelter for the night. They were courteously
received; Goldmund's bed was moved out of the
guest room into the writing room; his room was
made up for the visitors, chickens were killed, servants ran to the millpond to get fish. With pleasure
Goldmund took part in the festivities and the excitement; he immediately felt the unknown lady's
awareness of him. And as soon as he noticed her
interest in him and her desire, by a certain something in her voice and in her eyes, he also noticed
with growing interest how changed Lydia was,
how silent and remote she became and how she sat
watching him and the unknown lady. During the
elaborate dinner the lady's foot came to play with
Goldmund's under the table; he took great delight
in this game, but still greater delight in the brooding, silent tension with which Lydia watched it,
with inquisitive, burning eyes. Finally he dropped
a knife on purpose, bent down to reach for it under
the table and touched the lady's foot and calf with

a caressing hand. He saw Lydia turn pale and bite her lip as he continued to tell anecdotes from his cloister days and felt the unknown lady listen intently, not so much to his stories as to the wooing in his voice. The others, too, sat listening, his master with benevolence, the guest with a stony face, although he, too, was affected by the fire that burned in the young man. Lydia had never heard him speak this way. He had blossomed, lust hung in the air, his eyes shone, ecstasy sang in his voice, love pleaded. The three women felt it, each in her own fashion: little Julie with violent resistance and rejection, the knight's wife with radiant satisfaction, and Lydia with a painful commotion in her heart, a mixture of deep longing, soft resistance, and the most violent jealousy, which made her face look narrow and her eyes burn. Goldmund felt all these waves. Like secret answers to his courtship they came flooding back to him. Like birds, thoughts of love fluttered about him, giving in, resisting, fighting each other.

After the meal Julie withdrew; night had long since fallen; with her candle in a clay candlestick, she left the hall, frigid as a little cloister woman. The others stayed up for another hour, and while the two men discussed the harvest, the emperor, and the bishop, Lydia listened ardently to the idle chatter that was being spun between Goldmund and the unknown lady, among the loose threads of which a thick sweet net of give and take, of glances and intonations and small gestures had come into being, each one overcharged with meaning, overheated with desire. Greedily the girl drank in the atmosphere, but also felt disgust when she saw, or sensed, Goldmund touch the unknown lady's knee under the table. She felt the contact on her own flesh and gave a start. Afterwards she could not fall asleep and lay listening half the night, with pounding heart, sure that the two would come together. In her imagination she performed what was denied them, saw them embrace, heard their kisses, trembling with excitement all the while, wishing as much as fearing that the betrayed knight might surprise the lovers and sink his knife into the odious Goldmund's heart.

The next morning the sky was overcast, a wet wind blew, the guests declined all urging to stay longer and insisted on immediate departure. Lydia stood by while the guests mounted. She shook hands and spoke words of farewell, but she was not aware of what she was doing. All her senses were focused in her eyes as she watched the knight's wife place her foot in Goldmund's proffered hands, watched his right hand wrap around the shoe, wide and firm, and clutch the woman's foot forcefully for an instant.

The strangers had ridden off; Goldmund was in the study, working. Half an hour later he heard Lydia's voice giving orders under the window, heard a horse being led from the stable. His master stepped to the window, looking down, smiling, shaking his head. Then both watched Lydia ride out of the courtyard. They seemed to be making less progress in their Latin composition today. Goldmund was distracted; with a friendly word, his master released him earlier than usual.

No one saw Goldmund sneak a horse out of the courtyard. He rode against the cool wet wind into the discolored landscape, galloping faster and faster; he felt the horse grow warm under him, felt his own blood catch fire. He rode through the gray day, across stubble fields, heath, and swampy spots overgrown with shave grass and reeds, breathed deeply, crossed small valleys of alder, rotting pine forest, and once again brownish, bare heath.

On the high ridge of a hill, sharply outlined against the pale gray, cloudy sky, he saw Lydia's silhouette, sitting high on her slowly trotting horse.

He raced toward her; she saw that he was following her and spurred her horse and fled. She would appear and then disappear, her hair flowing behind her. He gave chase as though she were a fox; his heart laughed. With brief, tender calls he encouraged his horse, scanned the landscape with happy eyes as he flew past low-crouching fields, an alder forest, maples, the clay-covered banks of ponds. Again and again his eyes returned to his target, to the beautiful, fleeing woman. Soon he would catch up with her.

When Lydia saw that he was close, she abandoned the race and let her horse walk. She did not turn her head to look at her pursuer. Proudly, apparently casually, she trotted ahead of him as though nothing had happened, as though she were alone. He pushed his horse up to hers; the two horses walked gently side by side, but the animals and their riders were hot from the chase.

"Lydia!" he called softly.

There was no answer.

"Lydia!"

She remained silent.

"How beautiful that was, Lydia, to watch you ride from a distance, your hair trailing after you like a golden flash of lightning. That was so beautiful! How wonderful of you to flee from me. That's when I realized that you care for me a little. I didn't know, I doubted until last night. But when you tried to flee from me suddenly, I understood. You must be tired, my beauty, my love, let's dismount."

He jumped from his horse, seizing the reins of her horse in the same motion to keep her from galloping off once more. Her snow-white face looked down at him. As he lifted her from her saddle, she broke into tears. Carefully he led her a few steps, made her sit down in the wilted grass, and knelt beside her. There she sat, fighting her sobs. She fought bravely and overcame them.

"Oh, why are you so bad?" she began when she was able to speak. She could hardly utter the words.

"Am I so bad?"

"You are a seducer of women, Goldmund. Let me forget those words you said to me; they were impudent words; it does not become you to speak to me that way. How can you imagine that I care for you? Let us forget that! But how am I to forget the things I was forced to see last night?"

"Last night? But what did you see last night?"

"Oh, stop pretending, don't lie like that! It was horrible and shameless, the way you played up to that woman under my eyes! Have you no shame? You even stroked her leg under the table, under our table! Before me, under my eyes! And now that she's gone, you come chasing after me. You really don't know what shame means."

Goldmund had long since regretted the words he had said before lifting her off her horse. How stupid of him; words were unnecessary in love; he should have kept silent.

He said no more. He knelt by her side; she looked at him, so beautiful and unhappy that her misery became his misery; he, too, felt that there was something to be deplored. But in spite of all she had said, he still saw love in her eyes, and the pain on her quivering lips was also love. He believed her eyes more than he believed her words.

But she had expected an answer. As it was not forthcoming, Lydia's lips took on an even more bitter expression. She looked at him somewhat tearfully and repeated: "Have you really no shame?"

"Forgive me," he said humbly. "We're talking about things that should not be talked about. It is my fault, forgive me. You ask if I have no shame.

Yes, I have shame. But I also love you, and love knows nothing of shame. Don't be angry with me."

She seemed hardly to hear him. She sat with a bitter mouth, looking into the distance, as though she were alone. He had never been in such a situation. This was the result of using words.

Gently he laid his face against her knee; immediately the contact made things better. Yet he felt a little confused and sad, and she too seemed to be sad. She sat motionless, saying nothing, looking into the distance. All this embarrassment and sadness! But the knee accepted his leaning cheek with friendliness; it did not reject him. Eyes closed, his face lay on her knee; slowly it took in the knee's noble shape. With joy and emotion Goldmund thought how much this knee with its distinguished youthful form corresponded to her long, beautiful, neatly rounded fingernails. Gratefully he embraced the knee, let his cheek and mouth speak to it.

Now he felt her hand posing itself bird-light and fearful on his hair. Dear hand, he could feel her softly, childishly stroke his hair. Many times before, he had examined her hand in great detail and admired it; he knew it almost as well as his own, the long, slender fingers with their long, beautifully rounded pink nails. Now the long, delicate fingers were having a timid conversation with his curls. Their language was childlike and fearful, but it was love. Gratefully he nestled his head into her hand, feeling her palm with his neck, with his cheeks.

Then she said: "It's time, we must go."

He raised his head and looked at her tenderly. Gently he kissed her slender fingers.

"Please, get up," she said. "We must go home."

He obeyed instantly. They stood up, mounted, rode.

Goldmund's heart was filled with joy. How beautiful Lydia was, how like a child, pure and delicate! He had not even kissed her, and yet he felt so showered with gifts by her, and fulfilled. They rode briskly.

Only at their arrival a few yards before the entrance to the court she grew fearful and said: "We shouldn't have both come back at the same time. How foolish we are!" And at the last moment, while they dismounted and a servant came running, she whispered quickly and hotly in his ear: "Tell me if you were with that woman last night!" He shook his head many times and began unsaddling the horse.

In the afternoon, after her father had gone out, she appeared in the study.

"Is it really true?" she asked at once and with passion. He knew what she meant.

"But then, why did you play with her like that, in that disgusting fashion, and make her fall in love with you?"

"That was for you," he said. "Believe me, I would have a thousand times rather caressed your foot than hers. But your foot never came to me under the table; it never asked me if I loved you."

"Do you really love me, Goldmund?"

"Yes, indeed."

"But what will happen?"

"I don't know, Lydia. Nor do I worry about it. It makes me happy to love you. I don't think of what will happen. I am happy when I see you ride, and when I hear your voice, and when your fingers caress my hair. I'll be happy when you'll allow me to kiss you."

"A man is only allowed to kiss his bride, Goldmund. Have you never thought of that?"

"No, I've never thought of that. Why should I? You know as well as I that you cannot become my bride."

"That's true. And since you cannot become my husband and stay with me forever, it was very wrong of you to speak to me about love. Did you think that you would be able to seduce me?"

"I thought and believed nothing, Lydia. I think much less than you imagine. I wish nothing except that you might wish to kiss me. We talk so much. Lovers don't do that. I think you don't love me."

"This morning you said just the opposite."

"And you did just the opposite!"

"I? What do you mean?"

"First you fled before me when you saw me. That's when I thought that you loved me. Then you cried, and I thought that was because you loved me. Then my head lay on your knee and you caressed me, and I thought that was love. But now you're not behaving in a loving manner with me."

"I'm not like that woman whose foot you stroked yesterday. You seem to be accustomed to women like that."

"No, thank God you're much more beautiful and refined than she is."

"That's not what I meant."

"Oh, but it's true. Don't you know how beautiful you are?"

"I have a mirror."

"Have you ever looked at your forehead in the mirror, Lydia? And at your shoulders, at your fingernails, at your knees? And have you ever noticed how each part blends into and rhymes with each part, how they all have the same shape, an elongated, taut, firm, very slender shape? Have you noticed that?"

"The way you talk! I've never noticed that, actually, but now that you say it, I do know what you mean. Listen, you really are a seducer. Now you're trying to make me vain."

"What a shame that I can do nothing right with you. Why should I be interested in making you vain? You're beautiful and I'd like to try to show you that I'm grateful for your beauty. You force me to tell you with words; I could say it a thousand times better without words. With words I can give you nothing! With words I can't learn from you, nor you from me."

"What is there for me to learn from you?"

"For me from you, Lydia, and for you from me. But you don't want to. You only want to love the man whose bride you'll be. He'll laugh when he discovers that you haven't learned anything, not even how to kiss."

"So you wish to give me kissing lessons, you learned man?"

He smiled at her. He didn't like her words, but he could sense her girlhood from behind her slightly brusque, false-ringing talk, could sense desire taking possession of her and fear fighting against it.

He gave no answer. He smiled at her, caught her restless glance in his eyes, and while she surrendered to the spell, not without resistance, he slowly brought his face close to hers until their lips met. Gently he brushed her mouth; it answered with a little childlike kiss and opened, as though in painful surprise, when he did not let it go. Gently courting, he followed her retreating mouth until it hesitatingly came back to meet his and then he taught the spellbound girl without violence the receiving and giving of a kiss, until, exhausted, she pressed her face against his shoulder. There he let it rest, smelled with delight her thick blond hair, murmured tender, calming sounds into her ear and remembered how he, an ignorant pupil, had once been introduced to the secret by Lise, the gypsy. How black her hair had been, how brown her skin, how the sun had burned down on him, how the wilting John's-wort had smelled! And how far back it was, from what distance it came flashing across his memory. That was how fast everything wilted, it had hardly time to bloom!

Slowly Lydia stood up straight, her face was

transformed, her loving eyes looked large and earnest.

"Let me go, Goldmund," she said. "I've stayed with you so long, my love."

Every day they found their secret hour, and Goldmund let himself be guided in everything by her. This girlish love touched and delighted him most wonderfully. Sometimes she'd only hold his hand in hers for a whole hour and look into his eyes and depart with a child's kiss. Other times, on the contrary, she'd kiss him insatiably but would not permit him to touch her. Once, deeply blushing and struggling with herself, she let him see one of her breasts, with the intention of giving him a great joy; timidly she brought the small white fruit out of her dress; he knelt and kissed it and she carefully covered it up again, still blushing all the way down to her neck. They also spoke, but in a new way, differently than on the first day. They invented names for each other; she liked to tell him about her childhood, her dreams and games. She also often said that her love was wrong since he could not marry her; sadly and with resignation she spoke of it and draped her love with the secrecy of this sadness as with a black veil.

For the first time Goldmund felt not only desired by a woman but loved.

Once Lydia said: "You are so handsome and you look so happy. But deep inside your eyes there is no gaiety, there is only sorrow, as though your eyes knew that happiness did not exist and that all that is beautiful and lovely does not stay with us long. You have the most beautiful eyes of anyone I know, and the saddest. I think that that's because you're homeless. You came to me out of the woods, and one day you'll go off again and sleep on moss and walk the roads. —But where is *my* home? When you go away, I'll still have my father and my sister and my room and a window where I can sit and think of you; but I'll no longer have a home."

He'd let her talk. Sometimes he'd smile at her words, and sometimes he'd grow sad. He never consoled her with words, only with gentle caresses, only by holding her head against his chest, humming soft, meaningless, magic sounds that nurses hum to comfort children when they cry. Once Lydia said: "I'd really like to know what will become of you, Goldmund. I often think about it. You'll have no ordinary life, and it won't be easy. Oh, I hope you'll do well! Sometimes I think you ought to become a poet, a man who has visions and dreams and knows how to describe them beautifully. Ah, you'll wander over the whole world and all women will love you, and yet you'll always remain alone. You'd better go back to the cloister to your friend of whom you've told me so much! I'll pray for you that you will not be made to die alone in the forest."

She'd speak that way, in deep earnest, with lost eyes. But then again she'd ride laughingly with him across the late-autumn land or ask him funny riddles, or throw dead leaves and shiny acorns at him.

One night Goldmund was lying in his bed in his room, waiting for sleep. His heart was heavy with a soft pain; full and heavy it was beating in his chest, brimming over with love, and with grief; he didn't know what to do. He heard the November wind rattle at the roof; he had grown accustomed to lying like that for quite some time before falling asleep; sleep would not come. Softly, as was his custom in the evening, he intoned a chant to the Virgin:

tu advocata peccatorum!
et macula originalis non est in te.

Tu laetitia Israel,
tu advocata peccatorum!

With its soft music the song sank into his soul,
but at the same time the wind sang outside, a song
of strife and wandering, of wood, autumn, of the
life of the homeless. He thought of Lydia and of
Narcissus and of his mother. Full and heavy was
his restless heart.

Suddenly he started and stared, not believing.
The door of his room had opened, in the dark a
figure in a long white gown came in; soundlessly
Lydia came walking on bare feet across the stone
floor, gently closed the door, and sat down on his
bed.

"Lydia," he whispered, "my little doe, my white
flower! Lydia, what are you doing?"

"I've come to you only for an instant," she said.
"Just once I wanted to see my Goldmund in his
bed, my goldheart."

She lay down beside him, they didn't move,
their hearts were beating heavily. She let him kiss
her, let his admiring hands play with her body, but
more was not permitted. After a short while
she gently pushed his hands away, kissed him on
the eyes, got up soundlessly, and vanished. The
door creaked, the wind tinkled and thumped in
the attic. Everything was under a spell, full of
secrecy and anguish, promise and menace. Goldmund did not know what he was thinking, what
he was doing. When he woke again after a troubled
slumber, his pillow was wet with tears.

A few nights later she came back, the sweet
white ghost, lay down beside him for fifteen minutes, as she had the last time. In whispers she spoke
into his ear as she lay folded in his arms. She had
much to tell, much to complain about. Tenderly he
listened; she was lying on his left arm; his right
hand caressed her knees.

"Little Goldmouth," she said in a completely muffled voice near his cheek, "it is so sad that I may never belong to you. Our small happiness won't last much longer, our small secret. Julie is already suspicious; soon she'll force me to tell her. Or my father will notice. If he found me here in your bed, my little golden bird, your Lydia would fare ill; with tear-swollen eyes she would stand and look up to the trees to see her lover hang high up there, swaying in the wind. Oh, you had better run away, right now would be best, rather than let my father have you bound and hanged. I saw a man hanged once, a thief. I could not bear to see you hanged. You had better run away and forget me; I don't want you to die, my golden one, I don't want the birds to hack out your blue eyes! Oh no, my treasure, you must not go away. Ah, what am I to do if you leave me all alone?"

"Won't you come with me, Lydia? We'll flee together, the world is wide!"

"That would be wonderful," she sighed, "oh, so wonderful to wander into the world with you! But I can't. I can't sleep in the forest and be homeless and have straw in my hair, I can't do that. Nor can I bring such shame upon my father. No, don't speak, that's not just my imagination. I can't. I couldn't do it any more than eat off a dirty plate or sleep in a leper's bed. Ah, everything good and beautiful is forbidden us, we were both born for sadness. My golden one, my poor little boy, I should have to see you hanged after all. And I, I'll be locked up in my room and later sent to a convent. You must leave me, sweetheart, and sleep with the gypsies again and the peasant women. Oh, leave, go before they catch you and bind you! We'll never be happy, never!"

Softly he stroked her knee, touched her sex very delicately, and begged: "My little flower, we could be so very happy. Won't you let me?"

Not angrily but firmly she pushed his hand aside and drew away slightly.

"No," she said, "no, I won't let you. It is forbidden me. Perhaps you can't understand that, you little gypsy. I am doing wrong, I'm a bad girl, I'm bringing shame upon the whole house. But somewhere inside my soul I still have pride, and nobody may enter there. You must let me keep that, or else I can never again come to your room."

He would never have ignored an interdiction, a wish, a hint from her. He himself was surprised that she had so much power over him. But he was suffering. His senses remained stirred up, often his heart fought violently against his dependence. Sometimes he made efforts to free himself. Sometimes he'd court little Julie with elaborate flattery, and it was indeed most important to remain on good terms with this powerful person and to dupe her if possible. He had a strange relationship with this little Julie, who often behaved like a child and often seemed omniscient. She really had more beauty than Lydia, an extraordinary beauty which, combined with her somewhat precocious child-innocence, was a great attraction for Goldmund; he was often deeply in love with Julie. In this strong attraction he felt for the little sister, he recognized with surprise the difference between loving and desiring. In the beginning he had looked at both sisters with the same eyes, had found both desirable, but Julie more beautiful and seductive, had courted both equally, always kept an eye on both. And now Lydia had gained this power over him! Now he loved her so much that he had even renounced full possession of her, out of love. Her soul had become familiar and dear to him. In its childlike tenderness and inclination to sadness it seemed similar to his own. He was often deeply astonished and delighted to see how much her own soul corresponded to her body; she'd do something, say something, express a wish or an opinion, and her words and the attitude of her soul were molded in the same shape as the slant of her eyes and the form of her fingers.

These instants during which he thought he recognized the basic forms and laws that constituted her being, her soul as well as her body, had more than once roused in Goldmund the desire to retain something of this form and to re-create it. On a few sheets of paper that he kept most secret, he had made several attempts to draw from memory the outline of her head with the strokes of a pen—the line of her eyebrows, her hand, her knee.

With young Julie the situation was becoming rather difficult. She obviously sensed the wave of love in which her older sister was swimming, and her senses turned toward this paradise with curiosity and greed, while her stubborn mind refused to admit it. She treated Goldmund with exaggerated coolness and dislike. Yet, during moments of forgetfulness, she'd watch him with admiration and desiring curiosity. With Lydia she was often most tender, and occasionally even came to visit her in her bed, to breathe in the atmosphere of love and sex with wordless greed, purposely brushing against the forbidden and longed-for secret. Then again she'd make clear with almost offensive brusqueness that she knew of Lydia's secret transgression and felt contempt for it.

Attractive and disturbing, the beautiful, capricious child flittered between the two lovers, tasted of love's secrecy in thirsty dreams, played innocent, and then again dangerously knowing. The child rapidly gained a kind of power over them. Lydia suffered from it more than Goldmund, who rarely saw the younger sister except during meals. And Lydia also realized that Goldmund was not insensitive to Julie's charms; sometimes she'd see his appreciative, delighted eyes gazing at her. She could not say anything about it, everything was so complicated, so filled with danger. Julie must especially not be offended or angered; alas, any day, any hour the secret of her love could be discovered and an end put to her heavy, anguished bliss, perhaps a dreadful end.

Sometimes Goldmund asked himself why he had not left long ago. It was difficult to live the way he was now living: loved, but without hope for either a sanctioned, lasting happiness, or the easy fulfillments to which his love desires had been accustomed until now. His senses were constantly excited and hungry, never stilled; moreover, he lived in permanent danger. Why was he staying and accepting it all, all these entanglements and confused emotions? These were experiences, emotions, and states of mind for the sedentary, the lawful, for people in heated rooms. Had he not the right of the homeless, of the nonpossessing, to extricate himself from these delicate complications and to laugh at them? Yes, he had that right, and he was a fool to look for a kind of home here and to be paying for it with so much suffering, so much embarrassment. And yet he did. He not only put up with it, but was secretly happy to do so. It was foolish, difficult, a strain to live this way, but it was also wonderful. The darkly beautiful sadness of his love was wonderful, in its foolishness and hopelessness; his sleepless, thought-filled nights were beautiful; it was all as beautiful and delectable as the fold of suffering on Lydia's lips, or like the lost, resigned tone of her voice when she spoke of her love and sorrow. In a few weeks, lines of suffering had appeared on Lydia's young face. It seemed so beautiful and so important to him to retrace the lines of this face with a pen, and he felt he himself had become another person in these few weeks: much older; not more intelligent, yet more experienced;

not happier, yet much more mature, much richer in his soul. He was no longer a boy.

In her gentle, lost voice Lydia said to him: "You mustn't be sad, not because of me; I want to bring you only joy, to see you happy. Forgive me, I've made you sad, I've infected you with my fears and my grief. I have such strange dreams at night: I'm always walking in a desert, it is vast and dark, I can't tell you how vast and dark, and I walk there, looking for you, but you're not there and I know that I have lost you and that I will have to walk like that forever and ever, alone like that. Then I wake up and think: oh, how good, how wonderful that he's still here, that I'll see him, perhaps for many weeks more, or days, it doesn't matter, it only matters that he's still here!"

One morning Goldmund awoke shortly after dawn and continued to lie in his bed for a while, musing. Images from a dream hovered about him, disconnected. He had dreamed of his mother and of Narcissus; he could still see both figures clearly. As he extricated himself from the strands of the dream, a peculiar light caught his attention, a strange kind of brightness was filtering through the small window. He jumped up, ran to the window, and saw that the windowsill, the roof of the stable, the gate to the courtyard, the entire landscape beyond was shimmering bluish-white, covered by the first snow of winter. He was struck by the contrast between his agitated heart and the quiet, resigned winter landscape: how quiet, how gracefully and piously field and forest, hill and heath gave in to sun, wind, rain, draft and snow, how beautifully and gently maple and ash bore the burden of winter! Could one not become as they, could one learn nothing from them? Deep in thought, he walked out to the courtyard, waded in the snow, touched it with his hands, went into the garden and looked over the high, snow-covered fence at the snow-bent rose branches.

As they ate their gruel for breakfast, everybody mentioned the first snow. Everyone—even the girls—had already been outside. Snow had come late this year, Christmas was not far off. The knight spoke about the lands to the south that were strangers to snow. But the event that made this first winter day unforgettable for Goldmund occurred long after nightfall.

The two sisters had quarreled during the day, but Goldmund knew nothing of it. At night, after the house had grown quiet and dark, Lydia came to his room in accord with her custom. Wordlessly she lay down beside him, leaned her head against his chest to hear his heartbeat and to console herself with his nearness. She was sad and full of apprehension; she feared that Julie might betray her; yet she could not make up her mind to speak to her lover about it and to cause him sorrow. She was lying quietly against his heart, listening to the tender words he whispered to her from time to time, feeling his hand in her hair.

But suddenly—she had not been lying there for very long—she had a terrible shock and sat up, her eyes growing wide. Goldmund was also greatly frightened when he saw the door of his room open and a figure enter. His shock kept him from recognizing immediately who it was. Only when the apparition stood close beside his bed and bent over it did he recognize with anguish in his heart that it was Julie. She slipped out of the coat she had thrown over her nightgown and let it drop to the floor. With a cry of pain, as though cut by a knife, Lydia sank back and clung to Goldmund.

In a mocking, triumphant, though shaking voice Julie said: "I don't enjoy being in my room by myself all the time. Either you take me in with you, and we lie together all three of us, or I go and wake father."

"Well, come in then," said Goldmund, folding back the cover. "You'll freeze your feet off there." She climbed in and he had trouble making room for her in the narrow bed, because Lydia had buried her face in the pillow and was lying motionless. Finally, all three were in the bed, a girl on each side of Goldmund. For a second he could not resist the thought that not so long ago this situation corresponded to his most secret wishes. With strange anguish and secret delight, he felt Julie's hip against his side.

"I just had to see," she began again, "how it feels to lie in your bed, since my sister enjoys coming here so much."

In order to calm her, Goldmund softly rubbed his cheek against her hair and caressed her hip and knee with a quiet hand, the way one caresses a cat. Silent and curious she surrendered to his probing hand, felt the magic with curious reverence, offered no resistance. But while he cast his spell, he also took pains to comfort Lydia, hummed soft, familiar love sounds into her ear and finally made her lift her face and turn it toward him. Soundlessly he kissed her mouth and eyes, while his hand kept her sister spellbound on the other side. He was aware how embarrassing and grotesque the whole situation was; it was becoming almost unbearable.

It was his left hand that taught him the truth: while it explored the beautiful, quietly waiting body of Julie, he felt for the first time not only the deep hopelessness of his love for Lydia, but how ridiculous it was. While his lips were with Lydia and his hand with Julie, he felt that he should either force Lydia to give in to him, or he should leave. To love her and yet renounce her had been wrong, had been nonsense.

"My heart," he whispered into Lydia's ear, "we

are suffering unnecessarily. How happy all three of
us could be now! Let us do what our blood demands!"

She drew back, shrinking, and his desire fled to
the other girl. His hand was doing such pleasing
things to Julie that she answered with a long quivering sigh of lust.

Lydia heard the sigh and her heart contracted
with jealousy, as though poison had been dropped
into it. She sat up abruptly, tore the cover off the
bed, jumped to her feet and cried: "Julie, let's
leave!"

Julie was startled. The thoughtless violence of
Lydia's cry, which might betray them all, showed
her the danger. Silently she got up.

But Goldmund, offended and betrayed in all his
senses, quickly put his arms around Julie as she sat
up, kissed her on each breast, and hotly whispered
into her ear: "Tomorrow, Julie, tomorrow!"

Barefoot, in her nightgown, Lydia stood on the
stone floor, her feet blue with cold. She picked up
Julie's coat and hung it around her sister with a
gesture of suffering and submission that did not
escape Julie in spite of the darkness; it touched
and reconciled her. Softly the sisters vanished from
the room. With conflicting emotions, Goldmund
listened intently and breathed with relief as the
house remained deathly quiet.

The three young people were forced to meditate
in solitude over their strange and unnatural association. The two sisters found nothing to say to each
other, after they hurried back to their bedroom.
They lay awake in their respective beds, each
alone, silent, and stubborn. A spirit of grief, contradiction, nonsense, alienation, and innermost confusion seemed to have taken hold of the house.
Goldmund did not fall asleep until after midnight; Julie not until the early hours of morning.
Lydia lay torturously awake until the pale day rose

over the snow. Then she got up, dressed, knelt for a long time in prayer before the small wooden Saviour in her room, and as soon as she heard her father's step on the stairs went out and asked him to hear her. Without trying to distinguish between her fears for Julie's virginity and her own jealousy, she had decided during the night to put an end to the matter. Goldmund and Julie were still asleep when the knight was informed of everything Lydia had decided to tell him. She did not mention Julie's part in the adventure.

When Goldmund appeared in the writing room at the usual hour that morning, he found the knight in boots, vest, and girdled sword, instead of the slippers and housecoat he usually wore while they wrote. At once he knew the meaning of this.

"Put on your cap," said the knight. "I have a walk to take with you."

Goldmund took his cap from the nail and followed his master down the stairs, across the courtyard, and out the gate. Their soles made crunching noises on the slightly frozen snow; the sky was still red with dawn. The knight walked ahead in silence; the young man followed. Several times he looked back at the house, at the window of his room, at the steep, snow-covered roof, until all disappeared and there was nothing more to see. He would never see that roof, those windows again, never again the study, the bedroom, the two sisters. He had so often toyed with the thought of sudden departure. Now his heart contracted with pain, and it hurt bitterly to leave this way.

For an hour they walked in this fashion, the master going on ahead. Neither spoke, and Goldmund began to think about his fate. The knight was armed; perhaps he would kill him. But he did not believe that he would. The danger was small; he'd only have to run and the old man would stand there helpless with his sword. No, his life was not in danger. But this silent walking behind the offended, solemn man, this being led away wordlessly pained him more with every step. Finally the knight halted.

"From here on," he said in a broken voice, "you will continue alone, always in the same direction, you'll lead the wanderer's life you did before. If you ever show your face again in the neighborhood of my house, you will be killed. I have no desire to take revenge on you; I should have been more intelligent than to allow so young a man to live intimately with my daughters. But if you have the audacity to come back, your life is lost. Go now, and may God forgive you!"

As he stood in the sallow light of the snowy morning, his gray-bearded face looked almost dead. Like a ghost he stood there, and did not move until Goldmund had disappeared over the next ridge. The reddish tint in the cloudy sky had faded, the sun did not come out, and snow began to fall in thin, hesitant flakes.

9

Goldmund knew the area from many previous rides. The knight owned a barn beyond the frozen marsh, and farther on there was a farmhouse where he was known; he'd be able to rest and spend the night in one of those places. Everything else had to wait until tomorrow. Gradually, the feeling of freedom and detachment took hold of him again; he had grown unaccustomed to it. It did not have a pleasant taste on this icy, gloomy winter day; it smelled strongly of hardship, hunger, and want, and yet the vastness of it, its great expanse, its merciless harshness was almost comforting and soothing to his spoiled, confused heart.

He walked until he felt tired. My riding days are over, he thought. Oh, wide world! A little snow was falling. In the distance the edges of the forest fused with gray clouds; infinite silence stretched to the end of the world. What was happening to Lydia, that poor, anguished heart? He felt bitterly sorry for her; he thought of her tenderly as he rested under a bare, lonely ash in the middle of the deserted marshland. Finally the cold drove him on. Stiff-legged, he stood up, forced himself to a brisk pace; the meager light of the drab day already seemed to be dwindling. The slow trot across the bare fields put an end to his musing. It was not a question of thinking now, or of having emotions, no matter how delicate and beautiful; it was now a question of keeping alive, of reaching a spot for the night in time, of getting through this cold, inhospitable world like a marten or a fox, and not giving out too soon, in the open fields. Everything else was unimportant.

He thought he heard the sound of distant hoofs and looked around in surprise. Could anyone be following him? He reached for the small hunting knife in his pocket and slipped off the wooden sheath. The rider became visible; he recognized a horse from the knight's stable; stubbornly it was heading toward him. Fleeing would have been useless. He stopped and waited, without actual fear, but very tense and curious, his heart beating faster. For a second a thought shot through his head: "If I killed this rider, how well off I'd be; I'd have a horse and the world would be mine." But when he recognized the rider, the young stable-boy Hans, with his light-blue, watery eyes and the good, embarrassed boy's face, he had to laugh; to murder this good dear fellow, one would have to have a heart of stone. He greeted Hans with a friendly hand and tenderly patted Hannibal, the horse, on its warm, moist neck; it recognized him immediately.

"Where are you headed, Hans?" he asked.

"To you," laughed the boy with shining teeth. "You've run a good distance. I can't stay; I'm only here to give you regards and this."

"Regards from whom?"

"From Lady Lydia. Well, you certainly gave us a nasty day, Master Goldmund, I was glad to get away for a while. But the squire must not know that I've been gone, and with an errand that could cost me my neck. Here!"

He handed him a small package; Goldmund took it.

"I say, Hans, you don't happen to have a piece of bread in one of your pockets that you might give me?"

"Bread? I might find a crust." He rummaged in his pockets and pulled out a piece of black bread. Then he wanted to ride off again.

"How is the lady?" asked Goldmund. "Didn't she give you any message? No little letter?"

"Nothing. I saw her only for a moment. There's a storm at the house, you know; the squire is pacing like King Saul. She told me to give you these things, and nothing else. I've got to get back now."

"All right, all right, just a moment more! Say, Hans, you couldn't let me have your hunting knife? I've only a small one. When the wolves come and all that—it would be better if I had something solid in hand."

But Hans would not hear of that. He'd be very sorry, he said, if something should happen to Master Goldmund. But he could not part with his jackknife, no, never, not for money, nor a swap either, no, no, not even if Saint Genevieve in person asked him for it. There, and now he had to get a move on, and he did wish him well, and he did feel sorry about everything.

They shook hands and the boy rode off. Goldmund looked after him with a strange pain in his heart. Then he unpacked the things, happy to have the strong calf's-leather cord that held them together. Inside he found a knitted undervest of thick gray wool, which apparently Lydia had made for him herself, and there was also something hard, well wrapped in the wool, a piece of ham: a small slit had been cut into the ham and a shiny gold piece had been stuck into the slit. There was no written message. He stood in the snow, undecided, holding Lydia's gifts in his hands. Then he took off his jacket and slipped into the knitted vest; it felt pleasantly warm. Quickly he put his jacket back on, hid the gold piece in his safest pocket, wound the cord around his waist, and continued his walk across the fields. It was time he reached a place to rest; he had grown very tired. But he didn't feel like going to the farmhouse, although it would have been warmer and he'd probably also have found some milk there; he didn't feel like chatting and being asked questions. He spent the night in the barn, continued on his way early the next morning, in frost and sharp wind, driven to long marches by the cold. For many nights he dreamed of the knight with his sword and of the two sisters; for many days loneliness and melancholy weighed on his heart.

The following evening he found a place for the night in a village, where the peasants were so poor they had no bread, only gruel. Here, new adventures awaited him. During the night, the peasant woman whose guest he was gave birth to a child. Goldmund was present while it happened; they had waked him in the straw to come and help, although there was nothing for him to do finally, except hold the light while the midwife went about her business. For the first time he witnessed a birth. With astonished, burning eyes he gazed at the face of the woman in labor, richer suddenly by this new experience. At any rate the expression in the woman's face seemed most remarkable to him. In the light of the torch, as he stared with great curiosity into the face of the screaming woman, lying there in pain, he was struck by something unexpected: the lines in the screaming woman's distorted face were little different from those he had seen in other women's faces during the moment of love's ecstasy. True, the expression of great pain was more violent and disfiguring than the expression of ultimate passion—but essentially it was not different, it was the same slightly grinning contraction, the same sudden glow and extinction. Miraculously, without understanding why, he was surprised by the realization that pain and joy could resemble each other so closely.

And yet another experience awaited him in that village. The morning after the birth, he ran into the neighbor's wife, who soon replied to the amorous questioning of his eyes. He stayed a second night and made the woman very happy since it was the first time in many weeks of excitation and disappointment that his desires were finally stilled. This delay led to a new experience: he found a companion on that second day in the village, a lanky, daring fellow named Viktor, who looked half like a priest and half like a highway robber.

Viktor greeted him with scraps of Latin, claiming to be a traveling student, although he was long past his student years. He wore a pointed beard and treated Goldmund with a certain heartiness and highway humor that quickly won the younger man.

To Goldmund's questions, where he had studied and where he was headed, this strange fellow replied: "By my destitute soul, I have visited enough places of high learning. I've been to Cologne and to Paris, and few scholars have expressed deeper thoughts on the metaphysics of liverwurst than I in my dissertation at Leyden. Since then, *amicus*, I, poor bastard that I am, have crossed and recrossed the German Empire in all directions, my dear soul tortured by immeasurable hunger and thirst. Viktor, the peasant terror, they call me. My profession is teaching Latin to young wives and tricking sausages out of chimneys and into my belly. My goal is the bed of the mayor's wife, and if the crows don't chew me up beforehand, I'll hardly be able to avoid the obligation of dedicating myself to the tiresome profession of archbishop. It is better, my dear young colleague, to live from hand to mouth than the other way round, and, after all, a roasted hare has never felt better than in my humble stomach. The king of Bohemia is my brother, and our father in heaven feeds him as he does me, although he insists that I lend him a hand, and the day before yesterday this father, hardhearted as fathers are, tried to misuse me in order to save the life of a half-starved wolf. If I hadn't killed the beast, you, my dear colleague, would not have the honor of making my fascinating acquaintance. *In saecula saeculorum, amen.*"

Goldmund was still unfamiliar with the gallows humor and wayfaring Latin of this wanderer. He felt a bit scared of the lanky, bristly rascal and the rasping laughter with which he applauded his own jokes, yet there was something about this hardboiled vagrant that did please him, and he readily let himself be persuaded to continue the journey with him, because, whether the vanquished wolf was boasting or the truth, two were indisputably stronger than one and had less to fear. But before continuing the journey, brother Viktor wanted to speak a bit of Latin to the people, as he called it, and installed himself in the house of one of the poorer peasants. He did not follow the practice Goldmund had so far applied on the road, wherever he had been the guest of a farmhouse or a village; Viktor went from hut to hut, chatted with every woman, stuck his nose into every stable and kitchen, and did not seem willing to leave before each house had paid him a toll and a tribute. He told the peasants about the war in Italy and sang, beside their hearths, the song of the battle of Pavia. He recommended remedies for arthritis and loose teeth to the grandmothers; he seemed to know everything, to have been everywhere. He stuffed his shirt above the belt full to bursting with the pieces of bread, nuts, and dried pears the peasants had given him. With surprise Goldmund watched him wage his campaign, listened to him now frighten, now flatter the people, boast and win their admiration, speak broken Latin and play the scholar, and the next moment impress them with brash, colorful thieves' slang, saw how, in the middle of a tale or learned talk his sharp, watchful eyes recorded every face, every table drawer that was pulled open, every dish, every loaf of bread. He saw that this was a seasoned adventurer who had been exposed to all walks of life, who had seen and lived through much, who had starved a good deal, and shivered, and grown shrewd and impudent in the bitter struggle for a meager, dangerous existence. So this was what became of people who led a wanderer's life for a long time! Would he, too, be like that one day?

The next morning, as they moved on, for the first time Goldmund had a taste of walking in company. For three days they were on the road together, and Goldmund found this and that to learn from Viktor. Applying everything to the three basic needs of the homeless skirting death, finding a place for the night, and a source of food—had become an instinct with Viktor. He had learned much during the many years of roaming the world. To recognize the proximity of human habitation by almost invisible signs, even in winter; at night, to inspect every nook and cranny in forest or field as a potential resting or sleeping place; to sense instantly, upon entering a room, the degree of prosperity or misery of the owner, as well as the degree of his goodheartedness, or his curiosity, or fear—these were tricks which Viktor had long since mastered. He told his young companion many instructive things. Once Goldmund replied that he would not like to approach people from such a purposeful point of view and that, although he was unfamiliar with all these tricks, he had only rarely been refused hospitality upon his friendly request. Lanky Viktor laughed and said good-humoredly: "Well sure, little Goldmund, you may not have to, you're so young and pretty, you look so innocent, your face is a good recommendation. The women like you and the men think: 'Oh Lord, he's harmless, he wouldn't hurt a fly.' But look here, little brother, a man gets older, the baby face grows a beard and wrinkles, your pants wear out and before you know it you are an ugly, unwelcome guest, and instead of youth and innocence, nothing but hunger is staring out of your eyes. At that point you've got to be hard, you've got to have learned a few things about the world; or else you'll soon find yourself lying on the dung heap and the dogs'll come and pee on you. But I don't think that you'll be running around for too long anyhow, your hands are too delicate and your curls too pretty, you'll crawl back to where life is easier, into a nice warm conjugal bed or a good fat cloister or some beautifully heated writing room. And your clothes are so fine, you could be taken for a squire."

Still laughing, he ran his hands over Goldmund's clothes. Goldmund could feel these hands grope and search along every seam and pocket; he drew back and thought of his gold piece. He told of his stay at the knight's house, that he had earned his fine clothes by writing Latin. Viktor wanted to know why he had left such a warm nest in the middle of winter, and Goldmund, who was not accustomed to lying, told him a little about the knight's two daughters. This led to their first quarrel. Viktor thought Goldmund an incomparable fool for having run off and left the castle and the ladies to the care of the good Lord. That situation had to be remedied, he'd see to that. They'd visit the castle; of course Goldmund could not be seen there, but he should leave that to him. Goldmund was to write a little letter to Lydia, saying this and that, and he, Viktor, would take it to the castle and, by the Saviour's wounds, he would not come back without a little something of this and that, money and loot. And so on. Goldmund refused and finally became violent; he did not want to hear

another word about the matter, nor did he tell
Viktor the name of the knight or the way to the
castle.

When Viktor saw him so angry, he laughed
again and played the jovial companion. "Well," he
said, "don't bite your teeth out! I'm merely telling
you that you're letting a good catch slip through
our fingers, my boy. That's not very nice and broth-
erly of you. But you don't want to, you're a noble-
man, you'll return to your castle on a high horse
and marry the lady! Boy, your head is bursting
with nonsense! Well, it's all right with me, let's
walk on and freeze our toes off."

Goldmund remained grumpy and silent until
evening, but since they came neither upon a house
nor upon people that day, he gratefully let Viktor
pick a place for the night, let him build a wind-
break between two trees at the edge of the forest
and make a bed with an abundance of pine
branches. They ate bread and cheese from Viktor's
full pockets. Goldmund felt ashamed of his anger
and tried to be polite and helpful; he offered his
companion his woolen jacket for the night. They
agreed to take turns keeping watch against the
animals, and Goldmund took over the first vigil
while Viktor lay down on the pine branches. For a
long time Goldmund stood quietly with his back
against a fir trunk in order not to keep the other
man from falling asleep. Then he felt cold and
began to pace. He ran back and forth at greater
and greater distances, saw the tips of firs jut sharply into the pale sky, felt the deep silence of the
solemn and slightly awesome winter night, heard
his warm living heart beat lonely in the cold,
echoless silence, walked quietly back and listened
to the breathing of his sleeping companion. More
powerfully than ever he was seized by a feeling of
homelessness, without a house, castle, or cloister
wall between him and the great fear, running

naked and alone through the incomprehensible, hostile world, alone under the cool mocking stars, among the watchful animals, the patient, steady trees.

No, he thought, he would never become like Viktor, even if he wandered for the rest of his life. He would never be able to learn Viktor's way of fighting the horror, his sly, thievish squeaking by, his loud brazen jests and wordy humor. Perhaps this shrewd, impudent man was right; perhaps Goldmund would never completely become his equal, never altogether a vagrant. Perhaps he would some day creep back behind some sort of wall. Although even then he would remain homeless and aimless, never feel really safe and protected, the world would always surround him with mysterious beauty and eeriness; again and again he would be made to listen to this silence in which his heartbeat sounded anguished and fleeting. Few stars were visible, there was no wind, but way up high the clouds seemed to be moving.

After a long time Viktor awoke—Goldmund had not felt like waking him—and called to him.

"Come," he called, "your turn to catch some sleep, or you'll be no good tomorrow."

Goldmund obeyed; he stretched out on the pine bed and closed his eyes. He was extremely tired but did not fall asleep. His thoughts kept him awake, and something else besides thoughts, a feeling he did not admit to himself, an uneasiness and distrust that had to do with his companion. It was inconceivable to him now that he had told this crude, loud-laughing man, this jester and brazen beggar, about Lydia. He was angry with him and with himself and wondered how he could find a way and an opportunity to get rid of him.

After an hour or so, Viktor bent over him and again began feeling his pockets and seams; Goldmund froze with rage. He did not move, he merely opened his eyes and said disdainfully: "Go away, I have nothing worth stealing."

His words shocked the thief; he grabbed Goldmund by the throat and squeezed. Goldmund fought back and tried to get up, but Viktor pressed harder, kneeling on his chest. Goldmund could hardly breathe. Violently he writhed and jerked with his whole body, and when he could not free himself, the fear of death shot through him and made his mind sharp and lucid. He managed to slip one hand in his pocket, pull out his small hunting knife, and while the other man continued strangling him he thrust the knife several times into the body that was kneeling on him. After a moment, Viktor's hands let go; there was air again and Goldmund breathed it deeply, wildly, savoring his rescued life. He tried to sit up; limp and soft, his lanky companion sank into a heap on top of him with a ghastly sigh. His blood ran over Goldmund's face. Only now was he able to sit up. In the gray shimmer of the night he saw the long man lying in a huddle; he reached out to him and touched only blood. He lifted the man's head; it fell back, heavy and soft like a bag. Blood spilled from his chest and neck; from his mouth life ran out in delirious, weakening sighs.

"Now I have murdered a man," thought Goldmund. Again and again he thought it, as he knelt over the dying man and saw pallor spread over his face. "Dear Mother of God, I have killed a man," he heard himself say.

Suddenly he could not bear to stay a moment longer. He picked up his knife, wiped it across the woolen vest which the other man was wearing, which Lydia's hands had knitted for her beloved; he slipped the knife back into its wooden sheath and into his pocket, jumped up and ran away as fast as he could.

The death of the cheerful wayfarer lay heavy on

his soul; shuddering, as the day grew light he
washed away in the snow the blood he had spilled;
and then he wandered about for another day and
another night, aimless and anguished. Finally his
body's needs shocked him out of his fear-filled
repentance.

Lost in the deserted, snow-covered landscape,
without shelter, without a path, without food and
almost without sleep, he fell into a bottomless
despair. Hunger cried in his belly like a wild beast;
several times exhaustion overcame him in the middle of a field. He closed his eyes and thought that
his end had come, wished only to fall asleep, to die
in the snow. But again and again something forced
him back on his feet. Desperately, greedily he ran
for his life, delighted and intoxicated in the midst
of bitter want by this insane, savage strength of
will not to die, by this monstrous force of the
naked drive to live. With frost-blue hands he
picked tiny, dried-up berries off the snow-covered
juniper bushes and chewed the brittle, bitter stuff,
together with pine needles. The taste was exciting-
ly sharp; he devoured handfuls of snow against his
thirst. Breathless, blowing into his stiff hands, he
sat on top of the hill for a brief rest. Avidly he
looked about: nothing but heath and forest, no
trace of a human being. A few crows circled above
him; he looked at them angrily. No, they were not
going to feed on him, not as long as there was an
ounce of strength left in his legs, a spark of warmth
in his blood. He got up and resumed his merciless
race with death. He ran on and on, in a fever of
exhaustion and ultimate effort. Strange thoughts
took hold of him; he held mad conversations with
himself, now silent, now loud. He spoke to Viktor,
whom he had stabbed to death. Harshly and ironically he spoke to him: "Well, my shrewd brother,
how is it with you? Is the moon shining through
your bowels, old fellow? Are the foxes pulling your

ears? You killed a wolf, you say? Did you bite him
through the throat, or tear off his tail, or what? You
wanted to steal my gold piece, you old guzzler!
But little Goldmouth surprised you, didn't he, old
friend, he tickled you in the ribs! And all the while
you still had bags full of bread and sausage and
cheese, you stuffed pig!" He coughed and barked
mockeries; he insulted the dead man, he tri-
umphed over him, he jeered at him because he
had let himself be slaughtered, the fool, the stupid
braggart!

But after a while his thoughts and words turned
away from lanky Viktor. He saw Julie walking
ahead of him, beautiful little Julie, as she had left
him that night; he called countless endearments
to her, tried to seduce her with delirious, shameless
cajoleries, to make her come to him, to make her
drop her nightgown, to ride up to heaven with him
during this last hour before death, for a short moment before his miserable end. He implored and
commanded her high little breasts, her legs, the
blond kinky hair under her arms.

Trotting through the barren, snow-covered heath
with stiff, stumbling legs, drunk with misery, triumphant with the flickering desire to live, he began to whisper. Now it was Narcissus to whom he
spoke, to whom he communicated his recent reve-
lations, insights, and ironies.

"Are you scared, Narcissus," he said to him, "are
you shuddering, did you notice something? Yes, my
respected friend, the world is full of death, full of
death. Death sits on every fence, stands behind
every tree. Building walls and dormitories and
chapels and churches won't keep death out; death
looks in through the window, laughing, knowing
every one of you. In the middle of the night you
hear laughter under your window and someone
calls your name. Go ahead, sing your psalms, burn
pretty candles at the altar, say your evening prayers

and your morning prayers, gather herbs in your
laboratory, collect books in your libraries. Are you
fasting, dear friend? Are you depriving yourself of
sleep? He'll lend you a hand, our old friend the
Reaper, he'll strip you to the bones. Run, dear
friend, run as fast as you can, death is giving a
party in the fields, run and see that your bones stay
together, they're trying to escape, they don't want
to stay with us. Oh, our poor bones, our poor throat
and belly, our poor little scraps of brains under
our skulls! It all wants to become free, it all wants
to go to the devil, the crows are sitting in the trees,
those black-frocked priests."

He had long since lost all sense of direction; he
didn't know where he was running, what he was
saying, whether he was lying or standing. He stumbled over bushes, ran into trees; falling, he groped
for snow and thorns. But the drive was strong in
him. Again and again it pulled him forward,
spurred his blind flight. When he collapsed for the
last time, it was in the same little village in which
he had met the wayfaring charlatan a few days
earlier, where he had held the torch during the
night for the woman who was giving birth. There
he lay and people came running and stood about
him and talked, yet he did not hear them. The
woman whose love he had enjoyed earlier recognized him; she was shocked by the way he looked,
and took pity. Let her husband scold her; she
dragged the half-dead Goldmund into the stable.

It was not long before he was back on his feet.
The warmth of the stable, sleep, and the goat's
milk the woman gave him to drink revived him
and let him recover his strength; but all recent
events had been pushed back in his mind as
though much time had passed since they happened. His journey with Viktor, the cold, anguished
winter night under the pines, the dreadful struggle
on the bed of boughs, his companion's horrible

death, the days and nights lost and cold and hungry—it had all become the past. He had almost forgotten it; although it was not wiped out, it had been lived through and was nearly over. Something remained, something inexpressibly horrible but also precious, something drowned and yet unforgettable, an experience, a taste on the tongue, a ring around the heart. In less than two years he had learned all the joys and sorrows of homeless life: loneliness, freedom, the sounds of forests and beasts, wandering, faithless loving, bitter deathly want. For days he had been the guest of the summery fields, of the forest, of the snow, had spent days in fear of death, close to death. Fighting death had been the strongest emotion of all, the strangest, knowing how small and miserable and threatened one was, and yet feeling this beautiful, terrifying force, this tenacity of life inside one during the last desperate struggle. It echoed, it remained etched in his heart, as did the gestures and expressions of ecstasy that so much resembled the gestures and expressions of birth-giving and dying. He remembered how the woman had screamed that night in childbirth, distorting her face; how Viktor had collapsed, how quietly and quickly his blood had run out! Oh, and how he himself had felt death snooping around him on hungry days, and how cold he had been, how cold! And how he had fought, how he had struck death in the face, with what mortal fear, what grim ecstasy he had defended himself! There was nothing more to be lived through, it seemed to him. Perhaps he could talk about it with Narcissus, but with no one else.

When Goldmund first came to his senses on his bed of straw in the stable, he missed the gold piece in his pocket. Had he lost it during the terrible, half-unconscious stumbling march during those final days of hunger? He thought about it for a long time. He had been fond of the gold piece; he did not want to think it lost. Money meant little to him; he hardly knew its value. But this gold piece had become important to him for two reasons. It was the only gift from Lydia that was left him, since the woolen vest was lying in the forest with Viktor, soaked in Viktor's blood. And then, keeping the gold coin had been the reason for defending himself against Viktor; he had murdered Viktor because of it. If the gold piece was lost, the whole experience of that ghastly night would be useless, would have no value. After much thinking about it, he confided in the peasant woman.

"Christine," he whispered to her, "I had a gold piece in my pocket, and now it's no longer there."

"Oh, so you noticed?" she asked with a loving smile that was both sly and clever. It delighted him so much that he put his arm around her in spite of his weakness.

"What a strange boy you are," she said tenderly. "So intelligent and refined, and yet so stupid. Does one run around the world with a loose gold piece in one's open pocket? Oh, you childish boy, you darling fool! I found your gold piece as soon as I laid you down on the straw."

"You did? Where is it?"

"Find it," she laughed and let him search for quite a while before she showed him the spot in his jacket where she had sewed it. She added good motherly advice too, which he quickly forgot, but he never forgot her loving care and the sly-kind look in her peasant face, and he tried hard to show her his gratitude. Soon he was able to walk again and eager to move on, but she held him back because on that day the moon was changing and the weather would be turning milder the next. And so it was. By the time he left, the snow lay soiled and gray, the air was heavy with wetness. High up, one could hear the spring winds groan.

10

Again ice was floating down the rivers, and a scent
of violets rose from under the rotten leaves.
Goldmund walked through the colorful seasons: his
insatiable eyes drank in the forests, the mountains,
the clouds; he wandered from farm to farm, from
village to village, from woman to woman. Many a
cool evening he'd sit anguished, with aching heart,
under a lighted window; from its rosy shimmer
radiated all that was happiness and home and
peace on earth, all that was lovely and unreachable
for him. Everything repeated itself over and over,
all the things he thought he had come to know so
well; everything returned, and yet different each
time: the long walks across field and heath, or
along stony roads, sleeping in the summer forest,
strolls through villages, trailing after bands of
young girls coming home, hand in hand, from turning over the hay or gathering hops; the first shudder of autumn, the first angry frosts—everything
came back: once, twice, endlessly the colorful ribbon rolled past his eyes.

Much rain, much snow had fallen on Goldmund.
One day he climbed uphill through a sparse beech
forest already light green with buds. From the
mountain ridge he saw a new landscape lying at
his feet; it gladdened his eyes and a flood of expectations, desires, and hopes gushed through his
heart. For several days he had known that he was
close to this region; he had been looking forward

to it. Now, during this noon hour, it came as a surprise and his first visual impression confirmed and strengthened his expectations. Through gray trunks and softly swaying branches he looked down into a valley lying green and brown, furrowed by a wide river that shimmered like blue glass. He felt that his pathless roaming through landscapes of heath, forest, and solitude, with an isolated farm here and there, or a shabby village, was over for a long time. Down there the river flowed, and along the river ran one of the most beautiful and famous roads in the empire. A rich and bountiful land lay there, barges and boats sailed there, the road led to beautiful villages, castles, cloisters, and prosperous towns, and anyone who so desired could travel along that road for days and weeks and not fear that it would suddenly peter out in a forest or in humid reeds like those miserable peasant paths. Something new lay ahead and he was looking forward to it.

That evening he came to a beautiful village, wedged between the river and red vineyards along the wide highway. The pretty woodwork on the gabled houses was painted red; there were arched entranceways and narrow alleys full of stone steps. A forge threw a red fiery glow across the street; he heard the clear ringing of the anvil. Goldmund snooped about in every alley and corner, sniffed at cellar doors for the smell of wine barrels and along the riverbank for the cool fish odor of the water; he inspected church and cemetery and did not forget to look for a good barn for the night. But first he wanted to try his luck at the priest's house and ask for food. A plump, red-headed priest asked him questions and Goldmund told him the story of his life, with a few omissions and additions. Thereupon he was given a friendly reception and spent the evening in long conversation over good food and wine. The next day he continued his journey on the highway, along the river. He saw barges and rafts float by; he passed horse carts, and some of them gave him a ride for a stretch of the way. The spring days sped by, filled with color: villages and small towns received him; women smiled behind garden fences, knelt in the brown earth, planting bulbs; young girls sang in the village streets in the evening.

A young servant girl in a mill pleased him so much he spent two days in the area and tried to get to know her. She liked to laugh and chat with him; he thought he would have been happy to work at the mill and stay there forever. He sat with the fishermen; he helped the carters feed and comb their horses, was given bread and meat and a ride in exchange. The sociable world of travelers did him good after the long loneliness; with a good meal every day, after so much hunger, he gladly let himself be carried along by the joyous wave. It swept him on, and the closer he got to the bishop's city, the more crowded and joyful the highway became.

In one village he took an evening stroll along the river, with the trees already in leaf. The water ran quietly, mightily; the current sighed and gushed under the overhanging roots of trees; the moon came up over the hill, casting light on the river and shadows under the trees. He came upon a girl who was sitting there, weeping: she had quarreled with her lover; he had walked off and left her. Goldmund sat down beside her and listened to her sorrowful tale; he caressed her hand, told her about the forest and the deer, comforted her a little, made her laugh a little, and she permitted him a kiss. But at that point her young man came back looking for her; he had calmed down and regretted the quarrel. When he found Goldmund sitting beside her, he threw himself upon him and hammered at him with both fists. Goldmund had

difficulty defending himself, but finally he fought
the fellow off, and watched him run cursing
toward the village; the girl had long since fled. But
Goldmund did not trust the truce; he renounced
his bed for the night and wandered on half the
night in the moonlight, through a silent silver
world, extremely content, glad of his strong legs,
until the dew washed the white dust from his shoes
and he suddenly felt tired, lay down under the
next tree, and fell asleep. It was broad daylight
when he was awakened by something tickling his
face. He brushed it aside with a sleepy, groping
hand, fell asleep again, was once more awakened
by the tickling; a peasant girl was standing there,
looking at him, tickling him with the tip of a
willow switch. He stumbled to his feet. With a
smile they nodded to each other; she led him into
a shed, where the sleeping was more comfortable.
There they lay together for a while, then she ran
off and came back with a small pail of milk, still
warm from the cow. He gave her a blue hair ribbon
he had recently found in the street, and they
kissed once more before he wandered on. Her name
was Franziska; he was sorry to leave her.

That evening he found shelter in a cloister, and
the next morning he went to mass. A thousand
memories welled up in his heart; the cool stone air
of the dome and the flapping of sandals in the
marble corridors felt movingly familiar. After mass,
when the cloister church had grown quiet,
Goldmund remained on his knees. His heart was
strangely moved; he had had many dreams that
night. He felt the urge to unburden himself of his
past, to change his life somehow, he knew not
why; perhaps it was only the memory of Mariabronn and of his pious youth that moved him. He
felt the urge to confess and purify himself. Many
small sins, many small vices had to be admitted,
. but most heavily he felt burdened by the death of

Viktor, who had died by his hand. He found a
father and confessed to him, especially the knife
stabs in poor Viktor's neck and back. Oh, how long
since he had been to confession! The number and
weight of his sins seemed considerable to him; he
was willing to do a stiff penance for them. But his
confessor seemed familiar with the life of the wayfarers: he was not shocked; he listened calmly.
Earnest and friendly, he reprimanded and warned
without speaking of damnation.

Relieved, Goldmund stood up, prayed in front of
the altar as the father had ordered and was about
to leave the church when a ray of sunshine fell
through one of the windows. His eyes followed it;
in a side chapel he saw a statue that spoke to him
so strongly and attracted him so much that he
turned toward it with loving eyes and looked at it
with reverence and deep emotion. It was a wooden
madonna. Delicately, gently she leaned forward;
the blue cloak hung from her narrow shoulders; she
stretched out a delicate, girlish hand, and the expression of her eyes above the grieving mouth and
the gracefully rounded forehead were so alive and
beautiful, so deeply permeated with spirit that
Goldmund thought he had never seen anything
like it anywhere before. He could not look enough
at the mouth, at the lovely angle of the inclined
neck. It seemed to him that he saw something
standing there that he had often seen in dreams
and inklings, something he had often wished for.
Several times he turned to go; again and again the
statue drew him back.

When he finally turned to leave, the father confessor was standing behind him.

"Do you find her beautiful?" he asked in a
friendly tone.

"Inexpressibly beautiful," said Goldmund.

"That's what some people say," said the priest.
"Others say that this is no mother of God, that she

is much too modern and worldly, that the whole thing is untrue and exaggerated. There is a great deal of controversy about it. So you like her; I'm glad. We've had her only for a year, a donation from a benefactor of our order. She was made by Master Niklaus."

"Master Niklaus? Who is he, where does he live? Do you know him? Tell me about him, please! What a magnificent, blessed man who can create a work like that."

"I don't know much about him. He is a carver in our bishop's city, a day's journey from here; he has a great reputation as an artist. Artists usually are no saints, he's probably no saint either, but he certainly is a gifted, high-minded man. I have seen him a few times ..."

"Oh, you have seen him! What does he look like?"

"You seem completely fascinated with him, my son. Well, go to see him then, and give him regards from Father Bonifazius."

Goldmund thanked him exuberantly. The father walked off with a smile; for a long time Goldmund stood before the mysterious statue, whose bosom seemed to heave and in whose face so much pain and sweetness were living side by side that it made his heart ache.

He left the church a changed man. His feet carried him through a completely changed world. Since that moment in front of the sweet saintly wooden figure, Goldmund possessed something he had not possessed before, something he had so often mocked or envied in others: a goal! He had a goal. Perhaps he would reach it; perhaps his whole, ragged existence would grow meaningful and worthwhile. This new feeling filled him with joy and fear and gave wings to his steps. The gay, beautiful highway on which he was walking was no longer what it had been the day before, a festive playground, a cozy place to be. Now it was only a road that led to the city, to the master. Impatiently he hurried on. He arrived before evening: towers rose from behind walls; he saw chiseled escutcheons and painted signs over the city gates, entered with pounding heart, hardly noticing the noise and bustle in the streets, the knights on their horses, the carts and carriages. Neither knights nor carriages, city nor bishop mattered to him. He asked the very first person he met where Master Niklaus lived, and was deeply disappointed when the man didn't know who Master Niklaus was.

He came to a square surrounded by stately houses, many painted or decorated with images. Over the door of a house stood the figure of a lansquenet in robust, laughing colors. It was not as beautiful as the statue in the cloister church, but it had such a way of pushing out its calves and sticking its bearded chin into the world that Goldmund thought this figure might have been made by the same master. He walked into the house, knocked at doors, climbed stairs; finally he ran into a squire in a fur-trimmed velvet coat and asked him where he might find Master Niklaus. What did he want from him, the squire asked in return. Goldmund had difficulty holding himself back, to say merely that he had a message for him. Thereupon the squire told him the name of the street on which the master lived. By the time Goldmund had asked his way there, night had fallen. Anxious but happy, he stood outside the master's house, looking up at the windows; he almost ran up to the door. But it was already late, he was sweaty and dusty from the day's march. He mastered his impatience and waited. For a long time he stood outside the house. He saw a light go on in a window, and just as he was about to leave, he saw a figure step to the window, a very beauti-

ful blond girl with the gentle shimmer of lamplight
flowing through her hair from the back.

The next morning, after the city had awakened
and become noisy, Goldmund washed his face and
hands in the cloister where he had been a guest for
the night, slapped the dust from his clothes and
shoes, found his way back to the master's street
and knocked at the door of the house. A servant
appeared who first refused to lead him to the
master, but he managed to soften the old woman's
resistance, and finally she led him into a small hall.
It was a workshop and the master was standing
there, a leather apron around his waist: a bearded,
tall man of forty or fifty, Goldmund thought. He
scanned the stranger with piercing, pale blue eyes
and asked curtly what he desired. Goldmund delivered Father Bonifazius's greetings.

"Is that all?"

"Master," Goldmund said with baited breath, "I
saw your madonna in the cloister there. Oh, don't
give me such an unfriendly look; nothing but love
and veneration have brought me to you. I am not a
fearful man, I have lived a wanderer's life, sam-
pled forest, snow, and hunger; I'm not afraid of
anyone, but I am afraid of you. I have only a
single gigantic desire, which fills my heart to the
point of pain."

"And what desire is that?"

"To become your apprentice and learn with
you."

"You are not the only young man to wish that.
But I don't like apprentices, and I already have
two assistants. Where do you come from and who
are your parents?"

"I have no parents, I come from nowhere. I was
a student in a cloister, where I learned Latin and
Greek. Then I ran away, and for years I have
wandered the roads, until today."

"And what makes you think you should become

an image carver? Have you ever tried anything similar before? Have you any drawings?"

"I've made many drawings, but I no longer have them. But let me tell you why I wish to learn this art. I have done a great deal of thinking and seen many faces and figures and thought about them, and some of these thoughts have tormented me and given me no peace. It has struck me how a certain shape, a certain line recurs in a person's structure, how a forehead corresponds to the knee, a shoulder to the hip, and how, deep down, it corresponds to the nature and temperament of the person who possesses that knee, that shoulder, that forehead, and fuses with it. And another thing has struck me: one night, as I had to hold a light for a woman who was giving birth, I saw that the greatest pain and the most intense ecstasy have almost the same expression."

The master gave the stranger a piercing look. "Do you know what you are saying?"

"Yes, Master, it is the truth. And it was that precisely that I found expressed in your madonna, to my utter delight and consternation, that is why I have come. Oh, there is such suffering in the beautiful delicate face, and at the same time all the suffering is also pure joy, a smile. When I saw that, a fire shot through me; all my year-long thoughts and dreams seemed confirmed. Suddenly they were no longer useless; I knew immediately what I had to do and where I had to go. Dear Master Niklaus, I beg you with all my heart, let me learn with you!"

Niklaus had listened attentively, without making a friendlier face.

"Young man," he said, "you know surprisingly well how to speak about art, and it puzzles me that, young as you are, you have so much to say about ecstasy and pain. I'd gladly chat with you about this some evening over a mug of wine. But

look: to speak pleasantly and intelligently with
each other is not the same as living and working
together for a couple of years. This is a workshop.
Work is carved here, not conversation. What a man
may have thought up and know how to express
does not count here; here only what he can make
with his hands counts. You seem to mean what you
say. Therefore I'll not simply send you on your
way again. We'll see if you can do anything at all.
Did you ever shape anything in clay or wax?"

Goldmund found himself thinking of a dream he
had long ago in which he had modeled small clay
figures that had stood up and grown into giants.
But he did not mention it and said that he had
never tried.

"Good. You'll draw something then. There is a
table; you'll find paper and charcoal. Sit down and
draw, take your time, you can stay till noon or
evening. Perhaps that will tell me what you are
good for. Now then, we have talked enough. I'll do
my work; you'll do yours."

Goldmund sat in the chair Niklaus had indicated
to him, in front of the drawing table. He was in no
hurry to accomplish his task. First he sat, waiting
and silent like an apprehensive student. With curiosity and love he stared toward the master, whose
back was half turned and who continued to work
at a small clay figure. Attentively he studied this
man, whose stern, already slightly graying head
and hard, though noble and animated artisan's
hands held such graceful magic. He looked different than Goldmund had imagined: older, more
modest, soberer, much less radiant and heart-win-
ning, and not in the least happy. The merciless
sharpness of his probing eyes was now concen-
trated on his work. Freed from it, Goldmund
minutely took in the master's entire figure. This
man, he thought, might also have been a scholar,
a quiet earnest searcher, who has dedicated him-

self to a task that many predecessors have begun before him, that he will one day leave to
his successors, a tenacious, long-lived never-end-
ing work, the accumulation of the effort and
dedication of many generations. At least this
was what Goldmund read from the master's head:
great patience, years of study and thinking, great
modesty, and an awareness of the dubious value of
all human undertaking, but also faith in his mission. The language of his hands was something
else again; there was a contradiction between
the hands and the head. These hands reached
with firm but extremely sensitive fingers into the
clay they were molding. They treated the clay
like a lover's hands treat the willing mistress:
lovingly, with tenderly swaying emotion, greedy
but without distinguishing between taking and giving, filled with desire but also with piety, masterful
and sure as though from the depth of ancient
experience. Goldmund watched these blessed
hands with delighted admiration. He would have
liked to draw the master, had it not been for the
contradiction between face and hands which par-
alyzed him.

For about an hour he watched the steadily working artist, full of searching thoughts about the
secret of this man. Then another image began
to form inside him, to become visible in front
of his soul, the image of the man he knew best
of all, whom he had loved deeply and greatly admired; and this image was without flaw or contradiction, although it too bore many lines and
recalled many struggles. It was the image of his
friend Narcissus. It grew more and more tangible,
became an entity, a whole. The inner law of the
beloved person appeared more and more clearly
in his picture: the noble head shaped by the
mind; the beautiful controlled mouth, tightened
and ennobled by the service to the mind; the

slightly sad eyes; the haggard shoulders animated
with the fight for spirituality; the long neck; the
delicate, distinguished hands. Not since his departure from the cloister had he seen his friend so
clearly, possessed his image so completely within
him.

As though in a dream, will-less and yet eager,
Goldmund cautiously began to draw. With loving
fingers he brushed reverently over the figure that
lived in his heart; he forgot the master, himself,
and the place at which he sat. He did not notice
the light slowly wandering across the workshop, or
the master looking over at him several times. Like
a sacrificial ritual he accomplished the task that
had been given him, that his heart had given him:
to gather his friend's image and preserve it the
way it lived in his soul today. Without thinking of it, he felt he was paying back a debt,
showing his gratitude.

Niklaus stepped up to the drawing table and
said: "It's noon. I'm going to eat; you can come
along. Let's see—did you draw something?"

He stepped behind Goldmund and looked at the
large sheet. Then he pushed him aside and carefully took the sheet in his able hands. Goldmund had
come out of his dream and was now looking at the
master with anxious expectation. The master stood,
holding the drawing in both hands, looking at it
very carefully with his sharp stern light-blue eyes.

"Who is the man you have drawn here?" he
asked after a while.

"My friend, a young monk and scholar."

"Fine. Wash your hands, there's a well in the
yard. Then we'll go and eat. My assistants aren't
here, they're working outside the city."

Obediently Goldmund went out, found the courtyard and the well, washed his hands and would
have given much to know the master's thoughts.
When he came back, the master was gone; he

heard him rummaging about in the adjoining room. When he reappeared, he too had washed himself and wore a beautiful cloth jacket instead of the apron; he looked solemn and imposing. He led the way, up a flight of stairs—there were small carved angels' heads on the walnut banister posts—lined with old and new statues, into a beautiful room with floor, walls, and ceiling of polished wood; a table had been in the window corner. A young girl came running in. Goldmund knew her; it was the beautiful girl of the evening before.

"Lisbeth," the master said, "bring another plate. I've brought a guest. He is—well, I don't even know his name yet."

Goldmund said his name.

"Goldmund then. Is dinner ready?"

"In a minute, Father."

She fetched a plate, ran out and soon returned with the maid, who served the meal: pork with lentils and white bread. During the meal the father spoke of this and that with the girl, Goldmund sat in silence, ate a little and felt very ill at ease and apprehensive. The girl pleased him greatly, a stately, beautiful figure, almost as tall as her father, but she sat, well-mannered and completely inaccessible as though behind glass, and did not speak to the stranger, or look at him.

When they finished eating, the master said: "I'll rest for half an hour. You go down to the workshop or stroll around a bit outside. Afterwards we'll talk."

Goldmund bowed slightly and went out. It had been an hour or more since the master had seen his drawing, and he had not said a word about it. Now he had to wait another half hour! Well, there was nothing he could do about it; he waited. He did not go into the workshop; he did not want to see his drawing again just now. He went into the court-

yard, sat down on the edge of the well, and
watched the thread of water trickling endlessly
from the pipe into the deep stone dish, making
tiny waves as it fell, always carrying a little air
down with it, which kept rising up in white pearls.
He saw his own face in the dark mirror of the well
and thought that the Goldmund who was looking
up at him from the water had long since ceased
being the Goldmund of cloister days, or Lydia's
Goldmund, or even the Goldmund of the forests.
He thought that he, that all men, trickled away,
changing constantly, until they finally dissolved,
while their artist-created images remained un-
changeably the same.

He thought that fear of death was perhaps the
root of all art, perhaps also of all things of the
mind. We fear death, we shudder at life's insta-
bility, we grieve to see the flowers wilt again and
again, and the leaves fall, and in our hearts we
know that we, too, are transitory and will soon
disappear. When artists create pictures and thinkers search for laws and formulate thoughts, it is
in order to salvage something from the great dance
of death, to make something that lasts longer than
we do. Perhaps the woman after whom the master shaped his beautiful madonna is already wilted
or dead, and soon he, too, will be dead; others
will live in his house and eat at his table—but
his work will still be standing a hundred years
from now, and longer. It will go on shimmering
in the quiet cloister church, unchangingly beautiful, forever smiling with the same sad, flowering
mouth.

He heard the master come downstairs and ran
into the workshop. Master Niklaus was pacing;
several times he looked at Goldmund's drawing;
finally he walked to the window and said, in his
somewhat hesitant, dry manner: "It is customary

for an apprentice to study at least four years, and
for his father to pay for the apprenticeship."

He paused and Goldmund thought the master
was afraid that he could not pay him. Quick as
lightning, he pulled out his knife, cut the stitches
around the hidden gold piece, and held it up.
Niklaus watched him in surprise and broke out
laughing when Goldmund handed him the coin.

"Ah, is that what you thought?" he laughed. "No,
young man, you keep your gold piece. Listen now.
I told you how our guild customarily deals with
apprentices. But I am no ordinary master, nor are
you an ordinary apprentice. Usually an apprentice
begins his apprenticeship at thirteen or fourteen,
fifteen at the latest, and half of his learning years
are spent running errands and playing the servant.
But you are a grown man; according to your age,
you could long have been journeyman or master
even. Our guild has never had a bearded apprentice. Besides, as I told you before, I don't like to
keep an apprentice in my house. Nor do you look
like a man who lets himself be ordered about."

Goldmund's impatience was at its peak. Every
new thoughtful word from the master put him on
tenterhooks; it all seemed disgustingly boring and
pedantic to him. Vehemently he cried: "Why do
you tell me all this, if you don't want to make me
your apprentice?"

Firmly the master continued: "I have thought
about your request for an hour. Now you must
have the patience to listen to me. I have seen your
drawing. It has faults, but it is beautiful. If it
were not beautiful, I would have given you half
a guilder and sent you on your way and forgotten
about you. That is all I wish to say about the
drawing. I would like to help you become an
artist; perhaps that is your destiny. But you're
too old to become an apprentice. And only an
apprentice who has served his time can become

journeyman and master in our guild. Now you know the conditions. But you shall be allowed to give it a try. If you can maintain yourself in this city for a while, you may come to me and learn a few things. There will be no obligation, no contract, you can leave again whenever you choose. You may break a couple of carving knives in my workshop and ruin a couple of woodblocks, and if we see that you're no wood carver, you'll have to try your skill at other things. Does that satisfy you?"

Ashamed and moved, Goldmund had heard his words.

"I thank you with all my heart," he cried. "I am homeless; I'll be able to keep alive in this city as well as in the woods. I understand that you don't wish to assume responsibility for me as for a young apprentice. I consider it a great fortune to be allowed to learn from you. I thank you from the bottom of my heart for doing this for me."

11

New images surrounded Goldmund in this city; a new life began for him. Landscape and city had received him happily, enticingly, generously, and so did this new life, with joy and many promises. Although sorrow and awareness remained essentially untouched in his soul, life, on the surface, played for him in rainbow colors. The gayest and lightest period in Goldmund's life had begun. Outwardly, the rich bishop's city offered itself in all its arts; there were women, and hundreds of pleasant games and images. On the inside, his awakening craftsmanship offered new sensations and experiences. With the master's help he found lodgings in the house of a gilder at the fish market, and at the master's as well as at the gilder's he learned how to handle wood, plaster, colors, varnish, and gold leaf.

Goldmund was not one of those forsaken artists who, though highly gifted, never find the right means of expression. Quite a number of people are able to feel the beauty of the world profoundly and vastly, and to carry high, noble images in their souls, but they are unable to exteriorize these images, to create them for the enjoyment of others, to communicate them. Goldmund did not suffer from this lack. The use of his hands came easily to him; he enjoyed learning the tricks and practices of the craft, and he easily learned to play the lute with companions in the evening after work and to dance on Sundays in the village. He learned it easily; it came by itself. He worked hard at wood carving, met with difficulties and disappointments, spoiled a few pieces of good wood, and severely cut his fingers several times. But he quickly surmounted the beginnings and acquired skill. Still, the master was often dissatisfied with him and would say: "Fortunately we know that you're not my apprentice or my assistant, Goldmund. Fortunately we know that you've wandered in from the woods and that you'll go back there some day. Anybody who didn't know that you're a homeless drifter and not a burgher or artisan might easily succumb to the temptation to ask this or that of you, the things every master demands of his men. You don't work badly at all when you're in the mood. But last week you loafed for two days. Yesterday you slept half the day in the courtyard workshop, instead of polishing the two angels you were supposed to polish."

The master was right, and Goldmund listened in silence, without justifying himself. He knew he was not a reliable, hard-working man. As long as a task fascinated him, posed problems, or made him happily aware of his skill, he'd work zealously. He did not like heavy manual work, or chores that were not difficult but demanded time and application. Many of the faithful, patient parts of craftsmanship were often completely unbearable to him. It sometimes made him wonder. Had those few years of wandering been enough to make him lazy and unreliable? Was his mother's inheritance growing in him and gaining the upper hand? Or was something else missing? He thought of his first years in the cloister, when he had been such a good and zealous student. Why had he managed so much patience then? Why did he lack it now; why had he been able to learn Latin syntax and all those Greek aorists indefatigably, although, at the bottom of his heart, they were quite unimportant to him? Occasionally he'd muse about that. Love had steeled his will; love had given him wings. His life had been a constant courtship of Narcissus, whose love one could woo only by esteem and recognition. In those days he was able to slave for hours and days in exchange for an appreciative glance from the beloved teacher. Finally the desired goal had been reached: Narcissus had become his friend and, strangely enough, it had been that learned Narcissus who had shown him his lack of aptitude for learning, who had conjured up his lost mother's image. Instead of learning, monkhood, and virtue, powerful drives and instincts had become his masters: sex, women, desire for independence, wandering. Then he saw the master's madonna and discovered the artist within himself. He had taken a new road, had settled down again. Where did he stand now? Where was his road leading him? Where did the obstacles stem from?

At first he was unable to define it. He knew only this: that he greatly admired Master Niklaus, but in no way loved him as he had Narcissus, and that he took occasional delight in disappointing and annoying him. This, it seemed, was linked to the contrasts in the master's nature. The figures by Niklaus's hand, at least the best among them, were revered examples for Goldmund, but the master himself was not an example.

Beside the artist who had carved the madonna with the saddest, most beautiful mouth, beside the knowing seer whose hands knew magically how to transform deep experience and intuition into tangible forms, there was another Master Niklaus: a somewhat stern and fearful father and guildsman, a widower who led a quiet, slightly cowering life with his daughter and an ugly servant in his quiet house, who violently resisted Goldmund's strongest impulses, who had settled into a calm, moderate, orderly, respectable life.

Although Goldmund venerated his master, although he would never have permitted himself to question others about him or to judge him in front of others, he knew after a year to the smallest detail all that was to be known about Niklaus. This master meant much to him. He loved him as much as he hated him; he could not stay away from him. Gradually, with love and with suspicion, with always vigilant curiosity, the pupil penetrated the hidden corners of the master's nature and of his life. He saw that Niklaus allowed neither apprentice nor assistant to live in his house, although there would have been room enough. He saw that he rarely went out and equally rarely invited guests to his house. He observed that he loved his beautiful daughter with touching jealousy, and that he tried to hide her from everyone. He also knew that behind the strict, premature abstinence of the widower's life, instincts were still at play, that the master could strangely transform and rejuvenate himself when an order occasionally called him to travel for a few days. And once, in a strange little town where they were setting up a carved pulpit, he had also observed that Niklaus had clandestinely visited a whore one evening and that he had been restless and ill-humored for days afterwards.

As time went on, something other than this curiosity tied Goldmund to the master's house and preoccupied his mind. The master's beautiful daughter Lisbeth attracted him greatly. He rarely got to see her; she never came into the workshop and he could not determine whether her brittleness and reserve with men was imposed by her father or was part of her own nature. He could not overlook the fact that the master never again invited him for a meal, that he tried to make any meeting with her difficult. Lisbeth was a most precious, sheltered young girl; he could not hope to have a love affair with her, or a marriage. Besides, anyone who wanted to marry her would have to come from a good family, be a member of one of the higher guilds and probably have money and a house besides.

Lisbeth's beauty, so different from that of the gypsies and peasant women, had attracted Goldmund's eyes that first day. There was something about her that he could not decipher, something strange that violently attracted him but also made him suspicious, irritated him even. Her great calm and innocence, her well-mannered purity were not childlike. Behind all her courtesy and ease lay a hidden coldness, a condescension, and for that reason her innocence did not move him, or make him defenseless (he could never have seduced a child), but annoyed and provoked him. As soon as her figure became slightly familiar to him as an inner image, he felt the urge to create a statue of her, not the way she was now, but an awakened, sensuous, suffering face, a Magdalene, not a young virgin. He often dreamed of seeing her calm, beautiful, immobile face distorted in ecstasy or pain, of seeing it unfold and yield its secret.

There was another face alive in his soul, although it did not altogether belong to him, a face he longed to capture and re-create artistically, but again and again it drew back and shrouded itself: his mother's face. It was no longer the face that had appeared to him one day, from the depths of lost memories, after his conversation with Narcissus. It had slowly changed during his days of wandering, his nights of love, during his spells of longing, while his life was in danger, when he was close to death: it had grown richer, deeper, subtler. This was no longer his own mother; her traits and colors had by and by given way to an impersonal mother image, of Eve, of the mother of men.

The way some of Master Niklaus's madonnas powerfully expressed the suffering mother of God with a perfection that seemed unsurpassable to Goldmund, he hoped that one day, when he was more mature and surer of his craft, he would be able to create the image of the worldly mother, the Eve-mother, as she lived in his heart, his oldest, most cherished image; an inner image that had once been the memory of his own mother, of his love of her, but was now in constant transformation and growth. The faces of Lise, the gypsy, of the knight's daughter Lydia, of many other women had fused with that original image. Each new woman added to it, each new insight, each experience and event worked at it and fashioned its traits. The figure he hoped to be able to make visible some day was not to represent any specific woman, but the source of life itself, the original mother. Many times he thought he saw it; often it appeared in his dreams. But he could not have said anything about this Eve's face, or about what it was to express, except that he wanted it to show the intimate relationship of ecstasy to pain and death.

Goldmund learned a great deal in the course of a year. He became an able draftsman; occasionally, beside wood carving, Niklaus also let him try his hand at modeling with clay. His first successful work was a clay figure, a good two spans high. It was the sweet, seductive figure of little Julie, Lydia's sister. The master praised this work but did not fulfill Goldmund's wish to have it cast in metal; he found the figure too unchaste and worldly to become its godfather. Then Goldmund started working on a statue of Narcissus, in wood, portraying the Apostle John. If successful, Niklaus wanted to include the figure in a crucifixion group he had been commissioned to execute and on which his two assistants had been working exclusively for quite some time, leaving the final touches to the master.

Goldmund worked with profound love at the statue of Narcissus. He rediscovered himself in this work, found his skill and his soul again every time he got off the track, which happened often enough. Love affairs, dances, drinking with working companions, dice playing, and many brawls would get him violently involved; he'd stay away from the workshop for a day or more, or stand distracted and grumpy over his bench. But at his St. John, whose cherished, pensive features came to meet him out of the wood with greater and greater purity, he worked only during hours of readiness, with devotion and humility. During these hours he was neither glad nor sad, knew neither carnal longings nor the flight of time. Again he felt the reverent, light, crystal feeling in his heart with which he had once abandoned himself to his friend, happy to be guided by him. It was not he who was standing there, creating an image of his own will. It was the other man rather; it was Narcissus who was making use of the artist's hands in order to step out of the fleeting transitions of life, to express the pure image of his being.

This, Goldmund sometimes felt with a shudder, was the way true art came about. This was how the master's unforgettable madonna had been made, which he had visited in the cloister again and again on many a Sunday. The few good pieces among the old statues which were standing upstairs in the master's foyer had come into being in this secret, sacred manner. And one day that other, the unique image, the one that was even more hidden and venerable to him, the mother of men, would come about in the same manner. Ah, if only the hand of man could create such works of art, such holy, essential images, untainted by will or vanity. But it was not that way. Other images were created: pretty, delightful things, made with great mastery, the joy of art lovers, the ornament of churches and town halls—beautiful things certainly, but not sacred, not true images of the soul. He knew many such works, not only by Niklaus and other masters—works that, in spite of their delicacy and craftsmanship, were nothing but playthings. To his shame and sorrow he had already felt that in his own heart, had felt in his hands how an artist can put such pretty things in the world, out of delight in his own skill, out of ambition and dissipation.

When he realized this for the first time, he grew deathly sad. Ah, it was not worth being an artist in order to make little angel figures and similar frivolities, no matter how beautiful. Perhaps the others, the artisans, the burghers, those calm, satisfied souls might find it worthwhile, but not ho. To him, art and craftsmanship were worthless unless they burned like the sun and had the power of storms. He had no use for anything that brought only comfort, pleasantness, only small joys. He was searching for other things. A dainty crown for a madonna, fashioned like lacework and beautifully goldleafed, was no task for him, no matter how well paid. Why did Master Niklaus accept all these orders? Why did he have two assistants? Why did he listen for hours to those senators and prelates who ordered a pulpit or a portal from him with their measuring sticks in their hands? He had two reasons, two shabby reasons: he wanted to be a famous artist flooded with commissions, and he wanted to pile up money, not for any great achievement or pleasure but for his daughter, who had long since become a rich girl, money for her dowry, for lace collars and brocade gowns and a walnut conjugal bed with precious covers and linens. As though the beautiful girl could not come to know love just as well in a hayloft.

His mother's blood stirred deeply in Goldmund in the course of such reflections; he felt the pride and disdain of the homeless for the settled, the proprietors. At times craft and master were so repulsive to him that he often came close to running away. More than once the master angrily regretted having taken on this difficult, unreliable fellow who often tried his patience to the utmost. The things he learned about Goldmund's life, about his indifference to money and ownership, his desire to squander, his many love affairs, his frequent brawls, did not make him more sympathetic; he had taken a gypsy into his house, a stranger. Nor had it escaped him with what eyes this vagrant looked at his daughter Lisbeth. If he, nevertheless, forced himself to be patient, it was not out of a sense of duty or out of fear, but because of the St. John's statue, which he watched come into being. With a feeling of love and kinship of the soul that he did not quite admit to himself, the master watched this gypsy, who had run to him out of the forest, shape his wooden disciple after the moving, beautiful, yet clumsy drawing that had made him keep Goldmund at the time. He saw how slowly and capriciously, but tenaciously, unerringly, Goldmund fashioned the wooden statue of the disciple. The master did not doubt that it would be finished some day, in spite of all Goldmund's moods and interruptions, that it would be a work the like of which not one of his assistants was able to make, a work that even great masters did not often accomplish. In spite of the many things the master disliked in his pupil, of the many scoldings he gave him, of his frequent fits of rage—he never said a word about the St. John.

During these years Goldmund had gradually lost the rest of the adolescent grace and boyishness that had pleased so many. He had become a beautiful, strong man, much desired by women, little popular with men. His mind, his inner face, had greatly changed as well since the days Narcissus awakened him from the happy sleep of his cloister years. World and wandering had molded him. From the pretty, gentle, pious, willing cloister student whom everybody liked, another being had emerged. Narcissus had awakened him, women had made him aware, the wandering had brushed the down from him. He had no friends; his heart belonged to women. They could win him easily: one longing look was enough. He found it hard to resist a woman and responded to the slightest hint. In spite of his strong sense of beauty, of his preference for the very young in the bloom of spring, he'd let himself be moved and seduced by women of little beauty who were no longer young. On the dance floor he'd sometimes end up with a discouraged elderly girl whom no one wanted, who'd win him by the pity he felt for her, and not pity alone, but also a constantly vigilant curiosity. As soon as he gave himself to a woman—whether it lasted weeks or just hours—she became beautiful to him, and he gave himself completely. Experience taught him that every woman was beautiful and able to bring joy, that a mousy creature whom men ignored was capable of extraordinary fire and devotion, that the wilted had a more maternal, mourningly sweet tenderness, that each woman had her secrets and her charms, and to unlock these made him happy. In that respect, all women were alike. Lack of youth or beauty was always balanced by some special gesture. But not every woman could hold him equally long. He was just as loving and grateful toward the ugly as toward the youngest and prettiest; he never loved halfway. But some women tied him to them more strongly after three or ten nights of love; others were exhausted after the first time and forgotten.

Love and ecstasy were to him the only truly

warming things that gave life its value. Ambition
was unknown to him; he did not distinguish between bishop and beggar. Acquisition and ownership had no hold over him; he felt contempt for
them. Never would he have made the smallest
sacrifice for them; he was earning ample money
and thought nothing of it. Women, the game of the
sexes, came first on his list, and his frequent ac-
cesses of melancholy and disgust grew out of the
knowledge that desire was a transitory, fleeting
experience. The rapid, soaring, blissful burning of
desire, its brief, longing flame, its rapid extinction—
this seemed to him to contain the kernel of all
experience, became to him the image of all the joys
and sufferings of life. He could give in to this
melancholy and shudder at all things transitory
with the same abandonment with which he gave in
to love. This melancholy was also a form of love, of
desire. As ecstasy, at the peak of blissful tension, is
certain that it must vanish and die with the next
breath, his innermost loneliness and abandonment
to melancholy was certain that it would suddenly
be swallowed by desire, by new abandonment to
the light side of life. Death and ecstasy were one.
The mother of life could be called love or desire;
she could also be called death, grave, or decay.
Eve was the mother. She was the source of bliss as
well as of death; eternally she gave birth and
eternally she killed; her love was fused with cruelty. The longer he carried her image within him,
the more it became a parable and a sacred symbol
to him.

Not with words and consciousness, but with a
deeper knowledge of his blood, he knew that his
road led to his mother, to desire and to death. The
father side of life—mind and will—were not his
home. Narcissus was at home there, and only now
Goldmund felt penetrated by his friend's words
and understood them fully, saw in him his counter-

part, and this he also expressed in the statue of St. John and made it visible. He could long for Narcissus to the point of tears; he could dream of him wonderfully—but he could not reach him, he could not become like him.

Secretly Goldmund also sensed what being an artist meant to him, how his intense love of art could also occasionally turn to hatred. He could, not with thoughts but with emotions, make many different distinctions: art was a union of the father and mother worlds, of mind and blood. It might start in utter sensuality and lead to total abstraction; then again it might originate in pure concept and end in bleeding flesh. Any work of art that was truly sublime, not just a good juggler's trick; that was filled with the eternal secret, like the master's madonna; every obviously genuine work of art had this dangerous, smiling double face, was male-female, a merging of instinct and pure spirituality. One day his Eve-mother would bear this double face more than any other statue, if he succeeded in making her.

In art, in being an artist, Goldmund saw the possibility of reconciling his deepest contradictions, or at least of expressing newly and magnificently the split in his nature. But art was not just a gift. It could not be had for nothing; it cost a great deal; it demanded sacrifices. For over three years Goldmund sacrificed his most essential need, the thing he needed most next to desire and love: his freedom. Being free, drifting in a limitless world, the hazards of wandering, being alone and independent—all that he had renounced. Others might judge him fickle, insubordinate, and overly independent when he neglected workshop and work during an occasional furious fling. To him, this life was slavery; often it embittered him and seemed unbearable. Neither the master nor his future nor need demanded his obedience—it was art itself.

Art, such a spiritual goddess in appearance, required so many petty things! One needed a roof over one's head, and tools, woods, clay, colors, gold, effort and patience. He had sacrificed the wild freedom of the woods to this goddess, the intoxication of the wide world, the harsh joys of danger, the pride of misery, and this sacrifice had to be made again and again, chokingly, with clenched teeth.

Part of this sacrifice was recoverable. A few of his love adventures, his fights with rivals constituted a small revenge against the slavelike sedentary order of his present life. All his emprisoned wildness, all the caged-in strength of his nature steamed out of this escape valve; he became a known and feared rowdy. A sudden attack in a dark side street, on his way to see a girl or on the way home from a dance; a couple of blows from a stick, throwing himself around with lightning swiftness to pass from defense to attack, to press the panting enemy to him, to land a fist under the enemy's chin, or drag him by the hair, or throttle him mightily—all these things tasted good to Goldmund and cured his dark moods for a while. And the women liked it, too.

All this gave him plenty to do, and it all made sense as long as he was working on his St. John. It took a long time. The last delicate shapings of face and hands were done in solemn, patient concentration. He finished the statue in a small wooden shed behind the assistants' workshop. Then the hour of morning came when the work was finished. Goldmund fetched a broom, swept the shed meticulously clean, gently brushed the last sawdust from his Saint's hair, and stood in front of his statue for a long time, an hour or longer, filled with the solemn feeling of a rare and great experience which he might perhaps know one more time in the course of his life or which might remain unique. A man on the day of his wedding or on the day he is knighted, a woman after the birth of her first child might feel such emotions in the heart: a deep reverence, a great earnestness, and at the same time a secret fear of the moment when this high, unique experience would be over, classified, swallowed by the routine of the days.

He saw his friend Narcissus, the guide of his adolescent years, clad in the robe and role of the beautiful, favorite disciple, stand listening with lifted face and an expression of stillness, devotion, and reverence that was like the budding of a smile. Suffering and death were not unknown to this beautiful, pious, spiritualized face, to this slender figure that seemed to be floating, to these graceful, piously raised long hands, although they were filled with youth and inner music; but despair was unknown to them, and disorder, and rebellion. The soul of those noble traits might be gay or sad, but its pitch was pure, it suffered no discordant note.

Goldmund stood and contemplated his work. His contemplation began as a meditation in front of the monument to his youth and friendship, but it ended in a tempest of sorrow and heavy thoughts. There his work was, the beautiful disciple would remain, his delicate flowering would never end. But he, the maker, would have to part with his work; tomorrow it would no longer be his, would no longer be waiting for his hands, would grow and unfold under them no longer, was no longer a refuge to him, a consolation, a purpose in his life. He remained behind, empty. And therefore it seemed to him that it would be best to say farewell today not only to his St. John but also to the master, to the city, to art. There was nothing here for him to do any more; no images filled his soul that he might have carved. The longed-for image of images, the figure of the mother of men, was not yet accessible to him, would not be accessible for a long time. Should he go back to polishing little angel figures now and carving ornaments?

He tore himself away and walked over to the master's workshop. Softly he entered and stood at the door, until Niklaus noticed him and called out to him.

"What is it, Goldmund?"

"My statue is finished. Perhaps you'll come and take a look at it before you go up to eat."

"Gladly. I'll come right now."

Together they walked over, leaving the door open for more light. Niklaus had not seen the figure for a while; he had left Goldmund undisturbed at his work. Now he examined it with silent attention. His closed face grew beautiful and light; Goldmund saw his stern eyes grow happy.

"It is good," the master said. "It is very good. It is your assistant's piece, Goldmund. Now you have finished learning. I'll show your figure to the men at the guild and demand that they make you a master for it; you deserve it."

Goldmund did not value the guild very highly, but he knew how much appreciation the master's words meant, and he was glad.

While Niklaus walked slowly around the figure of St. John, he said with a sigh: "This figure is full of piety and light. It is grave, but filled with joy and peace. One might think that the man who made this had nothing but light and joy in his heart."

Goldmund smiled.

"You know that I did not portray myself in this figure, but my dearest friend. It is he who brought light and peace to the picture, not I. It was not really I who made the statue; he gave it into my soul."

"That may be so," said Niklaus. "It is a secret how such a work comes into being. I am not partic-

ularly humble, but I must say: I have made many
works that fall far behind yours, not in craft and
care, but in truth. No, you probably know yourself
that such a work cannot be repeated. It is a
secret."

"Yes," Goldmund said. "When the figure was
finished and I looked at it, I thought: you can't
make that again. And therefore I think, Master,
that I'll soon go back to wandering."

Astonished and annoyed, Niklaus looked at him.
His eyes had grown stern again.

"We'll speak about that. For you, work should
really begin now. This is not the moment to run
away. But take this day off, and at noon you'll be
my guest."

At noon Goldmund appeared washed and
combed, in his Sunday clothes. This time he knew
how much it meant and what a rare honor it was
to be invited to the master's table. As he climbed
the stairs to the foyer that was crowded with statues, his heart was far from being filled with the
reverence and anxious joy of the other time, that
first time when he had stepped into these beautiful
quiet rooms with pounding heart.

Lisbeth, too, was dressed up and wore a chain of
stones around her neck, and besides carp and wine
there was another surprise for dinner: the master
gave Goldmund a leather purse containing two
gold pieces, his salary for the finished statue.

This time he did not sit in silence while father
and daughter talked. Both spoke to him, they
drank toasts. Goldmund's eyes were busy. He used
this opportunity to study carefully the beautiful
girl with the distinguished, slightly contemptuous
face, and his eyes did not conceal how much she
pleased him. She treated him courteously, but he
felt disappointed that she did not blush or grow
animated. Again he wished fervently to make this

beautiful immobile face speak, to force it to surrender its secret.

After the meal he thanked them, lingering a while before the statues in the foyer. During the afternoon he strolled through the city, an aimless idler. He had been greatly honored by the master, beyond all expectation. Why did it not make him happy? Why did all this honor have such an unfestive taste?

Heeding a whim, he rented a horse and rode out to the cloister where he had first seen work by the master and heard his name. That had been a few years ago; it seemed unthinkably longer. He visited the madonna in the cloister church and again the statue delighted and conquered him. It was more beautiful than his St. John. It was similar in depth and mystery, and superior in craft, in free, gravityless floating. Now he saw details in the work that only an artist sees, soft delicate movements in the gown, audacities in the formation of the long hands and fingers, sensitive utilization of the grain of the wood. All these beauties werc nothing compared to the whole, to the simplicity and depth of the vision, but they were there nevertheless, beauties of which only the blessed were capable, those who knew their craft completely. In order to be able to create a work like this, one had not only to carry images in one's soul; one also had to have inexpressibly trained, practiced eyes and hands. Perhaps it was after all worthwhile to place one's entire life at the service of art, at the expense of freedom and broad experience, if only in order to be able once to make something this beautiful, something that had not only been experienced and envisioned and received in love, but also executed to the last detail with absolute mastery? It was an important question.

Late at night Goldmund returned to the city on

a tired horse. A tavern still stood open. There he took bread and wine. Then he climbed up to his room at the fish market, not at peace with himself, full of questions, full of doubts.

12

The next day Goldmund could not bring himself to go to work. As on many other joyless days, he roamed about the city. He saw housewives and servants go to market. He loitered around the fountain at the fish market and watched the fish venders and their burly wives praise their wares, watched them pull the cool silvery fish out of the barrels and offer them for sale, saw the fish open their mouths in pain, their gold eyes rigid with fear as they quietly gave in to death, or resisted it with furious desperation. He was gripped by pity for these animals and by a sad annoyance with human beings. Why were people so numb and crude, so unthinkably stupid and insensitive? How could those fishermen and fishwives, those haggling shoppers not see these mouths, the deathly frightened eyes and wildly flailing tails, the gruesome, useless, desperate battle, this unbearable transformation from mysterious, miraculously beautiful animals— the quiet last shiver that ran across the dying skin before they lay dead and spent—into flattened, miserable slabs of meat for the tables of those jovial paunches? These people saw nothing, knew nothing, and noticed nothing; nothing touched them. A poor, graceful animal could expire under their very eyes, or a master could express all the hope, nobility, and suffering, all the dark tense anguish of human life, in the statue of a saint with shudder-inducing tangibility—they saw nothing,

nothing moved them! They were gay; they were busy, important, in a hurry; they shouted, laughed, bumped into each other, made noise, told jokes, screamed over two pennies, felt fine, were orderly citizens, highly satisfied with themselves and the world. Pigs, that's what they were, filthier and viler than pigs! Of course he had only too often been one of them, had felt happy among them, had pursued their girls, had gaily eaten baked fish from his plate without being horrified. But sooner or later, as though by magic, joy and calm would suddenly desert him; all fat plump illusions, all his self-satisfaction and self-importance, and idle peace of mind fell away. Something plunged him into solitude and brooding, made him contemplate suffering and death, the vanity of all undertaking, as he stared into the abyss. At other times a sudden joy blossomed from the hopeless depth of uselessness and horror, a violent infatuation, the desire to sing a beautiful song, to draw. He had only to smell a flower or play with a cat, and his childlike agreement with life came back to him. This time, too, it would come back. Tomorrow or the day after, the world would be good again, it would be wonderful. At least it was so until the sadness returned, the brooding, the remorse for dying fish and wilting flowers, the horror of insensitive, pig-like, staring-but-not-seeing human existence. It was at such moments that Viktor always came to his mind. With torturing curiosity and deep anguish, he would think of the lanky wayfarer whom he had stabbed between the ribs and left lying on pine boughs covered with blood. And he wondered what had become of Viktor. Had the animals eaten him completely, had anything remained of him? The bones probably, and perhaps a few handfuls of hair. And what would become of the bones? How long was it, decades or just years, until bones lost their shape and crumbled into the earth?

As he watched the goings-on in the marketplace, feeling pity for the fish and disgust for the people, anguished by the melancholy in his heart and a bitter hatred against the world and himself, he once more thought of Viktor. Perhaps someone had found and buried him? And in that case, had all the flesh fallen from the bones, had it all rotted off, had the worms devoured everything? Was there still hair on the skull, and brows above the hollows of the eyes? And what had remained of Viktor's life, which had been so full of adventures and stories, the fantastic playfulness of his odd jests? Was there nothing else left alive of this human existence, which had, after all, not been ordinary, other than the few stray memories his murderer had of him? Was there still a Viktor in the dreams of women who had once loved him? Or had every vestige of him disappeared and dissolved? Thus it happened to everyone and everything: a brief flowering that soon wilted and was soon covered by snow. All the things that had flowered in him when he arrived in this city a few years ago, burning with desire for art, with deep anxious respect for Master Niklaus—what was still alive of them? Nothing, nothing more than was left of poor lanky Viktor's boastful silhouette. If somebody had told him a few years ago that the day would come when Niklaus would recognize him as an equal and demand his master's licence from the guild, he would have believed all the happiness in the world was in his hands. And now this achievement was nothing but a faded flower, a dried-up, joyless thing.

In the middle of these thoughts Goldmund suddenly had a vision. It lasted only an instant, a lightning flash: he saw the face of the universal mother, leaning over the abyss of life, with a lost smile that was both beautiful and gruesome. She was looking at birth and death, at flowers, at rustling autumn leaves, at art, at decay.

Everything had the same meaning to the universal mother. Her chilling smile hung above everything like a moon, sad and pensive. The dying carp on the cobblestones of the fish market was as dear to her as Goldmund; she was as fond of the scattered bones of the Viktor who had once tried to steal his gold as she was of his master's proud cool young daughter Lisbeth.

The lightning flash was gone; the mysterious mother face had vanished. But the pale glow continued to tremble deep in Goldmund's soul, the beat of life, of pain, of longing agitated his heart. No, no, he did not want the satiated happiness of the others, of fish venders, of burghers, of busy people. Let them go to hell. Oh, her twitching pale face, her fully ripe late-summer mouth, her heavy lips on which the immense fatal smile trembled like wind and moonlight!

Goldmund went to the master's house. It was toward noon, and he waited until he heard Niklaus leave his work and go to wash his hands. Then he went in.

"May I say a few words to you, Master, while you're washing your hands and putting on your jacket? I'm starving for a mouthful of truth. I want to say something to you that I might perhaps be able to say right now and never again. I must speak to a human being and perhaps you are the only one who can understand. I'm not speaking to the man with the famous workshop who is honored by so many assignments from great cities and cloisters, who has two assistants and a rich, beautiful house. I'm speaking to the master who made the madonna in the cloister outside the city, the most beautiful statue I know. I have loved and venerated this man; to become like him seemed to me the highest goal on earth. Now I have made a statue, my statue of St. John. It's not made as perfectly as your madonna; but that can't be helped. I have no plans for other statues, no idea that demands execution. Or rather, there is one, the remote image of a saint that I'll have to make some day, but not just yet. In order to be able to make it, I must see and experience much, much more. Perhaps I'll be able to make it in three or four years, or in ten years, or later, or never. But until then, Master, I don't want to work as an artisan, lacquering statues and carving pulpits and leading an artisan's life in the workshop. I don't want to earn money and become like other artisans. I don't want that. I want to live and roam, to feel summer and winter, experience the world, taste its beauty and its horrors. I want to suffer hunger and thirst, and to rid and purge myself of all I have lived and learned here with you. One day I would like to make something as beautiful and deeply moving as your madonna— but I don't want to become like you and lead your kind of life."

The master had washed and dried his hands. He turned and looked at Goldmund. His face was stern, but not angry.

"You have spoken," he said, "and I have listened. Don't worry now. I'm not expecting you to come to work, although there is much to be done. I don't consider you an assistant; you need freedom. I'd like to discuss a few things with you, dear Goldmund; not now, in a couple of days. In the meantime, you may spend your hours as you please. You see, I am much older than you and have learned a few things. I think differently than you do, but I understand you and what goes on in your mind. In a few days I'll send for you. We'll talk about your future; I have all kinds of plans. Until then, be patient! I know only too well how one feels when one has finished a piece of work that was important to one; I know this emptiness. It passes, believe me."

Goldmund left, dissatisfied. The master meant well, but how could he be of help? Goldmund knew a spot along the river where the water was not deep; its bed was covered with shards and all kinds of rubbish that fishermen had thrown there. He sat down on the embankment wall and looked into the water. He loved water very much; all water attracted him. From this spot, one could look through the streaming, crystal-threaded water and see the dark vague bottom, see a vague golden glitter here and there, an enticing sparkle, bits of a broken plate perhaps or a worn-out sickle, or a smooth flat stone or a polished tile, or it might be a mud fish, a fat turbot or redeye turning around down there, a ray of light catching for an instant the bright fins of its scales and belly—one could never make out what precisely was there, but there were always enchantingly beautiful, enticing, brief vague glints of drowned golden treasure in the wet black ground. All true mysteries, it seemed to him, were just like this mysterious water; all true images of the soul were like this: they had no precise contour or shape: they only could be guessed at, a beautiful distant possibility that was veiled in many meanings. Just as something inexpressibly golden or silvery blinked for a quivering instant in the twilight of the green river depths, an illusion that contained, nevertheless, the most blissful promise, so the fleeting profile of a person, seen half from the back, could sometimes promise something infinitely beautiful, something unbearably sad. In the same way a lantern hung under a cart at night, painting giant spinning shadows of wheel spokes on walls, could for a moment create a shadow play that seemed as full of incidents and stories as the work of Homer. And one's nightly dreams were woven of the same unreal, magic stuff, a nothing that contained all the images in the world, an ocean in whose crystal the forms of all human beings, animals, angels, and demons lived as ever ready possibilities.

He was absorbed in the game. With lost eyes he stared into the drifting river, saw shapeless shimmerings at the bottom, kings' crowns and women's bare shoulders. One day in Mariabronn, he recalled, he had seen similar shape-dreams and magical transformations in Greek and Latin letters. Hadn't he once talked about it with Narcissus? When had that been, how many hundred years ago? Oh, Narcissus! To be able to see him, to speak with him for an hour, hold his hand, hear his calm, intelligent voice, he would gladly have given his two gold pieces.

How could these things be so beautiful, this golden glow underneath the water, these shadows and insinuations, all these unreal, fairylike apparitions— so inexpressibly beautiful and delightful, when they were the exact opposite of the beauty an artist might create? The beauty of those undistinguishable objects was without form and consisted of nothing but mystery. This was the very opposite of the form and absolute precision of works of art. Nothing was as mercilessly clear and definite as the line of a drawn mouth or a head carved in wood. Precisely to the fraction of an inch, he could have retraced the underlip or the eyelids of Niklaus's madonna statue; nothing was indefinite there, nothing deceptive, nothing vague.

Goldmund was absorbed in his thoughts. He could not understand how that which was so definite and formal could affect the soul in the same manner as that which was intangible and formless. One thing, however, did become clear to him— why so many perfect works of art did not please him at all, why they were almost hateful and boring to him, in spite of a certain undeniable beauty.

Workshops, churches, and palaces were full of
these fatal works of art; he had even helped with
a few himself. They were deeply disappointing because they aroused the desire for the highest and
did not fulfill it. They lacked the most essential
thing—mystery. That was what dreams and truly
great works of art had in common: mystery.

Goldmund continued his thought: It is mystery
I love and pursue. Several times I have seen it
beginning to take shape; as an artist, I would like
to capture and express it. Some day, perhaps, I'll be
able to. The figure of the universal mother, the
great birthgiver, for example. Unlike other figures,
her mystery does not consist of this or that detail,
of a particular voluptuousness or sparseness,
coarseness or delicacy, power or gracefulness. It
consists of a fusion of the greatest contrasts of the
world, those that cannot otherwise be combined,
that have made peace only in this figure. They live
in it together: birth and death, tenderness and
cruelty, life and destruction. If I only imagined this
figure, and were she merely the play of my
thoughts, it would not matter about her, I could
dismiss her as a mistake and forget about her. But
the universal mother is not an idea of mine; I did
not think her up, I saw her! She lives inside me.
I've met her again and again. She appeared to me
one winter night in a village when I was asked to
hold a light over the bed of a peasant woman
giving birth: that's when the image came to life
within me. I often lose it; for long periods it remains remote; but suddenly it flashes clear again,
as it did today. The image of my own mother,
whom I loved most of all, has transformed itself
into this new image, and lies encased within the
new one like the pit in the cherry.

As his present situation became clear to him,
Goldmund was afraid to make a decision. It was as
difficult as when he had said farewell to Narcissus

and to the cloister. Once more he was on an important road: the road to his mother. Would this mother-image one day take shape, a work of his hands, and become visible to all? Perhaps that was his goal, the hidden meaning of his life. Perhaps; he didn't know. But one thing he did know: it was good to travel toward his mother, to be drawn and called by her. He felt alive. Perhaps he'd never be able to shape her image, perhaps she'd always remain a dream, an intuition, a golden shimmer, a sacred mystery. At any rate, he had to follow her and submit his fate to her. She was his star.

And now the decision was at his fingertips; everything had become clear. Art was a beautiful thing, but it was no goddess, no goal—not for him. He was not to follow art, but only the call of his mother. Why continue to perfect the ability of his hands? Master Niklaus was an example of such perfection, and where did it lead? It led to fame and reputation, to money and a settled life, and to a drying up and dwarfing of one's inner senses, to which alone the mystery was accessible. It led to making pretty, precious toys, all kinds of ornate altars and pulpits, St. Sebastians and cute, curly angels' heads at four guilders a piece. Oh, the gold in the eye of a carp, the sweet thin silvery down at the edge of a butterfly's wing were infinitely more beautiful, alive, and precious than a whole roomful of such works of art.

A boy came singing down the river road. Sometimes his singing was interrupted by a bite into a big piece of white bread he was carrying in his hand. Goldmund saw him and asked him for a small piece of bread, scratched out some of the soft crumb with two fingers, and formed tiny balls with it. He leaned over the embankment railing and threw the bread balls slowly, one by one, into the water, saw the white ball sink into the darkness, saw pushing fish heads swarm around it until it disappeared into one of the mouths. With deep satisfaction he saw ball after ball go under and disappear. Then he felt hungry and went to see one of his loves who served as a maid in a butcher's house and whom he called "My Lady of Sausages and Hams." With the usual whistle he called her to the window of her kitchen, expecting her to give him a little nourishing something to slip in his pockets and eat outdoors, high above the river on one of the vine-covered hills where thick red soil glistened healthily under the full grape leaves, where small blue hyacinths with the delicate scent of fruit blossomed in the spring.

But this seemed to be his day of decisions and realizations. As Kathrine appeared at the window, smiling down to him out of her coarsened face, as he stretched out his hand to make the habitual signal, he suddenly remembered all the other times he had stood waiting in the same manner. With boring precision he foresaw everything that would happen in the next few minutes: she would recognize his signal, step back, reappear promptly at the back door with a morsel in her hand, smoked sausages perhaps, which he would accept, and, he'd stroke her a little and press her to him as she expected of him. Suddenly it seemed infinitely stupid and ugly to provoke this whole mechanical sequence of often experienced things and play his part in it, to receive the sausage, to feel her sturdy breasts press against him, and squeeze her a little as though in payment. Suddenly he thought he saw a trait of soul-less habit in her dear coarse face, something mechanical and unmysterious in her friendly smile, something unworthy of him. His gesture froze in mid-air; the smile froze on his face. Was he still in love with her, did he really still desire her? No, he had been there too often. All too often he had seen this selfsame smile and smiled back without a prompting from his heart. What had still been all right yesterday was suddenly no longer possible today. The girl was still standing there, looking, but he had turned away, vanished from the street, determined never to go back there again. Let someone else stroke those breasts! Let someone else eat those delicious sausages! How this fat, happy city stuffed and squandered day in, day out! How lazy, spoiled, and fastidious these fat burghers were, for whom so many sows and calves were killed every day, so many poor, beautiful fish pulled from the river! And he—how spoiled and rotten he had become, how disgustingly like the fat burghers! To a wanderer in a snow-covered field, a dried-up prune or an old crust of bread tasted more delicious than a whole meal here with the prosperous guildsmen. Oh, the roaming life, freedom, the heath in the moonlight, the animal tracks peered at attentively in the gray-dewed morning grass! Here in the city, among the well-established burghers, everything was so easy and cost so little, even love. He had had enough of it. Suddenly he spat on it. Life here had lost its meaning; it was a marrowless bone. As long as the master had been an example and Lisbeth a princess, it had been beautiful, it had made sense; it had been bearable as long as he was working on his St. John. Now that it was over, the perfume was gone and the flower had wilted. He was swept up in a violent wave. A sudden awareness of impermanence washed over him, a feeling that often deeply tortured and intoxicated him. Everything was soon wilted, every desire quickly exhausted; nothing remained but bones and dust. But one thing did remain: the eternal mother, basic, ancient, forever young, with her sad, cruel smile of love. Again he saw her for an instant: a giant figure with stars in her hair. Dreamily she sat on the edge of the world, plucking flower after flower, life after life, with a playful hand, slowly dropping them into the bottomless void.

During these days, while Goldmund floated through the familiar city in a drunken depression of bidding farewell, watching a wilted piece of life fade away behind him, Master Niklaus took great pains to provide for his future and tried to make his restless guest settle down forever. He persuaded the guild to issue Goldmund a master's diploma and conceived a plan to tie Goldmund to him forever, not as a subordinate, but as an associate, with whom he would discuss and execute all important orders and share in the earnings. It might be a risk, not least because of Lisbeth, because the young man would of course soon become his son-in-law. But even the best assistant Niklaus had ever paid wages to could not have made a statue like Goldmund's St. John. Besides, he was growing old; had fewer ideas and less creative force, and he did not want to see his famous workshop sink to the level of ordinary craftsmanship. Goldmund would not be easy to handle, but he had to take the risk.

The master worried and speculated. He would enlarge the back workroom for Goldmund, give him the room in the attic and present him with beautiful new clothes for his acceptance by the guild. Carefully he sounded out Lisbeth's feelings. She had been expecting something of the sort since the meal that noon. And Lisbeth was not opposed to it. If the fellow could be persuaded to settle down and become a master of his craft, she had no objection. There were no obstacles on her side. And if Master Niklaus and his craft did not fully succeed in taming this gypsy, Lisbeth was sure she could achieve the rest.

Everything was ready, the bait had been laid appetizingly before the trap for the bird to walk in. The master sent for Goldmund, who had not shown himself of late. Once more he was invited to dinner. Again he appeared brushed and pressed; again he sat in the beautiful, somewhat oversolemn room; again he drank toasts to master and daughter, until finally the daughter left the room and Niklaus brought forth his great plan and made his offer.

"I think you've understood me," he said, concluding his surprising disclosure, "and I need not tell you that probably no young man has ever been promoted to master as rapidly, without even serving the required apprenticeship, and then placed in such a warm nest. Your fortune is made, Goldmund."

Goldmund looked at his master with embarrassed surprise, pushed the mug away although it was still half full. He had expected that Niklaus would scold him a little because of the days he had lost loafing, and then propose that he stay with him as his assistant. And now this. He felt sad and constrained, sitting across the table from this man. He could not find a ready answer.

The master's face grew slightly tense and disappointed when his honorable offer was not accepted immediately with joyful modesty. He stood up and said: "Well, my proposal comes unexpectedly. Perhaps you'd like to think about it. It does offend me a little that it should be this way; I had thought I was giving you a great joy. But never mind, take your time and think it over."

"Master," Goldmund said, fighting for words, "don't be angry with me! I thank you with all my heart for your goodwill, and even more for the patience with which you have taught me. I'll never forget how deeply indebted I am to you. But I need no time to think it over, I have long since decided."

"Decided what?"

"I had made my decision before I accepted your invitation and before I had any idea of your honor-

able offer. I'm not going to remain here any longer,
I'm going back on the road."

Niklaus turned pale and looked at him darkly.

"Master," begged Goldmund, "I do not wish to
offend you, believe me. I have told you my decision. Nothing can change it. I must leave, I must
travel, I must be free. Let me thank you cordially
once again, and let us bid each other a friendly
farewell."

He held out his hand; he was close to tears.
Niklaus did not take his hand. His face had turned
white; he was pacing the room, faster and faster,
his steps echoing with rage. Never had Goldmund
seen him like that.

Suddenly the master stopped, made a dreadful
effort to control himself, and said, looking past
Goldmund, through clenched teeth: "All right, go
then if you must! But go at once! Do not force me
ever to see you again! I don't want to do or say
anything that I might regret later. Go!"

Once more Goldmund held out his hand. The
master looked as though he were going to spit at it.
Goldmund turned, now also pale, and walked softly out of the room. Outside he put on his cap and
crept down the stairs, letting his hand brush over
the carved heads; downstairs he entered the small
workshop in the courtyard, stood for a while in
farewell in front of his St. John, and left the house
with a pain in his heart that was deeper than when
he left the knight's castle and poor Lydia.

At least it had gone quickly! At least nothing
unnecessary had been said! That was his only consolation as he crossed the threshold. Suddenly
street and city became transformed, had the unfamiliar face that familiar things take on when our
heart has taken leave of them. He looked back at
the door of the house: it had become the door to
a strange house that was now closed to him.

Back in his room Goldmund began to prepare

for his departure. Not much preparation was
necessary; he merely had to say farewell. There
was a picture on the wall that he had painted, a
gentle madonna, and a few trifles that he had
acquired: a Sunday hat, a pair of dancing shoes, a
roll of drawings, a small lute, a number of small
clay figures he had modeled; a few presents from
women: a bunch of artificial flowers, a ruby-
red drinking glass, a hard old heart-shaped cookie,
and similar odds and ends. Each piece had a
meaning and a story, had been dear to him and
was now only cumbersome clutter, of which he
could take nothing along. He traded the ruby glass
for his landlord's good strong hunting knife, which
he sharpened at the whetting stone in the courtyard. He crumbled up the cookie and fed it to the
chickens in the yard next door, gave the painting
of the madonna to his landlady and was given a
useful gift in exchange: an old leather satchel and
ample provisions for the road. He packed his few
shirts in the satchel with a couple of small
drawings rolled over a piece of broomstick, and
put in the food. Everything else had to stay behind.

There were several women in the city to whom
he should have said farewell; he had slept with
one of them only yesterday, without telling her of
his plans. Romantic souvenirs had a way of at-
taching themselves to one when one wanted to
move on, but they were not to be taken seriously.
He said farewell to no one but the owners of the
house. He did that in the evening, so he could leave
very early the next morning.

And yet there was someone who got up in the
morning and asked him into the kitchen for a cup
of hot milk just as he was about to sneak out. It
was the daughter of the house, a child of fifteen, a
quiet sickly creature with beautiful eyes who had a
defect of the hip that made her limp. Her name

was Marie. With a sleepless face, completely pale but carefully dressed and combed, she served him hot milk and bread in the kitchen and seemed very sad to see him leave. He thanked her and out of pity kissed her goodbye on her narrow mouth. Reverently, with closed eyes, she received his kiss.

13

During the first days of his new wandering life, in the first greedy whirl of regained freedom, Goldmund had to relearn to live the homeless, timeless life of the traveler. Obedient to no man, dependent only on weather and season, without a goal before them or a roof above them, owning nothing, open to every whim of fate, the homeless wanderers lead their childlike, brave, shabby existence. They are the sons of Adam, who was driven out of Paradise; the brothers of the animals, of innocence. Out of heaven's hand they accept what is given them from moment to moment: sun, rain, fog, snow, warmth, cold, comfort, and hardship; time does not exist for them and neither does history, or ambition, or that bizarre idol called progress and evolution, in which houseowners believe so desperately. A wayfarer may be delicate or crude, artful or awkward, brave or cowardly—he is always a child at heart, living in the first day of creation, before the beginning of the history of the world, his life always guided by a few simple instincts and needs. He may be intelligent or stupid; he may be deeply aware of the fleeting fragility of all living things, of how pettily and fearfully each living creature carries its bit of warm blood through the glaciers of cosmic space, or he may merely follow the commands of his poor stomach with childlike greed—he is always the opponent, the deadly enemy of the established proprietor, who hates him, despises him, or fears him, because he does not wish to be reminded that all existence is transitory, that life is constantly wilting, that merciless icy death fills the cosmos all around.

The childlike life of the wanderer, its mother-origin, its turning away from law and mind, its openness and constant secret intimacy with death had long since deeply impregnated and molded Goldmund's soul. But mind and will lived within him nevertheless; he was an artist, and this made his life rich and difficult. Any life expands and flowers only through division and contradiction. What are reason and sobriety without the knowledge of intoxication? What is sensuality without death standing behind it? What is love without the eternal mortal enmity of the sexes?

Summer sank away, and autumn; painfully Goldmund struggled through the bitter months, wandered drunkenly through the sweet-smelling spring. Hastily the seasons fled; again and again high summer sun sank down. Years passed. Goldmund seemed to have forgotten that there were other things on earth besides hunger and love, and this silent, eerie onrush of the seasons; he seemed completely drowned in the motherly, instinctive basic world. But in his dreams or his thought-filled moments of rest, overlooking a flowering or wilting valley, he was all eyes, an artist. He longed desperately to halt the gracefully drifting nonsense of life with his mind and transform it into sense.

One day he found a companion. After his bloody adventure with Viktor he never traveled any way but by himself, yet this man surreptitiously attached himself to him and he could not get rid of him for quite some time. This man was not like Viktor. He was a pilgrim who had been to Rome, a still young man, wearing pilgrim's cloak and hat.

His name was Robert and his home was on Lake
Constance. Robert was the son of an artisan. For a
time he had attended the school of the St. Gallus
monks, and while still a boy had made up his mind
to go on a pilgrimage to Rome. It was his favorite
ambition and he seized the first opportunity to
carry it out. This opportunity presented itself with
the death of his father, in whose shop he had
worked as a cabinetmaker. The old man was hardly under the ground when Robert announced to his
mother and sister that nothing could stop him from
setting out on his pilgrimage to Rome, to satisfy his
urge and atone for his and his father's sins. In vain
the women complained; in vain they scolded. He
remained stubborn, and instead of taking care of
them, he set out on his journey without his mother's blessing and with the curses of his sister. He
was driven mainly by a desire to travel, and to this
was added a kind of superficial piety, an inclination to linger in the vicinity of churches and
churchly rituals, a delight in masses, baptisms,
burials, incense, and burning candles. He knew a
little Latin, but his childish soul was not striving
for learning but rather for contemplation and
quiet adoration in the shadows of church vaults.
He had been a passionately zealous altar boy.
Goldmund did not take him very seriously, but he
liked him. He felt a slight kinship with his instinctive surrender to wandering and new places.
At the time of his father's death, Robert had con-
tentedly set out and had indeed reached Rome,
where he had accepted the hospitality of cloisters
and parsonages, looked at the mountains and at
the south and felt very happy. He had heard
hundreds of masses, prayed at all famous holy
places, received the sacraments, and breathed in
more incense than his small youthful sins and
those of his father required. He had stayed away
for a year or more, and when he finally returned

and entered his father's little house, he was hardly received like the prodigal son. His sister had meantime taken over the duties and privileges of the household. She had hired and then married an industrious cabinetmaker's assistant, and ruled over house and workshop so thoroughly that the returned pilgrim soon realized he was not needed. When he mentioned setting out on new travels, no one asked him to stay. He did not take it too much to heart. His mother gave him a few pennies, and again he put on pilgrim's clothes and set out without a goal, straight through the empire, a half-priestly vagrant. Copper souvenir coins from well-known pilgrim shrines and blessed rosaries tinkled around his body.

He met Goldmund, wandered with him for a day, exchanged wayfarers' memories with him, disappeared in the next small town, reappeared here and there, and finally stayed with him, an amiable, dependable traveling companion. Goldmund pleased him greatly. He wooed his favor with small services, admired his knowledge, his audacity, his mind, and loved his health, strength, and frankness. They got used to each other, and Goldmund was also easy to get along with. There was only one thing he would not tolerate: when his melancholy and brooding moods seized him, he remained stubbornly silent and ignored the other man as though he did not exist. During these moods one could neither chat nor ask questions nor console Goldmund; one had to let him be and remain silent. Robert was not long in learning this. He had noticed that Goldmund knew a lot of Latin verses and songs by heart. He had heard him explain the stone figures outside the portals of a cathedral, had seen him draw life-size figures on an empty wall in rapid, bold strokes, and he thought his companion was a favorite of God and practically a magician. Robert also saw that Goldmund was a favorite of women and could obtain their favors with a glance and a smile; though he liked this less well, still he had to admire him for it.

One day their journey was interrupted in an unexpected manner. They were approaching a village when they were received by a small group of peasants armed with cudgels, poles, and flails. From far off the leader shouted to them that they should turn around at once and never come back, that they should run like the devil or else they'd be beaten to death. Goldmund stopped and wished to know what this was all about; the reply was a stone against his chest. He turned to Robert, but Robert had already started running. The peasants advanced threateningly, and Goldmund had no choice but to follow his fleeing companion. Trembling, Robert waited for him under a crucifix in the middle of a field.

"You ran like a hero," laughed Goldmund. "But what do those pigs have in their thick heads? Is there a war on? To place armed sentinels outside their rotten little town, refusing to let people in—I wonder what it all means."

Robert didn't know either. But certain experiences in an isolated farmhouse the next morning made them guess the secret. The farm, which consisted of a hut, a stable, and a barn surrounded by a green crop with high grass and many fruit trees, lay strangely still and asleep: there were no voices, no footfalls, no children screaming, no scythes being sharpened, not a sound. In the courtyard, a cow stood in the grass, lowing furiously. It was obviously time to milk her. They stepped up to the door, knocked, received no answer, walked into the stable; it was open and abandoned. They went to the barn. On its straw roof, light green moss glistened in the sun—but they didn't find a soul there either. They walked back to the house, astonished and depressed by the deserted homestead. Several times they hammered against the door with their fists; no answer. Goldmund tried to open it. To his surprise he found it unlocked, and he pushed and entered the pitch-dark room. "God bless you," he called loudly. "Nobody home?" The hut remained silent. Robert stayed outside. Impelled by curiosity, Goldmund advanced further. There was a bad smell in the hut, a strange, disgusting smell. The hearth was full of ash. He blew into it: sparks still gleamed at the bottom under charred logs. Then he noticed someone sitting in the half light beside the hearth. Someone was sitting there in an armchair, asleep: it looked like an old woman. Calling did no good: the house seemed to be under a spell. With a friendly tap he touched the seated woman on the shoulder, but she did not stir and he saw that she was sitting in a cobweb, with threads running from her hair to her chin. "She is dead," he thought with a slight shudder. To make sure, he tried to revive the fire, scratched and blew until a flame shot up and he was able to light a long piece of kindling. He held it up to the woman and saw a blue-black cadaver's face under gray hair, one eye still open, staring empty and leaden. The woman had died sitting in the chair. Well, she was beyond help.

With the burning stick in his hand, Goldmund searched further. In the same room, across the threshold to a back room, he found another corpse, a boy perhaps eight or nine, with a swollen, disfigured face, dressed only in a shirt. He lay with his belly across the doorsill, both hands clenched in firm furious little fists. The second one, thought Goldmund. As though in a hideous dream, he walked into the back room. There the shutters were open, the daylight pouring in. Carefully he extinguished his torch and ground the sparks out on the floor.

There were three beds in the back room. One

was empty, and the straw peeked out from under coarse gray sheets. In the second bed another person, a bearded man, lay stiffly on his back, his head bent backward and his chin and beard pointing at the ceiling; it was probably the farmer. His haggard face shimmered faintly in unfamiliar colors of death, one arm dangling to the floor, where an earthen water jug had been pushed over. The water had run out and had not yet been completely absorbed by the floor; it had run into a hollow and made a small puddle. In the second bed, completely entangled in sheets and blanket, lay a big, husky woman. Her face was pressed into the bed, and coarse, straw-blond hair glistened in the bright light. With her, wrapped around her as though caught and throttled in the tousled linen, lay a half-grown girl as straw-blond as she, with gray-blue stains in her dead face.

Goldmund's eyes traveled from corpse to corpse. The girl's face was already terribly disfigured, but he could see something of her helpless horror of death. In the neck and hair of the mother, who had dug herself so deeply into the bed, one could read rage, fear, and a passionate desire to flee, especially in the wild hair, which could not resign itself to dying. The farmer's face showed stubbornness and held-in pain. He had died a hard death, but his bearded chin rose steeply, rigidly into the air like that of a warrior lying on the battlefield. His quiet, taut, stubbornly controlled posture was beautiful; it had probably not been a petty, cowardly man who had received death in this manner. Most touching was the little corpse of the boy lying on its belly across the threshold. The face told nothing, but the posture across the threshold and the clenched child fists told a great deal: incomprehensible suffering, unavailing struggle against unheard-of pain. Beside his head, a cat hole had been sawed into the door. Goldmund examined everything attentively. The sights in this hut were ghastly and the stench of the corpses dreadful; still, it all held a deep attraction for him. Everything spoke of greatness, of fate. It was real, uncompromising. Something about it stirred his heart and penetrated his soul.

Robert had begun calling him from outside, with impatience and fear. Goldmund was fond of Robert, but at this moment he thought how petty and cheap a living person could be in his childish fear and curiosity, compared to the nobility of the dead. He did not answer Robert's calls; he gave himself completely to the sight of the dead, with that strange mixture of heart-felt compassion and cold observation of the artist. He took in all the details: the sprawled-out figures, their heads and hands, the patterns in which they had frozen. How still it was in the spellbound hut, and what a strange, terrible smell! How sad and ghostlike was this small home, with the remains of the hearth fire still glowing, inhabited by corpses, completely filled with death, penetrated by death. Soon the flesh would fall off these quiet faces; rats would eat the bodies. What other people performed in the privacy of their coffins, in the graves, well hidden and invisible, the last and poorest performance, this falling apart and decaying, was performed here at home by five people in their rooms, in broad daylight, behind an unlocked door, thoughtlessly, shamelessly, vulnerably. Goldmund had seen many corpses, but never an example like this of the merciless workings of death. Deeply he studied it.

Finally Robert's yelling outside the house began to disturb him, and he went out. His companion looked at him with fright.

"What happened?" he asked in a low, fear-strangled voice. "Isn't there anyone in the house? Oh, and what eyes you have! Say something!"

Goldmund measured him coolly.

"Go in and take a look. This is a strange farm-house all right. Afterward we'll milk the beautiful cow over there. Go ahead!"

Hesitantly Robert entered the hut, discovered the old woman sitting at the hearth, and let out a loud scream when he realized that she was dead. As he came out, he was wide-eyed with fright.

"For heaven's sake! A dead woman is sitting there by the hearth. How can it be? Why isn't anyone with her? Why don't they bury her? Oh God, she's already begun to smell."

Goldmund smiled.

"You're a great hero, Robert; but you came back out too fast. A dead old woman sitting in a chair like that is indeed a strange sight; but if you'd walked a few steps farther, you'd see something stranger still. There are five corpses, Robert. Three in bed, a dead boy lying across the threshold, and the old woman. They're all dead, the entire family. The whole household is gone. That's why nobody milked the cow."

Horrified, Robert stared at him and suddenly cried in a choking voice: "Now I understand why the peasants didn't want to let us into their village yesterday. Oh God, now it's all clear to me. The plague! By my poor soul, it's the plague, Goldmund, and you've stayed in there all this time, maybe you even touched those corpses! Get away, don't come near me, I'm sure you're infected. I'm sorry, Goldmund, but I must go, I can't stay with you."

He turned to run but was held back by his pilgrim's cloak. Goldmund looked at him sternly, with silent reprimand, and mercilessly held on to the man, who pulled and tugged.

"My dear little boy," he said in a friendly-ironic tone, "you're more intelligent than one might think, you're probably right. Well, we'll find out in the next farm or village. Yes, it's probably the plague.

We'll see if we escape it safe and sound. But, little Robert, I can't let you run away now. Look, I have a soft heart, much too soft, and when I think that you might have contaminated yourself in there I cannot let you run off to lie down somewhere in a field and die, all alone, with no one to close your eyes and dig you a grave and throw a bit of earth over you. No, dear friend, that would be too sad to bear. Listen then, and pay careful attention to what I am saying, because I'm not going to say it twice: we two are in the same danger; it can hit you or it can hit me. Therefore we are staying together; we will either perish together or escape this cursed plague together. If you fall ill and die, I'll bury you; that's a promise. And if I die, then you do as you please: you can bury me or run off; I don't care. But until then, my friend, no one runs off, remember that! We need each other. And now shut your trap; I don't want to hear another word. Now go and find a bucket somewhere in the stable so that we can milk the cow."

They did this, and from that moment on Goldmund commanded and Robert obeyed, and both fared well for it. Robert made no more attempts to flee. He only said soothingly: "You frightened me for a moment. I didn't like your face when you came out of that house of death. I thought you had caught the plague. And even if it isn't the plague, your face has changed completely. Was it so terrible, what you saw in there?"

"It was not terrible," Goldmund said slowly. "I saw nothing in there that does not await you and me and everybody, even if we don't catch the plague."

As they wandered on, the Black Death was everywhere they went, reigning over the land. Some villages did not let strangers in; others let them walk unhindered through every street. Many farms

stood deserted; many unburied corpses lay rotting
in the fields and in the houses. Unmilked cows
lowed and starved in stables; other livestock ran
wild in the fields. They milked and fed many a
cow and goat; they killed and roasted many a
goatlet or piglet at the edge of the forest and
drank wine and cider in many a masterless cellar.
They had a good life. There was abundance everywhere. But it tasted only half good to them. Robert
lived in constant fear of the disease, and he felt
sick at the sight of the corpses. Often he was
completely beside himself with fear. Again and
again he thought that he had caught the plague,
and held his head and hands in the smoke of their
campfire for a long time, for this was supposed to
be a preventative, and felt his body (even in his
sleep) to see if bumps were forming on his legs or
in his armpits.

Goldmund often scolded and made fun of him.
He did not share his fear or his disgust. Fascinated
and depressed, he walked through the stricken
country, attracted by the sight of the great death,
his soul filled with the autumn, his heart heavy
with the song of the mowing scythe. Sometimes the
image of the universal mother would reappear to
him, a pale, gigantic face with Medusa eyes and a
smile thick with suffering and death.

One day they came to a small town that was
heavily fortified. Outside the gates defensive ramparts ran house-high around the entire city wall,
but there was no sentinel standing up there or at
the wide-open gates. Robert refused to enter the
town, and he implored his companion not to go in
either. Just then a bell tolled. A priest came out of
the city gates, a cross in his hands, and behind him
came three carts, two drawn by horses and one by
a pair of oxen. The carts were piled high with
corpses. A couple of men in strange coats, their

faces shrouded in hoods, ran alongside and spurred the animals on.

Robert disappeared, white-faced. Goldmund followed the death carts at a short distance. They advanced a few hundred steps farther; there was no cemetery: a hole had been dug in the middle of the deserted heath, only three spades deep but vast as a hall. Goldmund stood and looked on as the men pulled the corpses from the carts with staffs and boat hooks and tossed them into the vast hole. He saw the murmuring priest swing his cross over them and walk away, saw the men light huge fires all around the flat grave and silently creep back into the city. No one had tried to throw any earth over the pit. Goldmund looked in: fifty or more persons lay there, piled one on top of the other, many of them naked. Stiff and accusing, an arm or a leg rose in the air, a shirt fluttered timidly in the wind.

When he came back, Robert begged him almost on his knees to flee this place. He had good reason to beg, for he saw in Goldmund's absent look the absorption in and concentration on horror, that dreadful curiosity that had become all too familiar. He was not able to hold his friend back. Alone, Goldmund walked into the town.

He walked through the unguarded gates, and at the echo of his steps many towns and gates rose up in his memory. He remembered how he had walked through them, how he had been received by screaming children, playing boys, quarreling women, the hammering of a forge, the crystal sound of the anvil, the rattling of carts and many other sounds, delicate and coarse, all braided together as though into a web that bore witness to many forms of human labor, joy, bustle, and communication. Here, under this yellow gate, in this empty street, nothing echoed, no one laughed, no one cried, everything lay frozen in deathly silence, cut by the overloud, almost noisy chatter of a running well. Behind an open window he saw a baker amid his loafs and rolls. Goldmund pointed to a roll; the baker carefully handed it out to him on a long baking shovel, waited for Goldmund to place money into the shovel, and angrily, but without cursing, closed his little window when the stranger bit into the roll and walked on without paying. Before the windows of a pretty house stood a row of earthen jars in which flowers had once bloomed. Now wilted leaves hung down over scraps of pottery. From another house came the sound of sobbing, the misery of children's voices crying. In the next street Goldmund saw a pretty girl standing behind an upper-floor window, combing her hair. He watched her until she felt his eyes and looked down, blushing, and when he gave her a friendly smile, slowly a faint smile spread over her blushing face.

"Soon through combing?" he called up. Smiling, she leaned her light face out of the darkness of the window.

"Not sick yet?" he asked, and she shook her head. "Then leave this city of death with me. We'll go into the woods and live a good life."

Her eyes asked questions.

"Don't think it over too long. I mean it," Goldmund called up to her. "Are you with your father and mother, or are you in the service of strangers? Strangers, I see. Come along then, dear child. Let the old people die; we are young and healthy and want to have a bit of fun while there's still time. Come along, little brown hair, I mean it."

She gave him a probing look, hesitant and surprised. Slowly he walked on, strolled through a deserted street and through another. Slowly he came back. The girl was still at the window, leaning forward, glad to see him return. She waved to him. Slowly he walked on, and soon she came running after him, caught up with him before the gates, a small bundle in her hand, a red kerchief tied around her head.

"What's your name?" he asked.

"Lene. I'll go with you. Oh, it's so horrible here in the city; everybody is dying. Let's leave. Let's leave."

Not far from the gates Robert was crouching moodily on the ground. When Goldmund appeared, he jumped to his feet and stared when he caught sight of the girl. This time he did not give in at once. He whined and made a scene. How could a man bring a person with him from that cursed plague hole and impose her company on his companion? It was not only crazy, it was tempting God. He, Robert, was not going to stay with him any longer; his patience had come to an end.

Goldmund let him curse and lament until he found nothing more to say.

"There," he said, "now you've sung your song. Now you'll come with us, and be glad that we have such pretty company. Her name is Lene and she stays with me. But I want to do you a favor too, Robert. Listen: for a while we'll live in peace and health and stay away from the plague. We'll find a nice place for ourselves, an empty hut, or we'll build one, and I'll be the head of the household and Lene will be the mistress, and you'll be our friend and live with us. Our life is going to be a little pleasant and friendly now. All right?"

Oh yes, Robert was delighted. As long as no one asked him to shake Lene's hand or touch her clothes . . .

No, said Goldmund, no one would ask him to. In fact, it was strictly forbidden to touch Lene, even with a finger. "Don't you dare!"

All three walked on, first in silence, then gradually the girl began to talk. How happy she was to see sky and trees and meadows again. It had been so gruesome in the plague-stricken city, more horrible than she could tell. And she began to clear her heart of all the sad, horrible things she had seen. She told so many awful stories: the little town must have been hell. One of the two doctors had died; the other only looked after the rich. In many houses the dead lay rotting, because nobody came to take them away. In other houses looters stole, pillaged, and whored. Often they pulled the sick from their beds, threw them onto the death carts with the corpses, and down into the pit of the dead. Many a horror tale she had to tell, and no one interrupted her. Robert listened with voluptuous terror, Goldmund silent and unruffled, letting the horrors pour out and making no comment. What was there to say? Finally Lene grew tired, the stream dried up, she was out of words.

Goldmund began to walk more slowly. Softly he began to sing, a song with many couplets, and with each couplet his voice grew fuller. Lene began to smile; Robert listened, delighted and deeply surprised. Never before had he heard Goldmund sing. He could do everything, this Goldmund. There he was singing, strange man! He sang well; his voice was pure, though muffled. At the second song Lene was humming with him, and soon she joined in with full voice. Evening was coming on. Black forests rose up far over the heath, and behind them low blue mountains, which grew bluer and bluer as though from within. Now gay, now solemn, their song followed the rhythm of their steps.

"You're in such a good mood today," said Robert.

"Of course I'm in a good mood today, I found such a pretty love. Oh, Lene, how nice that the ghouls left you behind for me. Tomorrow we'll find a little house where we'll have a good life and be happy to have flesh and bone still together. Lene, did you ever see those fat mushrooms in the woods in autumn, the edible ones that the snails love?"

"Oh yes," she laughed, "I've seen lots of them."

"Your hair is that same mushroom brown, Lene, and it smells just as good. Shall we sing another song? Or are you hungry? I still have a few good things in my satchel."

The next day they found what they were looking for: a log cabin in a small birch forest. Perhaps some woodcutters had built it. It stood empty, and the door was soon broken open. Robert agreed that this was a good hut and a healthy region. On the road they had met stray goats and had taken a fine one along with them.

"Well, Robert," said Goldmund, "although you're no carpenter, you were once a cabinetmaker. We're going to live here. You must build us a partition for our castle, to make two rooms, one for Lene and me, and one for you and the goat. We don't have very much left to eat; today we must be satisfied with goat's milk, no matter how little there is. You'll build the wall, and we'll make up beds for all of us. Tomorrow I'll go out to look for food."

Immediately everybody set to work. Goldmund and Lene went to find straw, fern, and moss for their sleeping places, and Robert sharpened his knife on a piece of flint and cut small birch posts to make a wall. But he could not finish it in one day and that evening he went outside to sleep in the open. Goldmund had found a sweet playmate in Lene, shy and inexperienced but deeply loving. Gently he took her to his bosom and lay awake for a long time, listening to her heart, long after she had fallen asleep, tired and satiated. He smelled her brown hair, nestled close to her, all the while thinking of the vast flat pit into which the hooded devils had dumped their carts of corpses. Life was beautiful, beautiful and fleeting as happiness. Youth was beautiful and wilted fast.

The partition of the hut was very pretty. All three worked at it finally. Robert wanted to show what he could do and eagerly talked about all the things he wanted to build, if only he had a planing bench and tools, a straight edge and nails. But he had only his knife and his hands and had to be satisfied with cutting a dozen small birch posts and building a coarse sturdy fence in the hut. But, he decreed, the openings had to be filled in with plaited juniper. That took time, but it became gay and pretty; everybody helped. In between, Lene went to gather berries and look after the goat, and Goldmund scoured the region for food, explored the neighborhood, and came back with a few little things. The region seemed uninhabited. Robert was especially pleased about that: they were safe from contamination as well as from quarrels; but it had one disadvantage: there was very little to eat. They found an abandoned peasant hut not far away, without corpses this time, and Goldmund proposed to move to the hut rather than stay in the log cabin, but Robert shudderingly refused. He didn't like to see Goldmund enter the empty house, and every piece he brought over had first to be smoked and washed before Robert touched it. Goldmund didn't find much—two posts, a milk pail, a few pieces of crockery, a hatchet, but one day he caught two stray chickens in the fields. Lene was in love and happy. All three enjoyed improving their small home, making it a little prettier each day. They had no bread, but they took another goat into service and also found a small field full of turnips. The days passed, the wall was finished, the beds were improved, they built a hearth. The brook was not far and had clear sweet water. They often sang as they worked.

One day, as they sat together drinking their milk and praising their settled life, Lene said suddenly in a dreamy tone: "But what will we do when winter comes?"

No one answered. Robert laughed; Goldmund stared strangely ahead of him. Eventually Lene noticed that neither of them thought of winter, that neither seriously thought of remaining such a long time in the same place, that this home was no home, that she was among wayfarers. She hung her head.

Then Goldmund said, playfully and encouragingly as though to a child: "You're a peasant's daughter, Lene; peasants always worry. Don't be afraid. You'll find your way back home once this plague period is over; it can't last forever. Then you'll go back to your parents, or to whomever is still alive, or you'll return to the city and earn your bread as a maid. But now it's still summer. Death is rampant throughout the region, but here it is pretty, and we live well. That's why we can stay here for as long or as short a time as we like."

"And afterwards?" Lene asked violently. "Afterwards it is all over? And you go away? What about me?"

Goldmund caught her braid and pulled at it softly.

"Silly little girl," he said, "have you already forgotten the ghouls and the abandoned houses, and the big hole outside the gates where the fires burn? You should be happy not to be lying in that hole with the rain falling on your little nightshirt. Think of what you escaped, be glad that your dear life is still in your veins, that you can still laugh and sing."

She was still not satisfied.

"But I don't want to go away again," she complained. "Nor do I want to let you go. How can one be happy when one knows that soon all will be finished and over with!"

Once more Goldmund answered her, in a friendly tone but with a hidden threat in his voice.

"About that, little Lene, the wise men and saints
have wracked their brains. There is no lasting happiness. But if what we now have is not good
enough for you, if it no longer pleases you, then I'll
set fire to this hut this very minute and each of us
can go his way. Let things be as they are, Lene;
we've talked enough."

She gave in and that's where they left it, but a
shadow had fallen over her joy.

14

Before summer had wilted completely, life in the
hut came to an end in a way they had not imagined. One day Goldmund was roaming about the
area with a slingshot, hoping to wing a partridge or
some other fowl; their food had grown rather
scarce. Lene was not far away, gathering berries,
and from time to time he'd pass near her and see
her head, her brown neck rising out of her linen
shirt, or hear her sing. Once he stole a few of her
berries; then he wandered off and lost sight of her
for a while. He thought about her, half tenderly, half
annoyed, because she had again mentioned autumn and the future. She said that she thought she
was pregnant and she could not let him go off
again. Now it will soon be over, he thought. Soon
I'll have had enough and wander on alone. I'll
leave Robert, too. I'll try to get back to the big city
when the cold begins, to Master Niklaus. I'll spend
the winter there and next spring I'll buy myself a
new pair of shoes and walk and walk until I reach
our cloister in Mariabronn and say hello to Narcissus. It must be ten years since I last saw him, and I
must see him again, if only for a day or two.

An unfamiliar sound roused him from his
thoughts, and suddenly he realized that all his
thoughts and desires were already far away from
here. He listened intently. The sound of fear
repeated itself; he thought he recognized Lene's
voice and followed it, irritated that she was call-

ing him. Soon he was close enough—yes, it was Lene's voice. She was calling his name as though in great distress. He ran faster, still somewhat annoyed, but pity and worry gained the upper hand as her screaming continued. When he was finally able to see her, she was kneeling in the heather, her blouse completely torn, screaming and wrestling with a man who was trying to rape her. Goldmund ran forward with long leaps. All his pent-up anger, his restlessness, his sorrow broke out in a howling rage against the unknown attacker. He surprised the man as he tried to pin Lene to the ground. Her naked breasts were bleeding, and avidly the stranger held her in his grip. Goldmund threw himself upon him, his furious fingers grabbing the man's throat. It felt thin and stringy, covered with a woolly beard. With glee Goldmund pressed the throat until the man let go of the girl and hung limply between his hands; still throttling him, Goldmund dragged the exhausted, half-dead man along the ground to a few gray ribs of rock protruding from the earth. He raised the defeated man, heavy though he was, twice, three times in the air and smashed his head against the sharp-edged rocks, broke his neck, and threw the body down. His anger was still not fully vented; he would have liked to mangle the man further.

Radiant, Lene sat and watched. Her breasts were bleeding; she was still trembling all over and panting, but she soon gathered herself together. With a forlorn look of lust and admiration she watched her powerful lover dragging the intruder through the heather, throttling him, breaking his neck, and throwing his corpse down. Like a dead snake, limp and distorted, the body lay on the ground, the gray face with unkempt beard and thinning hair falling pitifully to one side. Triumphant Lene sat up and fell against Goldmund's heart, but suddenly she turned pale. Fright was still in her; she felt sick.

Exhausted, she sank into the blueberry bushes. But soon she was able to walk to the hut with Goldmund. He washed her breasts; one was scratched and the other bore a bite wound from the marauder's teeth.

The adventure excited Robert enormously. Hotly he asked for details of the combat. "You broke his neck, you say? Magnificent! Goldmund, you are a terrifying man."

But Goldmund did not feel like talking about it any more; he had cooled off. As he walked away from the dead man, poor boasting Viktor had come to his mind. This was the second person who had died at his hand. In order to shut Robert up, he said: "Now you might do something too; go over and get rid of the corpse. If it's too difficult to dig a hole for it, then drag it over to the reeds, or else cover it up with stones and earth." But Robert turned down the proposal. He wanted no commerce with corpses; you could never be sure they weren't infested with the plague.

Lene was lying down. The bite in her breast hurt, but soon she felt better, got up again, made a fire and cooked the evening milk; she was cheerful, but Goldmund sent her to bed early. She obeyed like a lamb, full of admiration for him. Goldmund was somber and taciturn; Robert realized it and left him alone. Much later Goldmund went to bed. Listening, he bent over Lene. She was asleep. He was restless; he kept thinking of Viktor, felt anguish and the urge to move on; playing house had come to an end. One thing made him particularly pensive. He had caught Lene's look while he bashed the man to death and tossed him down. A strange look. He knew that he would never forget it: pride and triumph had radiated from her wide, horrified, delighted eyes, a deep passionate desire to participate in the revenge and to kill. He had never seen anything like it in a

woman's face, and had never imagined such a
look. Had it not been for that look, he thought, he
might have forgotten Lene's face one day, after a
number of years. It had made her peasant-girl face
large, beautiful, and horrible. For months his eyes
had not experienced anything that made him quiver with the wish: "One ought to draw that!" That
look had caused this wish to quiver through him,
and a kind of terror.

He could not sleep, and finally he got up and
went outside. It was cool, and a light wind played
in the birches. He paced in the dark, sat down on a
stone, drowned in thoughts and deep sadness. He
felt sorry for Viktor and for the man he had killed
today. He regretted the lost innocence, the lost
childlike quality of his soul. Had he gone away
from the cloister, left Narcissus, offended Master
Niklaus and renounced beautiful Lisbeth merely to
camp in the heath, track stray cattle, and kill that
poor fellow back there on those stones? Did all this
make sense? Was it worth experiencing? His heart
grew tight with meaninglessness and self-con-
tempt. He let himself sink down and stared into
the pale night clouds, and as he stared, his
thoughts stopped; he didn't know whether he was
looking into the sky or into the drab world inside
him. Suddenly, just as he was falling asleep on the
stone, a large pale face appeared like far-away
lightning in the drifting clouds, the mother-face. It
looked heavy and veiled, but suddenly its eyes
opened wide, large eyes full of lust and murder.
Goldmund slept until the dew fell on him.

The next day Lene was ill. They made her stay
in bed, for there were many things to be done: in
the morning Robert had seen two sheep in the
small forest, but they had run from him. He called
Goldmund, and more than half the day they
hunted until they caught one of the sheep; they
came back exhausted. Lene felt very sick.

Goldmund examined her and found plague boils. He kept it secret, but Robert became suspicious when he heard that Lene had still not recovered. He would not stay in the hut. He'd find a sleeping place outside, he said, and he'd take the goat along too: why let it get infected.

"Go to hell," Goldmund yelled at him in fury. "I don't want to see you ever again." He grabbed the goat and pulled her to his side of the juniper partition. Robert disappeared without a word, without the goat. He was sick with fear: of the plague, of Goldmund, of loneliness and the night. He lay down close to the hut.

Goldmund said to Lene: "I'll stay with you, don't worry. You'll get well again."

She shook her head.

"Be careful, love. Don't catch this sickness too; you mustn't come so close to me. Don't try so hard to console me. I'm going to die, and I'd rather die than find your bed empty one morning because you have left me. I've thought of it every morning and been afraid of it. No, I'd rather die."

In the morning she was extremely weak. Goldmund had given her sips of water from time to time and napped a little in between. Now, in the growing light, he recognized the signs of approaching death in her face, it looked so wilted and flabby. For a moment he stepped outside to get some air and look at the sky. A few bent red fir trunks at the edge of the forest shone with the first rays of sun; the air tasted fresh and sweet; the distant hills were still shrouded in morning clouds. He walked a few steps, stretched his tired legs, and breathed deeply. The world was beautiful this morning. He'd probably soon be back on the road. It was time to say goodbye.

Robert called to him from the forest. Was she better? If it wasn't the plague, he'd stay.

Goldmund shouldn't be angry with him; he had watched the sheep in the meantime.

"Go to hell, you and your sheep!" Goldmund shouted over to him. "Lene is dying, and I too am infected."

This was a lie; he had said it to get rid of Robert. He might be a well-meaning man, but Goldmund had had enough of him. He was too cowardly for him, too petty; he had no place in this fateful, shocking scene. Robert vanished and did not return. The sun shone brightly.

When Goldmund came back to Lene, she lay asleep. He too fell asleep once more, and in his dream he saw his old horse Bless and the beautiful chestnut tree at the cloister; he felt as though he were gazing back upon his lost and beautiful home from an infinitely remote, deserted region, and when he woke, tears were running down his blond-bearded cheeks. He heard Lene speak in a weak voice. He thought she was calling out to him and sat up on his bed, but she was speaking to no one. She was stammering words, love words, curses, a little laugh, and began to heave deep sighs and swallow. Gradually she fell silent again. Goldmund got up and bent over her already disfigured face. With bitter curiosity his eyes retraced the lines that the scalding breath of death was so miserably distorting and muddying. Dear Lene, called his heart, dear sweet child, you too already want to leave me? Have you already had enough of me?

He would have liked to run away. To wander, roam, run, breathe the air, grow tired, see new images. It would have done him good; it might perhaps have got him over his deep melancholy. But he could not leave now. It was impossible for him to leave the child to lie there alone and dying. He scarcely dared go outside every few hours for a moment to breathe fresh air. Since Lene could no longer swallow any milk, he drank it himself.

There was no other food. A couple of times he led the goat outside, for it to feed and drink water and move around. Once more he stood at Lene's bed, murmured tender words to her, stared incessantly into her face, disconsolate but attentive, to watch her dying. She was conscious. Sometimes she slept, and when she woke up she only half opened her eyes; the lids were tired and limp. Around eyes and nose the young girl looked older and older by the hour. A rapidly wilting grandmother face sat on her fresh young neck. She spoke only rarely, said "Goldmund," or "lover," and tried to wet her swollen bluish lips with her tongue; when she did, he'd give her a few drops of water. She died the following night. She died without complaining. It was only a brief quiver; than her breath stopped and a shudder ran over her. Goldmund's heart heaved mightily at the sight. He recalled the dying fish he had so often pitied in the market: they had died in just that way, with a quiver, a soft woeful shudder, that ran over their skin and extinguished luster and life. For a while he knelt beside Lene. Then he went out and sat down in the bushes. He remembered the goat and walked back into the hut and let the animal out. After straying a short distance, it lay down on the ground. He lay down beside it, his head on its flank, and slept until the day grew bright. Then he went into the hut for the last time, stepped behind the braided wall, and looked for the last time at the poor dead face. It did not feel right to him to let the dead woman lie there. He went out, filled his arms with dry wood and underbrush, and threw it into the hut. Then he struck fire. From the hut he took nothing along but the flint. In an instant the dry juniper wall burned brightly. He stood outside and watched, his face reddened by the flames, until the whole roof was ablaze and the first beams crashed in. The goat jumped with fear and whined. He

knew he ought to kill the animal and roast a piece
of it and eat it, to have strength for his journey.
But he could not bring himself to kill the goat; he
drove it off into the heath and walked away. The
smoke of the fire followed him into the forest.
Never before had he felt so disconsolate setting out
on a journey.

And yet the things that lay in store for him were
far worse than he had imagined. It began with the
first farms and villages and continued to grow
more terrible as he walked on. The whole region,
the whole vast land lay under a cloud of death,
under a veil of horror, fear, and darkening of
the soul. And the empty houses, the farm dogs
starved on their chains and rotting, the scattered
unburied corpses, the begging children, the death
pits at the city gates were not the worst. The worst
were the survivors, who seemed to have lost their
eyes and souls under the weight of horror and the
fear of death. Everywhere the wanderer came
upon strange, dreadful things. Parents had abandoned their children, husbands their wives, when
they had fallen ill. The ghouls reigned like
hangmen; they pillaged the empty houses, left
corpses unburied or, following their whims, tore
the dying from their beds before they had
breathed their last and tossed them on the death
carts. Frightened fugitives wandered about alone,
turned primitive, avoiding all contact with other
people, hounded by fear of death. Others were
grouped together by an excited, terrified lust for
life, drinking and dancing and fornicating while
death played the fiddle. Still others cowered outside cemeteries, unkempt, mourning or cursing,
with insane eyes, or sat outside their empty houses.
And, worst of all, everybody looked for a scapegoat
for his unbearable misery; everybody swore that he
knew the criminal who had brought on the disease,
who had intentionally caused it. Grinning, evil

people, they said, were bent on spreading death
by extracting the disease poison from corpses
and smearing it on walls and doorknobs, by
poisoning wells and cattle with it. Whoever was
suspected of these horrors was lost, unless he was
warned and able to flee: either the law or the
mob condemned him to death. The rich blamed
the poor, or vice versa; both blamed the Jews,
or the French, or the doctors. In one town, Goldmund watched with grim heart while the entire ghetto was burned, house after house, with the
howling mob standing around, driving screaming
fugitives back into the fire with swords and clubs.
In the insanity of fear and bitterness, innocent
people were murdered, burned, and tortured everywhere. Goldmund watched it all with rage and
revulsion. The world seemed destroyed and poisoned; there seemed to be no more joy, no more
innocence, no more love on earth. Often he fled
the overly violent feasts of the desperate dancers.
Everywhere he heard the fiddle of death; he soon
learned to recognize its sound. Often he partici-
pated in mad orgies, played the lute or danced
through feverish nights in the glow of peat torches.

He was not afraid. He had first tasted the fear of
death during that winter night under the pines
when Viktor's fingers clutched at his throat, and
later in the cold and hunger of many a hard day.
That had been a death which one could fight,
against which one could defend oneself, and he
had defended himself, with trembling hands and
feet, with gaping stomach and exhausted body,
had fought, won, and escaped. But no one could
fight death by plague; one had to let it rage and
give in. Goldmund had given in long ago. He had
no fear. It seemed as though he was no longer
interested in life, since he had left Lene behind in
the burning hut, since his endless journey through
a land devastated by death. But enormous curiosity

drove him and kept him awake; he was indefatiga-
ble, watching the reaper, listening to the song of
the transitory. He did not go out of his way. Everywhere he felt the same quiet passion to participate, to walk through hell with wide-open eyes. He
ate moldy bread in empty houses, sang and drank
at the insane feasts, plucked the fast-wilting flower
of lust, looked into the fixed, drunken stares of the
women, into the fixed, stupid eyes of the drunk,
into the fading eyes of the dying. He loved the
desperate, feverish women, helped carry corpses in
exchange for a plate of soup, threw earth over
naked bodies for two pennies. It had grown dark
and wild in the world. Death howled its song, and
Goldmund heard it with burning passion.

His goal was Master Niklaus's city; that's where
the voice of his heart drew him. The road was long
and lined with decay, wilting, and dying. Sadly he
journeyed on, intoxicated by the song of death,
open to the loudly screaming misery of the world,
sad, and yet glowing, with eager senses.

In a cloister he came upon a recently painted
fresco. He had to look at it for a long time. A dance
of death had been painted on a wall: pale bony
death, dancing people out of life, king and bishop,
abbot and earl, knight, doctor, peasant, lansquenet—
everyone he took along with him, while skeleton
musicians played on hollow bones. Goldmund's curious eyes drank in the painting. An unknown colleague had applied the lesson he too had learned
from the Black Death, and was screaming the bitter lesson of the inevitable end shrilly into everyone's ear. It was a good picture, and a good ser-
mon; this unknown colleague had seen and painted
the subject rather well. A bony, ghastly echo rose
from his wild picture. And yet it was not what
Goldmund had seen and experienced. It was the
obligation to die that was painted here, the stern
and merciless end. But Goldmund would have pre-

ferred another picture. In him the wild song of
death had a completely different sound, not bony
and severe, but sweet rather, and seductive, motherly, an enticement to come home. Wherever the
hand of death reached into life, the sound was not
only shrill and warlike but also deep and loving,
autumnal, satiated, the little lamp of life glowed
brighter, more intensely at the approach of death.
To others death might be a warrior, a judge or
hangman, a stern father. To him death was also a
mother and a mistress; its call was a mating call, its
touch a shudder of love. After looking at the painted death dance, Goldmund felt drawn to the master and to his craft with renewed force. But everywhere there were delays, new sights and experiences. With quivering nostrils he breathed the air
of death. Everywhere pity or curiosity claimed an
extra hour from him, an extra day. For three days
he had a small bawling peasant boy with him. For
hours he carried him on his back, a half-starved
midget of five or six who caused him much trouble
and whom he didn't know how to get rid of. Finally
a peat digger's wife took the boy in. Her husband
had died, and she wanted to have a little life in the
house again. For days a masterless dog accompanied him, ate out of his hand, warmed him while he
slept, but one morning it too strayed off.
Goldmund was sorry. He had become accustomed
to speaking to the dog; for hours he'd have
thoughtful conversations with the animal about the
evil in people, the existence of God, about art,
about the breasts and hips of a knight's very young
daughter named Julie, whom he had known in his
youth. Goldmund had naturally grown a trifle mad
during his death journey: everyone within the
plague region was a trifle mad, and many were
completely insane. Perhaps young Rebekka was
also a trifle insane—a beautiful dark girl with burning eyes, with whom he had spent two days.

He found her outside a small town, crouching in the fields beside a heap of rubble, sobbing, beating her face, tearing her black hair. The hair stirred his pity. It was extremely beautiful, and he caught her furious hands and held them fast and talked to her, noting that her face and figure were also of great beauty. She was mourning her father, who had been burned to ash with fourteen other Jews by order of the town's authorities. She had been able to flee but had now returned in desperation and was accusing herself for not having been burned with the others. Patiently he held on to her twisting hands and talked to her gently, murmured sympathetically, and protectively offered his help. She asked him to help her bury her father. They gathered all the bones from the still warm ashes, carried them into a hiding place farther away in the field, and covered them with earth. In the meantime evening had fallen and Goldmund looked for a place to sleep. In a small oak forest he arranged a bed for the girl and promised to watch over her and listened to her moan and sob after she lay down; finally she fell asleep. Then he, too, slept a little, and in the morning he began his courtship. He told her that she could not stay alone like this, she might be recognized as a Jew and killed, or depraved wayfarers might misuse her, and the forest was full of wolves and gypsies. If he took her along, however, and protected her against wolf and man—because he felt sorry for her and was very fond of her, because he had eyes in his head and knew what beauty was—he would never allow her sweet intelligent eyelids and graceful shoulders to be devoured by animals or burned at the stake. Darkfaced, she listened to him, jumped up, and ran off. He had to chase after her and catch her before he could continue.

"Rebekka," he said, "can't you see that I don't

mean you any harm? You're sad, you're thinking of
your father, you don't want to hear about love right
now. But tomorrow or the day after, or later, I'll
ask you again. Until then I'll protect you and bring
you food and I won't touch you. Be sad as long as
you must. You shall be able to be sad with me, or
happy. You shall always do only what brings you
joy."

But his words were spoken to the wind. She
didn't want to do anything that brought joy, she
said bitterly and angrily. She wanted to do what
brought pain. Never again was she going to think
of anything resembling joy, and the sooner the wolf
ate her, the better. He should go now, there was
nothing he could do, they had already talked too
much.

"You," he said, "don't you see that death is everywhere, that people are dying in every house and
every town, that everything is full of misery. The
fury of those stupid people who burned your father
is nothing but misery; it is the result of too much
suffering. Look, soon death will get us too, and
we'll rot in the field and the moles will play dice
with our bones. Let us live a little before it comes
to that and be sweet to each other. Oh, it would be
such a pity for your white neck and small feet!
Dear beautiful girl, do come with me. I won't
touch you. I only want to see you and take care of
you."

He begged for a long time. Suddenly he understood how useless it was to court her with words
and arguments. He fell silent and looked at her
sadly. Her proud regal face was taut with rejection.

"That's how you are," she finally said in a voice
full of hatred and contempt. "That's how you
Christians are! First you help a daughter bury her
father whom your people have murdered and
whose last fingernail was worth more than all of
you together, and as soon as that is done, the

daughter must belong to you and go off whoring with you. That's how you are. At first I thought perhaps you were a good man. But how could you be! Oh, you are pigs!"

As she spoke, Goldmund saw glowing in her eyes, behind the hatred, something that touched him and shamed him and went deep to his heart. He saw death in her eyes, not the compulsion to die but the wish to die, the wish to be allowed to die, wordless obedience, abandonment to the call of the universal mother.

"Rebekka," he said softly, "perhaps you are right. I am not a good person, although I meant well with you. Forgive me. Only now have I understood you."

He raised his cap and bowed to her deeply as though to a countess, and walked off with heavy heart; he had to let her perish. For a long time he was sad and felt like speaking to no one. As little as they resembled each other, that proud Jewish girl did in some ways remind him of Lydia, the knight's daughter. To love such women brought suffering. But for a while it seemed to him as though he had never loved any other women, only these two, poor fearful Lydia and the shy, bitter Rebekka.

He thought of the black glowing girl for many days and dreamed many nights of the slender-burning beauty of her body that had been destined to joy and flowering and yet was resigned to dying. Oh, that those lips and breasts should fall prey to the "pigs" and rot in the fields! Was there no power or magic to save such precious flowers? Yes, there was such a magic; they continued to live in his soul and would be fashioned and preserved by him. With terror and delight he realized that his soul was filled with images, that this long journey through the land of death had filled him with ideas for drawings and statues. Oh, how this fullness strained at him, how he longed to come to himself quietly, to let them pour out, to convert them to lasting images! He pushed on, more glowing and eager, his eyes still open and his senses still curious, but now filled with a violent longing for paper and crayon, for clay and wood, for workroom and work.

Summer was over. Many people assumed that the epidemic would cease with autumn or the beginning of winter. It was an autumn without gaiety. Goldmund passed regions in which there was no one left to harvest the fruit. It fell off the trees and rotted in the grass. At other places savage hordes from the cities came to pillage, brutally robbing and squandering.

Slowly Goldmund neared his goal, and during the last stretch he was sometimes seized with the fear that he might be caught by the plague before he got there and die in some stable. He no longer wanted to die, not before tasting the joy of standing once more in a workshop and giving himself up to creation. For the first time in his life the world was too wide for him, the German Empire too large. No pretty town could entice him to stay; no pretty peasant girl retain him longer than a night.

At one point he passed a church. On its portal stood many stone figures in deep niches supported by ornamental small columns: very old figures of angels, disciples, and martyrs, like those he had seen many times. In his cloister in Mariabronn there had been a number of figures like this. Before, as an adolescent, he had looked at them, but without passion; they had seemed beautiful and dignified to him, but a little too solemn and stiff and old-fashioned. Later, after he had been moved and delighted by Master Niklaus's sweet sad madonna at the end of his first long journey, he had found these old solemn stone figures too heavy and rigid and foreign. He had looked at them with a certain contempt and had found his master's new type of art much more lively, intense, and animated. Now, returning from a world full of images, his soul marked by the scars and tracks of violent adventures and experiences, filled with painful nostalgia for consciousness and new creation, he was suddenly touched with extraordinary power by these strict, ancient figures. Reverently he stood before the venerable images, in which the heart of long-past days continued to live on, in which, still after centuries, the fears and delights of long-since-vanished generations, frozen to stone, offered resistance to the passage of time. A feeling of admiration rose with a humble shudder in his unwieldy heart, and of horror at his wasted, burned-up life. He did what he had not done for an infinitely long time. He walked up to a confessional to confess and be punished.

There were a number of confessionals in the church, but no priests. They had died, or they lay in the hospital, or they had fled for fear of contamination. The church was empty. Goldmund's steps echoed hollow under the stone vault. He knelt before an empty confessional, closed his eyes, and whispered into the grill: "Dear God, see what has become of me. I have returned from the world. I've become an evil, useless man. I have squandered my youth like a spendthrift and little remains. I have killed, I have stolen, I have whored, I have gone idle and have eaten the bread of others. Dear Lord, why did you create us thus, why do you lead us along such roads? Are we not your children? Did your son not die for us? Are there no saints and angels to guide us? Or are they all pretty, invented stories that we tell to children, at which priests themselves laugh? I have come to doubt you, Lord. You have ill-created the world; you are keeping it in bad order. I have seen houses and streets littered with corpses. I have seen the rich barricade themselves in their houses or flee, and the poor let their brothers lie unburied, each suspicious of the other. They slaughter the Jews like cattle; I have seen many innocent people suffer and die, and many a wicked man swim in prosperity. Have you completely forgotten and abandoned us, are you completely disgusted with your creation, do you want us all to perish?"

With a sigh he stepped out through the high portal and saw the silent statues, angels and saints stand haggard and tall in their stiffly folded gowns, immobile, inaccessible, superhuman and yet created by the hand and mind of man. Strict and deaf they stood there in their narrow niches, inaccessible to any request or question. And yet they were an infinite consolation, a triumphant victory over death and despair as they stood in their dignity and beauty, surviving one dying generation of men after another. Ah, poor beautiful Rebekka should be up there too, and poor Lene who had burned with their hut, and graceful Lydia, and Master Niklaus! One day they would stand up there and endure forever. He would put them there. These figures that meant love and torture to him today, fear and passion, would stand before later generations, nameless, without history, silent symbols of human life.

15

Finally the goal was reached. Goldmund entered the longed-for city by the same gate through which he had, so many years ago, stepped for the first time in search of his master. News from the bishop's city had already reached him on the road as he was approaching. He knew that the plague had been there too, that it was perhaps reigning still; people had told him of riots and unrest and that a governor had been sent by the Emperor to restore order, to enforce emergency laws and protect life and property. The bishop had left the city immediately after the outbreak of the epidemic and was living far away in one of his castles in the country. The wanderer had shown little interest in this news. As long as the city was still standing, and in it the workshop in which he wanted to work, everything else was unimportant to him. When he arrived, the plague had subsided; the people were waiting for the bishop's return and the governor's departure and looking forward to taking up their accustomed peaceful existence once more.

When Goldmund saw the city again, a feeling he had never before experienced—the emotion of homecoming—flooded through his heart and he made an unusually severe face to control himself. Everything was still in its place: the portals, the beautiful fountains, the clumsy old tower of the cathedral and the slender new one of the church of St. Mary, the clear bells of the church of St.

Lawrence, the broad-shining marketplace. Oh, how good that it had waited for him! Once, on the road, he had dreamed that he arrived and found everything unfamiliar and changed, some sections in decay and ruin and others equally unrecognizable because of new buildings and unpleasant landmarks. He walked through the streets close to tears, recognizing house after house. He found himself almost envying the solid burghers their pretty, secure houses, their fenced-in lives, the comforting, secure feeling of having a home, of belonging in a room, or in a workshop, among wives and children, servants and neighbors.

It was late afternoon. On the sunlit side of the street, houses, taverns, guild emblems, carved doors, and flower-pots were bathed in a warm glow. Nothing recalled the fact that death and madness had raged. Cool, light-green and light-blue, the clear river streamed under the resounding vaults of the bridge. For a while Goldmund sat on the embankment. Dark, shadowlike fish still glided by down there in the crystal greenness, or were motionless, their noses turned against the current. A feeble gold shimmer still blinked here and there from the twilight of the depths that promised so much and encouraged dreaming. Other waters had fish too, and other bridges and other towns offered pretty sights, and yet it seemed to him that he had seen nothing like this for a long time, that he had not felt anything similar.

Two butcher boys passed, pushing a calf. They were laughing, exchanging glances and jokes with a maid who was taking down wash above them on a balcony. How quickly everything passed! Not long ago the plague fires were still smoking here, and the dreadful body burners ruled; and now life went on, people laughed and joked. And he was no different. There he sat, delighted to see these things again, feeling grateful and even sensing warmth in the heart for the burghers, as though there had been no misery, no death, no Lene, no Jewish princess. Smiling, he stood up and walked on. Only when he approached Master Niklaus's house and walked again the street he had walked to work every day long ago did his heart begin to pound with anguish and worry. He walked faster. He wanted to call on the master that very day, to know where he stood; to wait until tomorrow seemed impossible. Was the master perhaps still angry with him? All that had been so long ago. It could no longer have any importance, but if it did, he would overcome it. If only the master was still there, he and his workshop, then all would be well. Hurriedly, as though afraid to miss something at the very last moment, he walked toward the familiar house, reached for the doorknob and had a terrible chill when he found the door locked. Was that a bad sign? Before, the door was never kept locked in broad daylight. Loudly he let the knocker fall and waited, sudden fear in his heart.

The old woman who had received him when he first entered this house came to open. She had not grown any uglier, only older and unfriendlier, and she did not recognize Goldmund. With anguish in his voice, he asked for the master. She looked at him, dumb and distrustful.

"Master? There's no master here. On your way, man. We let nobody in."

She tried to push him back out into the street, and he took her by the arm and yelled: "Speak, Margrit, for heaven's sake! I'm Goldmund, don't you know me? I must see Master Niklaus."

No welcome shone in her farsighted, half-blind eyes.

"There's no Master Niklaus here any more," she said coldly. "He's dead. Be on your way, I can't stand here and chat."

Everything collapsed inside Goldmund. He

shoved the old woman aside; she ran after him, screaming as he hurried through the dark hall toward the workshop. It was closed. Still followed by the nagging, scolding old woman, he ran up the stairs. In the twilight of the familiar room he saw the figures Niklaus had collected. Loudly he called for Mistress Lisbeth.

A door opened, and Lisbeth appeared. He recognized her only when he looked a second time: the sight contracted his heart. Ever since the moment he had been shocked to find the door bolted, everything in the house had seemed ghostlike, as though under a spell or in a nightmare, but now, at the sight of Lisbeth, a shudder went down his spine. Beautiful, proud Lisbeth had turned into a shy, bent-over old maid with a yellow, sickly face, a plain black dress, insecure eyes, and an attitude of fear.

"Forgive me," he said. "Margrit didn't want to let me in. Don't you know me? I'm Goldmund, tell me, oh tell me: is it true that your father is dead?"

He saw in her eyes that she had recognized him, and also that he was not in good standing here.

"Oh, so you are Goldmund," she said, and he recognized something of her proud manner in her voice. "You have troubled yourself in vain. My father is dead."

"And the workshop?" he blurted out.

"The workshop is closed. If you're looking for work, you must go elsewhere."

He tried to control himself.

"Mistress Lisbeth," he said in a friendly tone, "I'm not looking for work, I only wanted to say God bless you to the master, and to you. I am so sad to hear this! I can see that you have been through terrible times. If a grateful disciple of your father's can be of any service to you, please say so, it would be a joy to me. Ah, Mistress Lisbeth, my heart is breaking to find you this way—in such deep sorrow."

She withdrew to the door of the room.

"Thank you," she said hesitatingly. "You can no longer be of service to him, or to me. Margrit will show you out."

Her voice sounded bad, half angry, half fearful. He felt if she had the courage, she would have thrown him out cursing.

Soon he was downstairs, and the old woman slammed the door behind him and pushed the bolts. He could still hear the hard clicking of those two bolts. It sounded to him like the locking of a coffin lid.

Slowly he returned to the embankment. Again he sat at the old place above the river. The sun had gone down, cold came up from the water, the stone on which he sat felt cold. The street along the embankment had grown quiet. The stream foamed around the pillars of the bridge; the depths of the water were dark; no gold shimmer blinked up any more. Oh, he thought, if I fell over this wall and disappeared in the river! Again the world was filled with death. An hour passed, and the twilight turned to night. At last he was able to weep. He sat and wept, warm drops falling on his hands and knees. He wept for his dead master, for the lost beauty of Lisbeth, for Lene, for Robert, for Rebekka, for his wilted, squandered youth.

Later he found a tavern where he had once often drunk with friends. The owner recognized him. He asked her for a piece of bread and she gave it to him. She was friendly; she also gave him a mug of wine. He could not swallow the bread or drink the wine. That night he slept on a bench in the tavern. In the morning the owner waked him. He thanked her and left, eating the piece of bread in the street.

He walked to the fish market. There stood the

house in which he had once had a room. Beside the fountain, a few fishwives were offering their live wares; he stared into the barrels, at the beautifully glittering animals. He had often seen this before. He remembered how he had felt pity for the fish and anger against the fishwives and the shoppers. He remembered one morning when he had roamed here, admired the fish and felt sorry for them, when he had been very sad. Much time had passed since then; much water had washed down the river. He remembered his sadness well, but he could no longer remember what had made him so sad. It was that way with everything: even sadness passed, even pain and despair, as well as the joys. Everything passed, faded, lost its depth, its value, and finally there came a time when one could no longer remember what had pained one so. Pains, too, wilted and faded. Would today's pain also wilt one day and be meaningless, his deep despair at his master's death, at his dying in anger against him, his hurt that no workshop was open in which he could taste the joy of creating and roll the weight of images from his soul? Yes, doubtless this pain, this bitter need would also grow old and tired. It too would be forgotten. Nothing had permanence, and he regretted that, too.

As he stared at the fish, absorbed in these thoughts, he heard a low friendly voice speak his name.

"Goldmund," someone called shyly, and when he looked up, he saw a delicate, sickly young girl, with beautiful dark eyes, who was calling to him. He did not know her.

"Goldmund! It is you, isn't it?" said the timid voice. "How long have you been back in the city? Don't you know me any more? I'm Marie."

But he did not know her. She had to tell him that she was the daughter of his former landlord

who on that early morning of his departure had
warmed milk for him in the kitchen. She blushed,
telling this.

Yes, it was Marie, the sickly child with the lame
hip, who had taken care of him that day with such
timid sweetness. Now it all came back to him: she
had waited for him that cool morning and had
been so sad that he was leaving. She had cooked
milk for him, and he had given her a kiss which
she had received quietly and solemnly as if it were
a sacrament. He had never thought of her again.
Now she was grown up and had very beautiful
eyes, though she still limped. He shook hands with
her. He was so glad that someone in this city knew
and loved him.

Marie took him with her; he resisted only halfheartedly. He was invited to eat with her parents in
the room where his painting was still hung, where
his red ruby glass stood on the mantelpiece. They
asked him to stay a few days; they were glad to
see him again. Then he learned what had happened in his master's house. Niklaus had not died
of the plague, but beautiful Lisbeth had fallen ill
with it and for a long time lain deathly sick, and
her father had nursed her until he himself died, a
few weeks before she was quite cured. She was
saved, but her beauty had gone.

"The workshop stands empty," said the landlord.
"That'd be a nice home for a good image-carver
and there'd be plenty of money. Think about it,
Goldmund! She wouldn't say no. She no longer has
a choice."

He heard about the days of the plague, how the
mob had set fire to a hospital, had stormed and
pillaged several rich burghers' houses, how for a
while, after the bishop had fled, there had been no
order or safety in the city. That's when the Emper-
or, who happened to be in the region, sent the
governor, Count Heinrich. Well, he was a dapper

gentleman; he had restored order in the city with a couple of horsemen and soldiers. But now it was time his reign came to an end; the bishop was expected back. The count had imposed hardships on the citizens, and they had seen quite enough of his concubine, Agnes, who was a vixen. Well, soon they'd be off. The city council had long since got sick of having to deal with this courtier and warrior, who was the Emperor's favorite and received emissaries like a prince, instead of with the good bishop.

Now Goldmund was questioned about his adventures. "Ach," he said sadly, "let's not speak of it. I wandered and wandered, and the plague was everywhere and the dead lay all about, and everywhere the people grew mad and wicked with fear. I survived; perhaps one day we'll forget it all. Now I've come back and my master is dead! Let me stay here for a few days and rest, then I'll wander on."

He did not stay in order to rest. He stayed because he was disappointed and undecided, because memories of happier times made the city dear to him, and because poor Marie's love did him good. He could not return it, he could give her nothing but friendliness and pity, but her quiet, humble admiration warmed his heart. But more than all this, the burning need to be an artist once again kept him in this place, even without a workshop, even with only makeshift tools.

For a few days Goldmund did nothing but draw. Marie had found pen and paper, and he sat in his room and drew hour after hour, filling the large sheets now with hasty sketches, now with lovingly delicate figures, letting the overfilled picture book inside him flow out onto the paper. Many times he drew Lene's face: the way it had smiled with satisfaction, her love and murder lust after the vagrant's death, her face as it had been the last night, in the process of melting into formlessness, in its return to the earth. He drew the small peasant boy whom he had seen lying dead across his parents' threshold, with little clenched fists. He drew a cart full of corpses, with three pitifully straining nags pulling it, the death churls running beside it with long staffs, their eyes squinting darkly from the shadows of their black plague hoods. Again and again he drew Rebekka, the slender, black-eyed girl, her proud narrow mouth, her face full of sorrow and indignation, her graceful young figure that seemed created for loving, her proud bitter mouth. He drew himself as the wanderer, the lover, the fugitive from death's reaper, as a dancer at the orgies of the life-greedy. He sat absorbed over the white paper, drew the contemptuous face of Mistress Lisbeth the way he had known her in former days, the caricature of the old servant Margrit, the loved and feared face of Master Niklaus. Several times, with thin, intuitive strokes, he also sketched a large female figure, the earth mother, sitting with hands in her lap, a hint of a smile in her face under melancholy eyes. The outpouring of work, the mastering of these faces, did him great good. In a few days he filled with drawings all the sheets Marie had found for him. He cut off a piece of the last sheet and on it he drew Marie's face with sparing strokes, the beautiful eyes, the resigned mouth, and gave it to her.

Drawing had greatly lessened his feeling of heaviness and lightened the bursting fullness in his soul. As long as he was drawing, he did not know where he was. His world consisted of nothing but a table, white paper, and, at night, a candle. Now he awoke, remembered the most recent events, saw more hapless roaming ahead of him, and began strolling through the city with a strangely split sensation half of homecoming, half of departure.

On one of these strolls he met a woman. Seeing her refocused all his disordered feelings and gave them a new center. She was riding a horse, a tall, light-blond woman with curious, cool blue eyes, and a firm, strong body, a blossoming face full of eagerness for pleasure, and power, self-esteem, and a certain sniffing curiosity of the senses. She sat on her brown horse somewhat domineering and proud, accustomed to giving orders, but not withdrawn or haughty. Her nostrils seemed to be open to all the scents of the world, and her large loose mouth was obviously capable of taking and giving to the highest degree. The moment Goldmund saw this woman, he became fully awake and full of desire to measure himself against her. To conquer her suddenly seemed a noble goal to strive for, and if he were to break his neck on the way it would not have seemed a bad death to him. He felt that this blond lioness was his equal, rich in sensuality and soul, at the mercy of all storms, wild as well as delicate, well versed in passion from an ancient heritage of blood.

As she rode past, he followed her with his eyes. Between curly blond hair and blue velvet collar, he saw her firm neck strong and proud, yet covered by the tenderest skin. She was, he thought, the most beautiful woman he had ever seen. He wanted to hold this neck in his hands and wrest the blue-cool secret from her eyes. It was not difficult to find out who she was. He soon learned that she lived in the castle, that she was Agnes, the governor's mistress. It did not surprise him; she might have been the empress herself. At the fountain basin he stopped and looked at his mirror image. It matched the blond woman's face like a brother's, except that it was rather unkempt. That very hour he visited a barber he knew and persuaded him to cut his hair and beard and comb it clean.

The pursuit lasted two days. Whenever Agnes came out of the castle, the blond stranger was standing at the gates, looking admiringly into her eyes. Agnes rode around the ramparts and the stranger watched her from under the elms. Agnes visited a jeweler and, as she left the shop, she met the stranger. Light sparkled out of her masterful eyes; her nostrils quivered slightly. The next morning, when she again found him standing in readiness at her first ride, she smiled her challenge at him. He also saw the count, the governor, who looked bold and imposing. He had to be taken seriously, but there was gray in his beard and worry in his face, and Goldmund felt superior to him.

These two days made him happy; he was radiant with recovered youth. It was beautiful to show himself to this woman and to offer her combat. It was beautiful to lose his freedom to this beauty; beautiful and deeply exciting to gamble his existence on a single throw.

On the morning of the third day, Agnes rode out through the castle gates, accompanied by a groom on horseback. Immediately her eyes searched for the pursuer, ready for combat and a trifle concerned. There he was, and she sent the groom off on an errand. Slowly she rode ahead alone, out to the bridge gate and across the bridge. Only once did she look back, and saw the stranger following her. She waited for him on the road to the pilgrims' shrine of St. Vitus, which was deserted at this hour. She had to wait for half an hour, as the stranger walked slowly and did not want to arrive out of breath. Fresh and smiling he came walking up, a little twig with a bright red haw on it in his mouth. She had dismounted and tethered her horse and stood leaning against the ivy of the steep buttressing wall, gazing at her pursuer. He came up to her, looked her in the eye, and raised his cap.

"Why are you running after me?" she asked. "What do you want from me?"

"Oh," he said, "I'd much rather make you a present than accept one. I'd like to offer myself to you as a present, beautiful woman, to do with me as you will."

"All right, I'll see what can be done with you. But if you think that here is a little flower you can pluck without risk, you've made a mistake. I can only love men who risk their life if necessary."

"You may command me."

Slowly she detached a thin gold chain from her neck and handed it to him.

"What is your name?"

"Goldmund."

"Good, Goldmund; I shall have a taste of your golden mouth. Listen carefully: toward evening you'll take this chain to the castle and say that you found it. But don't let it out of your hands; I want to receive it directly from you. Come as you are, let them take you for a beggar. If one of the servants scolds you, remain calm. I have only two people in the castle who are trustworthy: the stable groom Max and my chambermaid Berta. You must reach one of these two and let them lead you to me. With all others in the castle, including the count, conduct yourself carefully; they are enemies. You've been warned. It may cost your life."

She held out her hand. He took it smilingly, kissed it gently, softly rubbed his cheek against it. Then he put the chain away and walked off downhill toward the river and the city. The vineyards were already bare; one yellow leaf after another floated from the trees. Laughingly, Goldmund shook his head and, looking down into the city, he found it friendly and lovable. Only a few days ago he had been sad, even sad that misery and suffering passed. And now indeed it had already passed, fluttered down like the golden leaf from a branch.

It seemed to him that love had never shone so brightly for him as it did from this woman, whose tall figure and blond joyful energy reminded him of the image of his mother as he had once, as a boy in Mariabronn, carried it in his heart. Two days ago he would not have thought possible that the world would laugh so gaily in his eyes, that he would once more feel the stream of life, of joy, of youth running so fully and urgently through his veins. What a joy to be still alive, to have been spared by death during all these gruesome months!

In the evening he went to the castle. There was a great bustle in the courtyard: horses were being unsaddled; messengers were scurrying about; servants were conducting a small procession of priests and church dignitaries through the inner door and up the stairs. Goldmund wanted to go after them, but the porter held him back. He pulled out the gold chain and said he had been ordered to hand it to no one but the lady herself or her chambermaid. He was given the escort of a servant and was made to wait for a long time in the corridors. Finally, a pretty, nimble woman appeared, walked past him, and asked in a low voice: "Are you Goldmund?" She motioned him to follow her. Quietly she vanished through a door, reappeared after a while, and motioned him in.

He entered a small room that smelled strongly of furs and perfume, and there were dresses and coats and ladies' hats on wooden stands, and all kinds of ladies' boots in an open chest. Here he stood and waited for half an hour perhaps. He sniffed at the scented gowns, brushed his hands over the furs, and smiled with curiosity at all the pretty stuff that hung there.

Finally the inner door opened, and it was not the chambermaid but Agnes herself, in a light blue dress, with white fur brimming around the neck. Slowly she walked up to the waiting man, marking each step, her cool blue eyes looking earnestly at him.

"You've had to wait," she whispered. "I think we're safe now. A committee of church officials is with the count. He is dining with them; they will probably have long discussions. Sessions with priests always last a long time. The hour is yours and mine. Welcome, Goldmund."

She bent toward him, her demanding lips approached his, silently they greeted each other in a first kiss. Slowly he closed his hand about her neck. She led him through the door into her bedchamber, which was high and brightly lit by candles. On a table a meal stood prepared. They sat down; she served him bread and butter and a little meat and poured white wine for him into a beautiful bluish glass. They ate, both drinking from the same bluish chalice, their hands playing probingly with each other.

"Whence have you flown, my beautiful bird?" she asked him. "Are you a warrior, or a musician, or are you just a poor wayfarer?"

"I'm everything you want me to be," he laughed softly. "I am all yours. I'll be a musician if you like, and you are my sweet lute, and when I put my fingers around your neck and play on you, we'll hear the angels sing. Come, my heart, I am not here to eat your cakes and drink your white wine. I've come only for you."

Gently he pulled the white fur from her neck and caressed the clothes off her body. Courtiers and priests held their sessions outside, servants crept about the halls, the thin sickle moon floated away behind the trees—the lovers knew nothing of it. For them paradise bloomed. Drawn toward each other and entangled in one another, they lost themselves in a perfumed night, saw its white flowering secrets shimmer in the darkness, plucked its longed-for fruit with tender and grateful hands.

Never had the musician played on such a lute; never had the lute sounded under such strong and knowing fingers.

"Goldmund," she whispered glowingly in his ear, "oh, what a sorcerer you are! I want to have a child by you, sweet Goldmund. And still more, I'd like to die with you. Drink me to the dregs, beloved, melt me, kill me!"

Deep in his throat a tone of happiness sounded as he saw the harshness in her cool eyes dissolve and grow weak. Like a tender expiring shiver, the shudder in the depth of her eyes spent itself like the silver shudder on the skin of a dying fish, golden as the sparkling of those magic shimmers deep down in the river. All the happiness a human being could experience seemed to come together in this moment.

Immediately afterward, as she lay with closed eyes, trembling, he got up and slipped into his clothes. With a sigh he spoke into her ear: "My beautiful treasure, I am leaving you. I don't feel like dying, I don't want to be killed by your count. First I want us to be as happy as we have been today. One more time, many more times."

She lay in silence until he was dressed. Gently he pulled the cover over her and kissed her eyes.

"Goldmund," she said, "oh, I am sorry that you must go! Do come back tomorrow! I'll let you know if there is danger. Come back, come back tomorrow!"

She pulled at a bellrope. The chambermaid received him at the door to the wardrobe and led him out of the castle. He would have liked to give her a gold piece; for a moment he felt ashamed of his poverty.

It was almost midnight when he got back to the fish market and looked up at the house. It was late, and nobody would be awake; probably he would have to spend the night outside. To his surprise he found the door open. Softly he crept inside and closed the door behind him. The way to his room led through the kitchen, which was lit. Marie sat at the kitchen table by a tiny oil lamp. She had just dozed off, after waiting for hours. When he entered, she started and sprang to her feet.

"Oh," he said, "Marie, are you still up?"

"I'm up," she said, "or you would have found the house locked."

"I'm sorry that you waited, Marie. It's late. Don't be angry with me."

"I'll never be angry with you, Goldmund. I'm only a little sad."

"You must not be sad. Why sad?"

"Oh, Goldmund, I'd so like to be healthy and beautiful and strong. Then you would not have to go to strange houses during the night and make love to other women. Then you would perhaps stay with me once and be a little sweet to me."

Her mild voice sounded hopeless, but not bitter, only sad. Embarrassed, he stood in front of her. He felt sorry for her; he did not know what to say. With a cautious hand, he reached for her head and stroked her hair. She stood very still and shuddered as she felt his hand on her hair. Then she wept a little, held her head up again, and said timidly: "Go to bed now, Goldmund, I've been talking nonsense, I was so sleepy. Good night."

16

Goldmund spent a day of happy impatience roaming in the hills. If he had owned a horse, he would have ridden to his master's beautiful madonna in the cloister. He felt the urge to see her again and thought that he had dreamed of Master Niklaus that night. Well, he'd go see the madonna another time. His bliss with Agnes might be of short duration, might lead to danger perhaps—but today it was in full bloom; he did not want to miss any of it. He did not want to see people, to be distracted; he wanted to spend the mild autumn day outside, with the trees and clouds. He told Marie that he was thinking of a hike in the countryside and might be back late. He asked her to give him a good chunk of bread for the road and not wait up for him in the evening. She made no comment, stuffed his pockets full of bread and apples, ran a brush over his old coat, which she had patched the very first day, and let him go.

He strolled across the river and climbed the steep-stepped paths through the empty vineyards, lost himself in the forest on the heights, and did not stop climbing until he had reached the last plateau. There the sun shone halfheartedly through bald trees. Blackbirds scurried before his steps; shyly they retreated into the bushes, looking at him with shiny black eyes. Far below, the river seemed a blue curve. The city looked like a toy; not a sound rose from it, except that of the bells ringing for prayers. Near him on the plateau there were small, grass-covered swellings, mounds from ancient pagan days, perhaps fortifications, perhaps tombs. He sat down in the dry, crackling autumn grass on the side of one of them. He could see the whole vast valley, the hills and mountains beyond the river, chain upon chain, all the way to the horizon, where mountains and sky merged in bluish uncertainty and could no longer be told apart. His feet had measured this sweeping distance much farther than the eye could see. All these regions, which were far away now and remembered, had once been close and present. A hundred times he had slept in those forests, eaten berries, been hungry and cold, crossed those mountain ridges, and stretches of heath, been happy or sad, fresh or fatigued. Somewhere in that distance, far out of the range of vision, lay the charred bones of good Lene; somewhere there his companion Robert might still be wandering, if the plague had not caught up with him; somewhere out there lay dead Viktor; and somewhere too, far off in the enchanted distance, was the cloister of his youth and the castle of the knight with the beautiful daughters, and poor, destitute, hounded Rebekka was still roaming there if she had not perished. So many widely scattered places, heaths and forests, towns and villages, castles and cloisters, and people alive and dead existed inside him in his memory, his love, his repentance, his longing. And if death caught him too, tomorrow, then all this would fall apart, would vanish, the whole picture book full of women and love, of summer mornings and winter nights. Oh, it was high time that he accomplished something, created something, left something behind that would survive him.

Up to now little remained of his life, of his wanderings, of all those years that had passed since he set out in the world. What remained were the few figures he had once made in the workshop, especially his St. John, and this picture book, this unreal world inside his head, this beautiful, aching image world of memories. Would he succeed in saving a few scraps of this inner world and making it visible to others? Or would things just go on the same way: new towns, new landscapes, new women, new experiences, new images, piled one on the other, experiences from which he gleaned nothing but a restless, torturous as well as beautiful overflowing of the heart?

It was shameless how life made fun of one; it was a joke, a cause for weeping! Either one lived and let one's senses play, drank full at the primitive mother's breast—which brought great bliss but was no protection against death; then one lived like a mushroom in the forest, colorful today and rotten tomorrow. Or else one put up a defense, imprisoned oneself for work and tried to build a monument to the fleeting passage of life—then one renounced life, was nothing but a tool; one enlisted in the service of that which endured, but one dried up in the process and lost one's freedom, scope, lust for life. That's what had happened to Master Niklaus.

Ach, life made sense only if one achieved both, only if it was not split by this brittle alternative! To create, without sacrificing one's senses for it. To live, without renouncing the nobility of creating. Was that impossible?

Perhaps there were people for whom this was possible. Perhaps there were husbands and heads of families who did not lose their sensuality by being faithful. Perhaps there were people who, though settled, did not have hearts dried up by lack of freedom and lack of risk. Perhaps. He had never met one.

All existence seemed to be based on duality, on contrast. Either one was a man or one was a woman, either a wanderer or a sedentary burgher, either a thinking person or a feeling person—no one could breathe in at the same time as he breathed out, be a man as well as a woman, experience freedom as well as order, combine instinct and mind. One always had to pay for the one with the loss of the other, and one thing was always just as important and desirable as the other. Perhaps women had it easier in this respect. Nature had created them in such a way that desire bore its fruit automatically, that the bliss of love became a child. For a man, eternal longing replaced this simple fertility. Was the god who had created everything in this manner an evil god, was he hostile, did he laugh ironically at his own creation? No, he could not be evil; he had created the hart and the roebuck, fish and birds, forests, flowers, the seasons. But the split ran through his entire creation. Perhaps it had not turned out right or was incomplete—or did God intend this lack, this longing in human life for a special purpose? Was this perhaps the seed of the enemy, of original sin? But why should this longing and this lack be sinful? Did not all that was beautiful and holy, all that man created and gave back to God as a sacrifice of thanks spring from this very lack, from this longing?

His thoughts depressed him. He turned his eyes toward the city, saw the marketplace, the fish market, the bridges, the churches, the town hall. And there was the castle, the proud bishop's palace, in which Count Heinrich was now ruling. Agnes lived under those towers and high roofs, his beautiful regal mistress, who looked so proud but who could nevertheless lose herself, abandon herself completely in love. He thought of her with joy, and gratefully remembered last night. To have been able to experience the happiness of that night, to have been able to make that marvelous woman happy, he had needed his entire life, all the things women had taught him, his many journeys, his needs, wandering through the snow at night, his friendship and familiarity with animals, flowers, trees, water, fish, butterflies. For this he had needed senses sharpened by ecstasy and danger, homelessness, all his inner world of images stored up during those many years. As long as his life was a garden in which such magic flowers as Agnes bloomed, he had no reason to complain.

He spent all day on the autumnal heights, walking, resting, eating bread, thinking of Agnes and the evening before him. Toward nightfall he was back in the city walking toward the castle. It had grown chilly; the houses stared out of quiet red window eyes; he met a small troop of singing boys carrying hollowed-out turnips with faces carved into them and candles inside. This little mummery left a scent of winter in its wake, and smiling, Goldmund looked after them. For a long time he strolled about outside the castle. The church dignitaries were still there; here and there he could see a priest silhouetted in one of the windows. Finally he was able to creep inside and find Berta, the chambermaid. Again she hid him in the little closet room until Agnes appeared and silently led him to her room. Tenderly her beautiful face received him, tenderly, but not happily; she was sad, worried, frightened. He had to try very hard to cheer her a little. Slowly his loving words and kisses restored a little of her confidence.

"How very sweet you can be," she said gratefully. "You have such deep sounds in your throat, my golden bird, when you're tender and chirp. I'm so fond of you, Goldmund. If only we were far from here! I no longer like it here. It will soon come to an end anyhow; the count has been called away; the silly bishop will soon return. The count is angry today. The priests have had harsh words with him.

Oh, my dear, he must not set eyes on you! You wouldn't live through the next hour. I'm so afraid for you."

Half-lost sounds rose in his memory—hadn't he heard this song before? That was how Lydia used to speak to him, so lovingly and full of fear, so tender-sad. That's how she used to come to his room at night, full of love and fear, full of worry, of gruesome images. He liked to hear it, that tender-anguished song. What would love be without secrecy? What would love be without risk?

Gently he drew Agnes to him, caressed her, held her hand, hummed low wooing sounds into her ear, kissed her eyebrows. It touched and delighted him to find her so frightened and worried because of him. Gratefully she received his caresses, almost humbly. Full of love, she clung to him, but her mood did not brighten.

Suddenly she started as a nearby door was slammed and rapid steps approached.

"Oh, my God, the count!" she cried in despair. "Quickly, you can escape through the closet room. Hurry! Don't betray me!"

She pushed him into the closet room. He stood alone groping hesitantly in the darkness. Behind the door he heard the count speak loudly to Agnes. He felt his way through the dresses to the other door; soundlessly he set one foot before the other. He reached the door to the corridor and tried to open it. And only at that moment, when he found the door locked from the outside, did he feel fear, did his heart beat wildly, painfully. It could be an unfortunate coincidence that someone had locked the door after he came in, but he did not believe so. He had walked into a trap; he was lost. Someone must have seen him sneak in here. It would cost him his life. Trembling, he stood in the darkness, and immediately thought of Agnes's last words: "Don't betray me!" No, he would not betray her. His heart pounded, but the decision steadied him. Angrily he clenched his teeth.

It all happened in seconds. A door opened and the count came in from Agnes's room, a candlestick in his left hand and an unsheathed sword in his right. At the same moment, Goldmund hastily scooped up a few dresses and coats that were hanging all around him and placed them over his arm. Let them take him for a thief—perhaps that was a way out.

The count saw him at once. Slowly he came closer.

"Who are you? What are you doing here? Answer, or I'll run this sword through you."

"Forgive me," whispered Goldmund. "I'm a poor man and you are so rich! I'll give it all back, my lord, everything I took. Here, see!"

And he put the coats on the floor.

"A thief, eh? It was not intelligent of you to risk your life for a few old coats. Are you a burgher of the city?"

"No, my lord, I'm homeless. I'm a poor man, you'll have mercy . . ."

"Silence! I want to know if perchance you were brazen enough to molest the lady. Ach, but since you'll be hanged anyhow, we won't have to pry into that. Theft is enough."

Violently he hammered against the locked door and called: "Are you there? Open up!"

The door opened from the outside, and three footmen stood in readiness with drawn blades.

"Tie him well," called the count in a voice that croaked with irony and pride. "He's a vagrant who came in here to steal. Put him in the dungeon, and tomorrow morning the rascal will dangle from the gallows."

Goldmund's hands were tied; he put up no resistance. He was led off, through the long corridor, down the stairs, through the inner courtyard, a

butler carrying a torch ahead of them. They
stopped in front of a round, iron-studded cellar
door, shouted and cursed because the key was not
in the lock. One of the footmen took the torch
while the butler ran back to fetch the key. There
they stood, three armed men and one bound one,
waiting outside the door. The one with the light
pushed it curiously on to Goldmund's face. At this
moment two of the priests who were guests in the
castle walked by on the way from the castle chapel. They stopped in front of the group; both looked
at the night scene attentively: the three footmen,
the bound man, the way they stood there, waiting.

Goldmund noticed neither the priests nor his
guards. He could see nothing but the low, flickering
light held close to his face. It was blinding his
eyes. And behind the light, in a twilight full of
horror, he saw something else, something formless,
large, ghostlike: the abyss, the end, death. With
staring eyes he stood there, seeing nothing, hearing
nothing. One of the priests was whispering intently
to one of the men. When he heard that the man
was a thief and condemned to death, he asked if
he had a confessor. No, they said, he had just been
caught in the act.

"Then I shall go to him in the morning," said the
priest. "Before early mass I'll bring him the holy
sacraments and hear his confession. You will swear
to me that he will not be led away before. I'll
speak to the count this very evening. The man may
be a thief; he still has the right to confession and
the sacraments like any other Christian."

The men dared not contradict. They knew the
clerical dignitary. He was one of the envoys; they
had seen him several times at the count's table.
And besides, why should the poor vagrant be deprived of confession?

The priests walked off. Goldmund stared. Finally the butler came with the key and unlocked the

door. The prisoner was led into a cellar, and stumbled down a few steps. A couple of three-legged stools were set around a table; it was the anteroom of a wine cellar. They pushed a stool toward him and told him to sit down.

"Tomorrow a priest is coming to confess you," one of the men said. Then they left and carefully locked the heavy door.

"Leave me the light, brother," begged Goldmund.

"No, fellow, you might do mischief with it. You'll get along without it. The wisest would be to get used to the dark. How long does such a light last anyway? It would be out within an hour. Good night."

Now he was alone in the blackness. He sat on the stool and laid his head on the table. It was painful to sit this way; the rope around his wrists hurt; but these feelings penetrated his consciousness only much later. At first he merely sat, with his head on the table as though he were about to be decapitated. He felt the urge to impress upon his body and senses what had been imposed upon his heart: to accept the inevitable, to accept dying.

For an eternity he sat that way, miserably bent over, trying to accept what had been imposed upon him, to realize it, to breathe it in, and fill himself with it. It was evening now. Night was beginning, and the end of this night would also be the end of him. That was what he had to realize. Tomorrow he would no longer be alive. He would be hanging, an object for birds to sit on and pick at. He would be what Master Niklaus was, what Lene was in the burned-out hut, like all those he had seen piled high on the death-carts. It was not easy to accept that, to let himself be filled with it. It was absolutely impossible to accept it. There were too many things he had not yet given up, to

which he had not yet said goodbye. The hours of
this night had been given him to do just that.

He had to say farewell to beautiful Agnes. Never
again would he see her tall figure, her light sunny
hair, her cool blue eyes, the diminishing quiver of
pride in these eyes, the soft gold down on her
sweet-smelling skin. Farewell, blue eyes, farewell
lovely mouth! He had hoped to kiss it many times
more. Oh, only this morning in the hills, in the late
autumn sun, he had thought of her, belonged to
her, longed for her! And he also had to say farewell to the hills, to the sun, the blue and white-
clouded sky, the trees and forests, to wandering,
the times of day, the seasons. Perhaps Marie was
still sitting up, even now: poor Marie with the
good loving eyes and hobbled gait, sitting and
waiting, falling asleep in her kitchen and waking
up again, but no Goldmund would ever come
home.

Oh, and his paper and drawing pen, and all the
figures he had wanted to make—gone, gone! And
the hope of seeing Narcissus again, his dear St.
John, that too had to be given up.

And he had to say farewell to his hands, his
eyes, to hunger and thirst, to love, to playing the
lute, to sleeping and waking, to everything. Tomorrow a bird would fly through the air and
Goldmund would no longer see it, a girl would sing
in a window and he would not hear her song, the
river would run and the dark fish would swim
silently, the wind would blow and sweep the yellow leaves on the ground, the sun would shine and
stars would blink in the sky, young men would go
dancing, the first snow would lie on the distant
mountains—everything would go on, trees would
cast their shadows, people would look gay or sad
out of their living eyes, dogs would bark, cows
would low in the barns of villages, and all of it

without Goldmund. Nothing belonged to him any more, he was being dispatched from it all.

He smelled the morning smell of the heath; he tasted the sweet young wine, the young firm walnuts; his memory spun a glowing panorama of the entire colorful world through his oppressed heart. In parting, all of life's beautiful confusion shone once more through his senses; grief welled up in him and he felt tear upon tear drop from his eyes. Sobbing, he gave in to the wave. His tears flooded out; collapsing, he abandoned himself to the infinite pain. Oh, valleys and wooded mountains, brooks among green elms, oh girls, oh moonlit evenings on the bridges, oh beautiful radiant image world, how can I leave you! Weeping, he lay across the table, a disconsolate boy. From the misery of his heart, a sigh, an imploring complaint rose: "Oh mother, oh mother!"

And as he spoke this magic word, an image answered him from the depths of his memory, the image of his mother. It was not the figure of his thoughts and artist's dreams. It was the image of his own mother, beautiful and alive, the way he had not seen it since his cloister days. To her he addressed his prayer, to her he cried his unbearable sorrow at having to die, to her he abandoned himself, to her he gave the forest, the sun, his eyes and hands; he placed his whole life and being in her motherly hands.

And so weeping he fell asleep; exhaustion and sleep held him in their arms like a mother. He slept an hour or two, escaping his misery.

He woke up and felt violent pain. His bound wrists burned horribly; a jagged pain shot through neck and back. He had trouble sitting up; then he came to and realized where he was again. Around him the darkness was complete. He did not know how long he had slept, how many hours he still had to live. Perhaps they'd come any moment to take him away to die. Then he remembered that he had been promised a priest. He didn't think that the sacraments would do him much good. He didn't know whether even complete absolution of his sins could bring him to heaven. He didn't know if there was a heaven, a God the father, a judgment, an eternity. He had long since lost all certitude about those things.

But whether there was an eternity or not: he did not desire it, he wanted nothing but his insecure, transitory life, this breathing, this being at home in his skin, he wanted to live. Furiously he sat up, groped his way to the wall in the dark, and began to think. There had to be an escape! Perhaps the priest was the answer. Perhaps he could convince him of his innocence, get him to say a good word on his behalf or help him secure a stay of execution or make his escape? He went over these ideas again and again. If they didn't work he could not give up; the game just couldn't be over yet. First he would try to win over the priest. He would try as hard as he could to charm him, to enlist him in his cause, to convince him, to flatter him. The priest was the one good card in his hand; all the other possibilities were dreams. Still, there were coincidence and destiny: the hangman might have a stomach-ache, the gallows might collapse, some unforeseeable possibility of escape might arise. In any case Goldmund refused to die; he had vainly tried to accept his fate, and he could not. He would resist, he would struggle, he'd trip the guard, he'd attack the hangman, he would fight for his life to the last moment, with every drop of blood in him. Oh, if he could only persuade the priest to untie his hands! A great deal would be gained.

In the meantime he tried, in spite of the pain, to work at the ropes with his teeth. With furious effort he succeeded, after a cruelly long time, in making them seem a little looser. Panting, he stood in the night of his prison, his swollen arms and hands hurting terribly. When he had gotten his breath again, he crept along the wall, step by step, exploring the humid cellar wall for a protruding edge. Then he remembered the steps over which he had stumbled down into this dungeon. He found them. He knelt and tried to rub the rope against the edge of one of the stones. It was difficult. Again and again his wrists instead of the rope hit the stone; they burned like fire and he felt his blood flow. But he did not give up. When a miserable strip of gray morning was visible between the door and the sill, he had succeeded. The rope had been rubbed through; he could untie it; his hands were free! But afterwards he could hardly move a finger. His hands were swollen and lifeless, and his arms were stiff with cramps all the way up to the shoulders. He had to exercise them. He forced himself to move them, to make the blood stream through them again. Now he had a plan that seemed good to him.

If he could not succeed in persuading the priest to help him, well then, if they left the man alone with him even for the shortest time, he had to kill him. He could do it with one of the stools. He could not strangle him, he no longer had enough strength in his hands and arms. First beat the priest to death, quickly slip into his robes and flee! When the others found the dead man, he'd have to be outside the castle, and then run, run. Marie would let him in and hide him. The plan would work.

Never in his life had Goldmund watched the grayish beginning of morning with such attention, longed for it and yet feared it. Quivering with tension and determination, he watched the miserable strip of light under the door growing slowly lighter. He walked back to the table and practiced crouching on the stool with his hands between his knees so that the missing ropes would not be noticed immediately. Since his hands had been freed, he no longer believed in his death. He was determined to get through, even if the whole world had to be smashed in the process. He was determined to live at any cost. His nose quivered with eagerness for freedom and life. And who could tell, perhaps someone on the outside would come to his aid? Agnes was a woman. Her power did not reach very far, nor perhaps did her courage; and it was possible that she would abandon him. But she loved him; perhaps she could do something for him. Perhaps her chambermaid Berta was hovering outside the door—and wasn't there also a groom she thought she could trust? And if nobody appeared and no sign was given him, well, then he'd go through with his plan. If it did not succeed, he'd kill the guards with the stool, two or three of them, as many as came in. He was certain of one advantage: his eyes had grown accustomed to the dark cellar. He now recognized instinctively all the shapes and shadows in the twilight, whereas the others would be completely blind for the first few minutes at least.

Feverishly he crouched at the table, thinking carefully what he would say to the priest to win his assistance, because that's how he had to begin. At the same time he eagerly watched the modest swelling of light in the slit. Now he longed desperately for the moment he had so dreaded hours ago. He could hardly wait; the terrible tension would not be bearable much longer. His strength, his vigilance, his power of decision would gradually diminish. The guard had to come soon with the priest, while his taut readiness, his determined will to be saved was still in the blossoming stage.

Finally the world outside awakened, the enemy approached. Steps resounded on the pavement in the court, a key was pushed into the lock and

turned: each sound boomed out like thunder after
the long deathly silence.

Slowly the heavy door opened a slit, creaking on
its hinges. A priest came in, alone, without a
guard, carrying a candlestick with two candles.
This was not at all what the prisoner had imagined.

How strangely moving: the priest who had entered, behind whom invisible hands pulled the
door shut, wore the habit of Mariabronn, the well-
known, familiar habit that Abbot Daniel, Father
Anselm, and Father Martin had once worn!

The sight stabbed at his heart; he had to look
away. Perhaps the habit of this cloister was the
promise of something friendly, a good omen. But
then again perhaps murder was still the only way
out. He clenched his teeth. It would be hard for
him to kill this friar.

17

"Praised be the Lord," said the priest and placed the candlestick on the table. Goldmund murmured the response, staring straight ahead.

The priest said nothing. He waited and said nothing, until Goldmund grew restless and searchingly raised his eyes to the man in front of him.

This man, he now saw to his confusion, was not only wearing the habit of the fathers of Mariabronn, ho also wore the insignia of the office of Abbot.

And now he looked into the Abbot's face. It was a bony face, firmly, clearly cut, with very thin lips. It was a face he knew. As though spellbound, Goldmund looked into this face that seemed completely formed by mind and will. With unsteady hand he reached for the candlestick, lifted it and held it closer to the stranger, to see his eyes. He saw them and the candlestick shook in his hand as he put it back on the table.

"Narcissus!" he whispered almost inaudibly. The cellar began to spin around him.

"Yes, Goldmund, I used to be Narcissus, but I abandoned that name a long time ago; you've probably forgotten. Since the day I took the vows, my name has been John."

Goldmund was shaken to the roots of his being. The whole world had changed, and the sudden collapse of his superhuman effort threatened to choke him. He trembled; dizziness made his head

feel like an empty bladder; his stomach contracted. Behind his eyes something burned like scalding
sobs. He longed to sink into himself, to dissolve in
tears, to faint.

But a warning rose from the depths of the memories of his youth, the memories that the sight of
Narcissus had conjured up: once, as a boy, he had
cried, had let himself go in front of this beautiful,
strict face, these dark omniscient eyes. He could
never do that again. Like a ghost, Narcissus had
reappeared at the strangest moment of his life,
probably to save his life—and now he was about to
break into sobs in front of him again, or faint? No,
no, no. He controlled himself. He subdued his heart,
forced his stomach to be calm, willed the dizziness
out of his head. He could not show any weakness
now.

In an artificially controlled voice, he managed to
say: "You must permit me to go on calling you
Narcissus."

"Do, my friend. And don't you want to shake my
hand?"

Again Goldmund dominated himself. With a
boyishly stubborn, slightly ironic tone, like the one
he had occasionally taken in his student days, he
forced out an answer.

"Forgive me, Narcissus," he said coldly and a
trifle blasé. "I see that you have become Abbot.
But I'm still a vagrant. And besides, our conversation, as much as I desire it, won't unfortunately last
very long. Because, Narcissus, I've been sentenced
to the gallows, and in an hour, or sooner, I'll probably be hanged. I say this only to clarify the situation for you."

Narcissus's expression did not change. He was
much amused by the boyish boasting streak in his
friend's attitude and at the same time touched. But
he understood and keenly appreciated the pride
that kept Goldmund from collapsing tearfully

against his chest. He, too, had imagined their reunion differently, but he had no objection whatsoever to this little comedy. Goldmund could not have charmed his way back into his heart any faster.

"Well yes," he said, with the same pretended casualness. "But I can reassure you about the gallows. You've been pardoned. I have been sent to tell you that, and to take you away with me. Because you cannot remain in this city. So we'll have plenty of time to chat with each other. Now will you shake my hand?"

They shook hands, holding on for a long time, pressing hard and feeling deeply moved, but their words stayed brittle and playful for a while longer.

"Fine, Narcissus, let's leave this scarcely honorable retreat, and I'll join your retinue. Are you traveling back to Mariabronn? You are. Wonderful. How? On horseback? Splendid. Then it will be a question of getting a horse for me."

"We'll get a horse for you, *amicus,* and in two hours we'll be on our way. Oh, but what happened to your hands! For heaven's sake, they are completely raw and swollen, and bleeding! Oh, Goldmund, what have they done to you!"

"Never mind, Narcissus. I did that to my hands myself. They had tied me up and I had to get free. It wasn't easy. Besides, it was rather courageous of you to come in here without an escort."

"Why courageous? There was no danger."

"Oh, only the slight danger of being murdered by me. Because that's what I had planned to do. They had told me a priest would come. I'd have murdered him and fled in his robes. A good plan."

"You didn't want to die then? You wanted to fight?"

"Indeed I did. Of course I could hardly guess that the priest would be you."

"Still," Narcissus said hesitantly, "that was a rather ugly plan. Would you really have been ca-

pable of murdering a priest who'd come to confess
you?"

"Not you, Narcissus, of course, and probably no
priest who wore the habit of Mariabronn. But any
other kind of priest, yes, I assure you." Suddenly
his voice grew sad and dark. "It would not have
been the first man I've murdered."

They were silent. Both felt embarrassed.

"Well, we'll talk about that some other time,"
Narcissus said in a cool voice. "You can confess to
me some day, if you feel like it. Or you can tell me
about your life. I, too, have this and that to tell you.
I'm looking forward to it. Shall we go?"

"One moment more, Narcissus! I just remembered something: I did call you John once before."

"I don't understand."

"No, of course you don't. How could you? It
happened quite a number of years ago. I gave you
the name John and it will be your name forever. I
was for a time a carver and a sculptor, and I think
I'd like to become one again. The first statue I
carved in those days was a wooden, life-size disciple with your face, but its name is not Narcissus, it
is John, a St. John under the cross."

He rose and walked to the door.

"So you did think of me?" Narcissus asked softly.

Goldmund answered just as softly: "Oh yes,
Narcissus, I have thought of you. Always, always."

He gave the heavy cellar door a strong push, and
the fallow morning looked in. They spoke no more.
Narcissus took him to his guest chamber. There a
young monk, his companion, was busy readying the
baggage. Goldmund was given food, and his hands
washed and bandaged. Soon the horses were
brought out.

Mounting, Goldmund said: "I have one more
request. Let us pass by the fish market; I have an
errand there."

They rode off and Goldmund looked up at every castle window to see if Agnes might perhaps be visible. He did not see her. They rode to the fish market; Marie had worried a great deal about him. He bade farewell to her and to her parents, thanked them a thousand times, promised to come back one day, and rode off. Marie stood in the doorway of her house until the riders were out of sight. Slowly she limped back inside.

They rode four abreast: Narcissus, Goldmund, the young monk, and an armed groom.

"Do you still remember my little horse Bless?" Goldmund asked. "He was in your stable at the cloister."

"Certainly. But you won't find him there any more, and you probably didn't expect to. It's been at least seven or eight years since we had to do away with him."

"And you remember that?"

"Oh yes, I remember."

Goldmund was not sad about Bless's death. He was glad that Narcissus knew so much about Bless, Narcissus who had never cared about animals and probably had never known another cloister horse by name. That made him very glad.

"With all the people in your cloister," he began again, "you'll laugh at me for asking first about that poor little horse. It wasn't nice of me. Actually I had wanted to ask about something else entirely, about our Abbot Daniel. But I suppose that he is dead since you are his successor. And I didn't intend to speak only of death to begin with. I'm not well inclined toward death at the moment, because of last night, and also because of the plague, of which I saw altogether too much. But now that we're on the subject, and since we'll have to speak about it some time, tell me when and how Abbot Daniel died. I revered him very much. And tell me also if Father Anselm and Father Martin are still alive. I'm prepared for the worst. But I'm glad the plague spared you at least. I never imagined that you might have died; I firmly believed that we would meet again. But belief can deceive, as I was unfortunate enough to learn by experience. I could not imagine that my master Niklaus, the image carver, would be dead either; I counted on seeing him again and working with him again. Nevertheless, he was dead when I got there."

"All is quickly told," said Narcissus. "Abbot Daniel died eight years ago, without illness or pain. I am not his successor; I've been Abbot only for a year. Father Martin was his successor, the former head of our school. He died last year; he was almost seventy. And Father Anselm is no longer with us either. He was fond of you, he often spoke of you. During his last years he could no longer walk at all, and lying in bed was a great torture to him; he died of dropsy. Yes, and we too had the plague; many died. Let's not speak of it. Have you any other questions?"

"Certainly, many more. Most of all: how do you happen to be here in the bishop's city at the governor's palace?"

"That is a long story, and you'd be bored with it; it is a matter of politics. The count is a favorite of the Emperor and his executor in many matters, and at this moment there are many things to be set to rights between the Emperor and our religious order. I was one of the delegates sent to treat with the count. Our success was small."

He fell silent and Goldmund asked nothing more. He had no need to know that last night, when Narcissus had pleaded for Goldmund's life, that life had been paid for with a number of concessions to the ruthless count.

They rode; Goldmund soon felt tired and had difficulty staying in the saddle.

After a long while Narcissus asked: "But is it

true that you were arrested for theft? The count said you had sneaked into the inner rooms of the castle, where you were caught stealing."

Goldmund laughed. "Well, it really looked as though I were a thief. But I had a meeting with the count's mistress; he doubtless knew that, too. I'm surprised that he let me go at all."

"Well, he wasn't above a little bargaining."

They could not cover the distance they had set themselves for that day. Goldmund was too exhausted; his hands could no longer hold the reins. They took rooms in a village for the night; he was put to bed running a slight fever, and they kept him in bed the next day, too. But then he was strong enough to ride on. Soon his hands were healed and he began to enjoy riding. How long since he had last ridden! He came to life again, grew young and animated, rode many a race with the groom, and during hours of conversation assaulted his friend Narcissus with hundreds of impatient questions. Calmly, yet joyously, Narcissus responded. Again he was charmed by Goldmund. He loved these vehement, childlike questions, all asked with unlimited confidence in his own ability to answer them.

"One question, Narcissus: did you also burn Jews?"

"Burn Jews? How could we? There are no Jews where we are."

"All right. But tell me: would you be capable of burning Jews? Can you imagine such a possibility?"

"No, why should I? Do you take me for a fanatic?"

"Understand me, Narcissus. I mean: can you imagine that, in certain circumstances, you might give the order to kill Jews, or consent to their being killed? So many dukes, mayors, bishops, and other authorities did give such orders."

"I would not give an order of that kind. On the other hand it is conceivable that I might have to witness and tolerate such cruelty."

"You'd tolerate it then?"

"Certainly, if I had no power to prevent it. You probably saw some Jews being burned, didn't you, Goldmund?"

"I did."

"Well, and did you prevent it? You didn't. You see."

Goldmund told the story of Rebekka in great detail; he grew hot and passionate in telling it.

"And so," he concluded violently, "what is this world in which we are made to live? Is it not hell? Is it not revolting and disgusting?"

"Certainly, that's how the world is."

"Ah!" Goldmund cried with indignation. "And how often you told me that the world was divine, that it was a great harmony of circles with the Creator enthroned in its midst, that what existed was good, and so forth. You told me Aristotle had said so, or Saint Thomas. I'm eager to hear you explain the contradiction."

Narcissus laughed.

"Your memory is surprising, and yet it has deceived you slightly. I have always adored our Creator as perfect, but never his creation. I have never denied the evil in the world. No true thinker has ever affirmed that life on earth is harmonious and just, or that man is good, my dear friend. On the contrary. The Holy Bible expressly states that the strivings and doings of man's heart are evil, and every day we see this confirmed anew."

"Very good. At last I see what you learned men mean. So man is evil, and life on earth is full of ugliness and trickery—you admit it. But somewhere behind all that, in your thoughts and books, justice and perfection exist. They exist, they can be proved, but only if they are never put to use."

"You have stored up a great deal of anger against us theologians, dear friend! But you have still not become a thinker; you've got it all topsy-turvy. You still have a few things to learn. But why do you say we don't put justice to use? We do that every day, every hour. I, for instance, am an abbot and I govern a cloister. Life in this cloister is just as imperfect and full of sin as it is in the world outside. And yet we constantly set the idea of justice against original sin and try to measure our imperfect lives by it and try to correct evil and put ourselves in everlasting relationship with God."

"All right, Narcissus. I don't mean you, nor did I mean that you were not a good abbot. But I'm thinking of Rebekka, of the burned Jews, the mass burials, the Great Death, of the alleys and rooms full of stinking corpses, of all the gruesome looting, the haggard, abandoned children, of dogs starved to death on their chains—and when I think of all that and see these images before me, then my heart aches and it seems to me that our mothers have borne us into a hopeless, cruel, devilish world, and that it would be better if they had never conceived, if God had not created this horrible world, if the Saviour had not let himself be nailed to the cross in vain."

Narcissus gave Goldmund a friendly nod.

"You are quite right," he said warmly. "Go ahead, say it all, get it all out. But in one thing you are quite wrong: you think that the things you have said are thoughts. But actually they are feelings. They are the feelings of a man preoccupied with the horror of life, and you must not forget that these sad, desperate emotions are balanced by completely different ones! When you feel happy on a horse, riding through a pretty landscape, or when you sneak somewhat recklessly into a castle at night to court a count's mistress, then the world looks altogether different to you, and no plague-stricken house or burned Jew can prevent you from fulfilling your desire. Is that not so?"

"Certainly that is so. Because the world is so full of death and horror, I try again and again to console my heart and to pick the flowers that grow in the midst of hell. I find bliss, and for an hour I forget the horror. But that does not mean that it does not exist."

"You expressed that very well. So you find yourself surrounded by death and horror in the world, and you escape it into lust. But lust has no duration; it leaves you again in the desert."

"Yes, that's true."

"Most people feel that way, but only a few feel it with such sharpness and violence as you do; few feel the need to become aware of these feelings. But tell me: besides this desperate coming and going between lust and horror, besides this seesaw between lust for life and sadness of death—have you tried no other road?"

"Oh yes, of course I have. I've tried art. I've already told you that, among other things, I also became an artist. One day, when I had roamed the world for three years perhaps, wandering almost all the time, I saw a wooden madonna in a cloister church. It was so beautiful, the sight moved me so deeply, that I asked the name of the sculptor who carved it and searched for him. I found him, he was a famous master; I became his apprentice and worked with him for a few years."

"You'll tell me more about that later. But what has art meant to you, what has art brought to you?"

"It was the overcoming of the transitory. I saw that something remained of the fools' play, the death dance of human life, something lasting: works of art. They too will probably perish some day; they'll burn or crumble or be destroyed. Still, they outlast many human lives; they form a silent empire of images and relics beyond the fleeting moment. To work at that seems good and comforting to me, because it almost succeeds in making the transitory eternal."

"I like that very much, Goldmund. I hope you will again make beautiful statues; my confidence in your strength is great. I hope you will be my guest in Mariabronn for a long time and permit me to set up a workshop for you; our cloister has long since been without an artist. But I do not think your definition quite encompassed the miracle of art. I believe that art is more than salvaging something mortal from death and transforming it into stone, wood, and color, so that it lasts a little longer. I have seen many works of art, many a saint and many a madonna, which did not seem to me merely faithful copies of a specific person who once lived and whose shapes or colors the artist has preserved."

"You are right in that," Goldmund cried eagerly. "I didn't think you were so well informed about art! The basic image of a good work of art is not a real, living figure, although it may inspire it. The basic image is not flesh and blood; it is mind. It is an image that has its home in the artist's soul. In me, too, Narcissus, such images are alive, which I hope to express one day and show to you."

"How lovely! And now, my dear Goldmund, you have strayed unknowingly into philosophy and have expressed one of its secrets."

"You're mocking me."

"Oh no. You spoke of 'basic images,' of images that exist nowhere except in the creative mind, but which can be realized and made visible in matter. Long before a figure becomes visible and gains reality, it exists as an image in the artist's soul. This image then, this 'basic image,' is exactly what the old philosophers call an 'idea.'"

"Yes, that sounds quite plausible."

"Well, and now that you have pledged yourself to ideas and to basic images, you are on mind-ground, in the world of philosophers and theologians, and you admit that, at the center of the confused, painful battlefield of life, at the center of the endless and meaningless death dance of fleshly existence, there exists the creative mind. Look, I have always addressed myself to this mind in you, ever since you came to me as a boy. In you, this mind is not that of a thinker but that of an artist. But it is mind, and it is the mind that will show you the way out of the blurred confusion of the world of the senses, out of the eternal seesaw between lust and despair. Ah, my dear friend, I am happy to have heard this confession from you. I have waited for it—since the day you left your teacher Narcissus and found the courage to be yourself. Now we can be friends anew."

It seemed to Goldmund that his life had been given a meaning. For a moment it was as though he were looking down on it from above, clearly seeing its three big steps: his dependence on Narcissus and his awakening; then the period of freedom and wandering; and now the return, the reflection, the beginning of maturity and harvest.

The vision faded again. But he had found a fitting relationship to Narcissus. It was no longer a relationship of dependence, but one of equality and reciprocity. He could be the guest of this superior mind without humiliation, since the other man had given recognition to the creative power in him. During their journey he looked forward with increasing eagerness to revealing himself to him, to making his inner world visible to him in works of images. But sometimes he also worried.

"Narcissus," he warned, "I'm afraid you don't know whom you're bringing into your cloister. I'm no monk, nor do I wish to become one. I know the three main vows. I gladly accept poverty, but I love neither chastity nor obedience; these virtues don't seem very manly to me. And I have nothing at all left of piety. I haven't confessed or prayed or taken communion in years."

Narcissus remained calm. "You seem to have become a pagan. But we are not afraid of that. You need not pride yourself any longer on your many sins. You have lived the usual life of the world. You have herded swine like the prodigal son; you no longer know what law and order mean. Surely you'd make a very bad monk. But I'm not inviting you to enter the order; I'm merely inviting you to be our guest and to set up a workshop for yourself in our cloister. And one thing more: don't forget that, during your adolescent years, it was I who awakened you and let you go into the worldly life. Whatever has become of you, good or bad, is my responsibility as well as yours. I want to see what has become of you; you will show me, in words, in life, in your works. After you have shown me, if I find that our house is no place for you, I shall be the first to ask you to leave again."

Goldmund was full of admiration every time his friend spoke in this manner, when he acted the abbot, with quiet assurance and a hint of mockery of people and life in the world, because then he saw what Narcissus had become: a man. True, a man of the mind and of the church, with delicate hands and a scholar's face, but a man full of assurance and courage, a leader, one who bore responsibility. This man Narcissus was no longer the adolescent of old times, no longer the gentle, devoted St. John; he wanted to carve this new Narcissus, the manly, knightly Narcissus. Many statues awaited him: Narcissus, Abbot Daniel, Father Anselm, Master Niklaus, beautiful Rebekka, beautiful Agnes, and still others, friends and enemies, alive and dead. No, he did not want to become a brother of the order, or a pious or learned man; he wanted to make statues, and the thought that his youthful home was to be the home of these works made him happy.

They rode through the chill of late autumn, and one day, on a morning when the bare trees hung thick with frost, they rode across a wide rolling land of deserted reddish moors, and the long chains of hills looked strangely familiar, and then came a high elm wood and a little stream and an old barn at the sight of which Goldmund's heart began to ache in happy anguish. He recognized the hills across which he had once ridden with the knight's daughter Lydia, and the heath across which he had walked that day of thinly falling snow, banished and deeply sad. The elm clumps emerged, and the mill, and the castle. With particular pain he recognized the window of the writing room in which he had then, during his legendary youth, corrected the knight's Latin and heard him tell of his pilgrimage. They rode into the courtyard; it was one of the regular stopping places of the journey. Goldmund asked the Abbot not to tell anyone there his name and to let him eat with the servants, as the groom did. That's how it was arranged. The old knight was no longer there and neither was Lydia, but a few of the old hunters and servants were still part of the household, and in the castle a very beautiful, proud, and domineering noblewoman, Julie, lived and reigned at her husband's side. She still looked wonderfully beautiful, and a little evil. Neither she nor the servants recognized Goldmund. After the meal, in the fading light of evening he crept into the garden, looked over the fence at the already wintery flower beds, crept to the stable door and looked in on the horses. He slept on the straw with the groom, and memories weighed heavily on his chest; he awakened many times. Scattered and infertile, the scenes of his life stretched out behind

him, rich in magnificent images but broken in so
many pieces, so poor in value, so poor in love! In
the morning, as they rode away, he looked anxiously up to the windows. Perhaps he could catch
another glimpse of Julie. A few days ago he had
looked just as anxiously up to the windows of the
bishop's palace to see if Agnes might not appear.
She had not shown herself, and neither did Julie.
His whole life had been like that, it seemed to him.
Saying farewell, escaping, being forgotten; finding
himself alone again, with empty hands and a frozen heart. He felt like that throughout the day,
sitting gloomily in the saddle, not speaking at all.
Narcissus let him be.

But now they were approaching their goal, and
after a few days they had reached it. Shortly before tower and roofs of the cloister became visible,
they rode across the fallow stony fields in which he
had, oh so long ago, gathered John's-wort for Father Anselm, where the gypsy Lise had made a
man of him. And now they rode through the gates
of Mariabronn and dismounted under the Italian
chestnut tree. Tenderly Goldmund touched the
trunk and stooped to pick up one of the prickly,
split husks that lay on the ground, brown and
withered.

18

During the first days Goldmund lived in the cloister, in one of the guest cells. Then, at his own request, he was given a room across the forge, in one of the administrative buildings that surrounded the main yard like a marketplace.

His homecoming put him under a spell, so violent that he himself was astonished by it. Outside the Abbot no one knew him here, no one knew who he was. The people, monks as well as lay brothers, lived a well-ordered life and had their own special occupations, and left him in peace. But the trees of the courtyard knew him, the portals and windows knew him, the mill and the water wheel, the flagstones of the corridors, the wilted rosebushes in the arcade, the storks' nests on the refectory and granary roofs. From every corner of his past, the scent of his early adolescence came toward him, sweetly and movingly. Love drove him to see everything again, to hear all the sounds again, the bells for evening prayer and Sunday mass, the gushing of the dark millstream between its narrow, mossy banks, the slapping of sandals on the stone floors, the twilight jangle of the key ring as the brother porter went to lock up. Beside the stone gutters, into which the rainwater fell from the roof of the lay refectory, the same herbs were still sprouting, crane's-bill and plantain, and the old apple tree in the forge garden was still holding its far-reaching branches in the same way. But more than anything else the tinkling of the little school bell moved him. It was the moment when, at the beginning of recess, all the cloister students came tumbling down the stairs into the courtyard. How young and dumb and pretty the boys' faces were—had he, too, once really been so young, so clumsy, so pretty and childish?

Beside this familiar cloister he had also found one that was unknown, one which even during the first days struck his attention and became more and more important to him until it slowly linked itself to the more familiar one. Because, if nothing new had been added, if everything was as it had been during his student days, and a hundred or more years before that, he was no longer seeing it with the eyes of a student. He saw and felt the dimension of these edifices, of the vaults of the church, the power of old paintings, of the stone and wood figures on the altars, in the portals, and although he saw nothing that had not been there before, he only now perceived the beauty of these things and of the mind that had created them. He saw the old stone Mother of God in the upper chapel. Even as a boy he had been fond of it, and had copied it, but only now did he see it with open eyes, and realize how miraculously beautiful it was, that his best and most successful work could never surpass it. There were many such wonderful things, and each was not placed there by chance but was born of the same mind and stood between the old columns and arches as though in its natural home. All that had been built, chiseled, painted, lived, thought and taught here in the course of hundreds of years had grown from the same roots, from the same spirit, and everything was held together and unified like the branches of a tree.

Goldmund felt very small in this world, in this quiet mighty unity, and never did he feel smaller than when he saw Abbot John, his friend Narcissus, rule over and govern this powerful yet quietly friendly order. There might be tremendous differences of character between the learned, thin-lipped Abbot John and the kindly simple Abbot Daniel, but each of them served the same unity, the same thought, the same order of existence, received his dignity from it, sacrificed his person to it. That made them as similar to one another as their priestly robes.

In the center of his cloister, Narcissus grew eerily tall in Goldmund's eyes, although he was never anything but a cordial friend and host. Soon Goldmund hardly dared call him Narcissus any more.

"Listen, Abbot John," he once said to him, "I'll have to get used to your new name eventually. I must tell you that I like it very much in your house. I almost feel like making a general confession to you and, after penance and absolution, asking to be received as a lay brother. But you see, then our friendship would be over; you'd be the Abbot and I a lay brother. But I can no longer bear to live next to you like this and see your work and not be or do anything myself. I too would like to work and show you who I am and what I can do, so that you can see if it was worth snatching me from the gallows."

"I'm glad to hear it," said Narcissus, pronouncing his words even more clearly and precisely than usual. "You may set up your workshop any time you wish. I'll put the blacksmith and the carpenter at your disposal immediately. Please use any material you find here and make a list of all the things you want brought in from the outside. And now hear what I think about you and your intentions! You must give me a little time to express myself: I am a scholar and would like to try to illustrate the matter to you from my own world of thought; I have no other language. So follow me once more, as you so often did so patiently in earlier years."

"I'll try to follow you. Go ahead and speak."

"Recall how, even in our student days, I sometimes told you that I thought you were an artist. In those days I thought you might become a poet; in your reading and writing you had a certain dislike for the intangible and the abstract, and a special love for words and sounds that had sensuous poetic qualities, words that appealed to the imagination."

Goldmund interrupted. "Forgive me, but aren't the concepts and abstractions which you prefer to use really images too? Or do you really prefer to think in words with which one cannot imagine anything? But can one think without imagining anything?"

"I'm glad you ask! Yes, certainly one can think without imagining anything! Thinking and imagining have nothing whatsoever in common. Thinking is done not in images but with concepts and formulae. At the exact point where images stop, philosophy begins. That was precisely the subject of our frequent quarrels as young men; for you, the world was made of images, for me of ideas. I always told you that you were not made to be a thinker, and I also told you that this was no lack since, in exchange, you were a master in the realm of images. Pay attention and I'll explain it to you. If, instead of immersing yourself in the world, you had become a thinker, you might have created evil. Because you would have become a mystic. Mystics are, to express it briefly and somewhat crudely, thinkers who cannot detach themselves from images, therefore not thinkers at all. They are secret artists: poets without verse, painters without brushes, musicians without sound. There are highly gifted, noble minds among them, but they are all without exception unhappy men. You, too, might have become such a man. Instead of which you have, thank God, become an artist and have taken possession of the image world in which you can be a creator and a master, instead of being stranded in discontentment as a thinker."

"I'm afraid," said Goldmund, "I'll never succeed in grasping the idea of your thought world, in which one thinks without images."

"Oh yes, you will, and right now. Listen: the thinker tries to determine and to represent the nature of the world through logic. He knows that reason and its tool, logic, are incomplete—the way an intelligent artist knows full well that his brushes or chisels will never be able to express perfectly the radiant nature of an angel or a saint. Still they both try, the thinker as well as the artist, each in his way. They cannot and may not do otherwise. Because when a man tries to realize himself through the gifts with which nature has endowed him, he does the best and only meaningful thing he can do. That's why, in former days, I often said to you: don't try to imitate the thinker or the ascetic man, but be yourself, try to realize yourself."

"I understand something of what you say, but what does it mean to realize oneself?"

"It is a philosophical concept, I can't express it in any other way. For us disciples of Aristotle and St. Thomas, it is the highest of all concepts: perfect being. God is perfect being. Everything else that exists is only half, only a part, is becoming, is mixed, is made up of potentialities. But God is not mixed. He is one, he has no potentialities but is the total, the complete reality. Whereas we are transitory, we are becoming, we are potentials; there is no perfection for us, no complete being. But wherever we go, from potential to deed, from possibility to realization, we participate in true being, become by a degree more similar to the perfect and divine. That is what it means to realize oneself. You must know this from your own experience, since you're an artist and have made many statues. If such a figure is really good, if you have released a man's image from the changeable and brought it to pure form—then you have, as an artist, realized this human image."

"I understand."

"You see me, friend Goldmund, in a place and function where it is made rather easy for me to realize myself. You see me living in a community and a tradition that corresponds to me and furthers me. A cloister is no heaven. It is filled with imperfections. Still, a decently run cloister life is infinitely more helpful to men of my nature than the worldly life. I don't wish to speak morally, but from a merely practical point of view, pure thinking, the practice and teaching of which is my task, offers a certain protection from the world. It was much easier for me to realize myself here in our house than it would have been for you. But, in spite of the difficulty, you found a way to become an artist, and I admire that a great deal. Your life has been much harder than mine."

This praise made Goldmund blush with embarrassment, and also with pleasure. In order to change the subject, he interrupted his friend: "I've been able to understand most of what you wanted to tell me. But there is one thing I still can't get through my head: the thing you call 'pure thinking.' I mean your so-called thinking without images, and the use of words with which one cannot imagine anything."

"Well, you'll be able to understand it with an example. Think of mathematics. What kind of images do figures contain? Or the plus and minus signs? What kind of images does an equation contain? None. When you solve a problem in arithmetic or algebra, no image will help you solve it, you execute a formal task within the codes of thought that you have learned."

"That's right, Narcissus. If you give me a row of figures and symbols, I can work through them without using my imagination, I can let myself be guided by plus and minus, square roots, and so on, and can solve the problem. That is—I once could, today I could no longer do it. But I can't imagine that solving such a formal problem can have any other value than exercising a student's brain. It's all right to learn how to count. But I'd find it meaningless and childish if a man spent his whole life counting and covering paper with rows of figures."

"You are wrong, Goldmund. You assume that this zealous problem-solver continuously solves problems a teacher poses for him. But he can also ask himself questions; they can arise within him as compelling forces. A man must have measured and puzzled over much real and much fictitious space mathematically before he can risk facing the problem of space itself."

"Well, yes. But attacking the problem of space with pure thought does not strike me as an occupation on which a man should waste his work and his years. The word 'space' means nothing to me and is not worth thinking about unless I can imagine real space, say the space between stars; now, studying and measuring star space does not seem an unworthy task to me."

Smilingly, Narcissus interrupted: "You are actually saying that you have a rather low opinion of thinking, but a rather high one of the application of thought to the practical, visible world. I can answer you: we lack no opportunities to apply our thinking, nor are we unwilling to do so. The thinker Narcissus has, for instance, applied the results of his thinking a hundred times to his friend Goldmund, as well as to each of his monks, and does so at every instant. But how would he be able to 'apply' something if he had not learned and practiced it before? And the artist also constantly exercises his eye and imagination, and we recognize this training, even if it finds realization only in a few good works. You cannot dismiss thinking as such and sanction only its 'application'! The contradiction is obvious. So let me go on thinking and judge my thoughts by their results, as I shall judge your art by your works. You are restless now and irritable because there are still obstacles between you and your works. Clear them out of the way. Find or build a workshop for yourself and get to work! Many problems will be solved automatically that way."

Goldmund wished nothing better.

Beside the courtyard gate he found a shed that was both empty and suitable for a workshop. He ordered a drawing board and other tools from the carpenter, all to be made after precise plans he drew himself. He made a list of the materials which the cloister carters were to bring him from nearby cities, a long list. He inspected all the felled timber at the carpenter's and in the forest, chose many pieces and had them carried to the grassy lot behind his workshop, where he piled them up to dry under a roof he built with his own hands. He also had much work to do with the blacksmith, whose son, a dreamy young man, was completely charmed and won over by him. Together they stood half the day at the forge, over the anvil, by the cooling trough or the whetstone, making all the bent or straight cutting knives, the chisels, drills, and planes he needed for his work. The smith's son, Erich, an adolescent of almost twenty, became Goldmund's friend. He helped him with everything and was full of glowing interest and curiosity. Goldmund promised to teach him to play the lute, which he fervently desired, and he also allowed him to try his hand at carving. If at times Goldmund felt rather useless and depressed in the cloister and in Narcissus's presence, he was able to recover in the presence of Erich, who loved him timidly and admired him immensely. He often asked him to tell him about Master Niklaus and the bishop's city. Sometimes Goldmund was glad to tell stories. Then he would be suddenly astonished to find himself sitting like an old man, talking about the travels and adventures of the past, when his true life was only now about to begin.

Recently he had changed greatly and aged far beyond his years, but this was visible to no one, since only one man here had known him before. The hardships of his wandering and unsettled life may already have undermined his strength, but the plague and its many horrors, and finally his captivity at the count's residence and that gruesome night in the castle cellar had shaken him to his roots, and several signs of these experiences stayed with him: gray hair in his blond beard, wrinkles on his face, periods of insomnia, and occasionally a certain fatigue inside the heart, a slackening of desire and curiosity, a gray shallow feeling of having had enough, of being fed up. During preparations for his work, during his conversations with Erich or his pursuits at the blacksmith's and at the carpenter's, he grew vivacious and young and all admired him and were fond of him; but at other times he'd sit for hours, exhausted, smiling and dreaming, given over to apathy and indifference.

The question of where to begin was very important to him. The first work he wanted to make here, and with which he wanted to pay for the cloister's hospitality, was not to be an arbitrary piece that one placed just anywhere for the sake of curiosity, no, it had to blend with the old works of the house and with the architecture and life of the cloister and become part of the whole. He would have especially liked to make an altar or perhaps a pulpit, but there was no need or room for either. He found another place instead. There was a raised niche in the refectory, from which a young brother read passages from the lives of the saints during meals. This niche had no ornament. Goldmund decided to carve for the steps to the lectern and for the lectern itself a set of wooden panels like those around a pulpit, with many figures in half-relief and others almost free-standing. He explained his plan to the Abbot, who praised and accepted it.

When finally he could begin—snow had fallen, Christmas was already over—Goldmund's life took on another form. He seemed to have disappeared from the cloister; nobody saw him any more. He no longer waited for the students at the end of classes, no longer drifted through the woods, no longer strolled under the arcades. He took his meals in the mill—it wasn't the same miller now whom he had often visited as a student. And he allowed no one but his assistant Erich to enter his workshop; and on certain days Erich did not hear a word out of him.

For this first work he had long since thought out the following design: it was to be in two parts, one representing the world, the other the word of God. The lower part, the stairs, growing out of a sturdy oak trunk and winding around it, was to represent creation, images of nature and of the simple life of the patriarchs and the prophets. The upper part, the parapet, would bear the pictures of the four apostles. One of the evangelists was to have the traits of blessed Abbot Daniel; another those of blessed Father Martin, his successor; and the statue of Luke was to eternalize Master Niklaus.

He met with great obstacles, greater than he had anticipated. And these obstacles gave him many worries, but they were sweet worries. Now enchanted and now despairing, he wooed his work as though it were a reluctant woman, struggled with it as firmly and gently as a fisherman struggling with a giant pike, and each resistance taught him and made him more sensitive. He forgot everything else. He forgot the cloister; he almost forgot Narcissus. Narcissus came a number of times, but was only shown drawings.

Then one day Goldmund surprised him with the request that he hear his confession.

"I could not bring myself to confess before," he admitted. "I felt too small, and I already felt small enough in front of you. Now I feel bigger, now I have my work and am no longer a nobody. And since I am living in a cloister, I'd like to submit myself to the rules."

Now he felt equal to the task and did not want to wait a moment longer. Those first meditative weeks at the cloister, the abandonment of all the homecoming, all the memories of youth, as well as the stories Erich asked him for, had allowed him to see his life with a certain order and clarity.

Without solemnity Narcissus received his confession. It lasted about two hours. With immobile face the Abbot listened to the adventures, sufferings, and sins of his friend, posed many questions, never interrupted, and listened passively also to the part of the confession in which Goldmund admitted that his faith in God's justice and goodness had disappeared. He was struck by many of the admissions of the confessing man. He could see how much he had been shaken and terrified, how close he had sometimes come to perishing. Then again he was moved to smile, touched when he found that his friend's nature had remained so innocent, when he found him worried and repentant because of impious thoughts which were harmless enough compared to his own dark abysses of doubt.

To Goldmund's surprise, to his disappointment even, the father confessor did not take his actual sins too seriously, but reprimanded and punished him unsparingly because of his neglect in praying, confession, and communion. He imposed the following penance upon him: to live moderately and chastely for a month before receiving communion, to hear early mass every morning, and to say three Our Fathers and one Hail Mary every evening.

Afterwards he said to him: "I exhort you, I beg you not to take this penance lightly. I don't know if you can still remember the exact text of the mass. You are to follow it word by word and give yourself up to its meaning. I will myself say the Our Father and a few canticles with you today, and give you instructions as to the words and meanings to which you are to direct your particular attention. You are to speak and hear the sacred words not the way one speaks and hears human words. Every time you catch yourself just reeling off the words, and this will happen more often than you expect, you are to remember this hour and my exhortation, and you are to begin all over again and speak the words in such a way as to let them enter your heart, as I am about to show you."

Whether it was a beautiful coincidence, or whether the Abbot's knowledge of souls was great enough to achieve it, a period of fulfillment and peace came for Goldmund from this confession and penance. It made him profoundly happy. Amid the many tensions, worries, and satisfactions of his work, he found himself morning and evening released by the easy but conscientiously executed spiritual exercises, relaxed after the excitements of the day, his entire being submitted to a higher order that lifted him out of the dangerous isolation of the creator and included him as a child in God's world. Although the battles of his work had to be overcome in solitude, and he had to give it all the passions of his senses, these hours of meditation let him return to innocence again and again. Still hot with the rage and impatience of his work, or moved to ecstasy, he would plunge into the pious exercises as though into deep, cool water that washed him clean of the arrogance of enthusiasm as well as the arrogance of despair.

It did not always succeed. Sometimes he did not become calm and relaxed in the evening, after burning hours of work. A few times he forgot the exercises, and several times, as he tried to immerse himself in them, he was tortured by the thought that saying prayers was, after all, perhaps only childish striving for a God who did not exist or could not help. He compained about it to his friend.

"Continue," said Narcissus. "You promised; you must keep your promise. You are not to think about whether God hears your prayers or whether there is a God such as you imagine. Nor are you to wonder whether your exercises are childish. Compared to Him to whom all our prayers are addressed, all our doing is childish. You must forbid yourself these foolish child's thoughts completely during the exercises. You are to speak the Our Father and the canticles, and give yourself up to the words and fill yourself with them just the way you play the lute or sing. You don't pursue clever thoughts and speculations then, do you? No, you execute one finger position after another as purely and perfectly as possible. While you sing, you don't wonder whether or not singing is useful; you sing. That's how you are to pray."

And once more it worked. Again his taut, avid ego extinguished itself in wide-vaulted order; again the venerable words floated above him like stars.

With great satisfaction, the Abbot saw Goldmund continue his daily exercises for weeks and months after his period of penance was over and after he had received the holy sacraments.

In the meantime Goldmund's work advanced. A small surging world grew from the thick spiral of the stairs: creatures, plants, animals, and people. In their midst stood Noah between grape leaves and grapes. The work was a picture book of praise for the creation of the world and its beauty, free in expression but directed by an inner order and discipline. During all these months no one but Erich saw the work; he was allowed to execute small tasks and thought of nothing but becoming an artist himself. But on certain days not even he was allowed to enter the workshop. On other days Goldmund took his time with him, showed him a few things and let him try, happy to have a believer and a disciple. If the work turned out successfully, he might ask Erich's father to release the boy and let him be trained as his permanent assistant.

He worked at the statues of the evangelists on his best days, when everything was harmonious and no doubts cast their shadows over him. It seemed to him that he was most successful with the figure that bore the traits of Abbot Daniel. He loved it very much; the face radiated kindness and purity. He was less satisfied with the statue of Master Niklaus, even though Erich admired it most of all. This figure revealed discord and sadness. It seemed to be brimming over with lofty plans for creation and yet there was also a desperate awareness of the futility of creating, and mourning for a lost unity and innocence.

When Abbot Daniel was finished, he had Erich clean up the workshop. He hid the remaining statues under a cloth and placed only that one figure in the light. Then he went to Narcissus, and when he found that he was busy, he waited patiently until the next day. At the noon hour he took his friend to see the statue.

Narcissus stood and looked. He stood there, taking his time, examining the work with the attention and care of the scholar. Goldmund stood behind him, in silence, trying to dominate the tempest in his heart. "Oh," he thought, "if one of us does not pass this test, it will be bad. If my work is not good enough, or if he cannot understand it, all my working here will have lost its value. I should have waited longer."

Minutes felt like hours to him, and he thought of the time when Master Niklaus had held his first drawing in his hands. He pressed his hot humid palms together in the effort of waiting.

Narcissus turned to him, and immediately he felt relieved. In his friend's narrow face he saw flower something that had not flowered there since his boyhood years: a smile, an almost timid smile on that face of mind and will, a smile of love and surrender, a shimmer, as though all its loneliness and pride had been pierced for a second and nothing shone from it but a heart full of joy.

"Goldmund," Narcissus said very softly, weighing his words even now, "you don't expect me to become an art expert all of a sudden. You know I'm not. I can tell you nothing about your art that you would not find ridiculous. But let me tell you one thing: at first glance I recognized our Abbot Daniel in this evangelist, and not only him, but also all the things he once meant to us: dignity, kindness, simplicity. As blessed Father Daniel stood before our youthful veneration, he stands here before me now and with him everything that was sacred to us then and that makes those years unforgettable to us. You have given me a generous gift, my friend, and not only have you given our Abbot Daniel back to me; you have opened yourself completely to me for the first time. Now I know who you are. Let us speak about it no longer; I cannot. Oh Goldmund, that this hour has been given us!"

It was quiet in the large room. His friend the Abbot was moved to the depth of his heart. Goldmund saw this and embarrassment choked his breathing.

"Yes," he said curtly, "I am happy. But now it's time to go and eat."

19

For two years Goldmund worked on this group and from the second year on he was given Erich as an apprentice. In the balustrade for the staircase he created a small paradise. With ecstasy he carved a graceful wilderness of trees, brush, and herbs, with birds in the branches, and the heads and bodies of animals emerging everywhere. In the midst of this peacefully sprouting primitive garden, he depicted several scenes from the life of the patriarchs. This industrious life was rarely interrupted. There was seldom a day now when working was impossible for him, when restlessness or boredom made him disgusted with his art. But when he did feel bored or restless he'd give his apprentice a chore and walk or ride into the countryside to breathe in the memory-filled perfume of the free and wandering life of the forest, or visit a peasant's daughter, or hunt, or lie for hours in the green staring into the vaulted halls of treetops, into the sprouting wilderness of ferns and juniper. He would always return after a day or two. Then he'd attack his work with renewed passion, greedily carve the luxuriant herbs, gently, tenderly coax human heads from the wood, forcefully cut a mouth, an eye, a pleated beard. Beside Erich only Narcissus knew the statues and he came often to the workshop, which at times was his favorite place in the cloister. He looked on with joy and astonishment. Everything his friend had carried in his restless, stubborn, boyish heart was coming to flower. There it grew and blossomed, a creation, a small surging world: a game perhaps, but certainly no less worthy a game than playing with logic, grammar, and theology.

Pensively he once said: "I'm learning a great deal from you, Goldmund. I'm beginning to understand what art is. Formerly it seemed to me that, compared to thinking and science, it could not be taken altogether seriously. I thought something like this: since man is a dubious mixture of mind and matter, since the mind unlocks recognition of the eternal to him, while matter pulls him down and binds him to the transitory, he should strive away from the senses and toward the mind if he wishes to elevate his life and give it meaning. I did pretend, out of habit, to hold art in high esteem, but actually I was arrogant and looked down upon it. Only now do I realize how many paths there are to knowledge and that the path of the mind is not the only one and perhaps not even the best one. It is my way, of course; and I'll stay on it. But I see that you, on the opposite road, on the road of the senses, have seized the secret of being just as deeply and can express it in a much more lively fashion than most thinkers are able to do."

"Now you understand," Goldmund said, "that I can't conceive of thoughts without images?"

"I have long since understood it. Our thinking is a constant process of converting things to abstractions, a looking away from the sensory, an attempt to construct a purely spiritual world. Whereas you take the least constant, the most mortal things to your heart, and in their very mortality show the meaning of the world. You don't look away from the world; you give yourself to it, and by your sacrifice to it raise it to the highest, a parable of eternity. We thinkers try to come closer to God by pulling the mask of the world away from His face.

You come closer to Him by loving His creation and re-creating it. Both are human endeavors, and necessarily imperfect, but art is more innocent."

"I don't know, Narcissus. But in overcoming life, in resisting despair, you thinkers and theologians seem to succeed better. I have long since stopped envying you for your learning, dear friend, but I do envy your calm, your detachment, your peace."

"You should not envy me, Goldmund. There is no peace of the sort you imagine. Oh, there is peace of course, but not anything that lives within us constantly and never leaves us. There is only the peace that must be won again and again, each new day of our lives. You don't see me fight, you don't know my struggles as Abbot, my struggles in the prayer cell. A good thing that you don't. You only see that I am less subject to moods than you, and you take that for peace. But my life is struggle; it is struggle and sacrifice like every decent life; like yours, too."

"Let's not quarrel about it, Narcissus. You don't see all my struggles either. And I don't know whether or not you are able to understand how I feel when I think that this work will soon be finished, that it will be taken away and set in its place. Then I will hear a few praises and return to a bare workroom, depressed about all the things that I did not achieve in my work, things you others can't even see, and inside I'll feel as robbed and empty as the workshop."

"That may be so," said Narcissus. "Neither of us can ever understand the other completely in such things. But there is one realization all men of good will share: in the end our works make us feel ashamed, we have to start out again, and each time the sacrifice has to be made anew."

A few weeks later Goldmund's big work was finished and set in its place. An old experience repeated itself: his work became the possession of others, was looked at, judged, praised; and he was lauded, honored, but his heart and his workshop stood empty and he no longer knew whether the work had been worth the sacrifice. On the day of the unveiling he was invited to the fathers' table for a festive meal at which the oldest wine of the house was served. Goldmund enjoyed the excellent fish and venison, and even more than by the old wine was warmed by the interest and joy of Narcissus, who praised him and honored his work.

A new work, which the Abbot had asked for and ordered, was already sketched out, an altar for the Mary chapel in Neuzell, which belonged to the cloister and in which a father from Mariabronn officiated as priest. For this altar Goldmund wanted to make a statue of the madonna, and to eternalize in her one of the unforgettable figures of his youth, beautiful fearful Lydia, the knight's daughter. Otherwise this commission was of little importance to him; it seemed suitable to him for Erich's assistant's project. If Erich did well, he'd have a good permanent partner who could replace him, free him to do those works that alone were still close to his heart. With Erich, he chose the wood for the altar and had him prepare it. Often Goldmund left him alone; he had resumed his roaming, his long walks in the woods. Once he was absent for several days, and Erich notified the Abbot, who also feared that Goldmund might have left for good. But he came back, worked for a week on the statue of Lydia, then began to roam again.

He was troubled. Since the completion of his big work his life had been in disorder. He missed early mass; he was deeply restless and dissatisfied. Now he often thought of Master Niklaus and wondered if he himself would not become soon what Niklaus had been, a hard-working and settled master in his craft, but unfree and unyoung. Recently a small adventure had given him food for thought: on one of his wandering days he had found a young peasant girl named Franziska, whom he liked. He had tried to charm her, had employed all the arts of seduction he knew. The girl listened gladly to his chatting, laughed delighted at his jokes, but she refused his advances, and for the first time he realized that, to a young woman, he seemed an old man. He had not gone back, but he had not forgotten. Franziska was right. He was older; he felt it himself, and it was not because of a few premature gray hairs and a few wrinkles around his eyes, but rather something in his being, in his mind. He found himself old, found that he had become strangely similar to Master Niklaus. With ill humor he observed himself and shrugged. He had grown cautious and tame; he was no longer an eagle or a hare; he had become a domestic animal. When he roamed about now, he was looking for the perfume of the past, for memories of his former adventures rather than for new freedom. Like a dog, he looked longingly and distrustfully for the lost scent. And after he had been away for a day or two, loafed a bit and caroused, something drew him irresistibly back. He had a bad conscience. He felt this workshop waiting for him, felt responsible for the altar he had begun, for the prepared wood, for his assistant Erich. He was no longer free, no longer young. He made a firm resolution: after the Lydia-Mary was finished, he wanted to go on a trip and try wandering once more. It was not good to live in a cloister for so long, with men only. It might be good for monks, but not for him. One could speak intelligently with men, and they understood an artist's work, but all the rest—chatting, tenderness, games, love, pleasure without thought—did not flourish among men, for that one needed women, wandering, freedom, and ever new impressions. Everything around him was a little gray and serious here, a little heavy and manly, and he had become contaminated; it had crept into his blood.

The thought of a trip consoled him. He kept to his work courageously in order to be free sooner. And as Lydia's figure gradually came toward him out of the wood, as he draped the strict folds of her dress over her knees, a deep, painful joy overtook him, a nostalgic falling in love with the image, with the beautiful shy girl figure, with his memory of that time, with his first love, his first travels, his youth. Reverently he worked at the delicate image, felt it one with the best within him, with his youth, with his most tender memories. It was a joy to form her inclined neck, her friendly-sad mouth, her elegant hands, the long fingers, the beautifully arched cups of her fingernails. Erich, too, would stare at the figure with admiration and loving respect whenever he had a free moment.

When she was almost finished, Goldmund showed her to the Abbot. Narcissus said: "That is a beautiful work, my dear friend. We have nothing in the whole cloister that measures up to it. I must confess to you that I worried about you on several occasions during the last months. I saw that you were restless and disturbed, and when you disappeared and stayed away for more than a day, I sometimes thought with sorrow: perhaps he's never coming back. And now you have carved this wonderful statue. I am happy for you and proud of you."

"Yes," Goldmund said, "the statue turned out rather well. But now listen to me, Narcissus. In order to make this a good statue, I needed my entire youth, my wandering, my love affairs, my courtship of many women. That is the source at which I have drunk. Soon the well will be empty; I feel dry in my heart. I'll finish this Mary, but then I'll take a good long vacation, I don't know for how long. I'll retrace my youth and all that was once so

dear to me. Can you understand that? Well, yes.
You know I was your guest, and I've never taken
any payment for my work here . . ."

"I often offered it to you," interrupted Narcissus.

"Yes, and now I'll accept it. I'll have new clothes
made, and when they're ready, I'll ask you for a
horse and a few gold pieces and then I'll ride out
into the world. Say nothing, Narcissus, and do not
be sad. It is not that I don't like it here any more; I
couldn't be better off anywhere else. Something
else is at stake. Will you fulfill my wish?"

They spoke about it no more. Goldmund had
made for himself a plain riding outfit and boots,
and as summer drew near, he completed the Mary
figure as though it were his last work. With loving
care he gave the hands, the face, the hair their
finishing touch. It might almost have seemed that
he was prolonging his work, that he was quite
happy to be slightly delayed again and again by
these final delicate touches to the figure. Days
passed, and always there was something new for
him to arrange. Although Narcissus felt deeply sad
about the approaching farewell, he sometimes
smiled a little about Goldmund's being in love,
about his not being able to tear himself away from
the Mary statue.

But one day Goldmund surprised him; suddenly
he came to take his leave. He had made up his
mind during the night. In his new clothes, with a
new cap, he came to Narcissus to say goodbye. He
had already confessed and communed some time
ago. Now he came to bid farewell and be given the
blessing for the road. The leavetaking came hard
to both of them, and Goldmund acted with a
brusqueness and indifference he did not feel in his
heart.

"Will I ever see you again?" asked Narcissus.

"Oh yes, if your pretty nag does not break my
neck, you will certainly see me again. Besides,

without me, there wouldn't be anyone left to call
you Narcissus and cause you to worry. So don't
fear. Yes, and don't forget to keep an eye on Erich.
And let no one touch my statue! She must remain
standing in my room, as I have said before, and you
are not to let the key out of your hand."

"Are you looking forward to the journey?"

Goldmund blinked.

"Well, I was looking forward to it; that's quite
true. But now that I'm about to ride off, it feels less
amusing than one might think. You'll laugh at me,
but I don't like going away; and this dependence
does not please me. It is like an illness; young
healthy men don't have that. Master Niklaus was
that way, too. Well, let's not chat about useless
stuff! Bless me, dear friend; I want to leave."

He rode off.

In his thoughts, Narcissus was greatly concerned
about his friend. He worried about him and missed
him. Would he ever come back? Now this strange
and lovable person was again following his
crooked, will-less path, roaming the world with
desire and curiosity, following his strong dark
drives, stormy and insatiable, a grown child. Might
God be with him; might he come back safe and
sound. Again he would fly hither and thither, the
butterfly, commit new sins, seduce women, follow
his instincts, would perhaps again be involved in
murder, danger, and imprisonment and might perish that way. How much worry this blond boy
caused one! He complained about growing old, all
the while looking out of such boyish eyes! How one
had to fear for him. And yet, deep down in his
heart, Narcissus was happy about Goldmund. It
pleased him very much that this stubborn child
was so difficult to tame, that he had such caprices,
that he had broken out again to shake off his
antlers.

Every day the Abbot's thoughts returned at one

time or another to his friend, with love and longing, gratitude and worry, occasionally also with
doubt and self-reproach. Should he not perhaps
have shown his friend more clearly how much he
loved him, how little he wished him to be other
than he was, how rich he had become through his
being and his art? He had not said much about it,
perhaps not enough—who could tell if he might
not have been able to keep him?

But he had not only been enriched by
Goldmund. He had also grown poorer because of
him, poorer and weaker, and it was certainly good
that he had not shown that to his friend. The world
in which he lived and made his home, his world,
his cloister life, his priestly office, his scholarly
being, his well-constructed thought edifice—all this
had often been shaken to its foundations by his
friend and was now filled with doubt. Certainly,
seen from the point of view of the cloister, from
the point of view of reason and morality, his own
life was better, righter, steadier, more orderly,
more exemplary. It was a life of order and strict
service, an unending sacrifice, a constantly renewed
striving for clarity and justice. It was much purer,
much better than the life of an artist, vagrant, and
seducer of women. But seen from above, with God's
eyes—was this exemplary life of order and discipline, of renunciation of the world and of the joys
of the senses, of remoteness from dirt and blood,
of withdrawal into philosophy and meditation any
better than Goldmund's life? Had man really
been created to live a regulated life, with hours
and duties indicated by prayer bells? Had man
really been created to study Aristotle and Saint
Thomas, to know Greek, to extinguish his senses, to
flee the world? Had God not created him with
senses and instincts, with blood-colored darknesses,
with the capacity for sin, lust, and despair? These

were the questions around which the Abbot's thoughts circled when they dwelt on his friend.

Yes, and was it not perhaps more childlike and human to lead a Goldmund-life, more courageous, more noble perhaps in the end to abandon oneself to the cruel stream of reality, to chaos, to commit sins and accept their bitter consequences rather than live a clean life with washed hands outside the world, laying out a lonely harmonious thought-garden, strolling sinlessly among one's sheltered flower beds. Perhaps it was harder, braver and nobler to wander through forests and along the highways with torn shoes, to suffer sun and rain, hunger and need, to play with the joys of the senses and pay for them with suffering.

At any rate, Goldmund had shown him that a man destined for high things can dip into the lowest depths of the bloody, drunken chaos of life, and soil himself with much dust and blood, without becoming small and common, without killing the divine spark within himself, that he can err through the thickest darkness without extinguishing the divine light and the creative force inside the shrine of his soul. Narcissus had looked deeply into his friend's chaotic life, and neither his love for him nor his respect for him dwindled. Oh no, since he had seen those miraculous still-life images, radiant with inner harmony, come into being under Goldmund's stained hands, those intent faces glowing with spirit, those innocent plants and flowers, those imploring or blessed hands, all those audacious, gentle, proud, or sacred gestures, since then he knew very well that an abundance of light and the gifts of God dwelt in the fickle heart of this artist and seducer.

It had been easy for him to seem superior to Goldmund in their conversations, to oppose his discipline and intellectual order to his friend's passions. But was not every small gesture of one of

Goldmund's figures, every eye, every mouth, every branch and fold of gown worth more? Was it not more real, alive, and irreplaceable than everything a thinker could achieve? Had not this artist, whose heart was so full of conflict and misery, fashioned symbols of need and striving for innumerable people, contemporary and future, figures to which the reverence and respect, the deepest anguish and longing of countless people would turn for consolation, confirmation, and strength?

Smiling and sad, Narcissus remembered all the times since their early youth when he had guided and taught his friend. Gratefully his friend had accepted, always admitting Narcissus's superiority and guidance. And then, quietly, he had fashioned his works, born of the tempest and suffering of his ragged life: no words, no instructions, no explanations, no warnings, but authentic, heightened life. How poor he himself was by comparison, with his knowledge, his cloister discipline, his dialectics!

These were the questions around which his thoughts turned. Just as he had once, many years ago, intervened roughly, almost brutally, in Goldmund's youth and placed his life in a new sphere, so his friend had preoccupied him since his return, had shaken him, had forced him to doubt and self-examination. He was his equal; Narcissus had given him nothing that had not been given back to him many times over.

The friend who had ridden off left him much time for thought. Weeks passed. The chestnut tree had long since lost its blossoms; the milky light-green beech leaves had long since turned dark, firm, and hard; the storks long since had hatched their young on the entrance tower and taught them to fly. The longer Goldmund stayed away, the more Narcissus realized how important he had been to him. He had several learned fathers in the house, an expert on Plato, an excellent grammari-

an, and one or two subtle theologians. And there
were among the monks a few faithful, serious, hon-
est souls. But he had no equal, no one with whom
he could seriously measure himself. This irreplaceable thing only Goldmund had given him. It was
hard to renounce it again now. He thought of his
absent friend with longing.

Often he went to the workshop, to encourage the
assistant Erich, who continued working at the altar
and eagerly awaited his master's return. Sometimes
the Abbot unlocked Goldmund's room, where the
Mary figure stood, lifted the cloth from the figure
carefully and stayed with her awhile. He knew
nothing of the figure's origin; Goldmund had never
told him Lydia's story. But he felt everything;
he saw that the girl's form had long lived in
Goldmund's heart. Perhaps he had seduced her,
perhaps betrayed and left her. But, truer than the
most faithful husband, he had taken her along in
his soul, preserving her image until finally, perhaps
after many years in which he had never seen her
again, he had fashioned this beautiful, touching
statue of a girl and captured in her face, her bearing, her hands all the tenderness, admiration, and
longing of their love. He read much of his friend's
history, too, in the figures of the lectern pulpit in
the refectory. It was the story of a wayfarer, of an
instinctive being, of a homeless, faithless man, but
what had remained of it here was all good and
faithful, filled with living love. How mysterious this
life was, how deep and muddy its waters ran, yet
how clear and noble what emerged from them.

Narcissus struggled. He mastered himself; he did
not betray his calling. He deviated in no way from
his strict service. But he suffered from a sense of
loss and from the recognition of how much his
heart, which was to belong only to God and to his
office, was attached to his friend.

20

The summer passed. Poppies and cornflowers, cockles and starwort wilted and vanished. The frogs grew silent in the pond and the storks flew high and prepared for departure. That's when Goldmund returned.

He arrived one afternoon, during a light rain, and did not go into the cloister; from the portal he went immediately to his workshop. He had come on foot, without the horse.

Erich felt a shock when he saw him come in. Although he recognized him at first glance, and his heart went out to greet him, the man who had come back seemed completely different: a false Goldmund, many years older, with a half-spent, dusty, gray face, sunken cheeks, and sick, suffering eyes, although there was no pain in them, but a smile rather, a kind-hearted, old, patient smile. He walked painfully; he dragged himself, and he seemed to be ill and very tired.

This changed, hardly recognizable Goldmund peered strangely at his assistant. He made no fuss about his return. He acted as though he had merely come in from another room, as though he had never left even for a minute. He shook hands and said nothing, no greeting, no question, no story. He merely said: "I must sleep," he seemed to be terribly tired. He sent Erich away and went into his room next to the workshop. There he pulled off his cap and let it drop, took off his shoes and walked over to the bed. Farther back in the room he saw his madonna standing under a cloth; he nodded but did not go up to her to take off the cloth and greet her. Instead he crept to the little window, saw Erich waiting uneasily outside, and called down to him: "Erich, you needn't tell anybody that I'm back. I'm very tired. It can wait until tomorrow."

Then he lay down on the bed in his clothes. After a while, since he could not fall asleep, he got up and walked heavily to the wall to look into a small mirror that hung there. Attentively he looked at the Goldmund who stared back at him out of the mirror, a weary Goldmund, a man who had grown tired and old and wilted, with much gray in his beard. It was an old, somewhat unkempt man who looked back at him from the little mirror's dull surface—but strangely unfamiliar. It did not seem to be properly present; it did not seem to be of much concern to him. It reminded him of other faces he had known, a little of Master Niklaus, a little of the old knight who had once had a page's outfit made for him, and also a little of St. Jacob in the church, of old bearded St. Jacob who looked so ancient and gray under his pilgrim's hat, and yet still joyous and good.

Carefully he read the mirror face, as though he were interested in finding out about this stranger. He nodded to him and knew him again: yes, it was he; it corresponded to the feeling he had about himself. An extremely tired old man, who had grown slightly numb, who had returned from a journey, an ordinary man in whom one could not take much pride. And yet he had nothing against him. He still liked him; there was something in his face that the earlier, pretty Goldmund had not had. In all the fatigue and disintegration there was a trace of contentment, or at least of detachment. He laughed softly to himself and saw the mirror

image join him: a fine fellow he had brought home
from his trip! Pretty much torn and burned out, he
was returning from his little excursion. He had not
only sacrificed his horse, his satchel, and his gold
pieces; other things, too, had gotten lost or deserted him: youth, health, self-confidence, the color in
his cheeks and the force in his eyes. Yet he liked
the image: this weak old fellow in the mirror was
dearer to him than the Goldmund he had been for
so long. He was older, weaker, more pitiable, but he
was more harmless, he was more content, it was
easier to get along with him. He laughed and
pulled down one of the eyelids that had become
wrinkled. Then he went back to bed and this time
fell asleep.

The next day he sat hunched over the table in
his room and tried to draw a little. Narcissus came
to visit him. He stood in the doorway and said:
"I've been told that you were back. Thank God,
I'm very glad. Since you did not come to see me,
I've come to you. Am I disturbing you in your
work?"

He came closer; Goldmund looked up from his
paper and held out his hand. Although Erich had
prepared him, the sight of his friend shocked Narcissus to the heart. Goldmund gave him a friendly
smile.

"Yes, I'm back. Welcome, Narcissus, we haven't
seen each other for a while. Forgive me for not
coming to you."

Narcissus looked into his eyes. He too saw not
only the exhaustion, the pitiful wilting of this face;
he saw other things besides, strangely pleasing
signs of acceptance, of detachment even, of surrender and old man's good humor. Experienced in
reading human faces, Narcissus also saw that this
changed, different Goldmund was not altogether
there any more, that either his soul was far withdrawn from reality and wandering dream roads or

already standing at the gates that lead to the beyond.

"Are you ill?" he asked cautiously.

"Yes. I am also ill. I fell ill at the very start of my journey, during the very first days. But you'll understand that I didn't want to come home again right away. You'd all have had a good laugh if I had come back so quickly and taken off my traveling boots. No, I didn't feel like it. I went on to roam about a bit; I felt ashamed because my journey was not working out. I had promised myself too much. Yes, I felt ashamed. Surely you understand that, you're an intelligent man. Forgive me, was that what you asked? It's like a curse; I keep forgetting what we're talking about. But that thing with my mother, you did that well. It hurt a lot, but . . ."

His murmuring ended in a smile.

"We'll make you well again, Goldmund, we'll take care of you. If only you had turned right around when you began feeling sick! You really don't have to feel ashamed in front of us. You should have come right back."

Goldmund laughed.

"Yes, now I remember. I didn't dare come back. It would have been shameful. But now I have come. Now I feel well again."

"Have you had great pain?"

"Pain? Yes, I have had pains enough. But you see, pains are not so bad; they've brought me to reason. Now I no longer feel ashamed, not even in front of you. The day you came to see me in prison, to save my life, I had to clench my teeth very hard, because I felt ashamed in front of you. But that is completely over now."

Narcissus put his hand on Goldmund's arm and immediately Goldmund stopped speaking and closed his eyes with a smile. He fell peacefully asleep. Disturbed, the Abbot ran to fetch the house physician, Father Anton, to look after the sick man. When they came back, Goldmund was still sitting fast asleep at his drawing table. They put him to bed and the physician stayed to examine him.

He found him hopelessly ill. He was carried into one of the sick rooms, where Erich kept a constant watch.

The whole story of his last journey was never known. He told a few details; others could be guessed. Often he lay listlessly. Sometimes he had a fever and was delirious; sometimes he was lucid, and then Narcissus was sent for each time. These last conversations with Goldmund became extremely important to him.

Narcissus set down a few fragments of Goldmund's reports and confessions. Others were told by Erich.

"When did the pain start? At the very beginning of my journey. I was riding in the forest and fell with my horse into a brook, where I lay the whole night in cold water. I must have broken several ribs; ever since, I've had pains in my chest. At that time I was not very far from here, but I didn't want to turn back. That was childish, I know, but I thought it would look foolish. So I rode on, and when I could ride no longer, because it hurt too much, I sold the horse, and then I was in a hospital for a long time.

"I'll stay here now, Narcissus. I'll never ride off again. No more wandering. No more dancing, no more women. Oh, otherwise I'd have stayed away much longer, years longer. But when I saw that there was no joy out there for me any more, I thought: before I go under, I want to draw a bit more, and make a few more figures. One does want to have some pleasure after all."

Narcissus said to him: "I'm very glad you've come back. I missed you very much. I thought of you every day, and I was often afraid that you would never want to come back."

Goldmund shook his head: "Well, the loss would not have been great."

Narcissus, his heart burning with grief and love, slowly bent down to him, and now he did what he had never done in the many years of their friendship. He touched Goldmund's hair and forehead with his lips. Astonished at first, and then moved, Goldmund knew what had happened.

"Goldmund," the Abbot whispered into his ear, "forgive me for not being able to tell you earlier. I should have said it to you the day I came to see you in your prison in the bishop's residence, or when I was shown your first statues, or at so many other times. Let me tell you today how much I love you, how much you have always meant to me, how rich you have made my life. It will not mean very much to you. You are used to love; it is not rare for you; so many women have loved and spoiled you. For me it is different. My life has been poor in love; I have lacked the best of life. Our Abbot Daniel once told me that he thought I was arrogant; he was probably right. I am not unjust toward people. I make efforts to be just and patient with them, but I have never loved them. Of two scholars in the cloister, I prefer the one who is more learned; I've never loved a weak scholar in spite of his weakness. If I know nevertheless what love is, it is because of you. I have been able to love you, you alone among all men. You cannot imagine what that means. It means a well in a desert, a blossoming tree in the wilderness. It is thanks to you alone that my heart has not dried up, that a place within me has remained open to grace."

Goldmund smiled happily; he was slightly embarrassed. With the soft, calm voice he had during his lucid hours, he said: "When you saved me from the gallows that day and we were riding home, I asked you about my horse Bless and you knew what had happened to him. That day I saw that you, who had never known one horse from another, had taken care of my little Bless. I understood that you had done it because of me, and I was very happy about it. Now I see that it was really so, that you really do love me. But I have always loved you, Narcissus. Half of my life was spent courting you. I knew that you, too, were fond of me, but I never dared hope that you would tell me some day, you're such a proud man. You give me your love in this moment when I have nothing left, when wandering and freedom, world and women have abandoned me. I accept it and I thank you for it."

The Lydia-madonna stood in the room, watching.

"Do you think constantly of death?" asked Narcissus.

"Yes, I think of it and of what has become of my life. As a young man, when I was still your pupil, I wished to become as spiritual as you were. You showed me that I had no calling for it. Then I threw myself into the other side of life, into the world of the senses, and women made it easy for me to find my joys there, they are so greedy and willing. But I don't wish to speak disdainfully of them, or of the joys of the senses; I have often been extremely happy. And I was also fortunate enough in my experiences to learn that sensuality can be given a soul. Of it art is born. But now both flames have died out in me. I no longer have the animal happiness of ecstasy, and I wouldn't want it now even if women were still running after me. And to create works of art is no longer my wish either. I've made enough statues; the number does not matter. Therefore it is time for me to die. I am ready, and I'm curious about it."

"Why curious?" asked Narcissus.

"Well, it may be a bit stupid of me. But I'm really curious about it. Not of the beyond, Narcissus. I think about that very little, and if I may say so openly, I no longer believe in it. There is no beyond. The dried-up tree is dead forever; the frozen bird does not come back to life, nor does a man after he has died. One may continue to think of him for a while after he's gone, but that doesn't last long either. No, I'm curious about dying only because it is still my belief or my dream that I am on the road toward my mother. I hope death will be a great happiness, a happiness as great as that of love, fulfilled love. I cannot give up the thought that, instead of death with his scythe, it will be my mother who will come to take me back to her, who will lead me back to nonbeing and innocence."

During one of his last visits, after Goldmund had not said anything for several days, Narcissus again found him awake and talkative.

"Father Anton thinks you must often be in great pain. How do you bear it so calmly, Goldmund? It seems to me you have found peace now."

"Do you mean peace with God? No, that peace I have not found. I don't want any peace with Him. He has made the world badly; we don't need to praise it, and He'll care little whether I praise Him or not. He has made the world badly. But I have made peace with the pain in my chest, yes. In former days I was not good at bearing pain, and although I sometimes thought dying would come easily to me, I was wrong. When death was so near me that night in Count Heinrich's prison, I saw that I simply could not face it. I was still much too strong and too wild to die; they would have had to break each one of my bones twice. But now it is different."

Speaking tired him. His voice grew weaker. Narcissus asked him to spare himself.

"No," he said, "I want to tell you. Before this I would have been ashamed to tell you. It'll make you laugh. When I mounted my horse that day and rode away, I was not just riding off into the blue. I had heard a rumor that Count Heinrich had returned to this region and that his mistress Agnes was with him. Well, all right, that does not seem important to you, and today it does not seem important to me either. But at that time the news burned itself into me, and I thought of nothing but Agnes. She was the most beautiful woman I had ever known and loved: I wanted to see her again, I wanted to be happy with her again. I rode off, and after a week I found her. And there, during that hour, the change in me took place. As I said, I found her. She had not grown less beautiful. I found her and found as well the opportunity to show myself to her and to speak to her. And just think, Narcissus: she no longer wanted to have anything to do with me. I was too old for her; I was no longer pretty enough, amusing enough; she no longer wanted anything from me. That, actually, was the end of my journey. But I rode on. I didn't want to come back to you so disappointed and ridiculous, and as I rode along, force and youth and intelligence had already completely abandoned me, because I stumbled into a gully with my horse and fell into a stream and broke several ribs and lay there helpless in the water. That's when I first learned about real pain. As I fell I felt something break inside my chest, and the breaking pleased me, I was glad to hear it, I was content with it. I lay there in the water and knew that I was about to die, but everything was completely different from that night in the count's prison. I had nothing against it; dying no longer seemed terrible to me. I felt those violent pains which I've often had since then, and with them I had a dream, or a vision, whatever you want to call it. I lay there and had burning pains in my chest and I was defending myself against them and screaming when I heard a laughing voice, a voice I had not heard since childhood. It was my mother's voice, a deep womanly voice, full of ecstasy and love. And then I saw that it was she, that she was with me, holding me in her lap, and that she had opened my breast and put her fingers between my ribs to pluck out my heart. When I saw and understood that, it no longer hurt. And now, when the pains come back, they are not pains, they are not enemies; they are my mother's fingers taking my heart out. She works hard at it. Sometimes she presses down and moans as though in ecstasy. Sometimes she laughs and hums tender sounds. Sometimes she is not with me, but high above in heaven, and I see her face among the clouds, as large as a cloud. She floats there, smiling sadly, and her sad smile pulls at me and draws my heart out of my chest."

Again and again he spoke of her, of his mother.

"Do you remember?" he murmured on one of the last days. "I had completely forgotten my mother until you conjured her up again. That day, too, it hurt very much, as though animal jaws were tearing at my intestines. We were still young then, pretty young boys. But even then my mother called me and I had to follow. She is everywhere. She was Lise, the gypsy; she was Master Niklaus's beautiful madonna; she was life, love, ecstasy. She also was fear, hunger, instinct. Now she is death; she has her fingers in my chest."

"Don't speak so much, my dear friend," said Narcissus. "Wait until tomorrow."

With his new smile Goldmund looked into Narcissus's eyes, with the smile that he had brought back from his journey, the smile that looked at times so old and fragile, a little senile perhaps, and then again like pure kindness and wisdom.

"My dear friend," he whispered, "I cannot wait until tomorrow. I must say farewell to you now, and as we part I must tell you everything. Listen to me another moment. I wanted to tell you about my mother, and how she keeps her fingers clasped around my heart. For many years it has been my most cherished, my secret dream to make a statue of the mother. She was to me the most sacred of all my images; I have carried her always inside me, a figure of love and mystery. Only a short while ago it would have been unbearable to me to think that I might die without having carved her statue; my life would have seemed useless to me. And now see how strangely things have turned out: it is not my hands that shape and form her; it is her hands that shape and form me. She is closing her fingers around my heart, she is loosening it, she is emptying me; she is seducing me into dying and with me dies my dream, the beautiful statue, the image of the great mother-Eve. I can still see it, and if I had force in my hands, I could carve it. But she doesn't want that; she doesn't want me to make her secret visible. She rather wants me to die. I'm glad to die; she is making it easy for me."

Deeply shaken, Narcissus listened to his words. He had to bend close to his friend's lips to be able to understand what they were saying. Some words he heard only indistinctly; others he heard clearly, but their meaning escaped him.

And now the sick man opened his eyes again and looked for a long while into his friend's face. He said farewell with his eyes. And with a sudden movement, as though he were trying to shake his head, he whispered: "But how will you die when your time comes, Narcissus, since you have no mother? Without a mother, one cannot love. Without a mother, one cannot die."

What he murmured after that could not be understood. Those last two days Narcissus sat by his bed day and night, watching his life ebb away. Goldmund's last words burned like fire in his heart.

ABOUT THE AUTHOR

Born in 1877 in Calw, on the edge of the Black Forest, HERMANN HESSE was brought up in a missionary household where it was assumed that he would study for the ministry. Hesse's religious crisis (which is often recorded in his novels) led to his fleeing from the Maulbronn seminary in 1892, an unsuccessful cure by a well-known theologian and faith healer, and an attempted suicide. After being expelled from high school, he worked in bookshops for several years—a usual occupation for budding German authors.

His first novel, *Peter Camenzind* (1904), describes the early manhood of a writer who leaves his Swiss mountain village to encounter the world. This was followed by *Beneath the Wheel* (1906), the story of a gifted adolescent crushed by the brutal expectations of his father and teachers, a novel which was Hesse's personal attack on the educational system of his time.

World War I came as a terrific shock, and Hesse joined the pacifist Romain Rolland in antiwar activities—not only writing antiwar tracts and novels, but editing newspapers for German prisoners of war. During this period, Hesse's first marriage broke up (reflected or discussed outright in *Knulp* and *Rosshalde*), he studied the works of Freud, eventually underwent analysis with Jung, and was for a time a patient in a sanatorium.

In 1919 he moved permanently to Switzerland, and brought out *Demian*, which reflects his preoccupation with the workings of the subconscious and with psychoanalysis. The book was an enormous success, and made Hesse famous throughout Europe.

In 1922 he turned his attention to the East, which he had visited several times before the war, and wrote *Siddhartha*, the story of an Indian youth's long spiritual quest for the answer to the enigma of man's role on this earth. In 1927 he wrote *Steppenwolf*, the account of a man torn between his individualism and his attraction to bourgeois respectability, and his conflict between self-affirmation and self-destruction. In 1930 he published *Narcissus and Goldmund*, regarded as "Hesse's greatest novel" (*The New York Times*), dealing with the friendship between two medieval priests, one contented with his religion, the other a wanderer endlessly in search of peace and salvation.

The Journey to the East appeared in 1932, and there was no major work until 1943, when he brought out *Magister Ludi*, which won him the Nobel Prize in 1946. Until his death in 1962 he lived in seclusion in Montagnola, Switzerland.

Special Offer
Buy a Bantam Book
for only 50¢.

Now you can have Bantam's catalog filled with hundreds of titles plus take advantage of our unique and exciting bonus book offer. A special offer which gives you the opportunity to purchase a Bantam book for only 50¢. Here's how!

By ordering any five books at the regular price per order, you can also choose any other single book listed (up to a $4.95 value) for just 50¢. Some restrictions do apply, but for further details why not send for Bantam's catalog of titles today!

Just send us your name and address and we will send you a catalog!